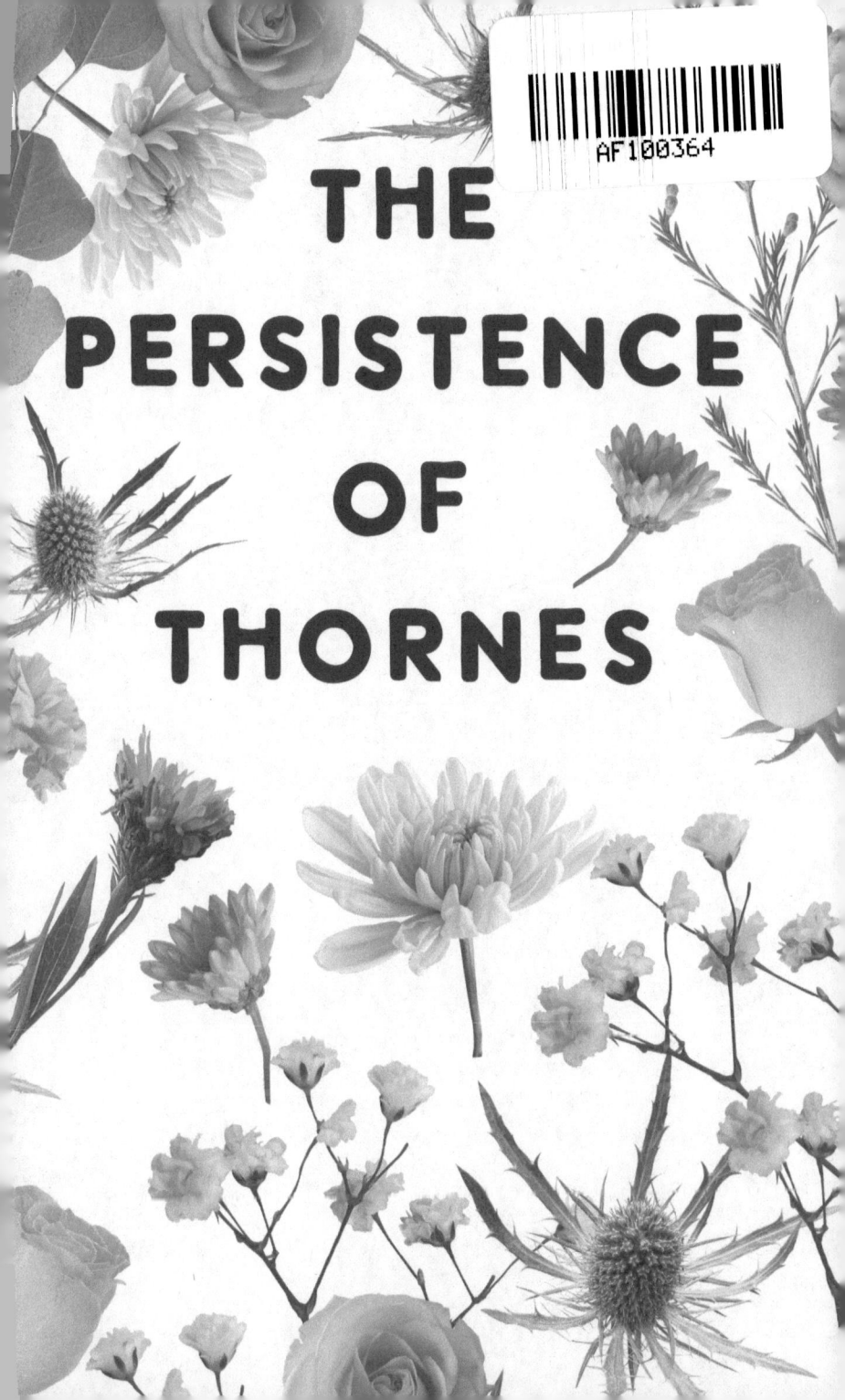

THE PERSISTENCE OF THORNES

Copyright © 2025 by Micalea Smeltzer

All rights reserved.

No part of this book may be reproduced in any form or by any electronic or mechanical means, including information storage and retrieval systems, without written permission from the author, except for the use of brief quotations in a book review.

Cover Design: Emily Wittig Designs

Editing (line editing, copying editing, and proofreading): VB Edits

Plotting and Outline help: Melanie with Made Me Blush Books

For the eldest daughters who struggle to let go and let anyone take care of them. I hope we all find our Caleb.

ONE

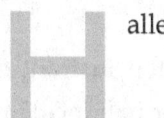alle

It's like a slow-motion replay of a lion attacking a gazelle, the way the ball sails through the air, arcing toward the man climbing out of his car next door.

Please, don't hit him! Don't hit him! Don't—
Smack.
The soccer ball ricochets off his head.
What an excellent first impression for my new neighbor.
The glower I turn on my fourteen-year-old brothers is deadly.

"I *said* to take the ball to the backyard."
The two of them take off, Quinn scooping up the ball on

his way, scattering for the broken fence and overgrown lawn beyond it.

I'm livid. Mostly because I'm exhausted. A bone-deep tired I've never felt. At twenty-three, I am now my brothers' legal guardian. This was not part of the plan, yet here we are. I couldn't let them end up in foster care. They're my brothers, my flesh and blood. They belong with me, even if taking responsibility for them puts an unbearable weight on my shoulders. I was barely getting by before. Now? I'll figure it out. I always do.

I set the box on the ground and cross the side lawn that separates my scraggly yard from the immaculate one next door.

The man rubs at his head, looking around for the source of his sudden concussion.

"I'm *so* sorry about that." I come to a stop in front of him, cringing. Not only because of the soccer ball incident, but because this man is dressed in an expensive, sharp-looking suit, while I'm standing here in ripped jean shorts and a t-shirt with a cartoon character on it I've owned since middle school. "My brothers ... I told them to play in the back, but they're fourteen and aren't too keen on listening to their sister."

He lowers his hand from his head and focuses his gaze on me. The move finally allows me to get a good look at his face.

Holy fuck.

He might be the best-looking man I've ever seen. Bright, expressive blue eyes. Sandy blond hair. Chiseled jaw with just a hint of stubble. And the posture of a man who's both confident and easy-going.

"It's okay," he says, voice deep and soothing. "I know how kids are. Your parents are moving in next door?"

"Oh, no. I mean yes, we're moving in next door, but no to the parents part. It's only me and my brothers."

"Ah." He nods, rubbing the spot on his head again. "I see."

The words aren't condescending, despite the way he eyes the house next door, *my* house. It looks like a verifiable dump compared to every other house on this street.

I straighten my shoulders. "It's not much, but I'm going to fix it up."

When I can afford it, which, at the rate I'm going, is never. But we'll have a roof over our heads. That's the most important part.

His blue eyes skate over my body. The move is perfunctory. Rather than checking me out, he's trying to commit me to memory so he can place me later. "If you need any help over there let me know. I did a lot of the work on my place."

I blink at him, surprised. "You did?"

He looks too clean-cut in his suit and tie. Though his hands are large and masculine with thick veins, they still don't look like the hands of a man who does manual labor. Though the sight of them makes me think I'd enjoy finding out all the things he can do with them.

He lets out an amused chuckle. "A fair amount, though I had help. Thayer"—he points to the house on the other side of his—"next door to me, owns a landscaping business. I'm sure he'd be happy to help with the yard."

Wincing, I eye the crab grass and dying plants. Our new place sticks out like a sore thumb in a row of well-maintained homes on this street. According to my realtor, this house sat vacant while family members fought over who would get the money from the sale. Apparently they never learned how to share. The fight dragged out so long, the house fell into disrepair, and that placed it squarely in my budget. It's in a good school district, though. I never thought I'd be thinking about things like that at my age, but here we are.

"That would be great." I paste on a smile even though I know there's zero chance I'll ever ask him or this other guy for help.

In many ways, I'm a stereotypical eldest daughter, which means I loathe the very thought of requesting help. If I can't figure it out, I'll die trying.

"I'm Caleb, by the way." He holds out a hand to me.

"Halle." I slip my hand into his. His palm is warm and surprisingly rough for how tidy his nails are. "These two dipshits are Quinn and Casen." I point to my brothers as they run back through the front yard and up a set of porch steps that groan beneath their weight.

"Halle," he repeats my name, and I feel it down in my toes. "Haven't heard that before. Do you need help with anything?" He motions to the small U-Haul in our driveway.

"Nah, it's okay." I wave at the white and orange trailer, dismissing his help even if I desperately need it.

The process would certainly go faster and be less painful with help, but I don't know anyone in town, and getting my brothers to help for more than a few minutes will be a feat. Their attention spans are nonexistent unless they're playing a video game.

He slips his hands into his pockets and wanders over to the open back of the U-Haul. Then, with an arched brow, he turns back to me. "Looks to me like you need help."

I press my lips together. The offer is well-meaning, but it's a trigger for me. The girl who's always had to do it all.

"It's really okay." I inhale deeply. "I can get the boys to help. We'll be fine."

Without another word, Caleb walks away. Shit. I didn't mean to piss him off. Just as I'm ready to call out an apology, he stops beside his car, leaning against its door, and pulls out his cell phone.

"Hey, can you come outside? Our new neighbor needs help unloading her U-Haul."

He pulls the device away from his ear, taps the screen, and slips it back into his pocket before he eyes me where I'm standing awkwardly in the halfway point between his yard and mine.

"Thayer's going to come help too."

Great. I do my best not to let my shoulders slump.

"You really didn't need to do that. It looks like you just got home from work." I wave a hand, gesturing to his suit. "I can figure it out."

He smiles slowly, like he sees right through my stubborn pride. "It's really not a problem."

I should probably be jumping for joy. It's supposed to

rain tomorrow, but with their help, I can get everything inside tonight. But that nagging part of my brain is still screaming at me to tell him that I'm fine on my own.

I give that internal voice a shove.

"Thanks," I say instead. "I'm going to check on the boys, and I'll be right back."

They've disappeared, and I don't hear them, which is never a good sign. At fourteen, they shouldn't need my constant supervision, but they prove time and time again that they're about as trustworthy on their own as a pair of toddlers, when, in reality, they're full-fledged teenagers.

That thought brings me up short.

They'll be fifteen in January, which means driver's ed and learner's permits and—

I tamp down on the spiraling thoughts. I'm getting ahead of myself.

"Take your time," Caleb says as I retreat. "I'm going to change real quick, and Thayer will be a few minutes."

I give him a thumbs-up and immediately wish the ground would open up and swallow me. A thumbs-up? What am I? Five?

I go in search of my brothers, stepping over the broken fence. The house is still locked, so they must be in the backyard. Unless they know how to pick locks.

My stomach plummets. *Crap! Can they pick locks?*

I wouldn't put it past them to learn in their free time.

"Boys?" I call out as I scan the yard. "The neighbors are going to help us unload. You two need to participate as well."

I push aside an overgrown bush, watching my step since

I'm a little scared I might encounter a snake. I'm a strong, independent woman until I encounter a snake or a spider.

"Casen? Quinn?"

I head for the massive tree, taking it in as I get closer. Head tipped back, I catch sight of a flash of color.

Of course they're in the tree. I wouldn't expect anything less.

"Get down from there before you break a bone and end up in the hospital. I need your help."

They're determined to give me a heart attack, I swear. I close my eyes and focus on my breathing, reminding myself that I'm doing the right thing by taking custody of them. That all this is worth it.

The boys laugh, shoving playfully in a mock effort to knock each other out of the tree.

"I mean it." I infuse my tone with all the firmness I can muster. "Get down and help or you're grounded."

That only earns a round of laughter.

I can't say I blame them. We're *siblings*. I'm not their parent. And for their whole lives, their parents have been deadbeats who never bothered to parent them. We share a mom, one who doesn't give a shit about being a mother, but while I have no idea who my dad is, theirs has been in and out of the picture over the years. Mostly when he wants money, which we never had, or a bed to crash in, which my mom was always willing to offer.

"Listen." I plant my hands on my hips. "I know this is a weird dynamic, and I know I'm not your mom, but I *am* your legal guardian. The two of you need to show some respect, and I'll do the same in return. Now, since our neighbors are being kind enough to help, would you please join us?"

Finally, reluctantly, they shimmy down the tree, both landing impressive jumps from branches too high for my liking.

"You're kind of a buzzkill," Casen says, sauntering past me.

Quinn stops beside me with a sigh. "We were going to help."

"But only after you gave me a minor heart attack over a potential broken bone, right?" I arch a brow, hands on my hips.

He cracks a half grin. "Exactly."

Out front, Caleb has returned, wearing a faded t-shirt and a pair of jeans that look way too good. And he's flanked by two other men. The first, a tall, good-looking man with a hint of gray in his stubble and at his temples, extends a hand and introduces himself as Thayer.

The other, who has hair the same shade as Thayer's and similar eyes, shakes my hand as well. "I'm Laith. This one's brother." He tosses a thumb in Thayer's direction.

He's tall and just as good-looking as his brother, but with an easier smile and softer eyes. Thayer's sharper edges make me think he's experienced some hardships, whereas Laith is full of a playful lightness. The other noticeable difference is a crook in Laith's nose that his brother doesn't have.

"I'm Halle." I tuck my hair behind my ears, cursing myself for somehow losing the hair band I always keep on my wrist. "I appreciate the help. You didn't have to do it."

Despite my desire to handle all my shit on my own, I can't say I'm not relieved.

"We're happy to do it," Laith says with a beaming smile.

Caleb, who was leaning against the U-Haul, straightens. "Put us to work."

I smooth my hands down my shirt and paste on a smile. "All right."

With their help, all our meager belongings are inside and in place in under two hours.

Now, I stand in the doorway of my bedroom, biting back the urge to cringe as Caleb assembles my bedframe, hands wringing, while I consider the best way to tell him he doesn't have to do that.

"You can go," I tell him. "I can figure out the bed."

There. That sounded okay, didn't it?

He glances over his shoulder, one of the pieces clasped in his hand. It would take me a while to figure out how to assemble it, but I could get it done. Eventually. And if I had to spend one night with my mattress on the floor, that wouldn't be so bad.

He arches a brow that's more brown than blond. "You really don't like help, do you?"

I frown, easing away from the wall. "Is it that obvious?"

In my experience, most people *don't* actually want to help, and when I suggest I can handle something on my own, they're way too quick to let me try.

He chuckles, sizing up the pieces. "Yeah, it is."

Across the hall, Laith and Thayer are putting together the boys' beds. The boys? They helped a little, but quickly lost interest, as I expected. Now they're outside doing who knows what. Terrorizing the poor squirrels in the tree? Figuring out how to roll the U-Haul down the hill? Plotting world domination?

I sit on the floor and bring my knees up to my chest. "I've always done things on my own. It's easier that way. So this is new for me."

He glances sidelong at me. "Get used to it here. This town is small, and we look after each other."

"That's ... nice." I wrinkle my nose. In reality, it sounds like my own personal hell.

He chuckles. "This may not be the right place for you, then."

I sigh, resting my chin on my knees and locking my arms around them tighter. "I did it for them. Good school district and low crime rates."

And this town is several hours away from our mother, so the chances of her showing up unexpectedly once she's out of prison are slim to none. Not that I'd give her the address.

He pauses, Allen wrench in hand, and assesses me.

Uncomfortable with the scrutiny, I eye the stained carpet. How is he not concerned that he's probably sitting on toxic waste? It's probably eating a hole in his expensive jeans as we speak. "I think you'll like it here."

I exhale, my breath causing my dark hair to flutter. "Do you want help, or should I get out of your way?"

He looks up from his work again, one hand frozen in midair. "What's going to make you feel better?"

"To help."

"Then I'd be happy to have it."

Thirty minutes later, the frame is assembled and we've positioned the queen-size mattress.

"Where are the sheets?"

"Oh." My face goes hot. "I can handle that."

The last thing I need is for my hot neighbor to see the holey, threadbare pink and white striped sheets. They were a girly indulgence I purchased with my first paycheck when I was sixteen. Even the TJ Maxx price was out of my budget, but their soft material made the splurge worth it and now I'm too attached to get rid of them.

He eyes me, raising his hands. "All right. Anything else you need?"

Lips pressed together, I pretend to ponder his question. "I think I'm good."

The amused look he gives me—lips half curled—tells me he sees right through me. "I ordered pizza. It should be here any minute," he announces, wiping his palms off on his pants.

I wince at the dust stains left behind in the shape of his massive hands.

"When did you have time to order pizza?"

"I used the app. Takes like two seconds," he says.

He did pull out his phone halfway through assembling the bed, but I figured he was checking in with a girlfriend or something. Because there's no way a guy this hot is single.

He only paused for a minute, but maybe that was enough time to text a girlfriend *and* order pizza.

I'm the one who should be providing a meal for him and his friends—

My stomach growls at the thought of food.

He grins, triumphant.

"I haven't eaten today." I bring a hand to my stomach and grimace.

He frowns at that. "Why not?"

"Too busy." And I spent more money feeding my brothers alone than I felt comfortable with. I figured I'd rather keep the additional ten dollars. Never know when I might need it, and hunger is something I've learned to deal with. "You really didn't need to do that, I could've…"

Could've what? Pizza for six people is not in my budget, and my fridge and cupboards are bare.

"Just say thank you." His tone is teasing, easygoing, but that doesn't stop me from feeling bad about once again stomping on his kind gesture.

"Thank you." The words are a pitiful squeak. "And thank you for the help. You really didn't have to do all this."

As much as I genuinely appreciate the help, dread has formed in my stomach, because I have no idea how I'll ever be able to repay him.

He dips his head. "You're welcome. I'm happy to help."

I shove my hands in my back pockets, rocking on my heels, unsure of what to say next.

He watches me, silent, his scrutiny making me itch. Thankfully, I'm saved by a knock on the front door.

He thumbs over his shoulder. "That'll be the food."

I puff out my lips. "Okay."

With a questioning glance, he leaves the room, then his feet pound down the stairs.

I blow out a breath and count to ten in an effort to center myself.

Across the hall, I poke my head into the boys' room and find the beds assembled and the dresser moved to beneath the window. But Thayer and Laith have disappeared.

Downstairs, I peek around, but I don't see them there either.

I follow Caleb into the kitchen, where he sets the pizzas down. "Where did your friends go?"

"Home, I guess."

"Oh, well, can you thank them for me?"

"Sure can."

"Listen." I clear my throat. "Like I said before, I'm not good with this whole ... friendly thing." I flick a finger between the two of us. "But I mean it, thank you. It would've taken me forever to do all this."

His eyes soften. "It's okay, Halle. To feel the way you do, you must have been disappointed by a lot of people in your life. When that happens, it's hard to trust again."

I nod, averting my gaze. "Thank you for understanding."

Most people take my behavior for stubborn pride, but it's not that at all. And somehow, this virtual stranger gets it.

He opens the top pizza box, then peers at me over top of the lid. "Let me guess, you don't have drinks."

I wince. "You'd guess right." This man helped move us in and bought dinner, and I don't even have *drinks*.

With a chuckle, he closes the box. "I'll be right back. You want a beer? You're legal, right?"

"I'm twenty-three," I say, a tad offended. Do I look that young? "But no thank you."

Watching my mom succumb to alcohol and drug abuse has made me wary of touching the stuff. That's not to say I've never had a drink, but the instances are few and far between. I tend to steer clear of any behavior that could cause me to be dependent on a foreign substance.

With a sheepish grin, he says, "I'll be back." Again. Like he's concerned I've forgotten in the two-point-five seconds that have passed.

"I'm going to go check on my brothers." I point to the living room, where their heads are just visible over the back of the couch.

The front door closes with a soft click as I approach them.

"Hungry? Caleb ordered pizza."

Quinn looks over at me. His dark brown hair is in need of a trim, but he refuses to let me take him anywhere.

"Pizza sounds good." He punches his brother, who removes one of his earbuds. "Pizza?"

It's the only word Casen needs to hear before he's up and moving toward the kitchen.

"We'll go to the grocery store tomorrow," I tell them. "Start thinking about what you want—but keep in mind the budget is tight."

"Sure thing, Cap." Casen salutes me.

I assume Cap is short for Captain, but honestly, one never knows when it comes to him.

The boys sit at the table, one of my better thrift-store finds, and dig into the pizza.

"Caleb went next door to get drinks for us, so be sure to tell him thank you when he gets back."

When neither looks up from the pizza they're inhaling or deigns to respond, I snap my fingers in front of each of their faces.

"Hey, did you hear me?"

"Yeah, yeah," Quinn says.

"We'll be sure to thank the new neighbor," Casen says, "but I think it's *you* he's hoping for a thank-you from, not us."

I frown. "What do you mean?"

Casen laughs, nearly choking on his pizza. "I mean, the new neighbor dude clearly wants in your pants."

I snort. That's preposterous. *I* might've checked him out, but there's no way he was doing the same. He's older by at least a few years and way out of my league. From what I've seen already, he has his life together. Me? I'm nowhere close. His clothes look expensive and his car is newer, so he must make good money.

A guy who looks like him and has a good job? There's no way he doesn't have a girlfriend.

I snort. "Yeah, right."

They exchange a look in that annoying, secret twin telepathy way they have.

With a huff, I change the subject. "I thought we could go

to the hardware store tomorrow. Pick out some paint. What do you think?"

Again, with the silent twin exchange.

"Okay," Quinn says. "Can we paint our room neon green?"

My instinct is to cringe, but I bite back the reaction. He's just trying to get under my skin. "Sure. Whatever color you want."

Hopefully they go with something more palatable than neon green, but they're the ones who'll have to live with it, not me. If they want to fuck with me, it'll be to their own detriment.

At the sound of the front door, I navigate my way through the kitchen to the foyer.

"Wow," I remark when I catch sight of the plastic bag full of drinks. "You didn't need to bring all that."

Caleb shrugs. "I always overstock when Costco has a sale."

"Right." I bite my lip. "Well, thank you."

He follows me back into the kitchen and opens the fridge. "What do you guys want?" he asks over his shoulder as he sets several waters and a variety of sodas on the top shelf.

"Coke."

"Beer."

I point a finger at Casen. "Case. Be for real."

His lips tip up in a sly smirk. "Coke for me too."

Caleb hands me two Cokes to pass to my brothers, and as I hold them out, I keep them just out of their reach, giving them both looks that say *be nice*.

"What do you want?" he asks, hand poised to grab another beverage.

As much as I want to copy my brothers and ask for a Coke, I'm more than likely dehydrated after all the work unloading the truck and setting up the house.

"Water for me, please."

Caleb straightens, holding a beer for himself and a bottle of water. He unscrews the top of the water bottle and hands it to me.

I take it and guzzle it down. It's half gone when I catch myself and set it on the counter. *God, Halle.* He's probably judging me for my excessive H2O consumption.

While Caleb pops the top on his beer and takes a careful sip, I swipe a slice of pizza and take a too large bite to occupy myself. With any luck, it'll keep me from doing or saying anything stupid.

"Hungry?" Caleb watches me with an amused smile.

"Starving," I say around the mouthful.

"I spoke to Thayer while I was next door. He said he'll have his guys take care of the lawn later this week."

His comment is like a bucket of ice water dumped over my head. I swipe my hands through the air. "No, no. That's okay. I'll get a lawn mower."

Mentally, I add it to the endless list of shit I need to buy.

Caleb shrugs, his demeanor easy. "It's not a big deal. He has the guys to do the work. Just let them handle it."

"But I—"

"We're broke, dude." Quinn says it in such a bold way, it silences the whole room.

It's not like our financial status isn't obvious, but my brother's blunt admission is like a swift kick to the gut.

Suddenly I'm not hungry anymore. I stick the half-eaten slice back in the box, the portion I did eat sitting like a lead ball in my stomach.

"He's not going to charge you." Caleb leans against the avocado green linoleum countertops.

That color was certainly a choice. I'd rather focus on that than on the implication of that statement.

"You're not a charity case," he says, as if reading my mind. "This is just neighbors helping neighbors. That's all."

In my periphery, Quinn elbows Casen, and then Casen clears his throat. "Do you want to get in our sister's pants?"

"Casen!" My face burns like I've been lit on fire.

Caleb brings a fist to his mouth, choking on his pizza.

I point a shaky finger at Caleb. "Don't you dare indulge him with an answer. And you." I swing my finger to Casen. "You know better than to ask things like that."

"It's a legitimate question," Quinn grumbles.

God help me. How am I supposed to do this? They're only fourteen. I've got to figure out how to keep them in line for another four years. At this rate, I can't imagine all three of us making it to their high school graduation.

With a ragged breath, Caleb straightens. He takes a sip from his beer, then clears his throat. "I'm just happy to help."

My brothers sear him with identical expressions. The same ones they gave when they were seven and skeptical that the spaghetti our mom smothered in ketchup instead of tomato sauce would be any good.

I pile slices on two plates, then hold them out to them. "Shoo. Go watch TV or something."

Before you embarrass me any further.

At least the internet was installed before we arrived. If it hadn't been, I have no idea what we would have done. It's not like they'll read a book.

"I'm sorry about them," I say to Caleb when the TV screen lights up. I sink onto a chair and pick up my pizza again. This time, I nibble on it, hoping it doesn't make my stomach churn.

He sits beside me and gives me a wry smile. "You don't need to apologize. It's funny, really. You're their sister, and they clearly want to embarrass you."

"Yeah," I sigh. "That's a problem. How can I be their guardian when they don't take me seriously?"

Caleb purses his lips slightly. It should look silly, but if anything, it's cute. "I'm sure they understand that when it comes to the important things."

The man has only known them for a few hours. He has no idea the kind of mischief they've gotten into over the past few years. If I can't keep them under control, I worry the state will change their mind and place them in foster care.

I give a small, miserable shrug. "We'll see, I guess."

Caleb takes another sip of beer, surveying the room. "Do you have a notepad handy?"

I snort and hold out an arm, gesturing to the stacks of boxes. "Pretty sure that's a no."

"Right. Phone, then?"

I pull it out of my pocket and set it on the table. "Why do you need my phone?"

Lips twisting in amusement, he says, "I was going to save my number to your contacts. Thayer's, Salem's, and Cynthia's too."

"I have no idea who those last two people are," I remind him.

"Salem is Thayer's wife and Cynthia is the elderly lady across the street. She and her partner, Thelma. They're too nosy for their own good, so you've been warned, but they're great if you need a hand."

I know good and well that I won't ask for help from any of these people, but I let him put all the numbers into my phone anyway.

Once we've finished eating, Caleb helps me straighten up the kitchen and heads for the front door.

"Wait," I call after him, picking up the pizza box we've put all the remaining slices in. "You should take the leftovers."

He shakes his head. "Nah, keep it. Your brothers might get hungry again, and cold pizza makes for great breakfast."

"It does, doesn't it?"

I can't count the number of slices I ate for breakfast as a kid.

As I follow him outside onto the front porch, I eye the flickering spiderweb-infested porch light and cringe, making a mental note to use a broom to clean it off and change the bulb tomorrow.

"Thanks again for your help."

As he descends the creaky steps, I hold my breath, afraid one might break beneath his feet.

Turning, he flashes me a disarming smile. "You're welcome. I'll see you around, Halle."

He strides across the yard, then bounds up his porch steps. When he turns my way, finding me watching, he smiles and throws his hand up. Then he disappears inside.

"People are way too friendly here," I mutter as I head inside and lock up behind me.

Hawthorne Mills might not be the place for us after all, but we have nowhere else to go, so for now, it'll have to do.

TWO

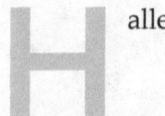alle

"Stop shoving each other," I hiss.

Ignoring me, Quinn and Casen continue arguing over what color to paint their room.

I pinch my brow and will the annoyance building inside me to abate. I have to keep my head on straight. For them. For me. I can't afford to fall apart.

And definitely not in the middle of a hardware store.

I'm *not* just their older sister anymore. I'm their guardian, and that means I have to act with a higher level of maturity than I have previously.

"I want yellow." Casen pulls out a swatch and thrusts it at Quinn.

Quinn slams it back into his chest. "And I want green."

"If you two can't figure this out civilly, then *I'm* picking the color, and I promise you won't like my choice."

There. That sounds more guardian-like. I'm providing them a solution while also being firm in my delivery.

That shuts them up quickly. They exchange a look, then Quinn says, "Can we do the room half yellow and half green?"

It's going to cost me more in paint, but at this point I don't care. "Sure."

"Sweet." They fist bump and bow their heads together, conspiring as if they weren't just arguing.

I leave them to it and go in search of an employee.

A man in a Thorne Hardware apron steps out from an aisle, kind smile already in place and a pair of reading glasses perched on his balding head. "Can I help you with something?"

"Do you have any clearance paint? Maybe colors people changed their minds about and returned?"

I mentally cross my fingers. It may not save me much, but right now, every dollar counts, and I'm hoping that a fresh layer of paint will help with the lingering stale smell inside the house.

He cocks his head and presses his lips together, thoughtful. "Sometimes we do. Follow me." With a wave, he turns and heads down the aisle. "If we've got any, they'll be over here." He takes a left and points to a shelf of miscellaneous items. "It may take a bit to sort through it all."

Cautious hope fills me as I eye the overflowing shelf. Hopeful or not, the smile I give the man is forced. Sometimes I wonder if once, maybe when I was young, before life wore me down, they were genuine. "Thank you."

He peers over my shoulder, neck craned. "Do you need a cart?"

Lip caught between my teeth, I half turn and follow his line of sight. "Yeah, I'll go get one."

He waves me off with a firm hand. "I've got it."

Before I can utter another word, he's headed toward the front of the store.

While I wait for him to return, I dig through the clearance items, setting aside a few cans of paint. The color options aren't great, but the discount is steep. There's a purple shade that will work for my room, even though I don't love it. A blue that will look okay for the main spaces. A yellow that's perhaps a bit *too* bright but will be fine for now in the kitchen and laundry room.

The man approaches with a cart. "Finding everything you need?"

"Yep, I think so." I grasp the handle of a gallon in each hand and heft them into the cart. "It's not perfect, but I'm on a budget."

He looks me up and down, brow furrowed in curiosity. "You're new in town." It's a statement, not a question.

"I am." I dip my chin. "My brothers and I just moved here."

He breaks into a wide smile. "Welcome. It's a close-knit community. You're going to love it."

"I'm realizing that." I give him a tight smile. "Anyway, thanks for the cart."

He waves. "Holler if you need anything, dear."

I peruse the clearance section a little longer, adding outlet covers and even a paint roller that's slightly dented but will still get the job done. When I make my way back over to the paint section, I'm not at all surprised to find my nerd brothers having a sword fight with wooden paint stirrers.

"Have you decided on a color?" I ask, holding out a hand for chips.

They cease their mock sword fight, and each one passes me a paint chip.

The colors are … disgusting, to say the least. But it's not my room, so I keep my mouth shut. If there's one thing I've learned since I took custody of them a month ago, it's to pick my battles.

"Why don't you grab paint rollers and tape while I get these mixed up?"

"Aye, aye, Cap. We'll get right on it." Casen tugs Quinn down the next aisle.

There's no one at the paint mixer, but there's a bell with a note that says *Ring for service*.

I tap the bell, and a moment later, the man from before appears behind the counter.

"Interesting choice of colors," he says when I hold out the paint chips.

"My brothers chose them for their room."

"Ah, I see. Do you know what brand you'd like to use? I recommend—"

It's rude of me, but I cut him off. "Whatever's cheapest."

Even if it's a dollar cheaper, that means I've got an extra dollar in my pocket.

"Of course, but—"

"Harold," I say, reading the name embroidered on his apron. "I'm on a budget. Just pick whatever is cheapest and covers well."

"Um." He taps his fingers. "That would probably be our Thorne's Promise in-house paint."

"Perfect. I'll take a gallon of each of these colors." I tap the chip cards. "Thank you," I add in hopes of smoothing the edges of my abrupt response.

"Is this it for the paint?" he asks, pulling the gallons off a shelf.

"Yep, that'll be all I need to have mixed."

"If you need to do any more shopping, I'll just bring these to the front, and you can pick them up when you're done. I can give those clearance gallons a good shake while I'm at it."

"That would be great," I say as I pull them out of the cart again.

As the mixing machine does its thing, making a loud whirring noise that makes me wince, I wheel the cart over to the next aisle. Instantly, I groan. Of course my brothers have knocked over a display, and dozens of sponges are scattered all over the floor.

Casen and Quinn, who are picking the cardboard display back up, freeze, eyes wide and locked on me.

"What did you do?" With a huff, I abandon the cart and drop to my knees, scooping up the sponges.

"It was an accident," Casen says.

"We're cleaning it up." That from Quinn.

It's silly. It's only a display. It's easily righted and nothing is broken. Even still, tears prick at the backs of my eyes. I'm *stressed*, and every time I turn around, one of my idiot brothers is doing something stupid.

"Hey," Quinn says softly. "Are you, like ... okay?"

"I'm fine," I snap, thrusting a handful of sponges at him.

"Maybe she's starting her period," Casen mutters. "She seems extra emotional."

"This has nothing to do with my period." I run my fingers through my hair, which is somehow tangled, even though I brushed it an hour or so ago.

I'd rather not let on just how stressed I am. Despite the way they worry me endlessly, they're kids with enough burdens of their own to deal with. And in reality, some of my worries are unfounded. Concerns like the one that hit me the second I saw the mess they'd created. That my brothers would be taken away from me because the powers that be will see that I'm not fit to take care of them. I feel entirely unworthy of them. Too young, too dumb, too fucking broke to raise them. But in my heart, I know they're better off with me. It's why I fought so hard for them after Mom went to prison.

The three of us get everything righted, and since they were wreaking havoc rather than picking out paint rollers, I toss a few of those into the cart along with plastic roller trays.

"Let's go," I say, pushing the cart forward.

At checkout, I find the paint cans, just as promised, and

the older gentleman loads them for me. When the total appears on the register, I balk a bit, but I bite my tongue and pay for it. The house smells musty and stale, and with any luck, a fresh coat of paint will fix the issue. I can't blame Thayer and Laith for leaving so quickly. I'm not sure how Caleb held out for as long as he did.

I'm worried that even the paint won't be enough. Not with the shape of the worn carpet in some of the rooms, but I have to try.

Outside, the boys help load the car without complaint. They're useful when they want to be.

Once it's all taken care of and they've returned the cart to the front of the store, I smooth my windblown hair off my forehead. "I'm going to walk around and see if any of these places is hiring. Why don't you hang out over there?" I ask, lifting my chin to the store down the street that looks like an arcade.

"Sure," they say in unison, giving me matching shrugs.

I pull out a ten-dollar bill and hand it to Quinn, but rather than take it, he just arches a brow.

"This isn't going to last long."

"I barely have that to spare, so make it last." I ruffle his hair and then Casen's.

With annoyed looks and hands roughing through their hair, they take off.

Once they're inside the arcade, I wander down the street, searching for help-wanted signs. With the number of businesses on this block and the next, someone is surely looking for part-time help.

The money I make doing scheduling for a doctor's

office is decent. On my own, it was good enough, and it's a remote position, which means I can be around for the boys when they need me. But it's not enough to support the three of us comfortably. They'll start school soon, and if they want to play sports or get involved in other extracurriculars, I don't want to have to tell them no. When I was growing up, we didn't have the money for that kind of stuff. I don't want the same for them if I can help it.

The first help-wanted sign I encounter is in the window of a musty-smelling thrift shop. I put in an application even if I'm not sure I can survive the smell. It might be worse than the house.

Next up is a hair salon, but they're only looking for a licensed hairstylist.

I continue on my way, passing a cute cupcake shop as I go. I'd love to surprise the boys with a half dozen, but my bank account is already screaming at me.

With a look one way, then the other, I cross the street and peruse the shops on the other side. The first few I try aren't looking for help. The coffee shop is next. It's a cute, quaint little place, and it smells like heaven.

"Hi," I say as I approach the barista. "I was wondering if I could put in an application? I saw the help wanted sign on the door."

"Oh." The young girl straightens and scans the small space. "Let me get my manager."

I step aside to wait so I'm not in the way if customers come in.

She comes back, her face lit up, and points to an empty

two-top by the front window. "She'll be out in a minute. You can sit over there if you'd like."

With a grateful smile, I shuffle to the table. I sit, my feet doing a nervous tap dance on the stamped concrete floor. A handful of minutes later, a woman several years older than me appears beside the table, holding a simple blue folder. Her dark hair is pulled back in a sleek bun and a pair of red glasses sit perched on her pert nose. She's dressed in a pair of adorable plaid pants and a short-sleeve shirt that shows off her full sleeve of tattoos.

I instantly like her.

"Hello, I'm Amy." She sits across from me and extends her hand. "Keeley said you were asking about a job?"

"I'm Halle." With a nod, I shake her offered hand. "I'm new in town and saw the sign out front. This place is adorable."

"I know it's unusual to go straight to the interview process, but since we're both here, I figured why not."

"That's great." I set my hands in my lap and lace my fingers. Hopefully that'll keep me from waving them around like I do when I'm nervous.

"Great." Amy pulls a piece of paper from the folder. "Have you worked in a coffee shop before?"

"No, but I'm a quick learner."

Her eyes dart away, and my heart sinks.

She looks back at me, and when her expression remains open, I exhale in relief. "Any experience with an espresso machine, at least?"

"Yes," I fib, keeping my shoulders back and my chin

high. If she hires me, I'll spend some time watching videos on YouTube. That way I won't look like a complete novice.

She arches a brow in doubt, and that confidence shrivels a bit.

So I double down and lie through my teeth. "M-my friend has one at her house," I stammer.

She moves on to other questions without calling me out, thankfully. Questions about my job history and skills that don't include making coffee. I've worked in retail and the backend of a restaurant, as well as a little waitressing. That should help sway things in my favor.

She taps her pen against the table and blows out a breath. "Experience as a barista is typically a must—"

My heart sinks.

"But"—my heart dares to soar—"I have a good feeling about you. When can you start?"

I resist the urge to get down on my knees and thank her. "As soon as you need me."

"How about Monday?"

That gives me four days to make some progress on the house and figure out how to use an espresso machine.

"Monday is perfect."

"Good." She breaks into a genuine smile. "Welcome to the team, Halle." Standing, she holds her hand out once again. "Order a coffee on your way out. On me."

"Thank you." I infuse the simple phrase with as much gratefulness as I can manage. "I'll see you Monday."

Normally I wouldn't take her up on the offer for a free coffee, but oh boy, do I need it.

I ordered an iced caramel latte and walk out with a pep in my step.

THREE

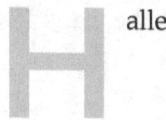alle

It looks like my old middle school mascot threw up in my brothers' bedroom. The yellow and green assault my eyes. So badly I have to literally raise a hand to shield them.

"It looks ... great."

The boys look at me, wearing matching grins and almost as much paint as they've managed to get on the walls. They won't hear any complaints from me. They got the job done, and it doesn't look half bad.

"Thanks." Casen scratches his nose, leaving behind a streak of paint.

"Would you be up for helping with painting the kitchen?"

They exchange a silent look and shrug. "Sure," Quinn replies.

"After, I thought we could go to the grocery store."

"Sounds good to me." Casen brushes past me on his way to the hall bathroom. "Can we get string cheese?" he yells as he turns on the water. "The kind that has the two colors twirled together?"

"Um…" My stomach tightens. "We'll see if it's in the budget. Okay?"

"Sure." The sink cuts off with a squeak.

The kitchen is tucked into the back corner, separated from the rest of the first floor.

"Yellow, huh?" Quinn peeks into one of the pans I've already prepped.

"It was the best I could find on clearance."

They blink at each other, doing the freaky silent twin talk thing for a moment. Then Casen says, "Ours weren't on clearance. We would've been okay with clearance paint."

I wave off his concern and pick up a roller, nodding at the tan wall I have a sneaky suspicion used to be white. "It's fine. This will be a whole lot better than what's here now. When money is less tight, maybe we can paint the cabinets white? What do you think?"

Quinn purses his lips, his head swaying from side to side. "That could look nice."

"Very basic-bitch white." Casen bobs his head. "I dig it."

"Casen!" I scold, though I can't stop the laughter that bubbles out of me.

"We can handle this since you got it all taped." Quinn picks up a roller.

I bite my lip. "I guess. Then I could start on the living room."

Another twin look.

Casen says, "Quinn can take care of the kitchen. I'll help with the living room."

"If you're sure?" The living room isn't huge, but it's quite a bit larger than this small space.

"I know we've only been here, like, a day," I ask Casen as we shuffle, single file, to the living room, "but what do you think so far?"

Casen picks up a roll of blue painter's tape and drops to his knees in front of the nearest baseboard. "Eh. It's a town, just like any other."

"Right," I sigh. "School doesn't start for a month. Maybe you guys can make some friends before then. Were there kids your age at the arcade?"

Before I'm even done speaking, I internally groan. I shouldn't have used the word *kids*. Teenagers don't like that kind of thing, do they? I can't remember what I was like at that age. I had to grow up fast, so I pretty much skipped over that whole phase of life. I went from being a kid to being the adult almost overnight. When Casen and Quinn were born, I was the one getting up with them in the middle of the night, making sure they were fed and changed.

"Some," he answers.

My shoulders slump. I really hate this one-word answer thing.

Too tired to force conversation, I get to work helping him tape so that we can get to the painting part. Already the smell of paint is stronger than the musty stench the house came with.

We're almost done with the first wall when he speaks again. "Halle?"

"Yeah, Case?" I keep my eyes on the roller as I coat the wall with paint, eager to get the work done. Painting the main walls of the house is going to be time-consuming.

"Quinn and I were talking. What if we got jobs? Then we could help you with bills and stuff."

Frozen in place, I squeeze my eyes shut. The heartbreak that his words triggers nearly brings me to my knees. Instantly, I'm transported back years. To when I was a girl, knowing we had no money for food or clothes, saying the same thing to my mom. She immediately jumped at the suggestion. And for a moment, it felt good. Knowing I could help her. Knowing I could make life better for my brothers. But I was way too young. Instead of just being a kid, I took on the brunt of responsibility for our entire family.

"No, Case." I exhale, letting the pain out with my breath. "Maybe when you're older. And only if you want to —a-and your money would be yours. I'm…" I don't want to lie to him. He's too smart for that. They both are. "Things are tight, but we're not that bad off. You two don't need to worry, I promise."

His eyes drop to the stained carpet beneath him. "Are you sure?"

My rambunctious, spunky, downright annoying little

brother looks like he's on the verge of tears. I hate the idea of either of them having to carry the burdens I did at their age. That was the whole point of my fight to gain guardianship.

"I promise. I might not be able to splurge on going out to dinner, and I may not get to spoil you with brand-new clothes, but the bills are paid, and we have money for necessities."

"You'll tell us if that changes? Promise?" My teenage brother holds out his pinky finger, wiggling it.

I loop my finger through his. "Promise."

The grocery store isn't busy, but the few shoppers here can't seem to take their eyes off us.

"I feel like a zoo exhibit," I mutter as we turn down another aisle.

Quinn snickers. "What kind of animal?"

I twist my lips and hum. "I don't know. Like a baboon or maybe a rhinoceros."

Casen barks out a laugh. "Those are two very different types of animals."

"Yeah, well." I shrug, examining a basket of apples that's been marked down. They're slightly bruised, but at the discounted price, they're worth the risk. I can't imagine fresh fruits will often be in the budget, and the boys will probably eat them before they can go bad anyway. They're *always* hungry. "I guess this is small-town life."

Our hometown was far from a big city, but Hawthorne

Mills is a speck of a town, and we're the shiny new toys everyone wants to speculate over.

"Are we really that interesting?" Casen asks as we move from the produce section to dairy. "They keep staring."

"Apparently we are." I open a refrigerator door, and as I pull a gallon of milk out, it takes effort not to cringe over the price. Jeesh. It's *milk*. How is it that expensive?

"Is it going to be like this when we start school?"

I turn to Quinn, no longer able to hold back the cringe. "Probably."

There's no point in sugarcoating it. They'll find out soon enough.

"Why do they care so much?" This from Casen.

I blow out a breath and carry on. "I guess they have nothing better to do."

Quinn punches Casen in the shoulder. "Maybe we should invite them all over. We can put them to work painting, then give them our whole sad backstory so they can move on."

I hate to admit it, but the kid might have a point.

"Come on," I say. "Let's get what we need so we can get out of here."

I hate that I can't make the transition easier for them. They've had to endure way more change than anyone should have to. I tried so hard to fill in the gaps left by Mom's parenting so they wouldn't have to experience what I did as a kid, but I worry I've failed epically.

We make it all the way to the ice cream aisle before we get stopped.

Every other person we've encountered has stared, but

this woman uses her shopping cart to block mine, blatantly cornering us by turning her cart so there's no way around her.

"I'm so sorry." I somehow keep my jaw from dropping, but the automatic apology escapes, even though our little collision wasn't my fault.

"I've seen you around." She wags an accusing finger, eyes narrowed. "You moved in across the street from me and my lover."

The boys snicker at the "my lover" comment.

I choke back my own laugh. "Did I? I haven't had the chance to meet many neighbors yet."

"I know," she replies, nose lifted a fraction. "You met that handsome man next door, though, I see."

"Uh…" My stomach twists at just the thought of him. "Caleb? Yeah, he helped us move in and so did…" Shit. What were their names?

"Thayer and Laith," she says.

Jeez. I live across from a nosy busybody. I have the rottenest luck ever.

"Yes," I say, inhaling deeply and searching for patience. "They helped too."

I search my brain for the name of the woman Caleb said lived across the street. "Are you Cynthia?"

"No," she snaps. "I'm Thelma. Cynthia's my wife. Well, we're not legally married, but it sounds nicer than admitting we're living in sin at our age."

My brothers, unable to help themselves, keel over in laughter. And I'm even closer to giving in and joining them.

"Laugh all you want, buddies," Thelma goes on. "I'm

finally living as my true, authentic self. I think that's what the young ones call it these days. To think I wasted so much time on *men*. They wouldn't know what the clitoris was if you smothered them with it."

"All right." Cheeks heating, I take an instinctive step back. "I really need to finish up here and get back home."

"I'm not done." She maneuvers her cart closer again. "I wanted to extend an invitation for dinner. My girl Cynthia is a great cook. She'll make you the best meatloaf you've ever had. Do you like meatloaf?" she asks, but before any of us can respond, she rambles on. "It doesn't matter." She waves a hand. "You'll like this one. Dinner is at six tonight. Don't come a minute sooner."

"I…" My words catch, my brain scrambling to catch up.

Before it can, she whips her cart around and scurries away. I have a feeling she did that on purpose so I'll feel too guilty not to come.

"What's a clitoris?" Quinn asks on one side of me. "Is that part of the vagina?"

"Is it where the pee comes out?" Casen adds.

I close my eyes, and even though I wouldn't consider myself a religious person, I send up a prayer. I'm going to need all the help I can get.

FOUR

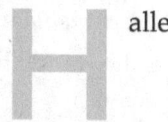alle

The box-made brownies hardly seem like the kind of neighborly thing Thelma will expect, but I hold on to them tightly as we cross the street anyway. She'd probably rather have an organ donation or a blood offering, but Betty Crocker brownies are all she's getting.

"Not sure this is a good idea," Casen mutters from my left.

On my right, Quinn adds, "Thelma gives 'I might murder you and bury you under my floors' vibes."

Teeth gritted, I look from one brother to the other.

"We'll be fine. She's like ninety pounds. We could take

her." I step to the side at the closed gate at the front of their yard, and Quinn swings it open.

He exchanges a look with his twin, and they give one another identical nods.

At least that's settled.

Caleb's car is gone again. Or still. It was gone early this morning. Not that it matters. I never asked what he did for work, but I feel guilty to have taken up so much of his time yesterday if he had to leave so early this morning. Especially since today has clearly been a long day out of the house for him.

The porch steps don't creak or groan as we go up. There's even a nice doorbell.

I peer over my shoulder and assess our run-down new home. *It's a work in progress. You'll get it all fixed eventually.*

It might take ten years, but eventually the raggedy house across the street will be my pride and joy.

I ring the doorbell and hold my breath. After the encounter earlier today in the grocery store, I'm not sure what to expect.

In a matter of seconds, the door swings open, revealing Thelma. "You're on time. I'm impressed."

She steps aside, allowing us to enter. The house is in better shape than mine, but it's a bit outdated. The living room to my left has pink carpet.

"I made these for dessert." I hold up the pan I'm still clutching tightly.

Lips pursed, she eyes it. "Brownies?"

"Yes?" For reasons unknown, it comes out as a question.

"Hmm." She takes the pan and shuffles down the hall. "Homemade?"

"I mean … I made it myself." I follow, assuming that's the right thing to do in this situation, the boys right behind me.

She comes to an abrupt stop, and I pull up short too. Poor Casen nearly trips on the rug but manages to catch himself.

"Out of a box, then, huh?"

I sigh. "Yes, it was Betty Crocker, if you must know."

Someone rescue me from this nightmare.

She harrumphs. "This way."

As we enter the kitchen, I have to admit that dinner does smell delicious.

In the kitchen, another woman sets a pair of oven mitts on the counter next to the range, and with a kind smile, smooths her hands down her apron. This must be Cynthia. "I hope this one isn't bothering you too much?" She tosses a thumb at Thelma. "She likes to mess with people."

Laughing, Thelma sets the pan of brownies on the counter. "Life's too boring not to." She grips my arm gently. "I hope I didn't annoy you too much."

I blink at her, head spinning. "I … huh?"

She goes on, undeterred by my general confusion. "There's no denying I'm nosy, but I'm not mean. Bossy? Yes. Otherwise, how would I have gotten you over here to have dinner with us? You're skin and bones, dear, but when we're done with you, you'll have some meat on you."

Again, I'm at a loss for words. "Oh. Okay."

It's perhaps the lamest thing that could've left my

mouth. In the past, I might've smarted back and told her how ridiculous she sounds, but frankly, I'm too exhausted to care. It's my natural state these days. I've been weary for over a decade now, the curse of having to grow up too soon and too fast.

Cynthia motions toward the dining room adjacent to the kitchen. "Go sit. This will just be a few more minutes."

I shoo the boys over to the table, but then turn back. "Are you sure you wouldn't like any help?"

"No, dear." She smiles, her eyes brimming with infinite kindness. It reminds me of my fifth-grade teacher. The woman who noticed I never brought a lunch and that my lunch account never had a balance. Who made sure I had something to eat every day. She always acted as if she'd packed too much. Back then, I took her actions at face value, secretly thrilled that this woman had such a bad habit of overpacking. It wasn't until years later that I realized what an unexpectedly kind gesture it was. I wasn't her kid or her problem, but she saw me. She saw beneath the façade I hid behind. The quiet girl who did her best not to be noticed. And when she looked at me, her eyes shone in the same way Cynthia's do now. Not with pity, but with care.

"Is it just me, or are these old ladies weird?" Quinn hisses under his breath as I sit across from him.

"Shush," I scold, giving him a light kick under the table.

I wouldn't put it past Thelma to have some kind of supersonic hearing.

After a minute or two, Cynthia appears with a loaf pan. Thelma is behind her with a bowl of salad and dressing.

"Can I help bring things to the table?" I ask, already halfway out of the chair.

"No," Cynthia says in a slightly scolding tone. "Stay where you are."

The two of them quickly head back into the kitchen.

Casen whimpers. "I think we've been kidnapped."

"Do you think they have a basement full of dead bodies?" Quinn adds.

I want to bang my head against the table, but I refrain. "Hush," I snap.

I'm tired, and the last thing I want to do is have to wrangle my brothers while also working on the motives of these women. I already hate this fucking town.

Cynthia and Thelma return, one carrying a bowl of mashed potatoes, the other with a tray of fresh rolls.

Okay, I may be questioning their sanity, but the dinner smells delicious. I will be gorging myself. Who knows when we'll have a meal like this again.

Even the boys exchange a look, eyes gleaming. It breaks my heart that I can't give them meals like this. Food is a luxury, regardless of what those who've never gone hungry say.

I scan the table, my mouth watering. "This looks incredible."

"Smells great too," Casen pipes in.

Quinn is too busy gazing at the spread with hearts in his eyes to say anything.

"Well, go on then. Dig in."

The words have barely left Thelma's mouth when the

boys are piling their plates high. She and Cynthia both watch, eyes wide in a mixture of fascination and terror.

"Hey, leave some for the rest of us." I try to keep my tone light, teasing, but it's a scolding, nonetheless. Any second, I expect our neighbors to change their minds about us and escort my brothers out of their house for acting like wild animals.

They slow, shooting sheepish looks around the table.

"Don't worry," Cynthia says with a nurturing smile aimed in my direction. "There's plenty more where that came from."

Once the boys have taken more than their fair share, the ladies nod for me to fill my plate. I'd much prefer they take the lead, but I do as I'm silently instructed, taking a small helping of each.

"Oh, honey, take more than that," Cynthia says, sympathy in her gaze.

"Are you sure?"

Thelma snorts. "We're positive."

I pile a little more onto my plate. I long ago got used to surviving without much food. On the rare occasions where we did have more than normal, I was reprimanded for being gluttonous if I took what my mother deemed as too much. I learned at an early age that it was better to eat less.

When the ladies ask the boys about whether they're excited for school to start in a month, Quinn shrugs, shoveling a forkful of mashed potatoes into his mouth. "I guess."

Casen's response isn't nearly as tempered. "School sucks."

I sigh, which triggers both ladies to look my way.

They go on asking question after question, curious about what I do and how I could possibly do it from home.

The dinner is delicious, but I find myself having trouble finishing my plate. I'm too busy fidgeting and trying to figure out the motivation behind all of their questions. And at the end of the night, despite my protests, Cynthia and Thelma send us home with all of the leftovers.

"Those old ladies might be weird," Casen says as I unlock the front door. "But they sure know how to cook."

He's not wrong.

As the boys file into the house, I peer over my shoulder, not at all surprised to see a set of eyes peering through the blinds across the street. I lift my hand, and they fall back into place.

FIVE

Halle

I haven't seen the neighbor, Caleb, in days, so I'm more than a little surprised when the porch light next door turns on, illuminating his tidy backyard, and he steps outside.

On instinct, I hunker down, like if I get low enough in the plastic chair, I can hide. I'm suddenly regretting turning on the shitty, flickering porch light. I should have gone with sitting in the dark as the sun set.

He braces his forearms on the railing of his deck, and his shoulders deflate like a several day-old balloon.

Since he hasn't noticed me, I take him in, cataloging his broad shoulders and his narrow waist. He's slender, but not lanky, his dark blond hair looking more honey brown beneath the darkening sky.

The last thing I should be doing is checking him out. Sleeping with a neighbor would only cause trouble. Maybe it'd scratch an itch, but then what? There's no way we could avoid one another after.

I'm trying not to notice how good his ass looks when he reaches into his back pocket and pulls out a rectangular pack.

Is that…?

He smacks it against the heel of his hand, then pulls out…yep, it is. He pulls out a cigarette, then slips the box back into his pocket. He holds the cigarette between his fingers for a few seconds, examining it like he's contemplating something. Eventually, he clamps his lips around one end and cups his hands around the other, lighting it.

With a sigh I can hear from here, he turns and leans against the railing, ankles crossed. He bows his head, his shoulders rounded in a way that makes him look sad, weary.

That's when he lifts his head and his eyes meet mine.

Fuck.

I've been caught.

And in a bad way. It's not like he just looked over and saw me. No, he caught me staring.

Kill me now.

A slow smile spreads across his face as he carefully pulls the cigarette from between his lips and waves.

I lift my hand in silent greeting, and when he starts down his porch steps, I curse myself. With each step he takes across the lawn, my heart hammers, and when he steps across the space where one entire fence panel is missing, my cheeks heat.

"Hey," he says in that deep timbre, sending a shiver down my spine.

I seriously need to get laid. It's been months. My last encounter was the opposite of memorable, clearly, or I'd remember how long it's been.

"I haven't seen you around," I blurt out like an idiot. Dammit. Now he knows I've been paying attention.

He takes another drag from his cigarette before tossing it to the ground and toeing it out in my grass. Before I can crack a joke about littering, he stoops and picks up the butt, then stuffs it into the pocket of his jeans.

"You wouldn't have. I work in Boston, and I stay there when I'm particularly busy."

"What do you do?" I point to the chair beside me. "It's not comfortable, but you can sit."

With a dip of his chin, he sits. As he settles, his scent washes over me. I have to hold my breath because, damn, he smells good, even with the hint of the cigarette still clinging to his white cotton shirt. His hair is damp, making me think the delicious scent is from his body wash.

"I'm an attorney." He leans back, the chair creaking beneath his weight.

"Ah," I breathe out. "I should've known."

Chuckling, he drums his fingers on the arms of the chair. "Why is that?"

"You have that look about you. Lawyer, doctor, architect, finance. Something big and important."

He cracks a grin, rubbing his fingers along the stubble lining his jaw. "You think I'm big and important?"

I roll my eyes. "I said you have the *look*." We're quiet for a long moment, my cheeks heating and his attention fixed on me. Eventually, I work up the nerve to ask, "What kind of attorney are you?"

"Family law." A haunted look crosses his face.

"Tough case?" I pick up my can of soda and take a long swallow. After the day I've had—my first at the coffee shop, then coming home to find the house a disaster—I probably need something stronger, but I refuse to touch alcohol. I've seen the worst side of it. I've seen how easy it is to move on to harder stuff. And I won't risk it.

"You have no idea." He lets out a weary sigh. One that sounds a lot like the noise my neighbor used to make. Back when he'd tell me to enjoy being a kid while I could, because adulthood sucked. He'd sit out on his stoop, sighing over everything. I never told him, but even back then, I was long past feeling like a kid. The minute I stepped into the house, I'd be responsible for taking care of my mom and my brothers. That's why I sat outside talking to him so often. "That's the reason for the cigarette. I only smoke when I'm feeling particularly troubled."

"You want to talk about it?" I ask.

He shakes his head. "Just a hard case is all. Reunification is typically what we hope for, but in this situation, I don't believe that's what's best for the kids. It's hard. I have a feeling they'll be back in the system again."

On instinct, I peer over my shoulder. On the other side of the sliding-glass door, the living room is awash in the soft glow of the TV, and I can just make out my brothers' forms on the couch.

"So." Caleb stretches his legs out, laying his large hands on his knees. "Tell me about your day. Surely it was better than mine."

I snort, a thread of unease working through me. "Today was my third day at the coffee shop in town, and I managed to mess up nearly every order. I spilled coffee on myself and dropped an entire tray of almond croissants. I'll be lucky if I'm not fired. I'm not making a good impression."

I spent my entire lunch break sitting in my car crying. Normally, I'm a master at keeping my shit together, but today got to me. I'm tired of trying so hard and nothing working out in my favor.

"I'm sorry," he murmurs.

I shrug. "It is what is."

Those four words make my chest constrict. I've been repeating them to myself for years. There's no point in wallowing when things don't go well.

Even if that's exactly what I came outside to do.

"Still, it's okay to admit it was a sucky day."

I sigh. "Fine. Today fucking sucked."

With a laugh, he crosses his arms over his chest. "Today fucking sucked."

"So," I begin, "if you have a place in Boston, why do you have a house here? Seems like it would be more convenient to live in Boston full time."

"It's a long story," he warns, dropping his head back.

I arch a brow, even if he's not looking at me. "And?"

Sighing, he straightens. "You sure you want it?"

"Please." I probably sound too eager, but honestly, my interest has more to do with needing a distraction than anything else.

"I grew up here. My family founded the town generations ago. Somewhere along the way, our last name morphed from Hawthorne to just Thorne." He rubs at his face, looking more haggard than even a moment ago. Dark circles haunt the space beneath his eyes, and his lids are heavy like he hasn't slept well in a while. "Anyway, my ex-wife moved back here and got married, so I bought the house next door."

A bark of laughter bursts out of me. "To what? Torment her?"

The way he flinches makes me instantly wish I could take that back.

"No." The word escapes him slowly, his eyes fixed on his hands clasped in front of him. "To be close to my daughter. If I stayed in Boston all the time, I'd barely have any time with her. I'm not here as much as I'd like to be, but this way, I get to see her at least once a week."

"That must be hard."

Clearly, he cares deeply for his daughter if he's willing to buy the house next door to his ex to be close to her.

"It is. Our situation is unconventional, to say the least." He spreads his fingers on his thighs and lets out a long exhale. "But it works for us."

"How old is she? Your daughter?"

He smiles softly, eyes distant. "Ten."

"Ten?" I try not to let my shock show. "How old are you?"

His low chuckle rumbles through me. "Twenty-nine."

Younger than I thought. When I think about it, I suppose he doesn't look over thirty, but the way he carries himself and the depth in his eyes make him appear older.

"Wow. I can't imagine having a baby at nineteen."

It's silly to say that, since I've been practically raising my brothers since I was nine, but still...

"Life happens." His reply is simple, and when he drums his fingers on the arms of the chair and looks out at the yard, I know that part of our conversation is over. "I see Thayer got your yard mowed."

"He really didn't have to do that." I tuck a stray strand of hair behind my ear.

After doing things on my own for so long, having people I don't even know offer to help is strange.

"I'm sure he didn't mind."

Coming home to a well-manicured lawn after my first day at the coffee shop had been surprisingly nice. The yard still needs a lot of work to look anything like Caleb's or Thayer's but this is still a huge upgrade.

Despite the dirt patches and ignore the broken fence.

Gaze averted, I play with the ends of my hair. "In case you haven't noticed, I don't do well with help."

He laughs, a deep, throaty sound. "I figured that out within five minutes of meeting you."

"I'm used to fending for myself."

Caleb's face softens, his shoulders lowering. "I'm sorry."

Normally those words make anger simmer in my veins. Pity gets my hackles up. But when I study him, that's not what I see. No, his expression is full of genuine concern instead.

He assesses me in return, those blue eyes seeing more than I want them to. It makes sense, I guess, knowing what he does. He probably sees right through me. He probably clocked our situation the night we met.

His eyes hold mine, the blue a gentle, swaying current. "You won't have to keep fending yourself. Not here. We all look after each other."

I flinch. "I'm not from here. None of you really know me."

"Doesn't matter." He stands and stretches, his white t-shirt riding up, showing off just a sliver of skin above his waistband. "You're one of us now."

Without another word, he turns and saunters back over to his house. At his back door, he lifts his hand in a wave, then he ducks inside.

After the door has shut, I say, "I'm not so sure about that."

SIX

Caleb

"I've missed you, Daddy," Seda says softly, perusing the menu even though she'll order French toast like she does every time we're here.

"I've missed you too."

Some might think it's strange that I coparent a child who isn't technically mine. To them, I would say that blood means little when it comes to love.

Salem and I broke up before I went to college, but when she came back to me, pregnant with Thayer's baby, I knew I'd be there for her and that child any way I could be. At the time, I didn't think we'd ever be more than just friends.

Eventually, though, we grew closer again. It probably helped that we had some distance from Hawthorne Mills. When it was just us, it didn't take long to get back to the way we'd been. Our connection had always been easy like that. Deep down, I knew she still cared for Thayer, but I loved her enough to look past it. After all, *I* had her, and he didn't.

Even still, I wasn't surprised when she asked for a divorce.

Sad? Sure.

Surprised? No.

But I wouldn't take that time back—our short marriage, raising Seda, none of it.

The day Seda was born was the happiest of my life. The memories are bittersweet, but recalling them always settles my soul.

"Caleb?" Salem stands in the doorway of the bedroom, holding her stomach, a pained expression contorting her face. "I think this is it."

I can't help but give her a skeptical look. We've had two false alarms already.

"For real this time," she says through gritted teeth. "I'm leaking..." Her cheeks flame. "I think my water broke. Or maybe it's breaking. I don't know. It's not a big gush like the movies, but I think that's what it is."

I move swiftly into action, grabbing the bags we packed in preparation for this day. "Get in the car," I tell her. "I'll get everything else."

In a matter of minutes, I've loaded our bags, along with the one for the baby, and several pillows. The car seat has already been installed. I specifically went to the firehouse to ensure it was done correctly. When I'm certain we have everything we could possibly need while we're at the hospital, I slide in behind the wheel.

"Do you think we're bringing too much?" she asks, her lip caught between her teeth.

"No." Yes. Way too much. But better safe than sorry. I don't want to leave her side if I don't have to.

Twenty minutes later, we pull into the hospital parking lot. Salem hasn't complained once, despite the pain contorting her face every few minutes.

"How far apart are they?" I ask.

"About six minutes, I think."

Once I've parked, I dart to the entrance in search of a wheelchair, and as I rush back and find she's already waddling toward me, I curse. She'd smack me if she knew I called her walk a waddle, but that's exactly what it is.

"Salem," I scold. "Get in the chair."

She does so without protest, clearly in a lot of pain. I hit the lock button on my fob and spin her around. I'll be back for our stuff later. Right now, I need to get her inside.

Check-in goes smoothly since we preregistered, and in triage, a nurse confirms that she's in active labor, adding that she's already at six centimeters.

Salem squeezes the life out of my hand, eyes squished shut.

"Breathe," I tell her when her face reddens.

"Shut up," she bites out. "It feels like a bowling ball is trying to force its way out of my vagina. It fucking hurts."

I press my lips together.

Silence.

Got it.

Several hours and one epidural later, it's time for Salem to push.

I hold one leg while a nurse takes the other.

"Come on, baby," I whisper, kissing the side of her head. "You've got this."

Her bottom lip wobbles, her eyes full of terror. "I'm scared."

"Don't be. On the other side of this, you get to meet your daughter."

*She squeezes my hand, lips quivering. "*Our *daughter."*

Fuck. Tears immediately burn my eyes. Those simple words mean more to me than she'll ever know. Despite my classes and work, I haven't missed a single appointment. I want to be involved in everything. The ultrasounds, the baby's movements, all of it. Night after night, I've talked to our child, more and more excited to meet her.

"Our daughter," I echo around the lump in my throat.

"All right, Salem," the doctor says. "Here comes another contraction. I want you to bear down and push. Trust your body. It knows what it's doing."

She does as she's instructed. When she pauses for a break, she brings those pleading eyes to mine. "Don't look down there."

I laugh. "A little late for that, sweetheart."

She groans. "You know what I mean."

Smiling, I smooth the sweaty blond hair off her forehead. Her eyes are tired, but there's a determination there too. "I want to watch. I don't want to miss a single detail of this. You're bringing our child into the world. Already, this is the most important thing I've ever been part of."

She bites her lip. "*Then don't judge whatever else may happen down there.*"

I laugh again. "*I won't, baby.*"

An hour later, a tired, teary-eyed Salem gives one last push, and finally, our daughter comes screaming into the world, arms flailing, covered in goo. And she's absolutely perfect.

Tears fall from my eyes of their own accord.

A nurse suctions stuff out of her mouth, then the doctor plops her onto Salem's chest.

Salem sobs, patting the baby's back and repeating "oh my God" over and over again.

I kiss her, murmuring, "*I love you so much. Look what you did. Look how amazing you are.*"

"*She's perfect,*" *she sobs.* "*Just look at her, Caleb.*"

And I do.

I feel it then.

That I'm this little girl's dad, not because she shares my DNA, but because I choose her.

"What are you thinking about?" Seda asks, playing with a strand of her blond hair.

She looks like a clone of her mother. I don't see a trace of Thayer in her. Or perhaps that's only wishful thinking on my part.

"How much I love you."

She beams. "I love you too, Daddy. Mom said I can hang out with you all day if you're free."

"I'm always free for you."

Even if I weren't in Hawthorne Mills, if my girl called me and said she needed me, I wouldn't hesitate to hop in the car and drive back to see her.

I swore I would be a different kind of parent to her than mine were for me. My parents weren't inherently terrible, but they put a lot of pressure on me to be the best at everything. It was too much for a kid, and it's my life's mission to make sure Seda doesn't have to experience that kind of overwhelming strain. If she's happy, then that's enough for me.

Seda smiles, her shoulders lowering in relief. "Good. Samson cries *so* much. Mom says he's teething."

"He probably is. Remember how it hurts when your adult teeth grow in?" I ask, leaning forward a fraction. "Now try being a baby and not knowing what's happening."

"But he's not a baby anymore," she argues. "He's almost two."

"Yes, but he's still a little guy, and he's probably getting his molars. That's gotta hurt. Have some sympathy."

She frowns. "So should I get him a stuffie or something?"

Smiling, I lift a shoulder. "We could if you want. It might cheer him up."

"Hmm." She tilts her head. "I think we should. Oh, and Mom said you should come over for dinner. She's making lasagna."

"Sounds good. What should we do between now and then?"

Her blue eyes light up and she bounces in her seat. "Could we go to the mall?"

The mall is nearly an hour away, but it's one of her favorite places. She isn't old enough for makeup yet—

though she'll argue over that point—but that doesn't stop her from perusing every store that sells the stuff.

I wind my straw wrapper around my finger absently. My dad once said it looked ridiculous for a man to use a straw in a restaurant. Dumbest shit I've ever heard. Who knows how many people handle the outside of these glasses. It feels more sanitary this way.

"If that's what you want."

"It is." She nods, her head bobbing a little too vigorously.

As our server sets our plates before us, Seda rubs her hands together eagerly. My girl *loves* French toast.

"Thanks," I say as I pick up the syrup and drizzle a generous amount over my pancakes.

A day like this, spent with Seda, is exactly what I need after a rough week. Sometimes I question my profession, or at least my specialty. I prefer my quiet life here in Hawthorne Mills—even if it gives my overbearing mother more access to me than I'd like—but I do what I do for the families I can help. If I stopped, the guilt would consume me. How many families wouldn't receive the proper help? Sure, there are other attorneys in Boston, but I'm good at what I do. It would be a disservice to so many if I gave it up.

But I'm too young to feel so weary. I'm not quite thirty, yet somehow, I feel closer to fifty.

Once we're finished, we step into the sunshine side by side. It's a beautiful summer day in Hawthorne Mills. It may only be seventy now, but it'll be eighty by the afternoon.

Seda starts toward my car, but I shake my head and grasp her arm. "I need coffee first."

The coffee at the diner is always too bitter and slightly burned-tasting, and the single cup I had first thing this morning isn't enough.

Seda scurries along beside me as I head down the sidewalk, a happy pep in her step. "Can I get coffee?"

"No," I say, just like I do every time she asks.

"When I'm older?"

"Yeah, when you're older."

She peers up at me as we cross the street. "Like next year?"

"Mm," I hedge. "Maybe a little longer."

She sighs, her steps turning heavier. "But that's forever from now."

"It'll be here before you know it, trust me."

I never believed my parents when they said that time flies, when they told me to enjoy things and not rush life. But somehow, I blinked and my newborn baby girl turned into a ten-year-old.

Seda steps in first, and I follow. There's a short line, and behind the counter, Halle works. Her brown hair is pulled back in a sloppy ponytail, a few stray hairs escaping from beneath her baseball cap.

Frazzled doesn't even begin to properly convey how she looks.

"Uh." She blinks at the person standing across the counter. "What did you say your name was again?"

"Darren."

"Right." Sharpie in hand, she takes a cup off the stack,

but he clears his throat, and she freezes. "Is something wrong?"

"I ordered an iced coffee. Not hot."

Halle slowly lowers the paper cup. "Right. I knew that."

She pulls a plastic cup next, then scrawls the man's name and sets it on the counter. "That'll be four dollars and seventy-five cents."

The man pays and moves to the side to wait, and Halle takes the next order.

When I finally step up to the counter, Halle lets out a frustrated groan. "How long have you been here witnessing my misery?"

"Long enough." I bite back a smile.

"What can I get you, then?" Halle asks, fingers shaking slightly against the touchscreen.

"A black coffee, please."

She taps on the screen and picks up a cup, though she stops with it lifted in midair. "Oh, wait. What size?"

"The one you have is fine."

"Okay," she says, staring at it.

The woman standing at the espresso machine sighs. "Just put an X for black coffee."

"Right." Halle's cheeks flame red, her head lowered as she marks my cup with an X and slides it down the counter.

"That'll be three dollars and fifty-five cents."

I hand her a five-dollar bill. When she passes me the change I stuff it in the tip jar. "I hope your day gets better, Halle."

"Do you two know each other?" Seda asks, squinting at me, then Halle.

"She and her brothers just moved in next door to us."

"Oh." Seda's face brightens. "I've seen you. Those boys are your brothers?"

Halle nods, swallowing thickly. "They are. I hope they haven't bothered you."

Seda shakes her head, blond hair swaying. "No. They're nice."

Halle's eyes go wide. "Oh. Well, good, then."

"They came over and swam at my house yesterday."

"They did?" My new neighbor's once flushed cheeks have lost most of their color. "They didn't tell me."

Seda bites her lip, her eyes flitting up to me, then down to the counter. "Maybe I wasn't supposed to say? I don't want to get them in trouble."

"No, no," Halle says, adjusting her cap. "It's fine." To me she says, "I take it this is your daughter?"

Pride fills my chest. "Yes, this is Seda."

"Nice to meet you," Seda says with a smile. "I should've said that first."

"Come on." I squeeze her shoulder. "Let's leave poor Halle alone."

For a moment, Halle watches us, but then between one blink and the next, she straightens and focuses on the woman who steps up to the register, pasting on a fake smile.

"You still want to go to the mall?" I ask Seda as the woman who sighed at Halle calls my name and sets my coffee on the pickup counter.

She scoffs. "Of course."

I should have known better than to hope she might have changed her mind.

"All right, kiddo, let's go then."

Hours later, I park in my driveway and follow Seda over to Salem and Thayer's house. Inside, it smells like a gourmet Italian restaurant, the scent of basil and mozzarella filling the air.

"Seda! Seda! Seda! I missed you!" Seda's little sister, Soleil, barrels into her, nearly knocking her off her feet. "You've been gone *forever*."

"Only since this morning, silly goose." Seda tugs on one of Soleil's pigtails.

Thayer pokes his head out from the kitchen, dishrag tossed over his shoulder. "You're back," he says to Seda. "Hey, Caleb. You staying for dinner?"

I dip my chin. "Thanks for having me."

He plucks the rag from his shoulder, wiping at his fingers. "You want a glass of wine? A beer?"

"Wine would be great."

Seda and Soleil scurry over to where their brother is playing in his toddler-sized ball pit in the corner of the living room. He throws one, and it hits Seda square in the forehead, but as I step into the kitchen, my little girl is unfazed, greeting the little guy with a hug.

"Hi," Salem says, pulling the lasagna out of the oven. "I'm glad you could come."

"I'll never say no to lasagna."

Unless my mom makes it, but it has nothing to do with her cooking skills. No, it's because every time I go over to their house, I'm subjected to a lecture. Even now that I'm pushing thirty, she still treats me like a child whose every move needs to be guided.

"Everything is ready. Want to toss the salad while I get the kids' plates fixed?" she asks, setting the pan down on a hot plate.

Without hesitation, I work to assemble the makings they've prepped and set out on the counter, only pausing when Thayer holds a glass of wine out to me.

"Thanks." I lift my glass in his direction. "Oh, and thanks for tending to Halle's yard."

"It wasn't a problem," he says, heading out of the kitchen. A moment later he returns with a giggling Samson tossed over his shoulder. "In you go." He sets the kid in his highchair and snaps his wriggling form into it in record time.

Sam finally notices me, reaching his chubby hands out. "Cal! Cal!"

"Hey, buddy." I bend down, meeting his eyes, and ruffle his hair. "What have you been up to today?"

"Snacks," he answers.

Salem laughs from where she's dishing out lasagna. "If the kid isn't walking around with a cracker in one hand and a drink in the other tormenting the pets, then I swear he's not happy."

"Aw, that's not true, is it?"

He giggles in response.

"All right, kids," Thayer hollers. "Get in here and grab

your plates."

Seda and Soleil tumble into the kitchen, dashing for Salem, and with a warning to walk carefully and use both hands, they take their plates to the table.

As I watch, an ache settles deep in my gut.

I've moved on from Salem.

I loved her, a part of me will always love her, but I realize now that she's not the love of my life. We never had the connection she shares with Thayer.

But I want that. A soul-deep special kind of connection.

And I miss *this*. The kids. Having a family to come home to every night.

Sure, I'm young.

I have plenty of time to find the right person. To settle down. Have more kids.

But some days the life I want feels out of reach, and it hurts.

"Here's your plate, Caleb," Salem says, breaking me out of my thoughts.

I take it from her with a quiet "thank you" and sit beside Seda.

Samson bangs his fists on his tray. "Lagna! Lagna! Lagna!" he demands.

His chant pulls at my heartstrings. I'll miss it when he begins to pronounce things correctly. Just like I miss all of Seda's mispronunciations.

When Thayer and Salem join us, it hits me that Thayer's brother isn't here, which is unusual.

"Where's Laith?"

Thayer groans.

Salem, on the other hand, singsongs, "He's on a date."

"Oh?" Though I arch a brow lazily, inside, my heart races with panic, and the strangest fear engulfs me. What if he's out with Halle?

I shake my head. The idea is ridiculous. And even so, why should I care?

Thayer stifles a snort. "It's one of his app buddies, don't get too excited."

By app buddies, he means one of the women Laith hooks up with.

"Shush." Salem swats at him. "He doesn't normally take them on dates. This is progress."

Thayer grumbles, "Whatever you want to call it."

Laith's refusal to settle down is a sore spot for his family. After spending an evening out with him and a few beers to many, I know there's more to the story, but I'm not about to spill his secrets.

"He'll get there," Salem says, wearing a small smile. "And what about you?" She zeroes in on me.

"What about me?" I feign confusion, suddenly feeling cornered.

"Are you dating anyone?"

"No."

It hurts, the way her eyes dim. She'd love to see me settle down, to find my person, but she also harbors guilt, worried that she wasted my time while we were married. Like maybe she kept me from meeting the woman I'm supposed to be with.

I dated one of Seda's teachers for about six months, but it just didn't work out. That's how it goes most of the time. I haven't given up hope, but between the stress that comes with my line of work and carving out all the time I can for Seda, just the idea of finding time to dedicate to another person is exhausting.

"Once things slow down at work," I say, hoping to assuage her guilt, "I'll have more time to date. Don't worry about me."

Seda clears her throat, bringing my attention to her. Her mouth is ringed in tomato sauce, and her eyes are bright. "What about Halle?" she asks. "Maybe you could ask her on a date."

My stomach knots in a weird way. Part denial and part interest. I stick with denial. "We're neighbors, sweetie. That could get complicated. And I'm sure she's still trying to get settled in. I doubt she's actively looking to date."

Thayer let's out an amused laugh. "Don't let being neighbors stop you if you're interested."

Another knot of my stomach. This one a little less pleasant. Right. That's how he and Salem met.

I run my fingers through my hair.

"I don't have time to date," I reiterate, keeping my tone firm. "So that's that."

Thayer and Salem exchange a look, but neither speaks.

It's rare that either of them genuinely irritates me, but at times like this, I can't help but feel a little rankled. They have their own secret, silent language, and they're clearly using it to talk about me without saying a word.

There's no point. My lack of a love life is not their burden to bear.

And I'm going to have to meet up with Laith soon so I

can warn him that these two seem interested in meddling in our love lives.

By some miracle, we make it through the rest of dinner without another mention of dating, and once I've gotten hugs from all the kids, I head home, carrying a plate full of cupcakes Salem insisted I take. I had the whole house renovated when I bought it. New paint and new floors, and I had the kitchen and bathrooms gutted and redone. On the inside, it doesn't even resemble the house I purchased, which is exactly what I was going for. I wanted to make this place mine.

I flick on the light in the foyer and pad to the kitchen, where I set the plate on the counter. I know I should shower and go to bed, but instead, I'm drawn to my back porch, unable to resist looking for Halle.

I step outside and drop into the rocker on my deck. As I lean back, I peer over, going for casual.

Sure enough, she's there and she's...

I sit up straight. Why the fuck is she crying?

Before I know what I'm doing, I'm off the porch and striding across the lawn.

SEVEN

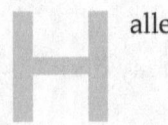alle

No, no, no. The words echo in my mind as Caleb steps onto his back porch, and when he spots me bawling my eyes out, I wish the ground would open up and swallow me whole.

The last thing I need is for him to witness my humiliation.

I dash my tears away and stand. I've got my hand on the doorknob, ready to slip inside and pretend I didn't see him, when he barks out, "What's wrong? Who hurt you?"

At the sound of genuine worry in his tone, my breath catches. Slowly, I turn and exhale. "No one."

He bounds up the three porch steps, each one groaning

beneath his feet. I'm pretty sure the whole decking is rotted out, but that's a problem for future Halle.

"Then what's wrong? You're crying."

Now that my escape has been thwarted, I brush past him and plop down in the plastic chair. "It's nothing."

"Listen," he says, easing into the other chair.

I don't know whether to be offended or pleased by the way he so easily invites himself over and gets comfortable.

"I know it's none of my business, but if there's anything I can do to help, please tell me."

I inhale a shaky breath, blinking back another round of tears, and force myself to meet his eye. "Has anyone ever told you that you're a bit of a fixer?"

He winces. "A time or two."

"You don't need to do that. Not with me. You don't know me. I don't expect you to swoop in like Superman and fix my life. My problems are mine to deal with."

I've dug myself out of shit more times than I can count, and I'll do it again the next time I find myself stuck. I've only ever had myself to rely on, and that won't change just because my new neighbor has a savior complex.

"I just ... I like to help," he says softly, almost brokenly.

Brow furrowed, I assess him. The light hair and the dusting of stubble shadows his achingly perfect jawline—

Stop. Good God. Stop thinking about his jawline! We have more pressing issues to deal with!

It hits me then. Caleb and I are a lot alike. I might not know him well, but it's obvious that he takes care of the people he cares about, probably to his own detriment, and I do the same. Time and again, I've put myself in a tough spot to help my mom out or take care of my brothers. Our situation now is the definition of that. I'm now fully responsible for them when, some days, I feel as though I can hardly look out for myself.

I clear my throat. "But who helps you?"

Brow furrowed, he lowers his gaze to his hands in his lap. For a long moment, he doesn't speak, like he's really considering my question. Finally, he straightens and says, "I don't know. No one, I guess. Not really anyway."

Though the candidness surprises the shit out of me, I keep my expression tempered, only giving him a small, sad smile. "It's tough being the fixer."

"The fixer?" He arches a brow.

"Yeah, the person who swoops in and takes care of everyone else, even as they continue to struggle on their own."

"That's what you think I am?" He cocks his head to the side, curiosity glimmering in his blue eyes.

"I don't just think it. It's been obvious since the day I met you. You helped a total stranger move in, then fed us, refusing to take no for an answer. And when I discovered that you bought a house beside your ex-wife and her husband to be close to your kid? That only confirmed the theory. It doesn't get any more fixer than that."

He frowns, lacing his fingers together. "Fuck, you're right."

I tip an imaginary cup in his direction in a mock toast. "Welcome to the club."

He watches me out of the corner of his eye for a few long seconds, then clears his throat. "Don't think you've distracted me from the reason I came over. You were over here crying."

I groan, burying my face in my hands. "I was really hoping you'd forget that."

"I forget nothing." He kicks his legs up on the railing.

My lungs squeeze tight, scared that the whole railing will crumble, taking the whole house down with it.

Miraculously, it holds. It's a wonder, really. If it collapsed, that would be the icing on the cake that is my epically shit-tastic day.

"I got fired," I say, throat burning with the threat of a fresh wave of tears. "From the coffee shop," I add. "It might not seem like much, but I need the extra income."

Though his eyes drill into the side of my face, I don't dare look at him. If I do, I'll break down again. Normally I'm better at keeping my shit together, but with the added stress of keeping a roof over my brothers' heads, I've reached my limit.

With a sigh, I stare out at the field behind our houses. It's filled with wildflowers, but tonight, all that's visible are the intermittent twinkling of fireflies.

I inhale, finding that my breath is embarrassingly shaky. I'm not even surprised I got fired. Normally I can toss myself into any situation and figure it out, but the chaos of the coffee shop, the constant noise and busyness, had me too flustered to function properly. I made a fool of myself.

"Would you like a cupcake?"

At the out-of-pocket question, I whip around to face him. "What?" I laugh. "Where did that question come from?"

Shrugging, he stands. "You sound like you could use a cupcake, and I happen to have some at home."

With my lips pressed together, I assess him, trying not to notice how delicious he looks. "This is feeling very much like a real-life *get in the van and I'll give you candy* moment."

His laughter floats around us on the night air. It's a nice laugh. Warm and sweet. It suits him.

"Do you want a cupcake or not?" he asks, eyes dancing in the moonlight. Hands in the pockets of his jeans, he leans against the railing. "I could always eat them all myself, but—"

I hold up a hand. "I'm a girl who's had a bad day. I'm not saying no to a cupcake."

Inside, the boys are still sprawled out in front of the TV, watching a movie. Knowing they won't even notice my absence, I follow Caleb down the stairs and across the yards. This is the first time I've crossed the invisible line that separates our homes. Despite the darkness, I try to eat up every detail. Like the small outdoor table set up close to the house with a variety of herbs on top of it.

"My daughter wanted to grow them," he says when he notices where my gaze has gone.

With a nod, I continue my inspection, taking in the swing set and ground-level trampoline.

His porch steps don't creak or groan beneath our weight, and his back door slides open silently as I follow him into his house.

"Wow." The word is out before I can stop it. "This is beautiful," I add, since there's no taking my awe back now.

The interior walls on the main level have been removed

so the dining room, kitchen, and living room are all open to one another. The wooden beams that crisscross the ceiling add warmth to the space. So does the fluffy-looking couch. It faces a tv that looks more like a framed piece of art than an expensive piece of electronics. The dining room boasts a table large enough for six. The kitchen is spacious, the chandelier above the island surprising for the home of a single man yet still fitting. The cabinets are a light brown wood color that pairs perfectly with what looks like marble countertops. The stairs near the front door have been hollowed out, and beneath them is a custom bookshelf, every inch of which is filled with books and knickknacks and photos.

This is what I want some day. A beautiful, updated house that still feels like a home.

"Thank you," he says, leaning against the side of the island. "I had help with the design. And though I did as much work as I could on my own, I had to hire more of it out than I would have liked."

"I'm sure, with your job, you don't have a lot of time for home improvement projects."

"Exactly." He nods toward one of the stools tucked against the island. "Take a seat."

I settle in and glide my finger along one of the veins in the stone countertop. Caleb doesn't move.

"So," I say, brow arched. "Where are these cupcakes you promised me?"

He grins, and a dimple I've never noticed before pops out, instantly causing my heart to skip a beat.

"I promised you *a* cupcake," he teases. "I didn't say anything about sharing any more than that." He shuffles to the other side of the kitchen, and when he turns, he's holding a plate completely full of cupcakes. "That one there is chocolate-chocolate." He sets the plate in front of me and points to the one with smooth chocolate icing. "Birthday cake, strawberry lemonade, cookie dough, brownie sundae, orange creamsicle, banana split, red velvet, and finally, peanut butter."

Mouth watering, I blink at the selection. "That's quite the random selection."

He shrugs. "Salem owns a cupcake shop. She always has extras."

"Salem is your ex, right? Seda's mom?"

"Yeah. Want a drink?" He steps back and pulls open a cabinet.

"Water would be great," I reply. "I haven't had a chance to meet her yet."

"I'm sure she'll introduce herself soon. And when she does, she'll probably show up with more of these." He gestures to the assortment of cupcakes. "I was kidding, by the way, when I said you could only have one. I'll never eat all of these. Take as many as you want."

"One is more than enough." I already feel indebted to this man. In a matter of days, he's done more for me than almost anyone ever has. And he's been gone for a good portion of the time that my brothers and I have been in Hawthorne Mills.

"At least take a few for your brothers."

I bite my lip, uncertainty swamping me. "You really wouldn't mind?"

His gaze softens, the blue of his irises darkening. "I don't mind at all."

I swipe the birthday cake flavor for Casen and brownie sundae for Quinn, then pick up my water and slowly sip it.

Caleb stares at me, waiting.

"What?" The question is pointless. I already know what he's going to say.

"You're supposed to take one for yourself too, Halle."

My stomach sinks a little. "I feel bad. I don't want to take all your cupcakes."

"Halle." His bossy, commanding tone should bother me. Instead, I feel it in places I don't want to think about.

To distract myself, I snag the red velvet.

"Good." With a nod, he picks up the peanut butter one. "Eat up."

Certain that he'll scold me again if I don't, I peel the paper from the cupcake and take a bite. "Mmm," I hum as the flavor of the cake and the rich cream cheese frosting register. "This might be the best red velvet cupcake I've ever had." I take another bite.

He chuckles, amusement lightening his eyes a hue. "And to think you held yourself back."

I purse my lips. "I was trying to be nice."

"Hey." He raises his hands. "I offered you a cupcake in the first place. You were always going to get one."

For the next several moments, we eat our cupcakes in silence. I have to hold back a moan more than once to keep from embarrassing myself, but the flavor is incredible, so it's not easy.

Eventually, he wipes his mouth and clears his throat. "If

you really do need another job, I might have a solution for you."

"Really?" I straighten and survey the house. "Do you need help cleaning?" Keeping this place clean wouldn't be so bad. From the sound of things, he's gone a lot, and—

"No." He drops his head and huffs a laugh. "I'm good on that front, but I do need an assistant. I've been putting off looking for someone, but now…" He shrugs. "It's yours if you want it."

"An assistant?" I fiddle with the cupcake wrapper while the thought settles in. But in seconds, my shoulders droop, and I shake my head. "I can't travel into Boston. The commute would be too long."

"No, you'd work from here." He straightens on his side of the island. "Answer emails, phone calls, keep up with my schedule. Things like that. I don't see any reason you'd need to come to Boston. You can use my home office. The computer is secure."

I press my lips together. Another remote position. It's tempting, but it feels like charity. Like he doesn't really need an assistant. He's just making this up because he's a fixer. And after what a disaster the coffee shop turned out to be, I can't help but doubt myself.

Caleb splays his hands on the marble countertop and ducks so we're eye to eye. "How about a trial run? That way we can make sure the situation works for both of us before I hire you on part time."

I twist the ring on my thumb. It's nothing special, a flea market find, but it's one of very few items my mom ever gave me just because. Maybe it's stupid to cherish it, but I do.

Lips pressed together, I nod. "A trial run would be good."

He pushes his hair off his forehead for what has to be the third or fourth time tonight, his focus fixed on me. "I'll be home until Sunday night. What day works best for you?"

"Tomorrow?" The sooner I know whether this will work, the better. "Around two?"

He picks up his phone, taps at the screen, and nods. "Works for me." After a few more taps, he slips his phone into his pocket. Then, without a word, he pulls plastic wrap out of a drawer and tears off a piece.

"Thanks for this. It did make me feel better." I wad up the cupcake liner and stand, and before I can ask where I should dispose of it, he pulls out a cabinet with a hidden trashcan. "Fancy," I mutter, tossing the wrapper in. "I better get going." I shuffle to the back door and peer back at him. "Make sure my brothers haven't killed each other."

He nods once. "I'll walk you home."

"It's literally next door. I'll be fine."

But Caleb can't be persuaded. He follows me outside, carrying the plate holding my brothers' cupcakes, only handing it to me when I've pulled the back door open.

"See you tomorrow," he says, carefully stepping off the porch. He eyes the foundation like he, too, worries the whole thing might fall apart.

"See you," I agree.

I lock up behind me, scared to admit to myself that maybe Caleb really is my guardian angel.

EIGHT

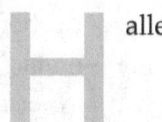alle

As I take in Caleb's front yard from up close, it's obvious he's put a great deal of time and energy into it. New pavers make up the walkway to the porch steps, and the front of the house is lined with bushes and wispy yellow flowers.

The siding is a warm gray blue that complements the brick on the foundation. My house looks positively pitiful next to this one, but with enough time and money, I'm hopeful I can change that.

The front door is a muted shade of orange—I've never been a fan of the color, but somehow it works—and the doorknocker is shaped like a dragonfly. It makes me think his daughter picked it out. Based on the little herb garden in the back, Caleb seems like the type to let his little girl have a say in things like that.

There's no doorbell, so I use the knocker to signal my arrival. When he doesn't answer, I try again, knocking harder this time.

When the door swings open, my breath catches at the sight I'm confronted with.

A shirtless, sweaty Caleb stands in front of me, wiping his face with a towel.

"Sorry about that." Smiling, he lowers the towel. "I was in the gym, and time got away from me. I'll shower really quick, then I'll be down."

Would it be wrong to ask him to stay like this? I'll gladly ogle him in all his gloriously sculpted, sweaty perfection. He's a slim guy, so I wasn't expecting so many muscles. I have to squeeze my hands into fists to resist the urge to poke his abs to see if they're real or a figment of my overactive imagination.

"Yeah, that's fine. I'll wait."

"Good." He smiles, that dimple appearing again. The dimple in combination with his current state of undress is almost too much. "Make yourself at home."

It's a throwaway sentiment, in most cases an empty offer. But I have a feeling that with Caleb, I could take over his kitchen and make myself a late lunch, then get into his liquor cabinet for a drink, and he wouldn't even bat an eye.

Caleb jogs up the stairs, and when a door shuts a moment later, I take a deep breath and slip my shoes off. I'm not a nosy person, but I can't help myself. I'm drawn to the sideboard on the left of the foyer and the photos hanging on the wall above it.

One is of a much younger Caleb dressed in a cap and gown and standing with a middle-aged man and woman I assume are his parents. In another, he doesn't look much older. His smile is even wider, and he's holding a newborn Seda. The next image is another of him and Seda. This time, he's kneeling, arms held out for a baby who looks wobbly on her feet. In another, Seda is covered in spaghetti sauce. My favorite is the one with Seda on Caleb's shoulders. They're standing in front of a carousel, and she's licking a rapidly melting ice cream cone. Caleb's face is alight with laughter, and the ice cream is dripping onto his hair and forehead.

I venture into the living room space next. Though our houses are similar in size, the lack of walls make his feel much larger than mine. The sectional couch looks like a cloud. It's low and white and fluffy, tempting me to dive onto it and sink into the cushions, never to be seen or heard from again.

The bookshelves are filled with everything from self-help books and law texts to children's and middle grade books. There are even a few fantasy novels tossed in. I pull out a thick tome and read the blurb before sliding it back onto the bookshelf.

The upright piano beneath the front window makes my heart ache with a long-forgotten desire. As a girl, I'd wanted to learn to play an instrument more than anything. But I quickly found out something like that took money and time we didn't have.

Gently, I tap a few keys. It sounds horrible, but it still makes me smile. Maybe one day, when things are better, I'll learn. That could be fun.

As much as I want to continue snooping, I rein in my curiosity and plop down on the couch.

Instantly, a sigh escapes me. *God*. It's so comfy.

I sink into the plush pillows, tipping my head back and closing my eyes. I could easily fall asleep here. It's like a cocoon, holding me gently and practically rocking me to sleep.

I wonder what Caleb would think if he came down and found me curled up asleep on his couch.

Again, he probably wouldn't bat an eye. Hell, he'd probably cover me with a blanket and go on about his day.

Luckily, I don't have to put that theory to the test. When I hear his feet on the stairs, I straighten. A heartbeat later, he appears, jogging down the steps, bringing with him the scent of his woodsy, masculine soap. Wet like this, his hair is light brown instead of blond. His gym clothes have been replaced by jeans and a t-shirt, and he's barefoot. It makes sense, this being his house and all, but the casualness of the sight is strangely intimate.

I scoot forward and push off the couch. Only it's so low and deep that I get up about halfway before I flop back down on the cushions.

He bursts into laughter, the sound low and rich, lighting up my nerve endings. Maybe I should be embarrassed. Instead, I'm filled with a sense of pride. I get the impression he doesn't laugh like that often, so it makes me unreasonably happy to be the one to make him sound like that.

"Your couch is trying to eat me."

He sidesteps the coffee table and holds out a hand. "It'll do that. I'll help."

I slide my hand into his, trying to ignore the warmth of his skin and the contentment that soaks into me on contact. Instead, I focus on using him as the stability I need to find my balance.

"Thanks." Only as I smooth my hand down the front of my t-shirt, do I wonder if I should've dressed up more, worn a more professional outfit. This is a trial run, after all, but there's nothing I can do about it now.

"Office is this way." He nods toward the stairs and heads that way, so, with a deep breath, I follow.

If he's really okay with this, then I'll get over my concerns about his tendency to fix the problems of others. Because I couldn't ask for a more ideal working situation. I'd be right next door, so if the boys needed me, I'd be easy to get to. And I can't imagine that Caleb would be upset if I needed to pop over and check on them on occasion. He has a kid of his own. He knows how it can be.

Upstairs, he leads me to the room at the very end of the hallway and gestures for me to step inside first.

Every aspect of this home is impressive. The walls, baseboards, crown molding, ceiling, and even the bookcases behind his desk are all painted the same shade of dark olive green. I never could have imagined a room this dark could feel anything but claustrophobia-inducing. But this space is the complete opposite. It's warm and cozy. Downright homey. Within seconds of setting foot inside, I itch to pluck a book off the shelf and curl into the leather chair in the corner.

"I love this room," I blurt out.

He chuckles, the low sound rumbling through me. "Thanks. Having a workspace I enjoy being in makes work a little less tedious."

"I bet."

He pulls out the chair behind the computer, gesturing for me to sit.

Once I've settled, he spins the chair so I'm facing the iMac on the desk. The screen practically beckons me to run my fingers along its sides. It's sleek, modern, and like everything else here, it's green.

The desk is bare of anything besides the desktop, keyboard, and mouse.

"Where are all your"—I wave a hand over the spotless surface—"knickknacks and stuff? Like sticky notes and pens and—"

Lips curling in amusement, he pulls out a drawer. It's extremely organized, but sure enough, there's a cup with blue pens, another with black, and a third with red. Sticky notes in a variety of colors, a stapler, and a jar of paperclips. He closes it and opens the next. Envelopes and mailers of varying size. The third drawer is full of printer paper. He moves behind me and opens the top drawer on my left. It's full of documents. The one below it is filled with files.

"If you need anything else, let me know, and I'll pick it up." He shuts the last drawer and turns to face the bookcase. He slips a small, thin book off the shelf and sets it in front of me.

"Any log-in information you need will be in here." He taps the cover. "And I'll set you up with your own, then add the information to it."

"Okay."

He leans in closer, one hand braced on the desk, the other resting on the back of the chair near my shoulder. The proximity makes my heart skip a beat, his scent overwhelming.

I clear my throat and inhale through my mouth. "Could you walk me through some of the things you'd need me to do?"

My knowledge of family law begins and ends with taking custody of my brothers. I suppose that may be more than most, but I'd say it's no more than basic.

"Sure." He reaches around me and wiggles the mouse. A heartbeat later, the computer screen glows. He quickly types in his password and then logs into his email. He scours through them and eventually clicks on one. "This is something like I'd have you reply to."

It's a short message, a client requesting a face-to-face.

"All you'd need to do is check my schedule and respond with times I'm available."

"Easy enough," I reply.

Almost too easy. I'm back to worrying that he's offered me this position out of pity.

But I *need* this job, so I don't dare speak up.

He shows me how to access his appointment book next. Then his email address book and mailing address catalog. After an hour of navigating and clicking and taking notes on where to find which kinds of files, my brain is spinning, but it seems doable.

And my worries about charity are assuaged, mostly, when he says, "Once you get a feel for that stuff, I'll give you more responsibilities, but for now, stick with this. I'm not great at explaining what I need done, so this will be a learning opportunity for both of us. Okay?"

"Okay," I echo, fighting a smile. He and I have that in common.

He leans away, and for the first time in an hour, it feels like I can breathe.

"When do you want me to start?" I ask as I follow him down the stairs.

Rather than lead me to the door, he heads for the kitchen and the fancy-looking coffee setup that's nearly as intimidating as the espresso machine at the coffee shop.

He scratches the back of his head. "I'm not technically working tomorrow, but why don't you come over whenever you want? You can respond to emails. That way I'll be around if you have any questions. I'll pay you for your time, of course, but how about you officially start Monday?"

"That's fine." With the elastic I always keep on my wrist, I pull my hair back and twist it into a low bun. Instantly, a little tension ebbs from my shoulders. I wanted to do it while I sat at the computer, but I worried I'd end up elbowing Caleb in the face or something.

"I'm making quesadillas for dinner," he says.

I frown at the comment. Why is he telling me this?

"You and your brothers," he says before I can ask, "are welcome to come over. It's just Seda and me, and I always make too much food."

The part of me that steadfastly hates any kind of handouts or help instantly bristles. But I tamp that emotion down. His suggestion feels genuine, and I swear he's surrounded by an aura of sadness. I've noticed it each time I've seen him. Like he's lonely.

It's that reason alone that makes me agree. "I'm sure my brothers would love that."

Caleb's whole face lights up with his smile, easing the underlying concern that he's doing this for my benefit alone. "Great. Want to head over at about five thirty? Feel free to let yourselves in."

"All right. Sounds good." Head ducked, I pad to the entryway.

Caleb skirts around me, beating me to it—his hand hovering at my waist; not quite touching, but close enough for me to feel his warmth—and opens the front door and follows me out onto the porch.

"Thanks for helping me out with this. I really appreciate it."

"It's not a problem." Even though I'm still not totally convinced it isn't a pity job.

He remains on the porch as I cross our yards and ease my way up the rickety front steps. With one hand on the doorknob, I wave. He lifts a hand in return, but rather than retreating, he continues to watch until I've stepped inside.

I close my front door behind me and lean against it.

Instantly, I'm assaulted by the sound of my brothers yelling at their video game. It's the antithesis of Caleb's silent house, but I can't help but be grateful for it. For the noise and the company. And my heart breaks a little for my neighbor.

NINE

Caleb

At five-thirty on the dot, the front door eases open.

"What's that?" Seda asks, swiveling around in her chair. Her mouth opens in surprise when Halle appears, but when Quinn and Casen step in behind her, that surprise quickly morphs into horror. "Dad!" she whisper-shrieks. "You didn't tell me they were coming." She looks down at her dirty shorts and top, eyes bulging, and hops to her feet. "I have to go change."

Lightning fast, she's off and running upstairs to her room.

Frowning, I follow her movements until she disappears, then assess our visitors.

What the fuck just happened?

"Is something wrong?" Halle asks, pulling me out of my confused stupor. "Did I get the time wrong? We can go if—"

"No, no." I usher her inside with a wave of my hand. "Come on in. Seda wanted to go change."

Quinn and Casen look around the house, taking it in with matching expressions of awe.

"This house is sick," Casen says.

"It's cool," Quinn adds, sliding his hands into the pockets of his pants.

The twins are identical, but when I met them the day they moved in, I noted that Quinn has a tiny mole above his lip. I'm impressed that I remembered. If not, there's no way I'd be able to tell them apart.

"Thanks, guys. Drinks are in the fridge. Take whatever you want."

"Sweet," they mutter in unison, rushing toward the refrigerator.

Quinn, naturally, pulls out a bottle of Corona first.

I chuckle and arch a brow at him as I step into the kitchen. "Nice try, kid."

He sends me a grin and puts it back.

"Quinn!" Halle scolds, her cheeks going pink. "I can't believe you did that."

"It was a joke," he grumbles, grabbing a soda. "Lighten up."

Halle shoots me an apologetic look, her fingers tangled together in front of her.

I shake my head. "I would've done the same thing at their age."

"They know better." She glowers at her brothers.

"Relax," Casen says, popping the tab on a Coke. "We're not going to turn into Mom. Have some faith in us."

Quinn taps his sister on the shoulder. "Laugh some." He pops the tab on a can of Sprite. "Try it with me. *Ha, ha, haaa.*"

With her lips turned down in a frown, she angles her body toward me. "I'm really sorry about that."

"Seriously, it's fine." I snag the dishrag from the sink and wipe down the counter. "I'm glad they feel comfortable enough to joke."

My words don't erase her frown.

"Why don't you head out back?" I suggest to the boys. "We'll eat out there."

"Cool." Casen shrugs. "Come on, Quinn."

Halle wraps her arms around her torso, watching them go. Once the door is shut behind them, she drops her focus to the floor in front of her. "I'm so embarrassed."

"Don't be. They're teenagers. I did worse at their age, I'm sure."

Between one blink and the next, she perks up. As if when she smiles, she's slipped a mask into place. "Is there anything I can help with?" She looks around at the various toppings I have laid out. "Please, put me out of my misery and give me a task."

Laughing, I point to a tray of condiments. "You could take that out back. Ask your brothers what kind of quesadillas they want. We've got beef, chicken, and cheese. And what kind do you want?"

"Um." With her lip caught between her teeth, she surveys all the fixings. "Cheese for me, please." With that, she picks up the tray, balancing it easily on one hand.

"Were you a waitress?"

She whips her head around, her expression full of confusion, until she eyes the tray, and her posture relaxes.

She gives a tiny nod. "Yeah, I was. Habit, I guess."

Halle heads out back, and I've barely gotten started on her quesadilla when Seda comes downstairs.

She's changed into a clean pair of jean shorts and a t-shirt. Her hair is freshly brushed, and I swear she's put on a bit of mascara and lip gloss. Though I didn't think she even owned mascara. I'll have to talk to Salem about that.

From the look of things, my daughter is crushing on the teen boys next door.

"You look nice." I leave it at that. The last thing I want is to embarrass her.

She freezes at the bottom of the stairs. "But not too nice, right?"

"Uh…" I feel like I'm caught in a trap. Is there a right answer for this situation? "No, not too nice," I hedge. "But nice enough."

Fuck, I'm not ready for this. It's inevitable that my baby girl will grow up and crush on boys, but that doesn't make witnessing the changes any easier. There's nothing like raising a kid to truly show a person how quickly time goes.

"Cool. That's good. I think," she mutters more to herself than me.

I arch a brow and leave it at that. "Cheese quesadilla for you, right?"

"Um…" She hedges, her eyes darting to the back door.

Halle breezes back in, tucking her light brown hair behind her ears. "They both want beef."

Seda brightens, her back straightening. "I'll have beef too."

I narrow my eyes. "You never want beef. You always want cheese or chicken."

Cheeks going pink, she darts a look at Halle. "I changed my mind." She lifts her chin, shoulders pulled back in defiance. "I want beef."

I lower my head to hide my amusement. "Seda, don't ever change yourself to impress others. The people who matter will like you just the way you are."

Brows knitted, Halle looks from my daughter to me and back again.

"Just give me freaking cheese then, Dad," Seda snaps.

I flinch on instinct.

"Stop making such a big deal out of it. God." She storms outside, the door shutting harder than normal behind her. Though she may not have slammed it, she still made her point.

Dad.

Seda *never* calls me Dad. I'm Daddy. Thayer is Dad. She's always used that distinction between us, so this hurts.

"Does she…" Halle starts, peeking outside. "Do you think she has a crush on my brothers?"

Groaning, I drop my head. "I believe she does."

Halle approaches me at the island, bringing her sweet

scent with her. Fuck, I worry Seda isn't the only one crushing on a neighbor.

She taps her nails on the counter. "Is this her first crush?"

With a huff, I flip the quesadilla in the pan. "I think so."

"And on my brothers?" She cringes. "I'm so sorry."

In one quick move, I slide the finished dish onto a plate and hand it to her. "It was bound to happen eventually. That one's for Seda."

She takes it outside while I get started on a beef quesadilla.

When Halle returns, she leans against the counter beside me. "I still remember my first crush."

"You do?" I ask, more curious than I probably should be.

"Yes." She presses her lips together, her eyes dancing. "His name was Thomas. It was fifth grade, and at the time, he was the cutest boy I'd ever seen."

"What happened?" It's a stupid question. She was in elementary school. Even so, I'm eager for the answer.

She snorts. "Nothing. I was ten."

"When did you have your first kiss?" The second the words are out, I wish I could suck them back in. But it's too late for that, so I backpedal. "I-I was just curious," I stutter. "Because Seda's ten, and you know ... I'm just going to shut up now." I focus on my task, hoping my face isn't as red as it feels.

Halle picks up the saltshaker and inspects it before putting it back down. "Sixteen. I was a late bloomer. Or maybe it's more that I just didn't have the time. It happened behind the school at the end of the day. In case you were curious about that too." She tries to hide her smirk but fails. "What about you?"

"Twelve," I admit. "It was at a soccer game."

"You played?"

"No. I played football."

"Ah." She nods. "Of course you did."

Chuckling, I get started on the next quesadilla. "What's that supposed to mean?"

She crosses her arms, the move highlighting her chest in a way I try to ignore. "You just have that look about you. Mr. Perfect. The popular guy."

With a grin, I flip the tortilla. While that side cooks, I get started on another. "You think I was popular?"

She arches a challenging brow. "Were you?"

I nod simply. "Yes."

Her laugh is loud and filled with amusement. "I knew it."

"What about you?" I point the spatula at her, then focus on removing the quesadilla from the pan.

"What about me?" she splays her hands on the counter, her chipped yellow nail polish catching my attention.

"Were you popular?"

She lets out an unladylike snort and doesn't bother trying to stop it. "Knowing what you do about me already, do you think there's any chance I was popular?" When I don't answer right away, she adds, "No, I most definitely was not."

"Why?" I turn her way again, only then noticing the twisted, almost tormented expression on her face.

Shit. Maybe I shouldn't have asked.

"I don't know," she huffs. "Maybe it was because my mom was an addict, or it could've been my ripped, dirty clothes, or maybe it was because sometimes we'd run out of shampoo and my hair would smell funny. Or—" She sighs. "Honestly, there were a lot of reasons I wasn't popular. That's only the tip of the iceberg."

Stomach knotting, I keep my focus fixed on the stovetop, cursing myself for upsetting her. For now, it seems best to just move on from the subject. When the quesadilla is perfectly browned, I slide it onto the plate. "Those are for your brothers."

With a small nod, she takes the plates, and while she's delivering them, I make quick work of preparing hers. By the time she comes back into the house, I'm already plating it and starting on mine.

"This is yours," I tell her. "Head out and eat it while it's hot. I'll be there in a minute."

She shakes her head. "That's okay. I'll wait with you."

If we've got another minute to ourselves, I figure I might as well check in, even if I'm hesitant about how she'll respond. "Do you still feel okay about everything?" It's not the end of the world if she doesn't want to work with me, but I *do* need the help. "The job, I mean."

She inhales deeply and searches my face. "Yeah." The word comes out slowly, drawn out, like she has more to say, so I wait it out while I assemble my dinner. "You're not just doing this because you feel sorry for me, right? I..." She looks down at her nails. "I don't want your pity. I can find another job."

I flip the quesadilla in the pan, buying myself a minute to get the words right. Honestly, maybe I did offer her the job because I felt sorry for her, but I *do* need the help. I've just been putting it off.

But I can't tell her that. She'll never accept my reasoning if she knows my initial intention.

"I need an assistant." Not a lie. "I haven't had the time to find one, so when you said you needed a job, it seemed like a no brainer." Also not a lie. "It's a convenient arrangement for both of us, don't you agree?"

"That's true." She plays with the ends of her hair, her fingers moving absently, like it's a nervous tic. "But if at any point I'm not performing as well as you'd like, please tell me. I wouldn't mind the opportunity to improve if that's the case, but if my work still isn't up to par, then fire me. Got it?"

There's no stopping the grin that spreads slowly across my face. "I'm sure your performance will be more than satisfactory."

If she catches my innuendo, she ignores it, which is for the best.

Once my dinner is plated, I snag a beer from the fridge and nod at the door. "We better get out there before my kid asks one of your brothers to marry her. Or worse, both."

She throws her head back and guffaws. "Oh, God. Can you imagine?"

I shake my head. "I refuse to imagine it. She's going to be a kid forever, lest I lose my sanity."

At the door, she peers at me over her shoulder and smiles softly. "I think it's too late for that."

"Oh." I arch an amused brow. "Are you saying I'm already insane?"

She shrugs and shuffles outside. "You said it, not me."

"Go home, Halle."

Without looking away from the dish she's rinsing, she shakes her head. "No. You made dinner and now I'm cleaning up."

Shaking my head, I swipe the dish from her and open the dishwasher. "No need. I have this magic appliance that'll do it for me."

Halle eyes the appliance with a healthy dose of skepticism. "Do those things actually work?"

I load another plate, trying not to show my amusement. "Yes."

Her lips turn down in a hint of a frown. "I've never had one."

Her answer freezes my movements. "Never?"

She shakes her head. "I don't know if I could get used to using one."

Wow. I've never *not* had a dishwasher. For some bizarre reason, that thought makes me realize just how privileged my life really has been.

"Believe me," I say, keeping my tone light, "you could."

"If I ever have one," she adds, passing me another dish. "The house needs a lot of updates, and a dishwasher falls pretty close to the end of my list of priorities."

I've officially lost it. Because all I want to do right now is drive over to the nearest home improvement store and buy a dishwasher for Halle.

She already has too much going on. She shouldn't have to worry about washing dishes too.

But I can't imagine she'd take it well if I made a purchase like that for her. "I'm sure you will one day," I remind myself. "You're young. You have time."

She snorts. "I'm twenty-three going on a hundred and three at this point."

I frown at her comment. I could tell from the moment she tried to blow off my offer to help her move in that she hasn't had an easy life, and every time we're together, the weary set of her shoulders silently urges me to take some of that weight from her so she can stand up straighter.

The thought is usually followed by my mother's voice, telling me that I've always wanted to fix everything and everyone.

It's not a compliment when she says it.

But it's true. I like helping people. If I have the power to ease another's burdens, then why wouldn't I?

But in this case, I absolutely cannot buy Halle a dishwasher.

I'm certain my pretty neighbor would never speak to me again if I tried.

"You've always had to take care of yourself, haven't you?" I close the dishwasher and press the start button.

Casen and Quinn are gone already. They went straight home after dinner so they could play video games, much to Seda's dismay. She dragged herself upstairs after their departure, sulking the whole way, to take a shower and read in bed.

With a sigh, Halle leans back against the counter, crossing her arms.

Of their own accord, my eyes drop to the swell of her breasts. I catch myself quickly, forcing my gaze up, finding her watching me wearing a hint of a smile.

"Yeah, I have," she says, letting me get away with checking her out. "There's one person in the world I can rely on, and it's me."

Her words are like a stab to the heart. The pain, though, is quickly followed by the desire to *be* someone for her.

I don't make the vow to her, but in that moment, I make it to myself.

Halle might think the only person she can count on is herself, but I'll prove to her that she can count on me too.

TEN

Halle

For three weeks, I've answered emails and scheduled meetings for Caleb. I've filed documents and set up depositions. And so far, it's been fairly smooth sailing. Certainly better than my coffee shop experience. I still haven't been brave enough to go back there to even order a drink.

Still sleepy, I pour coffee into my mug, then add the syrup I made yesterday. I'm not sure the brown sugar concoction will be life-changing like the recipe promised, but it smells good. I add a little creamer and stir, then take a tentative sip.

Pretty good.

Certainly better than anything I made at the coffee shop.

I blame the fancy machines. They're far more complicated than any kind of equipment has the right to be.

Caleb is working from home today, so now that I know the syrup isn't half bad, I pour a cup of coffee for him too.

"Boys," I call out. "I'm headed over to work. Be good. Call me if you need anything, and sandwiches are in the fridge."

On the couch, Quinn tips his head back and hollers, "See you."

"Yeah, see ya," Casen says without looking away from his video game.

Once again, I'm thankful I managed to rescue their gaming console when our mother went on a rampage and destroyed everything in sight.

It rained last night, making the pathway between our homes muddy, so I take careful steps the whole way. On Caleb's front porch, I set the coffees down and take my shoes off. No way am I dragging mud through Caleb's impeccably kept house.

After unlocking the front door, I scoop up the cups and let myself inside.

"Oh my God."

The words leave me without my permission.

Damn.

Caleb is partway down the stairs, dressed in a fitted navy suit, his hair slightly damp from a shower and curling at his collar. As he hits the bottom stair, he snaps his watch in place and looks up at me, his eyes dancing with mirth.

Caleb looks incredible in a t-shirt and jeans, but this

man in a suit and tie? He's on another level. I never thought I'd be attracted to the buttoned-up suit kind of man, yet here I am. Or maybe it's just Caleb that has this effect on me.

"Hey," he says, quickly eating up the space between us with his long legs. That one word serves as a bucket of cold water, pulling me out of my stupor. "Turns out I'm needed in Boston today. Are you good here?"

"Y-Yeah." I stutter. How is it that he can fluster me so easily?

"I brought you a coffee." I thrust the cup out to him, thankful I went with a travel mug.

"Thanks." With a grateful smile, he takes a sip. "Remind me how you got fired from the coffee shop again?"

"The barista life is not for me."

Also, the espresso machine is the devil in disguise. The hissing sound it made was not of this world.

He chuckles. "I left a stack of papers for you to go through on my desk. If I think of anything else, I'll call. The change of plans has me a bit frazzled." He blows out a breath. "Hopefully I'll be back later."

With that, he's gone. I lock the door behind him, then head upstairs to his office. The computer is already booted up, so all I have to do is click on the icon for my profile and use my fingerprint to log on.

While I wait for his email to load, I flip through the documents he's left behind for me to get an idea of what I need to get done. Then I sort through his inbox, responding to the ones I'm CC'd on and looking at the ones he's flagged for me. This is the first time I've been here working alone. All week, he's worked from home, setting himself up in the chair in the corner of the office with his laptop on his lap. Yesterday, when he took a call, he went downstairs like he typically does, earbuds in place so he can talk hands-free. But when he returned, he brought turkey sandwiches with the most incredible sauce. A sauce whose ingredients he refused to share.

"Secret recipe." He'd smirked, clearly pleased that I enjoyed the sandwich enough to ask.

I've only replied to one email when my phone rings.

"Hey," Caleb says when I answer, the background noise from his Bluetooth speaker almost deafening. "I think I left a folder I need. Can you check?"

"Sure." I slide the chair back and stand. "Where do you think it is?"

"Check my bedroom. I think it's on the dresser."

"Caleb." I bite my lip, trying and failing to keep my laughter at bay. "Why on earth would you have a work folder in your bedroom?"

He lets out a gruff sigh. "It's not like I have anything better to do."

"You could read a book. Or watch a movie. Or—"

"Okay, I get your point. Just look, please."

I head down the hall to the closed door across from the one whose door is open and clearly belongs to a little girl. I ease the bedroom door open, waiting for it to squeak, but the sound never comes. Caleb must have replaced the doors and hinges when he remodeled, because not a single one squeaks like mine do. One of these days I'll remember to pick up WD-40.

"Oh, wow," I gasp as I step into his room.

Caleb's chuckle echoes in my ear, but it barely registers. I'm too busy taking in the space. The walls are painted a dark charcoal, and the floor is layered with two rugs that overlap. The bed is huge—what size mattress is bigger than a king? Because this has to be it—with a black velvet headboard. The bed coverings are in shades of cream, with a black blanket at the foot. Most surprising are the throw pillows in complementary shades.

"I hope you gave your interior designer a massive tip. This room is gorgeous."

He huffs good-naturedly. "Just check for the folder, Halle."

Right. Folder.

I find it right away—resting on the dresser, like he said it would be—then tuck it under my arm and pad back out into the hall. "Do you need me to scan it and email it to you?"

"That would be great. Thanks."

"No problem. Call me if you need anything else."

I hang up and quickly scan the contents of the folder. I'm in the process of uploading them when my phone rings again.

"Hey," I answer. "Uploading the files now. I'll email them in just a minute."

"Uh…" The voice on the other end of the line is decidedly not Caleb's. "Halle, we have a problem."

My brother's tone instantly sends me into fight-or-flight mode. "Quinn, what is it?" Gripping the phone tighter, I book it out of the office and fly down the stairs.

"We were playing our game, and we kept hearing this sound. At first we didn't think anything of it. But then…"

"But then what?" I snap, my fingers fumbling with the dead bolt on the front door. It takes five tries to get the door unlocked because my hand won't stop shaking. "Are you okay?"

That's my biggest worry. That they're hurt. Is someone trying to break in? I can't imagine who. Our mom is still in prison, but there's always their dad.

"Yeah, we're okay, it's just … the house is kind of … wet."

Wet. I pull up short at the top of the porch steps. That wasn't what I was expecting him to say.

"What do you mean wet?"

"The floor's wet. Like *really* wet."

My stomach sinks. No, no, no, *no*. This can't be happening. I mumble nonsense, then disconnect the call and shove my phone into my pocket.

With a harsh inhale, I turn around and go back for the shoes I left just inside the door. Then I scurry across the yard far less delicately than before. The moment I enter the house, I step into a puddle.

"Where's it coming from?" I shriek at my brothers, who are standing, stunned, in front of the couch.

"No idea." Casen shrugs. "We got up, and the floor is wet."

A small cry climbs its way out of my throat as I dart to the kitchen. The panic already coursing through me has now been joined by annoyance. Why didn't they go looking when they first heard the noise? This is not a mess that can just be wiped away. This is full-on damage.

As thought after thought races through me, I spin in a circle, trying to figure out where to look first.

"Kitchen," I mutter, pulling myself to a stop.

I throw open the cabinet beneath the sink, but it's dry.

"Can you guys help me look?" I plead over my shoulder. Slamming the cabinet door, I straighten and head for the laundry room next.

Casen and Quinn are already there, standing side by side, watching water flow from behind the washer. Dammit. I whimper at the thought of what this month's bill will look like.

"I have to get the main water valve turned off." Without hesitation, I turn and dart to the back door. When I don't find it there, I run around the front of the house, suddenly thankful for the broken fence panels.

I don't find it there either there.

"Everything okay?"

Heart pounding, I whip around, finding Thayer standing beside his work truck, a hand shielding his eyes from the sun.

"A pipe broke, and the house is flooding. I need to turn the—"

Thayer eats up the distance between us faster than seems humanly possible. "Let's check the garage," he says. "That's where ours is."

"I can't open it from out here."

It's an old door, and it's locked from the inside. So I hustle in through the front door with Thayer hot on my heels. When he steps into the garage, his fingers find the light switch before mine do, flooding the space with light. And within seconds, he locates the valve and has the water shut off.

"Thank you." I breathe out a sigh of relief.

"You're welcome." He nods to the house, and I turn, following his silent direction.

Inside, the floor is covered in nearly two inches of water now. It could be so much worse, but even this is threatening to send me over the edge.

"Fuck," he curses, assessing the damage.

"Yeah," I sigh. "Fuck."

"I have a wet vac. I'll get it set up and start sucking out the water, but this…"

"Yeah, I know." I don't need him to finish his sentence to know how bad this is. A flood like this means the carpet will have to be torn out. The baseboards will need to go too. God only knows what else.

I press my lips together, holding back tears. Or maybe a scream.

Why this?

Why now?

Why *me*?

When my phone rings in my pocket, I bite back a groan and pull it out.

Caleb.

"Is everything okay?" he asks before I can greet him. "I'm at the office, but I don't see the files you were going to send me."

"No." My voice cracks embarrassingly, and my face heats an instant later. "It's not okay."

He's silent for a moment, but when he does speak, his voice has a steely edge. "What happened? Are you hurt?"

I press a hand to my aching forehead, a migraine already jackhammering its way through my skull. "My house flooded. There's about two inches of water and—"

"Fuck, I'll call Thayer. Maybe he's still home—"

"It's okay, he's already here." I run my trembling fingers through my hair. "I'm going to call my insurance company too. But I'll run over and email the papers first."

"Fuck the papers."

My heart lurches at the fury in his tone.

"I'm coming home."

"W-What?" I stutter. "You just got to Boston. You need to be there for work."

"It can wait."

With every word he speaks, the tears push against my defenses, determined to pour out. I've never been one to complain, but I've already endured more than my fair share of upset in my life. Now this? My brothers need a home, and…

"It sounded like it couldn't," I finally reply, tamping down my rising panic attack.

"Halle." His tone is stern, so unlike his typically gentle way. "You need help, don't you?"

I bite my tongue to hold back a whimper. Yes, I need help, but admitting that out loud is more than I can bear. I've always had to handle my own shit. I don't know *how* to let someone help me.

"Exactly," he says when I remain silent. "I'll get what I need from here and be on my way in thirty. Pack a bag. The boys too. Take it over to my place."

Before I can protest, Caleb hangs up on me.

I stare at my phone and give myself a solid three seconds to wonder what the fuck just happened before I move. He ended the call like that on purpose, so I couldn't argue with him. Smart man.

The boys have already unhooked their gaming console from where it was set up beneath the TV—naturally that was their main concern—and Casen is setting it on the kitchen table when I clap to get their attention. "Pack up your stuff. We're going to have to stay somewhere else tonight."

And tomorrow night too. And who knows how many nights after that.

They exchange a look, communicating in the silent way they do. "Are we going to have to sell the house?"

I snort. I was the only one stupid enough to buy the house, and that was before the water damage. "No, but..." I eye the water soaking into my sneakers and wiggle my toes, cringing at the way they squish. "I don't know what kind of repairs we're looking at. Water is serious. It means mold."

"The house is moldy!" Quinn practically shrieks. "Isn't mold deadly?"

I pinch the bridge of my nose, sending up a silent prayer. "I just meant that water *causes* mold, and it doesn't take a lot for that to happen. This much is enough to mold the floors and baseboards."

The worried look they exchange guts me. They're fourteen-year-old goofballs, but they're more perceptive than they let on. Their lives haven't been easy either, and I hate that I can't take away all the stressors. I want them to be teenagers, to enjoy being carefree at least a little before they have to grow up.

"Can we help?" Casen asks.

It's on the tip of my tongue to say no, but I won't infantilize them. They're strong boys, and they can clearly see that I need help. "Yeah, we need to get everything we can out of the water. With any luck, some of it will be salvageable." I gesture to the couch and other furniture downstairs. Most of our belongings may have been thrift-store finds, but it doesn't make the loss of it any easier to swallow.

Just as we're starting, Thayer returns with his wet vac.

"Thank you so much." If I can be thankful for one thing today, it's that he hadn't left for work yet.

"It's not a problem," he says, smoothing his hands down his jeans. "My wife is home, so if you need help or somewhere to hang out, just knock on the door. She knows what's going on."

"Thanks," I say, throat tight. "I really appreciate it."

The boys help me move furniture around, taking what we can upstairs and wiping each piece down. In the end, I think most of it will be fine. We use the wet vac to suck up all the standing water, then use every towel we own to soak up all we can. I tend to overreact, and honestly, I hope that's the case now. If anyone could use a break, it's me.

"There isn't much else we can do right now." Hands on my hips, I face my brothers.

Sweaty and a tad out of breath, my brothers eye me, but neither speaks. Casen pushes his hair out of his eyes.

"Are your bags packed yet?"

They nod in unison. I should be used to it by now, how in sync they are with each other, but I'm not sure I ever will be. "Okay, just hang out ... wherever while I do mine, and then we'll..." I trail off and sigh. I'm not sure how to even finish that thought.

I really don't want to take Caleb up on his declaration—it was far too blunt to be called an offer—to stay with him, but I can't afford a room at a hotel, regardless of whether insurance will eventually reimburse me.

With a deep breath in, I head to the stairs, resigned to accepting help. Maybe a normal person would do so easily, but my trauma response includes the need to be in control of every aspect of the emergency. How could it not when that's what's always been expected of me? And despite my self-awareness, it's still difficult to fight the urge.

The stairs creak beneath my feet, further quieting my brothers' whispers. They're worried, and that's the last thing I want. But the moment I enter my room, I freeze. Maybe because of the stress, but I can't be sure.

I give myself a minute to mentally reboot. Then I yank a bag out of the closet, toss it onto the bed, and start packing. I don't need much. We can easily come back over. But I find myself piling the bag full anyway.

As I zip it closed, a tear slides down my cheek.

Crap.

I straighten and sniff it back.

I *hate* crying.

"You're so sensitive." My mother's voice echoes in my mind.

For as long as I can remember, she told me I was too emotional. Too sensitive. Too tender-hearted. Just *too* everything. Eventually, I learned to shut those parts of myself off. I stopped crying years and years ago. Now, I *loathe* the sensation. The weakness it brings with it.

"Halle?"

At the sound of my name in that gentle tone, my breath catches, and I spin around.

Caleb is standing in the doorway, still dressed in those gorgeous blue suit pants and fitted white shirt, though he's shed the jacket. His head is lowered to keep from brushing the frame above him.

That tone, the genuine concern, causes the floodgates to open, and more tears fall.

I hastily swipe them away, frustrated with myself for showing him this weakness. Before I can turn away, he's standing in front of me, cradling my face. His blue eyes are locked on mine and swimming with concern, not judgment. Not annoyance or disgust or any of the emotions that would flit across my mom's face when I was sad.

"Can I hug you?" he asks.

Normally just the idea of being held would cause me to recoil. But in this moment, I can't think of a single thing I want more. So I nod, maybe a little too vigorously, and he pulls me in close.

On instinct, I melt against him. He wraps his arms around me, chin resting on my head, and holds me tight.

My arms hang like limp noodles at my sides, but he doesn't let that stop him.

I sniffle, the sound muffled by his shirt, the urge to cry so strong I worry I won't be able to keep the tears at bay any longer.

"Let it out, Hal."

"I don't want to ruin your shirt," I mutter, bottom lip wobbling.

"Who cares about my shirt?" He pulls me impossibly closer, using the right amount of pressure to help regulate my system. "I have a million more."

For some reason, that makes me giggle.

"I'm so sorry about the water," he whispers.

"Nothing ever goes right for me. I should've expected this."

He loosens his hold and ducks, meeting my eyes. "How could you have expected this? It was a freak accident, something your inspector probably should've caught. Not you."

I press my lips together. "I waived the inspection in return for a price reduction."

His shoulders sag. "Fuck." He tugs me in tighter again.

"I'm an idiot."

"No, you're not. You just wanted to put a roof over your brothers' heads. Who can blame you for that?"

My chest warms a fraction. He gets it. I've only known the man for a month, and he already sees more of me than anyone ever has.

He doesn't loosen his hold on me when he asks, "Are you ready to go?"

"No," I answer. With a thick swallow, I nuzzle into his chest a little more firmly. I'm feeling all kinds of vulnerable, but I force myself to ask for what I want. "I want you to hug me a little longer. Is that okay?"

"Yeah, Hal. I've got you."

Stepping into Caleb's guest bedroom is the closest I've ever come to being in a luxury hotel suite. Every detail is beautiful in an understated way. It's a far cry from the ratty old quilt I always sleep with—the one currently draped over my arm—and my hand-me-down furniture. I have to fight a cringe when I set my quilt down on the fluffy white duvet.

"Bathroom is there." He points to my left as he sets the bag he insisted on carrying on the bed. "You'll share with Seda when she's over. Hope that's okay."

"It's fine. I've never not shared a bathroom before." I exhale a heavy breath. There's no way I'll ever be able to repay Caleb for his generosity and kindness.

He moves in front of me, hands on his hips, and cocks his head. "What's that sigh about?" Before I can answer, he snaps his fingers. "Let me guess, you're worried that this is too much and you don't know how you'll return the favor. Am I right?"

I wrinkle my nose, chin jutted in the air. "Annoyingly spot-on."

His responding smile is blinding.

Asshole.

Except Caleb is the farthest thing from an asshole there is.

He reaches out like he's going to touch me, but when he's mere millimeters away, he drops his hands to his sides. "Please don't think you owe me anything. Anyone would do this."

That's the thing he doesn't realize—no, not everyone *would* do this. He's just that kind of guy.

Arms wrapped around my waist, I shrug. "I have no idea how long we'll have to be out of the house."

With any luck, there won't be too much damage. Maybe we discovered it in time and got it cleaned up before anything could be truly destroyed. But I don't dare hope. I learned long ago that my luck is too shitty for that.

"It'll make me feel better if we help out while we're here. I can buy groceries and cook dinner, and maybe Casen and Quinn can mow or—"

"I *like* cooking and Thayer takes care of the grass."

I frown up at him, gaze narrowing when I discover his blue eyes twinkling annoyingly with humor. "You're not gonna make this easy on me, are you?"

He shrugs and crosses his arms. The move makes his biceps strain against the white fabric of his dress shirt in a way that makes my mouth water. "No, I'm not." His top lip curls a little, like he's fighting a smile. "Get settled. I'm going to the office." He sidesteps me.

I whip around, hair flying behind me. "Do you need me to—"

He places one hand on the knob and holds the other up. "No." Then he's gone.

"Okay," I reply to the now empty room. With a clap of my hands, I turn to the bed. "Get settled."

I assess my bag, then peer over at the dresser beneath the wall-mounted TV. It seems silly to fill it with my stuff when there's a chance we'll be back home in a few days.

The door opens behind me, distracting me from my indecision. I half-expect to see Caleb back, but it's Casen.

"Hey, Case."

His eyes drop to the floor between us. "I'm really sorry I didn't get up and check the second I heard something. We were playing, and—" He sniffles.

That tiny sound shatters my heart. He's never been a crier.

I surge forward and wrap my arms around him. Any day now, he'll be taller than me, but for now, I'm thankful he's not. I don't know that holding him like this would feel as comforting as it does.

"It's okay, Case. I'm not mad."

Frustrated about the situation, sure. But not mad. They're just kids.

"It's just ... you're doing so much for us. You moved us all this way, you got a second job, the house..." He trails off, gaze averted. "We shouldn't be your responsibility. We're a burden."

I hold him tighter, like Caleb did for me. "You're my *family*. I *chose* this. I chose you. Both of you. I *want* this. Promise. You're not a burden to me, Case. Life likes to kick you when you're already down. That's just how it goes." I step back, cupping his shoulders. "Shit happens. It just so happens that we get more than our share of the shit. But we're not going to let it make us angry or bitter, okay? We're better than that."

He nods. "I love you. We're lucky to have you."

"Oh, Casen." I yank him into another hug and blink back fresh tears. "I'm the lucky one."

"Can I get in on the hugfest?"

I laugh at the sound of Quinn's voice and hold out one arm.

"Things will get better," I say as he crowds in close. "You'll see."

I have to believe that. Otherwise, I'll drown.

ELEVEN

Caleb

"Floor's ruined," the insurance adjuster says. "Looks like it's been leaking down the wall and under the floors for some time. The burst pipe just made it impossible to miss. My guess is when they start pulling carpet and laminate, they'll determine that the whole subfloor is beyond repair."

Beside me, Halle covers her mouth and closes her eyes.

"When will she know about the coverage?"

He sighs and glances at his clipboard. "Give me about a week."

"Thanks for your time." I shake hands with the man since Halle is—rightfully so—frozen in place.

He shuffles out and pulls away from the curb. A full minute later, when Halle still hasn't moved, worry sets in.

Gripping her elbow, I duck in front of her, catching her eye. "Hal, are you okay?"

She shakes her head. "No." Her voice is small.

Halle puts on a brave front. She doesn't let many people see her vulnerable side. But for some reason, she tends to lower her guard around me. And I fucking love it, even if I hate that she's hurting.

She tucks a strand of hair behind her ear and clears her throat. "I guess I just have to wait and see, right?"

"Right." I wish I could assure her that it'll all work out, but I can't promise that, so I keep my mouth shut.

She starts back over to my house, her steps slow and tentative, and I walk beside her.

I'm waffling between talking about it some more or keeping my mouth shut, unsure of which she'd prefer, when she says, "I need to go into town. I put off picking up school supplies for my brothers, but I can't wait any longer." She frowns up at me, squinting against the sun.

School starts in three days, so she's not kidding.

I wince. "You probably won't find much here. You'd be better off heading a couple of towns over. I know a place."

She wrinkles her nose, eyes still squinted. I move in front of her to keep the sun from blinding her.

"Do you just know everything there is to know?"

Fighting a laugh, I shrug and slide my hands into the pockets of my shorts. There's a slight chill to the air today, and it won't be long before summer is gone for good, but I'm not ready to let go of my shorts just yet. I only get three or four months of warm weather, so I'll take advantage of every one.

"Pretty much. Remember, I grew up here."

"Right." She licks her lips and looks away briefly. When she looks back, her expression is lighter. Fuck, it makes me happy to see that. "How could I forget your family founded the town?"

I rock back on my heels. "I don't know. I try to forget every day."

She cocks her head and scrutinizes me from head to toe, like she can see right through me. "Why's that?"

I lean in close, and when her breath catches at my proximity, I bite back a smile. "You haven't met my parents yet."

Taking a step back, I pull my keys out of my pocket and hold them up. "I took the whole day off. Grab the boys and we'll head out."

Her brow pinches. "You're going to take us?"

"That's what I said." A ghost of a grin slips out this time, but I tamp it down quickly. Her suspicion is amusing, but it also breaks my heart a little. Time and time again, she shows me that she's never even had the opportunity to rely on another person.

One day she'll see she can count on me.

"Are you sure?"

I dip my chin. "I wouldn't ask if I didn't mean it."

"All right." She flashes me a small, grateful smile.

My chest warms, and I pocket that smile like I'm saving it for a rainy day.

"I'll get them." She takes off, bounding up the stairs and into the house. Her tiny shorts only make her toned legs look longer, and her simple tight-fitted black t-shirt shows off her trim waist and perfect curves.

Shaking thoughts of her body from my head, I slide into the car. I crank the engine and adjust the AC vents so they won't blast in her face when she gets in. Minutes later, she appears with her bag slung crossways over her body and shuts the door behind her.

No brothers.

She opens the passenger door but doesn't get in. Instead, she ducks her head and says, "They don't want to go. Said they don't care what I get them—which is really trusting on their part because I could get them Barbie supplies just to spite them. If you don't want to go now, it's okay. I can go by myself."

Every time she makes a comment like that, my heart splinters a little more. Her natural reaction to shrug off any suggestion of help, to reject a notion before someone else can reject her, makes it obvious she's never been able to count on another person.

"Hal?"

She blinks, those warm brown eyes of hers making my stomach dip. "Yeah?"

"Get in the fucking car."

Surprised laughter bubbles out of her. "I didn't know you were capable of curse words. You're such a saint." She slides onto the leather seat and shuts the door.

There's no stopping the smile that splits my face. With the car in reverse, I press my hand to the back of her headrest and look over my shoulder. I don't think I'll ever get used to having a backup camera.

"Trust me, Halle"—I glance at her, then pull out onto the road—"I'm no saint."

If she only knew the very unsaintly thoughts I've had about her.

As I put the car in drive, I swear there's the briefest flash of desire heating her eyes. She hides it by focusing on her lap, fiddling with the frayed edges of her shorts.

As I pull away, I pass her my phone. "You can put whatever music you like on."

"Seriously?" She holds my phone and side-eyes me. "Most men like to be in control of the music choices."

I glance sideways at her. "I thought we'd established already that I'm not most men."

She presses her lips together. A habit, I've realized. Maybe a conditioned response to keep her mouth shut. A response I want to put an end to.

"What's your passcode?"

That simple question is enough to cause my shoulders to relax. She needs to let go more, especially if something as simple as being given the power to pick the music selection makes her nervous.

Halle is strong-willed and stubborn, yet surprisingly insecure at times. She's a lesson in contradictions, with so many complex facets to her personality. From what I've seen, I could dig and dig and never get to the bottom of her well of trauma, but I'll be damned if I'm not going to try.

"Don't have one," I answer.

She sighs, the sound one of resignation, like she knows she should've expected this answer. "Not like most men, got it."

I keep my smile to myself.

A few minutes later, when the opening bars of a country love song play through the speakers, she peers over at me. "Is this okay?"

"It's great." I adjust my hand on the wheel. "Ever been to a concert?"

She huffs a laugh. "No, definitely not."

"If you could go to one, who would you want to see?"

In my periphery, she purses her lips, thoughtful. "Probably Ford Parker."

"He's pretty new, right?"

"Mmm." She nods. "He only has two albums, but I like his sound. His lyrics are … well, they're poetry."

I make a mental note to check his tour schedule. "Who else do you like?"

"Asha Donavan. She's a little more pop than country, but I like her voice. She's got this rasp that adds feeling to all of her songs."

"Do you sing?" I ask.

I'm greedy to know all I can about her. The questions may be innocuous, but I've got to start somewhere.

With a light laugh, she tucks a piece of hair behind her ear. "In the shower and along to the radio, yeah. But I don't sing all that well, if that's what you're really asking."

"If you could go anywhere in the world right now, where would you go?"

I'm pushing it now, digging a little deeper, but to my surprise, she doesn't shut down.

"I've never thought about it." She gives a self-deprecating laugh. "Isn't that sad? I've never considered leaving my brothers, so I haven't put effort into dreams that'll never become a reality." She swallows audibly. "Where would you go?"

"Everywhere."

She pokes my arm, a pop of static electricity zinging between us. "Ow." She shakes her finger, giggling. "Sorry about that. But 'everywhere' is not an answer."

"You didn't give me one either," I counter.

She hums, peering out her window. We're silent then, but before I can move on to a safer topic, she says, "Scotland. I think I would go to Scotland." The words are quiet, hesitant, like she worries that by speaking the thought aloud, any chance of one day going will be snatched from her.

"Why there?"

"I'm not sure." She shrugs, making her hair slip over her shoulder. "I guess because it seems peaceful."

Once I've parked, I unbuckle my seat belt and shift her way. "I want to travel everywhere, because I feel like there's so much out there to see and do and experience and that I've barely touched the tip of the iceberg."

She studies my face, like she's really processing my answer.

"From here, it sounds like you're searching for something," she says softly. "But if I know one thing, it's that the answers you're looking for aren't out there in the world." She presses a hand to my chest. "They're right here."

My heart kicks up a notch in speed, and her fingers tremble slightly, like maybe she notices. Like she sees the way my heart reacts to her.

She pulls her hand away carefully and laces her fingers in her lap. "Sorry. I shouldn't have done that."

I probably shouldn't say it, but the words fall from my mouth before I can stop. "You can touch me anywhere, Halle. Anytime you want."

Her breath catches slightly, her eyes wide with a mixture of wonder and confusion.

Before I can regret my declaration, I turn and push my door open. She does the same, carefully closing hers behind her.

I slip my keys into my pocket, then round the car and guide her to the entrance.

While I swipe a cart, she pulls up a screenshot of a supply list. The store has organized back-to-school items together, making the process easy, and in no time, we've crossed off every item, even securing some pretty good deals.

At checkout, I have to shove my hands deep into my pockets to keep from whipping my wallet out and insisting that I pay. Halle would eviscerate me if I tried to pay for her brothers' things. It's not my place, anyway, but that doesn't stop me from wanting to help. If I can make things easier on someone else, why wouldn't I?

Before Halle can get to the bags, I scoop them all up and head for the exit.

"I could've gotten those," she says, her feet tapping against the pavement as she catches up with me.

"I know you could've, but I have them."

She narrows her eyes at me as I set the bags in the back seat.

"Has anyone ever told you that you have a savior complex?"

Savior complex?

Huh.

She might have a point.

"No."

She plants her hands on her hips. "I'm pretty sure you do."

"You're probably right," I give her a smirk. No sense in arguing. I can't seem to help myself when it comes to people I care about. "Hungry?"

She frowns. "Huh?"

"Are you hungry? You know, that thing where your stomach demands food?"

The smallest of smiles plays on her lips. "I think I like it when you're sarcastic."

I grin. "Good to know." I shut the door and hit the lock button on my fob. "There's a burger place over here. I can't come this way and not stop."

"You come this way often?" She crinkles her nose. "Never mind. That sounded like a cheesy pickup line."

I slow my steps so we're side by side and bump her arm lightly. "You got any others to try on me?"

"Oh, God." She lets out a groan, but in a matter of seconds her lips twitch like she's trying not to laugh. "One time, a guy approached me and said 'dating is a numbers game, so can I get yours?'"

I bark out a laugh. "Too bad you already have my number."

At the crosswalk, we pause, and she squints against the sun for what has to be the third or fourth time today.

Head bowed, I take my sunglasses off and hold them out. "Here."

She shoots me a funny look. "Huh?"

I wave them in front of her. "Take them. You're squinting."

"Oh, it's fine." The crosswalk lights up, and we carefully step out into the road. "This is the place, right?" She points at the Al's Burgers sign at the strip mall ahead.

"That'd be the one." I push the glasses closer again. "Take them. It'll make me feel better."

With a sigh, she slips them on. "Thank you, but I promise you I would've been fine without them."

As we approach the small mom-and-pop restaurant, I jog ahead of her and pull the door open.

"Thanks," she says again, taking off my sunglasses and holding them out to me.

"Keep them for now." I wave her off and navigate toward the counter to order. "What would you like?"

"I can get my own, Caleb."

Mouth pressed into a line, I stare down at her, and I don't let up until she starts to squirm. "It was my idea to get burgers. Ergo, I'll be buying."

"Ergo," she mutters. "Fine." With a huff, she takes a step closer to the counter. "Just a plain cheeseburger and small fry."

"How about I get a large fry and we share?"

"That's fine." She worries her bottom lip between her teeth, eyeing the order board.

"Drink?" I ask her.

"Um ... I'll take a Sprite."

"You got it,." I pull out my wallet and smile at the cashier approaching the counter. "Go pick a spot. I'll be there in a minute."

She hesitates, eyeing me, but rather than argue, she nods once. "Okay."

Other guys might find Halle's flippant responses and her need to remind me that she can take care of herself frustrating. But it doesn't bother me a bit. Maybe because I see it for what it really is. Self-reliance is a great quality to have, but she's never known anything different, so she holds a little too tight to it. It's ingrained in her. Being taken care of is as foreign to her as another language. It'll take time for her to overcome the need to reject my offers of help, but in time, I hope to prove that she can count on me too.

After I've ordered, I stand off to the side to wait, collecting salt, ketchup, and malt vinegar packets.

Halle scrolls on her phone from the booth she chose, sneaking looks my way every so often.

When she looks a third time and meets my eyes, she sticks her tongue out and mouths, "Stop staring at me."

Crossing my arms over my chest, I grin and shake my head.

"Here you go, dear," the older woman behind the counter says, getting my attention.

"Thanks." I flash her a smile and drop the condiments onto the tray.

"You were staring at me, Thorne," Halle accuses as I approach the table.

"I was." I slide into the seat across from her and pass her the burger with the red sticker that reads *Plain* on its wrapper.

"You don't even deny it." She shakes her head, lips twitching.

As I unwrap my burger, I arch a single brow at her. "Why would I?"

She presses her lips together, a silent war raging in her dark eyes, like she can't decide whether to answer the question truthfully or not. Eventually, she exhales and says, "I'm beginning to think my brothers were right when they said you have a crush on me."

As we stare at one another, a flush creeps up her neck and into her cheeks.

A thrill zips through me. "I do."

Her jaw drops, and she sputters nonsensically.

"And don't even think about believing that I only offered you a place to stay because of that. I would've done it for anyone in need. And don't worry, I'm not going to ask you out."

Voice small, she asks, "You're not?"

I swallow a bite of burger and wipe my mouth with a napkin. "No. I won't put you in that position. You work for me, and for now, you live with me. I don't want you to think that you owe me a shot because of that."

"What if..." She drops her attention to her untouched burger. "What if I wanted you to?"

My stomach drops in surprise, the sensation so sudden I feel like I'm free-falling off a cliff. "Wanted me to what?" I press. I'm pretty sure I know what she means, but I ask for clarification anyway.

"Ask me on a date."

Fuck. I want to whoop and jump for joy, but I don't want to scare her away.

Instead, I say, "No." Forcing the single syllable out is painful, but she has to see where I'm coming from.

"No?" She slides her burger away from her, straightening. "Why not? You just said—"

"Are you attracted to me?" I ask.

"Yes," she answers, shocking me with her honesty.

"At least we're on the same page there."

"Right, so why—"

I hold up a hand. "For all the reasons I mentioned. You like me? You want to kiss me? Date me? Fuck me?" I've never been so forward when it comes to a woman, not even Salem. "Then you make the move. I have to know it's what you want."

Her cheeks are crimson now. "Okay."

"Okay," I echo.

TWELVE

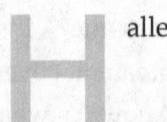alle

In the two weeks since Caleb and I had lunch at the burger joint, I haven't stopped thinking about our conversation. We admitted to our mutual attraction, and then he put the ball in my court.

Since then, what have I done about it? A big fat nothing.

Why?

Because I'm scared.

I've never met a man like him before, and it's impossible not to be on the lookout for ulterior motives. It's ridiculous, really. He's been nothing but transparent, and he literally put all the control in my hands.

All my life, men have come and gone, an almost constant rotation of not-so-great guys. Every one of them wanted something from my mom, usually sex or drugs or a place to crash.

While my experience has been wholly different, it's been pretty minimal. I've never had a serious relationship. In high school, I lost my virginity to a guy on the baseball team. Honestly, I just wanted to get it over with. He didn't care about me, and I certainly didn't care about him. All my interactions with men have involved sex in some way, so I guess I can't judge my mom too harshly in that department.

Caleb is different.

Maybe other men use tactics similar to his in an effort to gain a woman's trust for not so altruistic reasons, but Caleb? This is just the way he is. He's a giver. He just can't help himself.

"Stop thinking about this," I mutter as I shut the computer down at the end of the workday.

Caleb's been in Boston for the past few nights, but he'll be back this evening. The fridge was relatively barren when he left, but now it closely resembles a desert. A stop at the grocery store is a must. I want to restock the food the boys and I have eaten, plus I plan to make dinner. I'm sure he'll be hungry when he gets in.

I shuffle down the hall and pop my head into my brothers' room. "I'm going to the store. Want to come?"

They both shrug. "Why not," Casen says.

"You finished your homework, right?"

They nod in unison, wearing innocent expressions. "Show me."

School started less than two weeks ago, and I've already received a call from a teacher. Apparently, they haven't been turning in work, and more than once, they've been caught hanging out on the football bleachers instead of in class.

Clearly, they're determined to make sure I'm gray-haired before I'm thirty.

Casen slides off the bed and holds out the tablet the school issued him. When I note the tasks checked off in his virtual classroom, I hand it back and pad over to Quinn.

"Don't think I haven't forgotten about you."

With a groan, he rolls off the bed. His lanky body looks like it's suspended in air for the space of a heartbeat, and just before I'm certain he'll hit the ground, he catches himself and straightens. "Here."

I look it over and hand it back, then pad back into the hallway. "Thank you. I'm going to change before we go. Meet you guys in the car?"

I shut myself in the guest bedroom and change out of my comfy clothes. No one sees me for either job, so why bother dressing up? I yank a pair of jeans on, nearly tripping over my feet in the process, then, because the air is beginning to get that crisp edge to it, I pull on a sweater and boots.

Last week, I got a second opinion on the water damage. According to the man who came out and looked, it's not as bad as the adjuster thought. But it'll likely still be two or three months before repairs can even begin.

The boys are already in the car when I step outside, the

radio blasting. I slide into the driver's seat and immediately turn it off.

"Are you trying to bust my eardrums?" I glare at Casen in the passenger seat, then Quinn behind me. "Maybe irritate the whole neighborhood? It's like you want Thelma to storm over here and scold you."

Casen snorts as I buckle my belt. "Like she would."

"She loves us," Quinn adds, a hand on each of our seats.

"Yeah, she and Cynthia gave us cookies earlier."

I shift in my seat and frown at Casen. "When did that happen?"

"She waved us over when we got off the bus."

Thelma and Cynthia are harmless, but it hits me that my brothers are one hundred percent the kids who would get fooled into getting into a van with an offer of sweets or kittens.

"Where's my cookie?" I joke.

Quinn snickers at my shoulder. "You think we left any for you?"

Chin lifted, I grin at him in the rearview mirror. "I should've known better."

Casen pokes my arm. "I saved one for you."

I blink at him. "Seriously?"

He nods as I reverse out of the driveway. "Duh."

A handful of minutes later, I park outside the grocery store and tear my list in half.

The boys clamber out, causing a ruckus that's pretty standard for them, and Quinn darts for the cart corral.

"Divide and conquer." I hold one part out to Casen. "But no adding anything to the cart that's not on the list."

"You got it, sis." Quinn steers the cart inside, Casen on his heels.

In the vestibule, I grab my own cart and steer to the right side of the store. The total is probably going to make my stomach churn, but we've been eating Caleb's food since the day we moved our things over and he insisted that it was silly to keep things separate. I shake off the concern, then double check the list, making sure I'm not forgetting anything before I head toward checkout, where the boys are already waiting.

"How about spaghetti for dinner?"

"You know we're good with whatever," Casen grunts in reply.

He's right. They've never been picky eaters. Even when they were little.

As we're loading the car, we garner the attention of one couple, but that's it. We're far less intriguing than we were when we moved here. *Everyone* was staring then.

Though the day has gone smoothly, the whole way home, I'm hit with one concern after another about whether moving here was the right thing for them. After Mom's sentencing, it felt like a good idea to put some distance between us and our past. But sometimes I worry that I was being selfish, uprooting them because *I* needed a fresh start? I've always known that if I stayed in that town, I'd go nowhere in life, and for years, I've worried that the same would be the case for them.

I exhale, pushing away the concerns. The choices have already been made. Now all I can do is hope for the best.

At home, the boys hop out of the car, and instead of

heading for the trunk, they go straight to the front door and let themselves in.

I'm still gaping as the front door closes. "Seriously?" I mutter. "Unbelievable."

I know they're kids, but they're old enough to know they should help. Looks like it's my job to teach them.

Trunk popped, I pick up several bags, then I head in. The house is silent as I step inside, which means they've already gone upstairs, probably to play their video games.

"Quinn! Casen!" I yell as I set the bags on the counter. "Get your butts outside and help me carry in the groceries." Silence. "Now!"

Their steps are heavy as they run down the stairs and march straight out the front door.

I sigh, running my fingers through my hair. This is hard. Being their sister but also their parent. It's a weird line to toe, but it's an important one. Even before I was awarded guardianship, I felt like it was my responsibility to turn them into good adults.

When they reappear, loaded down with bags, they're griping with each other.

"Will you stay and help me put this stuff away?" I keep my tone light rather than demanding their help the way I want to.

Without responding, they get to work.

With the three of us working together, it only takes a few minutes, and as they help me collect all the bags, I smile and say, "Thank you. I appreciate the help."

"You're welcome," Casen says.

"Ditto." Quinn shoots finger guns my way.

"You guys are welcome to help me make dinner too."

They eye each other and Quinn laughs. "Nice try, sis."

With a shrug, I pull out a pot. "It was worth a shot."

The boys dash upstairs again, and I've just filled the pot and turned on the stove when the doorbell rings. I hesitate and consider ignoring it. This isn't my house, after all, but when it rings again a minute later, I carefully make my way over. Through the window, the figure of a woman with blond hair is visible.

My stomach sinks when her identity registers. Caleb's ex-wife.

Is it too late to hide?

She waves, unwittingly answering that question for me. So I force my feet forward and steel myself with a breath before I open it. I've seen her from a distance, and we've waved in passing, but we haven't formally met. Perhaps I should've made my way next door and introduced myself, especially since the boys have clearly met her if they've been swimming in her pool, but it's too late for that now.

I paste on a smile, then pull the door open. "Hello?" I sound like a scared five-year-old. I clear my throat. "You must be Salem." There. That sounds a little better.

"I am. It's so nice to finally meet you. I feel awful about not introducing myself sooner." She holds out a platter. "I made cupcakes to apologize."

"Cupcakes?" A thrill shoots through me.

Her smile grows. She's gorgeous. No wonder Caleb fell in love with her. Her face is round, with delicate features and freckles that make her look younger than what I assume is twenty-nine. I can't help but compare myself to her. I'm her complete opposite, with dark hair and dark eyes. I'm at least a couple of inches taller, and I have more curves. How could Caleb possibly be attracted to me? She and I wouldn't fall into the same category in any aspect when it comes to a man's type.

"Cupcakes are kind of my thing."

"Do you want to come in?" I take a step back. Shit. I should have asked as soon as I answered the door. Or maybe I shouldn't have offered at all, since this isn't my home. Though I'm sure she's been in this house more than I have.

She's kissed Caleb.

She's slept beside him.

Fucked him.

Married him.

It's like my brain is set on making sure I hate this woman. But I stomp the thoughts away. She might've had him once, but she doesn't now.

"Sure. I can't stay long, though. My husband is with the kids, and the terrible twos have a whole new meaning when it comes to our youngest. I'm not sure if it's a boy thing or a third child thing, but he's like the Energizer Bunny. He never stops. Yesterday, I turned away for two seconds, and when I turned back, he'd drawn on the wall with a Sharpie." She follows me through the house as she prattles on.

It's nice, really. Her chatter helps to ease some of my anxiety.

In the kitchen, she sets the cupcakes on the counter. "I'm really sorry to hear about your house."

I lift one shoulder. "It is what it is."

Ugh, there they are again. Those five annoying words.

"Still sucks." She slides onto a stool and rests her forearms on the counter. "And…" She winces. "I have to admit, I had a bit of an ulterior motive for coming over here."

"Oh?" I drop the pasta in the rapidly boiling water, willing my heart to remain steady. "What would that be?"

"Caleb likes you." She says it slowly, carefully, like she's placing a bomb between us.

I blink. That's it? By the caution, I expected something scandalous.

"I know."

She sits up straighter, surprise flickering over her face. "You do?"

"Yes." I pull another pan out of the cabinet and then snag the meat from the fridge. "We've discussed our mutual interest." Once the meat is sizzling on the stove, I turn and wash my hands, avoiding her gaze.

"Caleb is a really good guy," she says behind me. "The best. He has a big heart and he deserves to be happy." When I turn, I find she's wearing an almost sad expression. "I hope you'll give him a chance."

I crinkle my nose.

Is she trying to wingman her ex?

"You divorced him," I say, trying to keep my tone even. "But you're over here singing his praises. Why?"

Despite my efforts, the question comes out sounding more combative than I intend, but I can't take it back now.

She winces. "Yes, I divorced him, but the situation was

far from typical." She traces her fingers around a swooping line in the countertop.

"Explain."

I haven't asked Caleb for details. His marriage isn't any of my business. But if she's come all the way over here to talk to me about him, then I will press for details. It's best to be prepared with all the facts, and I can't help but be curious about her perspective of what went down between them. Caleb says he's over her and has moved on, but I can't help but wonder how she views the situation.

"Let me text my husband and let him know I'm going to be a little later than planned."

I set an onion on a cutting board and search for a knife. "It's that kind of story?"

"Oh, yeah." Her fingers fly across her phone's screen. Once she's hit send, she sets it on the counter, strides around the island, and pulls a wineglass from a cabinet. She procures a bottle of wine next, silently holding it up in question. When I shake my head, she fills her glass, then sits down and begins her tale.

"Caleb and I were high school sweethearts, though I hate that term." She takes a careful sip of wine while I chop the onion into fine pieces. "Thayer moved in the summer after our senior year." She nods in the direction of her house, then sets her glass down. "This is my childhood home."

My breath gets caught in my throat. Her *what?*

"Caleb didn't buy this house because of me," she says, clearly picking up on my shock. "After my mom passed away, my sister and I wanted to sell it. Caleb wanted to be close to Seda, so it made sense."

"He loves her a lot." I use my knife to slide the onions into the pan, then mix them in with the browning beef.

"He's an amazing father." She taps her fingers on the side of the glass. "Anyway, Thayer and I had this instant connection. It was more intense than anything I'd ever experienced. We were drawn to each other in a way that was impossible to fight, even though he's more than ten years older than me." She takes another sip of the wine, a larger one than the last, then gives me a sad smile. "I would watch his son sometimes, and Thayer and I gradually got close. Though it wasn't our intention, we fell in love."

She wipes at an invisible speck on the counter and clears her throat.

"It wasn't fair to Caleb, even though he and I had broken up when he left for college…" She takes a deep breath, ghosts of her past swimming in her eyes. "Thayer's son passed away…"

My heart lurches, my thoughts instantly going to my brothers. I can't imagine losing a child.

"It was…" She blows out a breath. "Hard, as you can imagine. Thayer's entire world imploded. Shit happened and we broke up. Then I found out I was pregnant." Her eyes mist over, but she blinks the moisture away. "I didn't know where else to go. Caleb had always been my safe space, so I went to him, and I told him everything. It hurt, telling him that I'd fallen in love with another man. But he accepted it. He forgave me, and then he stepped up to help me with Seda. First as friends. But it didn't take long to fall back into old habits. Then it was like we never ended in the first place."

"What made you get divorced?" I ask as I stir in the tomato sauce. I probably shouldn't ask, but she came here willing to share, so why not?

"He wanted to have more kids."

I spin on my heel, spatula in hand. "You divorced him because he wanted kids?" From where I'm standing, that makes no sense. He wanted more kids, so she divorced him, yet she now has *more kids*? "Surely you guys could've compromised."

She shakes her head, a soft sad smile settling on her lips. "When he broached the topic of kids, I knew I needed to end it, because I … I loved him. A part of me will *always* love him in a way. But that discussion made me realize that though I cared for Caleb, Thayer was it for me. It killed me. Realizing how selfish I'd been. All that time I'd been denying Caleb the chance to find the kind of love I'd had once. I didn't think Thayer and I would ever reconnect, and I never wanted to come back here, but when my mom got sick, I had no choice."

"Oh," I say softly. "I'm sorry about your mom."

"Thanks." She dips her chin and tucks her hair behind her ear. "Anyway," she sips the last of her wine, "maybe that will help you understand him a little better."

"You don't have to sell me on him. He's not a bachelor that needs to be put up for auction."

"No, he's not," she agrees, eyes dropping. "But he is a man who has *always* put the needs of others above his own, and he needs someone who won't take advantage of that. Someone who can meet him in the middle."

"And you think that's me?" I blurt. "You don't even know me."

"You're right. But I know Caleb, and I've seen the way you take care of yourself and your brothers."

With that, she stands, rinses her glass, and lets herself out.

All the while, I stand still, stunned speechless.

My stupor is only broken when Quinn shouts, "Is dinner ready yet?"

THIRTEEN

Caleb

My entire body sags once my car is in park in the driveway. Work was draining, and then traffic was a bitch. Every day, this job gets harder. I have a love-hate relationship with my profession. I enjoy helping people. It's fulfilling. But the tragedies I witness and the poor circumstances I have to be involved with can very easily weigh on me. And watching the justice system fail the people who need it most grates on me.

I drag myself out of the car, hit the lock button on my key fob, and trudge toward the front of the house.

The lights on the first floor are dimmed, like everyone's already in their respective rooms for the night.

The sight makes my heart drop. I *want* to see Halle. I want to talk with her about normal, mundane things. I haven't seen her in days and I'm more than a little desperate for normalcy.

Not that any of this is normal. I made my feelings for the woman clear. She reciprocated. Yet we're at a standstill. And on top of that, she's staying here temporarily. Soon enough, she and her brothers will go home. Honestly, I'm shocked she hasn't tried to go back while she waits for the repairs to begin.

Inside, I lock the door and head for the kitchen. The house smells incredible, making my stomach rumble. Damn. The turkey sandwich I grabbed from the deli for lunch was hardly sufficient.

I veer toward the stairs and set my stuff down, then make a beeline for the fridge. The lights above the island are on but dimmed, so it isn't until I'm passing it, on a mission to dig for leftovers, that I notice the containers on the marble countertop.

Spaghetti.

She made spaghetti for dinner.

This isn't the first time she's cooked, but it catches me off guard anyway.

The soft approach of feet snags my attention, then Halle appears in the doorway.

Her damp hair hangs past her shoulders and she's wearing an oversize blue t-shirt and what looks like blue and white boxers beneath.

I bristle at the sight of those. I've never been the jealous type, but the unbridled feeling rises up inside me anyway. I shove it down, way down, and smile.

"This looks delicious."

"I thought you'd be in sooner," she remarks, eating up the space between us with careful steps.

My shoulders sag. "There was an accident. It slowed traffic down."

"Ah, that makes sense. Do you want to shower before you eat? I can plate our food while you do that." She looks down at her toes, wiggling them against the hardwood floor.

I splay my hands on the counter. "You haven't eaten because you were waiting for me?" There's no hiding my disbelief or my hope. "Why?"

She shrugs her slender shoulders and drags her eyes up to mine. They're wide, doe-like, and swimming with uncertainty. "Because I wanted to."

Fuck if that doesn't feel like a shot straight to my heart. She waited because she *wants* to eat dinner with me? My mind runs with that, reading into the statement a little too deeply and pulling meaning from it—that she wants to spend time with me—that may only be wishful thinking.

"A shower would be nice."

"Okay." She blesses me with the tiniest of smiles. "I'll get this ready."

I take the quickest shower of my life, then change into a pair of sleep pants and a sweatshirt. I've never minded dressing up for work, but nothing beats the feeling of slipping into comfortable clothes at the end of the day.

On the way back, I pop my head into the twins' room. They're watching TV with the door open, sprawled out, lanky limbs everywhere. "Hey, guys."

As if the movement was choreographed, they glance over, heads tilted at the same angle.

"Hey." Casen waves.

"Good to have you back, landlord." Quinn chortles.

"Landlord." I stifle a snort and shake my head. "You're funny."

With a rap of my knuckles on the doorframe, I step back out into the hallway and let them get back to their movie. They have school in the morning, and it's getting late, but in the few days they've been here, I've already learned that there's really no controlling a teen's bedtime. I guess I can look forward to that experience with Seda.

Downstairs, Halle has set our food out on the dining room table. Our plates are on opposite sides, directly across from each other, and she's filled two glasses with ice water. She's even gone through the trouble of lighting a few candles.

It's ... romantic.

So much so that my steps come up short and my heart trips over itself.

Am I dreaming? Worse, am I dead?

"Don't look so shocked," she laughs.

Fuck if I don't fall in love with that sound. I didn't know it was possible to feel such deep emotion for a person's laugh, but hers is so rare that I can't help but treasure it.

"They're just candles. Don't overthink it."

Right. Just candles.

I ease into the seat across from her, taking her in. Her face is bare of any makeup. Her hair is mostly dry now, the ends curling slightly.

Lips puckered and attention fixed on her fork as she twists it in her noodles, she says, "I met Salem today. Like actually met her, not just in passing. She brought cupcakes."

"You finally met her, huh?" Though I force a smile, nerves assault my stomach.

Salem has been itching to meet Halle, especially since she knows I *like* her. It's thanks to sheer luck only that she hasn't until now.

"How'd that go?"

She lifts one shoulder, gaze still averted. "It was fine. She's really pretty."

You're prettier.

"She … uh … told me the whole story. About what happened between you two, I mean. And Thayer."

I take my time chewing and swallowing a bite of spaghetti. "It was a hard time for all of us."

"I'm sure. She told me about Thayer's son…" She audibly swallows. "I can't imagine. If something happened to one of my brothers, it would devastate me. I don't know how you ever recover from something like that."

"You don't," I answer simply. "He'll always carry that pain. He has good days and bad, but I think he chooses to live and love his life that much more *for* Forrest."

She sips her water, eyes trained on me. "You actually like him, don't you?"

Laughter flies out of me. "Now? Yeah. Didn't used to, though."

She cocks her head to the side. "You mean something actually managed to ruffle your feathers, Caleb Thorne?"

"My feathers get ruffled more often than you'd think," I admit. "But yeah, I was hurt and angry. Who wouldn't be? The divorce was a blow too."

She winces at that, making my heart sink.

Shit. I clear my throat. "But probably not in the ways you're thinking."

"Explain," she demands, her voice warbling slightly. "I want to understand you better."

Halle is so self-reliant, so independent. So this? Wanting to know more about me? It feels like a gift.

"I felt like I had failed Seda. My parents aren't divorced, but they probably should be. All my life, I've strived not to be anything like them. All I wanted was for Seda to have a better childhood than I did. Divorce meant separate homes, and even though I'd formally adopted her and Salem promised that she would never take my daughter from me, I was still scared. She's *not* my blood. I know exactly how that would play out if we ended up in court."

"Salem said you wanted more kids."

I sigh and set my fork down. I'm glad Halle is curious about my life, and if there's any chance of a future between us, she needs to know this stuff, but fuck if it doesn't dredge up pain that took a long time to abate.

"I did." There's no sense in lying. "Seda was getting older, and I wanted her to have siblings."

Halle takes a deep breath, then lets it out slowly. "Are you still in love with her? I need to know that."

"No," I answer easily. "I'm not. There will always be a

place in my heart for her. She's Seda's mom, after all. But that's where my feelings for her end."

"Are you sure?" she presses. "I-I need to know, because I … I have feelings for you. It's confusing, and I don't know what to make of them, but I can't … I refuse to fall for a man who's in love with someone else."

My heart stumbles over itself, and I'm pretty sure my jaw just hit the floor.

"You're falling for me?"

"I don't know!" Voice rising, she covers her face with her hands. "I don't know," she says, softer this time. "Like I said, I'm confused. I don't have experience with guys like you."

My chest tightens. "Like me?"

"You know." She waves a hand a little wildly. "Perfect."

The laugh that escapes me is sardonic. "Halle, I'm far from perfect."

"From where I'm sitting, you seem pretty dang close to it, while I'm the furthest thing from it. My family is a disaster. The town I lived in all my life is a giant ticket to nowhere. I only finished one year of community college because I couldn't handle the schoolwork while working multiple jobs and ensuring my brothers were taken care of."

Her shoulders droop.

"I used every penny I had to buy a house that probably should have been bulldozed. I'm still barely scraping by with two jobs while trying to build a life where my brothers can just be kids. I'm a *wreck*. I can't possibly be what you want or need, but there's a connection here I can't deny." She flicks a finger between us. "You said I had to make the first move, but I'm scared. Everyone in my life has let me down, Caleb. Everyone. I don't want you to let me down too. But I don't want to put that pressure on you. There will always be disappointments. No one is perfect. But if this would just be sex—"

"Halle. Shut up, please."

She presses her lips together at my command, her cheeks turning the brightest shade of red.

I straighten in my seat and angle forward. "You could never let me down. We've recognized that there's mutual attraction here. Now let's get on the same page. What do you want from me? Do you want to give this a serious try? Actually date? Or do you just want sex?"

Halle covers her face with her hands again, shaking her head.

I bite back a laugh as I watch her. I shouldn't find her turmoil so amusing, but damn if her transparency isn't refreshing.

"I could bend you over this table," I grit out. "Skim my hands up your thighs and slide your pants down. If I did, would I find you wet and waiting for me?"

Her hands drop with a thud to the table. We've both entirely forgotten to eat.

"Caleb," she breathes, her eyes wide. She looks toward the stairs. "My brothers—"

"I was kidding." I pick up my water glass and take a slow sip. "Not that I wouldn't love to bend you over and fuck you from behind, but now's not the time."

She ducks her head so her hair hides her face and shakes

it. "I … I thought I was confused before, but now you've really got me tangled up."

"Good." I choke back a laugh. "I like that I can take you by surprise."

In a town this small, we all know one another. Sometimes too well. Halle's status as a new resident isn't what intrigues me, but I can't deny that her lack of preconceived notions about me is refreshing. I've never been interested in the friends with benefits thing, so I'm hoping she'll shoot that proposal down, but if that's all she'll give me for now, then I'll take it.

"I've never dated anyone." Though she lets out a shaky breath once the words are out, she follows it by lifting her chin and pulling her shoulders back. "That's not to say I'm inexperienced in other ways. But relationships? It's all foreign to me, and I'm scared." She swallows thickly.

I keep my mouth shut, hands fisted in my lap to keep from reaching out for her. It took a great deal of guts for her to admit to her fear, and I want to show her that I'm listening, that I respect her feelings completely.

"But I'd like to go on a date with you. See where this thing goes. But"—she holds up a finger—"if this doesn't work out, you have to promise that we'll remain cordial. We're neighbors, after all."

I lean across the table and hold out my pinky.

"Promise."

She loops her finger through mine. "Promise."

FOURTEEN

Halle

"What do you mean?" There's no way I heard the school secretary correctly. "Please tell me you're joking."

She's not joking. No school secretary would waste their time making a call like this for no reason.

"They'll be here in the office when you arrive. They're suspended for three days."

My heart sinks. "I'll be there in about ten minutes."

When I end the call, I'm not at all surprised to find Caleb watching me, brow arched, from the chair in the corner where he's reading ... *is that* Percy Jackson? I swear he had a law text open on his lap earlier.

"What was that about?" he asks when all I do is blink back at him.

It takes several seconds to process the call and find the words to answer. "I have to get my brothers." I push back from the desk. "I'll be back soon. Shouldn't take more than thirty minutes. I hope."

Ten minutes there. Ten minutes back. That leaves ten minutes to get the rundown from the principal and potentially lay into the boys for their idiocy.

"I gathered that much. What happened, though?" He slides a bookmark between pages and shuts the book.

I take a deep breath, willing my nerves to remain settled, and blow it out. "They caught a snake and let it loose in the school."

Caleb stares at me for a long moment, then bursts into laughter, startling the shit out of me. "I'm so glad I have a daughter. Boys are something else."

"You're a boy," I argue.

"Yeah, and teen boys do dumb shit." He sets his book aside and gets up. "I'll drive."

I stomp my way into the school. Alone. By some miracle, I convinced Caleb to stay in the car. He was dead set on joining me, but I reminded him that I'm their guardian. I need to handle these kinds of things on my own if the boys are ever going to respect me.

I'm buzzed inside and head straight to the office, where I show my ID to the secretary.

"Halle—"

I snap my finger in my brothers' direction. "I don't want to hear anything from either of you right now."

Eyes wide, they look from me to each other, no doubt using that twin telepathy.

The woman behind the counter stands and smooths the front of her shirt. "The principal would like to talk to you."

"Lovely." The word is more sarcastic than I mean for it to be, but there's no taking it back now.

She leads me over to a closed door and knocks. When a gruff voice replies with a "come in," she gives me an encouraging smile. It only makes me more nervous.

Inside the office, I come face to face with a large man with a receding hairline and ruddy cheeks. His eyes seem kind, though, so that gives me hope.

"Hi, Principal Lewis." I hold out a hand. "It's nice to meet you, though I wish it was under different circumstances."

His grip is solid but not bruising. "I wish the same, Miss…?"

"Emerson," I reply. I have our mom's maiden name while the boys have their dad's. My dad didn't stick around long enough to even give me his name. Figures.

"Miss Emerson." He nods once. "I understand that moving and starting school in a new place can be a challenge. Your brothers may still be adjusting, and that isn't out of the ordinary, but catching and releasing a snake inside the school is inexcusable behavior."

A weight settles on my chest, making breathing painful. "Believe me, I know. I promise I'll deal with them."

"As I'm sure Mrs. Clemons informed you, they've received a three-day suspension. Being that it's Friday, it will begin on Monday. I don't often mete out this type of consequence, but in this case, it's necessary. There have been some … other incidents. Given the period of adjustment I believe students need, I chose to overlook them, but I'm afraid I can't keep turning a blind eye."

My stomach sinks. "What other incidents?" And why wasn't I notified?

He winces. Maybe realizing that this information shouldn't have been kept from me. "One of them took the plaque off my door."

What?

"They also stole paints from the art department. They've yet to turn up. So you'll see why I couldn't let the snake incident go without a fitting consequence."

With every transgression he ticks off, my blood heats further. I'm going to kill them.

How do parents do this shit? Where does the patience come from?

"Thank you for letting me know," I say, somehow keeping my tone even. "Is there anything else you need from me?"

"No, not today." He rests both palms on the desk. "But this behavior can't continue, Miss Emerson. I like to think of myself as a patient and understanding man. Hence the reason I haven't spoken to you about their behavior until now. My hope was that I could deter them by speaking with them myself. Clearly, I was wrong."

Standing, I blow out a breath and force a smile. "I'll talk

to them." I shake hands with him again, then let myself out. In the main area of the office, I level my waiting brothers with a glare. "Let's go."

Without a word, they follow, feet dragging and expressions stoic.

Outside, when they catch sight of Caleb's idling SUV, Quinn physically deflates. "You brought Caleb?"

"He insisted on coming. And you're in no position to complain about anything right now."

I wait until we're in the car and off school property before I turn around in my seat, ready to breathe fire.

"I'm so angry at you two." Rage makes my hands shake. "This shit is not okay. Stealing and letting wild animals go in the school? Seriously? Mom might have let this crap slide, but I won't. You're almost fifteen, for God's sake. Act like it."

"It was just a prank," Casen whispers, lowering his gaze. "It was supposed to be funny."

"Funny, huh? Did anyone laugh?" I bite out through gritted teeth. "Because I'm not laughing. Your principal certainly wasn't laughing. And when I walked in, neither of you were either."

"It's boring here," Quinn complains, flopped back against the seat. "Can you blame us for trying to liven things up?"

"Yes!" I practically shriek. "Yes, I can blame you. That behavior is unacceptable, and it reflects poorly on me. By tomorrow, everyone in this town will know what you did."

Caleb winces, glancing at the boys in the rearview mirror. "More like tonight. If they haven't already heard."

"Great," I snap. "We moved here for a second chance. Clean slate. A do-over. And you're already pulling the same crap. You're so, so smart, both of you, so maybe try using your brains for good instead of evil, okay?"

They exchange a look and give muttered agreements.

With a sharp inhale, I make a decision, and before I can second-guess myself, I force the words out. "You're grounded for a month. No video games and no television in your room."

"What?" Casen darts forward in his seat with so much force, the seat belt catches him. "You can't do that!"

"That's not fair," Quinn fires alongside him.

"Want to make it two months?" I threaten, my voice pure steel.

That gets them to shut up.

Once they've both slumped back again, I face forward, blinking back the tears I refuse to let fall. Anxiety claws its way up my throat and shrouds me in doubt. Maybe I'm not cut out for this.

Without a word, Caleb rests his hand on my knee and rubs soothing circles with his thumb. The light touch is surprisingly effective, quickly grounding me and making it easier to breathe.

Whether or not I'm cut out for this, I'm responsible for them, so I have to figure it out.

Caleb parks in the driveway, but none of us moves.

"Caleb?" I finally say, the quiet words piercing the silence. "Have any chores the boys could take care of for you? They'll have a whole lot of free time for the next month."

Caleb glances at them in the rearview mirror, and I swear he's managed to join in on their twin telepathy.

What the hell? I glare at him, but before I snap, he clears his throat.

"The deck needs to be power washed. I'll pull the power washer out."

FIFTEEN

Caleb

"What were you guys thinking?" I peer back at the boys as I tug on the power washer's handle. I stored it under the deck after I last used it.

Two sets of shoulders rise and fall. "Don't know," Quinn says.

"You must've been thinking something." With a grunt, I pull the power washer out completely. I haven't even turned thirty yet, but I can guarantee my back will be screaming later. The deck doesn't actually need to be cleaned, but it was the first thing that came to mind when she asked if I had any chores for them to do.

At the end of the day, they just need to know there are people in their life who care. They're begging for attention in the only way they apparently know how.

I set up the machine and show them what to do, then leave them to it, already thinking through other projects they could tackle to keep themselves occupied. Thelma and Cynthia could probably use some extra help too, and both boys seem to have a soft spot for the ladies.

The moment we got out of the SUV, Halle stormed inside. I stayed with the boys, figuring she could probably use a little time to cool down. Now, as I pad through the first floor, I don't see her.

Once I've climbed the stairs, I discover her in the place I should have looked first. She's sitting in front of the computer in my office, fingers flying furiously over the keyboard.

"Hey, what are you doing?"

"Working," she replies without looking up. "Need to send out a few more emails this afternoon."

"Halle." The carpeted floor silences my steps as I get closer. I lean against the desk, crossing my arms over my chest.

She ignores me.

"Halle. Look at me."

Her fingers slow and she looks up, her expression shuttered.

"You realize I'm your boss, right?"

With a huff, she rolls her eyes.

It takes effort to keep from smiling. God, I love her sass.

"I'm aware, yes."

"Do you really think I expected you to come back in here and work after that?"

"No." She lowers her focus to her hands, which are still poised over the keyboard. "But I needed to."

With a finger beneath her chin, I tilt her head up. "Why?"

"To distract myself," she admits. Her shoulders sag with a weariness she shouldn't possess at her age.

The response doesn't surprise me at all. What does is how easily she fessed up to it.

I sit on the edge of the desk, tugging at my pant leg when it strains against my knee. "I think we should talk about it."

"Ugh." She covers her face with her hands. "You're right, but I don't want to."

"What happened when you went into the school?"

She heaves a heavy sigh, her chest expanding, then falling dramatically, then shoves her fingers through her long dark hair and secures it with an elastic band from her wrist like she often does when she's working.

"The principal was nice enough, but he told me that they've had other incidents already. He just hadn't reported them to me, hoping they could sort it out at school. But leave it to the chaos twins to not take it seriously."

She drops her arms to the desk and buries her face in them, letting out a muffled scream.

"I'm sorry you're getting dragged into this mess."

Amusement courses through me. "I'm pretty sure I dragged myself into it, but whatever you need to tell yourself."

She cracks a small smile.

"So I know about the snake, but what else have they done?"

"They stole the principal's nameplate from his door."

I can't help but laugh. "Seems pretty trivial to me."

Her body deflates. "And they stole paint from the art class. It hasn't turned up yet, so who knows what they've done with that." She tosses her hands in the air. "Caleb." My name is a small whimper, a plea, and fuck if I wish she wasn't saying it under very different circumstances. Head lowered again, she sniffles. "I don't think I can do this."

"Hey," I crouch in front of her and angle in until she meets my eye. "Parenting isn't easy. For anyone. I can guarantee every parent has days they want to quit. But you're exactly what those boys need. You hear me?"

She nods brokenly. "I don't want them to end up like our mom, and I'm so scared that I'm one wrong decision away from forcing them in that direction. I don't have a dad, and my mom's in prison. They're all I have. I can't lose them too."

I cup her cheek, rubbing my thumb against her silky soft skin.

God, this girl. Her brain must be on a constant spin cycle of worry. "You're not going to lose them."

"You can't know that," she argues.

Chest tightening, I force her face up and hold her eyes. "I see the way they look at you. They admire you. This shit ... they're kids. Surely, they're probably confused and upset about all the changes, so they're acting out, but don't think for a second that you've caused any of it, okay?"

She gives a tiny jerk of a nod. The gesture lacks any confidence, making me think that she's placating me rather than agreeing.

I straighten and peer down at her. "Work if it makes you feel better, but I promise you don't need to."

"Thirty more minutes," she says, already turning back to the computer.

With a nod, I step back, then I let myself out of the room. After our talk the other night, I've been hoping to take her out this weekend. Now, I'm even more determined to make it happen. After a quick phone call to make a reservation, I jog across the street to visit with Cynthia and Thelma.

I ring the doorbell, and while I wait, I take in the overwhelming number of potted plants on the front porch. Despite how chilly the mornings are these days, their flowers are holding strong. Can't say the same for mine.

"Well, aren't you a sight for sore eyes." Cynthia opens the door wide and motions me inside. "Come in, come in. To what do we owe the pleasure of your company, Caleb Thorne?"

The floors creak beneath my boots. "It's good to see you, Cynthia. I have a favor to ask of you."

"I've got cookies in the oven. Let me pull them out, and then we'll chat."

I follow her into the kitchen, where Thelma sits at the table. The table covered in thick sheets of paper and a few canvases. And several small paint containers that bear stickers that say *Hawthorne Mills High School*.

Biting back laughter, I shake my head.

I settle at the table across from her, careful not to touch any wet paint. "What are you up to?"

The oven squeaks behind me as Cynthia opens it to take out the cookies.

"Painting," Thelma replies, dragging a paintbrush over the piece of paper she's working on, leaving a red streak behind. "Can you believe it? I mentioned to Casen and Quinn that I was thinking about painting again, and they brought me all these supplies."

I press a hand over my mouth to keep the laughter at bay. "Yes, very nice of them."

Thelma is a lot of things, but she's not stupid. She knows they stole the supplies, but frankly, she'd do the same thing.

Cynthia sits beside me, placing a gentle hand on my wrist. "The cookies need a minute to cool. What was it you came over to ask us?"

"Could you keep an eye on Casen and Quinn tomorrow evening? Around six? It'd only be for a couple of hours. I know this is short notice, and I can check with Salem and Thayer if it doesn't work for you, but I thought I'd ask you first, since the boys like spending time with you."

"That sounds wonderful," Cynthia says, her face lighting up.

"Send the delinquents over at 5:45. Dinner will be ready precisely at six," Thelma says without looking up from her painting.

Delinquents. Huh. Looks like my theory was correct. She definitely knows the art supplies are stolen.

"Will do. I really appreciate this."

"We're happy to help," Cynthia says, patting my hand.

At the same time, Thelma says, "You owe us one."

Cynthia scoffs. "Don't listen to her. We love those boys."

"What are you getting up to that you need us to be babysitters?" Thelma asks, finally looking up, eyes narrowed on me.

She has this way of looking at a person that's both accusatory and encouraging.

"I'm taking Halle on a date."

Beside me, Cynthia lets out a cry of joy and claps. "I knew it! I told you, love, didn't I?"

Thelma grumbles, pointing her dripping paintbrush at me. "You couldn't have held out a little longer? Now I'm down five bucks."

Fighting a smile, I look from her to her wife. "You two were betting on Halle and me?"

Cynthia hums, eyes dancing. "We wagered on how long it would take you to ask her out. I had faith in you." She squeezes my shoulder. "Thelma swore it would take you until the new year at least."

Thelma scoffs. "She's sugarcoating it for you to spare your feelings."

Frowning, I lean forward, elbows on what I hope is a paint-free spot of the table. "What was your prediction, then?"

Thelma's grin is downright evil. This woman is a menace. "I bet that it'd take you at least six months to work up the nerve."

Head tossed back, I laugh. "Well, that's mean. Glad I could surprise you, though."

"You really like her then?" Cynthia asks, one brow quirked.

Just the thought of Halle makes me smile. "Yes. A lot."

"Good. That teacher you dated was too mealy-mouthed for you. You need a girl with fire, and that Halle girl has got it."

"Fire, huh?" I bite back a grin.

"Reminds me of myself, if I'm being honest," Thelma muses. "You know what that means?"

"Yeah," I sigh.

It means I'm in for a world of trouble.

SIXTEEN

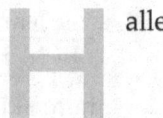alle

"You bought a dress for me?" I hold up the maroon-colored garment and turn, zeroing in on Caleb. "Where on earth are you taking me?"

When we agreed to give this a shot, I never imagined he would take me out quite so soon or that it would require me to dress up. The dress isn't the fanciest thing I've ever seen, but it is certainly nicer than anything I've ever owned.

Eyes twinkling, he takes a step closer. "I'll tell you when we're in the car."

Annoyance mixed with what might be excitement courses through me. "Why? Am I going to hate it?"

With a frown, he backs toward the door. "I hope not." He gives the doorframe a knock and steps into the hall. "I have to get ready too. Meet you downstairs in an hour?"

Nodding, I lay the dress out on the bed gently. There's no point in pressing him for more information. I'm learning that Caleb is incredibly stubborn when he wants to be.

I don't own much makeup, but I use what I've got, and when I'm done, I feel a little stronger. It's not that I *need* makeup, but in situations like this, it can be a confidence booster. And I can't deny I could use a little of that. I use my old curling iron, a hand-me-down from my mother, to set my hair in loose waves. It took far too long to understand that my curls were always tighter than I wanted because I was supposed to comb through them a bit to soften them. That's probably something most girls learn from their mothers. Not me.

I slip into the dress, surprised when it covers more skin than I expected. It shows off a bit of cleavage, but that's about it. The sleeves are short with a slight flutter, and it cinches in at the middle before flaring out and stopping just past my knees.

As I assess myself in the mirror, I can't help but wonder what Caleb was thinking when he picked it. And it's hard to imagine any man picking out a dress this simplistic yet flattering for a woman.

My single pair of black heels should work fine with this. They're a little scuffed, but it's not too obvious, so unless people stare at my feet, they shouldn't notice.

I give myself a final once-over in the mirror, fluffing my hair, then sling my purse over my shoulder. Only a little wobbly on my feet—mostly from nerves, not the heels—I pull the door open. When the two figures on the other side register, I let out a small yelp.

Quinn grins. "You look pretty."

Casen looks me up and down and nods. "I like the dress."

"Thank you. Caleb got it for me."

They exchange a look and bark out identical laughs.

Apprehension skitters down my spine. "What?"

Casen pats my arm, then steps back, headed for the stairs. "He's so down bad for you."

"No, he's not," I scoff.

Quinn snorts. "We're not blind." He follows his twin. "See you later."

Once they've disappeared, I take a moment to gather myself. They've got me even more out of sorts, and I need to focus if I want to make it down the stairs in these heels without rolling an ankle.

Halfway down, holding on to the banister for dear life, I realize I could have just taken them off.

I'm so focused on not falling that I don't even notice Caleb waiting for me at the landing until he lets out a low "fuck."

"What?" I freeze, heart lurching.

Did my lipstick smear on the way down? Did I leave a clip in my hair?

"You look ... beautiful."

I look down, assessing myself, trying to imagine what I look like from his perspective. Beautiful is not the first adjective that comes to mind. Awkward seems more fitting.

Rather than argue, I decide to take the compliment graciously. "Thank you."

When I finally reach him, he offers me his hand. Even like this, he towers over me. He's got to be six-foot-two.

He smells minty like he just brushed his teeth, and his face is freshly shaved. I want to run my fingers over his cheeks to determine whether they're as smooth as they look.

Before I can do it—thankfully, since I probably would have made a fool of myself—he clears his throat. "Your brothers are already across the street. Do you need anything before we go?" He entwines our fingers, tightening his hold.

I open my mouth to respond, but nothing comes out. When I try again, my voice is embarrassingly breathy. "I don't think so."

His touch alone causes my heart to jump and goose bumps to erupt up and down my arms. Outside, he opens the passenger door and waits for me to buckle my seat belt before shutting the door. I squeeze my eyes closed and count to five. When I open them again, he's sliding into the driver's seat. My heart flutters as his scent wafts over me. Men like Caleb don't exist in my world, so while the gesture—opening my door for me—is a simple one, it packs a powerful punch.

Would my mom have been different if a man had treated her right?

Not that the way a man treats a woman should have a major influence on her wellbeing, but I wonder if it would have helped. Or maybe it's easier to blame her behavior on bad situations than it is to accept that she's just a horrible person.

"Are you up for DJing again?" He holds his phone out to me.

I take it, noting how much heavier it is than mine. Probably because of the thick, expensive case.

I cue up a playlist and place his phone in the cupholder, then I slip off my heels. If I'm going to wear them all night, I'd rather delay the pain they'll inflict for as long as I can. "Do I get to know where we're going now?"

His shirt rustles with a roll of his shoulders. "I suppose. You're not going to jump out of a moving vehicle, are you?"

A small huff escapes me. "Should I?"

"I hope not." With a laugh, he rubs his jaw, but when he speaks again, his voice is subdued. "We're going to a ballroom dance class."

My stomach lurches. Oh yeah, I'm definitely contemplating jumping out of the car.

"Ballroom dancing?"

I've got to hand it to him. It's a creative date idea, but it's nothing like the simple dinner I was expecting.

Though I try to hide it, the horror I feel leaks out as I say, "What if I step on your toes?"

He scoffs. "What if *I* step on your toes?"

Focus averted, I pick at the edge of my nail. "I'd be okay."

"Exactly, so why would you think I wouldn't be if you did it?"

Stomach hollowing out, all I can do is shrug. "I'm not sure."

He comes to a stop at a light and zeroes in on me, once again using his fingers to gently tilt my face up. "I take it none of the men in your life have been very understanding."

I give him a sad smile. "Seems like all the guys my mom brought around had tempers."

As for my own experiences with men, I never let it get that far. Sex and nothing more. But I don't think Caleb wants to hear that.

"I'm sorry she did that."

I clear my throat and force myself to hold his gaze. "I'm sorry she thought she didn't deserve better."

The light changes and he eases off the brake. A moment later, we're on the interstate, and he's got one hand on the wheel, the other wrapped around mine again. "Do you want to talk about her?"

"There's not much to tell." I look out the window as the trees blur past. "She's my mom. Sometimes she was good, but most of the time she forgot I even existed. Then, for some dumb reason, she got pregnant again." The moment the words are out, I regret them. "I wouldn't change anything," I clarify. It's the truth. "I love my brothers, but she'd never shown more than a passing interest in me. Mostly, I was a burden or an inconvenience. So I don't understand what she was thinking. After the boys were born, she spiraled further. Year after year, it got worse. The drugs and alcohol. She didn't work and eventually turned to selling herself to pay for her habits. And when she tried to sell drugs to an undercover cop, then offered him sex to let her off, things didn't go well."

Caleb sucks in a harsh breath, his cheeks hollowing.

Shit. I've probably scared him enough to send him running. Maybe it's for the best. He clearly comes from a privileged family. Even if they're not perfect, like he's alluded to, he was certainly more taken care of than I was. He's the literal golden boy, while I'm the girl from the wrong side of the tracks.

"We can turn around," I say softly. The words cause a fissure in my heart, but offering him an out is the right thing to do. "If you don't want to go on a date with me anymore."

The car veers to the right sharply as Caleb takes the exit we almost pass, and I hold on to the dashboard for dear life. Rather than whip around and get back on the interstate headed back toward Hawthorne Mills, he brakes heavily and comes to a stop on the side of the road.

"What the fuck?"

He undoes his seat belt and shifts so his whole body is facing me. "You think that would deter me from taking you out? You think your past has any bearing on my feelings for you?" There's hurt in his voice and etched into the lines of his face. "Fuck, Hal. I'm just ... I'm trying to wrap my head around how your mom could take you and your brothers for granted like that. The three of you are incredible. You deserve to be cherished. She chose herself and her vices over you. That's shitty. And it breaks my heart that you grew up in that environment."

"But you were so quiet," I defend, turning to face him, arms crossed. "What was I supposed to think?"

Despite the way his nostrils flare and the passion in his

words, he doesn't scare me. Time and again, he's shown me that he won't hurt me.

"I needed a moment to process my thoughts," he says, voice gentler than before. "I didn't think I should come out and tell you I hate your mom while we're on our first date, but fuck, Halle, I really hate your mom."

A soft, disbelieving laugh leaves me. "Thank you. I think."

He cuffs my neck gently, his thumb rubbing soothing circles against my cheek.

"You expect me to run, and I get it. No one has ever stuck around. But I need you to know—I need you to *believe*—that I don't plan on going anywhere, not as long as you want me."

This man. His words suture up those cracks in my heart, just like that.

How does he always know exactly what to say to soothe my frayed edges? It's unfair when I feel like I constantly stumble over my own words.

I wet my lips and manage a breathy "okay."

"Okay," he echoes, nodding once.

Another ten seconds or so pass before he releases me.

He straightens, buckles up again, then pulls back onto the road. When we're on the interstate again, he settles his hand on my knee, a warm reassurance, but he makes no move to skim it higher.

His easy, carefree grin returns. "Now that that's settled, let's get on with our date."

The studio is located in a small building across from a small strip of stores, including a pizza shop, a liquor store, and a pharmacy.

The sign on the door reads *Frederica's Ballroom Dance Studio.*

As he creeps through the parking lot, I can't help but worry that I'm going to make a fool of myself. Step on toes. Fall. Or worse. I'm not even sure what *worse* is, but if it's possible, there's a chance I'll discover it.

Caleb gets out, and before I've even slipped into my shoes, he pulls my door open.

"Let me get that," he says, taking one heel from me.

I open my mouth to protest, but he arches a brow, silencing me, and slips it onto my foot. I feel like Cinderella.

"Thank you."

He offers me his hand, and though my instinct is to climb out on my own, to prove to him that I don't need the help, I take it.

Though the front of the studio is nothing but floor-to-ceiling windows, they're covered by curtains, so at least I don't have to worry about any passersby witnessing what I'm sure will be my ultimate humiliation.

Hand in hand, we enter the studio. The first thing I notice is the sweet vanilla scent from the diffuser on the check-in desk. The next is the kind smile radiating from the woman standing there.

"Hi," she says, her tone light. "Checking in for the beginner ballroom class?"

"Yes," Caleb answers, giving my hand a reassuring squeeze.

She slides a clipboard over to him. "Sign in here, please."

He scribbles both our names down in annoyingly neat handwriting that makes my penmanship look like that of a third-grader.

When he's finished, she spins the clipboard around, peers down at it, then writes our names in Sharpie on two nametag stickers. "Just put these on your shirts and enter through those doors there." She points to our left. "Enjoy."

Caleb finally releases my hand to peel the backing off my name sticker. He reaches out like he's going to affix it to my chest, but before he makes contact, he jerks his head once and pulls back. With a sheepish smile, he holds it out with a thumb and forefinger instead.

I struggle not to hide my smile. The man is almost thirty, incredibly intelligent and kind, but he gets flustered over the idea of accidentally touching my boob if he puts the sticker on me? It's adorable.

Once we're both wearing our nametags, he takes my hand again and leads me into the designated studio.

Holding his hand like this feels right, and that alone is terrifying.

If I let this man in and he changes his mind, he could so easily shatter my world. And a little voice in my head tells me that I'm more like my mom than I'd like to believe. If I'm dependent on a man for my self-worth, I'm no better than she is.

When I catch sight of several couples mingling near a refreshments table, my stomach cramps.

I *loathe* small talk.

Caleb, thankfully, doesn't drag me over to the other couples. Instead, we keep to the wall just the two of us.

I give his hand a squeeze in thanks. He may not realize it, but small gestures like this mean the world.

He looks down at me, his fingers grazing the curve of my jaw. "How are you doing?" he murmurs, a stray piece of blond hair falling over his forehead. "You're okay with this, right?"

Though I was pretty certain before, I know without a doubt now that if I wasn't okay with it, he wouldn't hesitate to escort me back out.

"Nervous, but I'm okay."

I *want* to put myself out there, do things that I normally wouldn't, and this is perfect. Though there are people here who may witness my embarrassment, I never have to see them again. And Caleb has shown me time and again that I'm safe to take risks when I'm with him.

"Good," he replies.

There are nine couples total waiting for class to begin when a beautiful woman in a cobalt blue dress in a similar design to mine breezes in. She looks like she's well into her fifties, and she carries herself with a confidence I can only hope to one day possess.

"Hello, hello my beauties," she greets, the bracelets on her wrists tinkling like chimes. "I'm so happy you're here. I'm eager to introduce you to the wonder that is ballroom dancing. My husband Matteo and I will be your instructors tonight. He's running a little behind, so we'll get introductions out of the way while we wait. I'm Frederica."

She points to a couple on her left and asks them to share

their names. Slowly, she works her way around the group, and when it's our turn, my voice comes out annoyingly high-pitched.

"Halle?" she repeats. "Not Hailey?"

"Nope, it's Halle."

I can't count the number of times I've been called Hailey, so I'm used to having to make the distinction.

"Beautiful name," she says, clapping once. "Ah, here comes my husband."

A middle-aged man with dark hair and toned muscles strides straight over to Frederica and tugs her against him, greeting her with a kiss to her cheek. "Sorry I'm late, my love."

Their eyes shine with pure love and adoration for each other. It's almost jarring to see a couple their age so clearly enraptured with the other.

He releases her, then surveys the rest of us. "I'm Matteo, and I've been dancing with my lovely wife here for thirty years. Would've been longer, but this one"—he wags his finger at her, chuckling—"is very stubborn. It took quite a bit of time to convince her to give me a chance."

Frederica rolls her eyes. "Only because I'd always heard you were a charmer."

"And were the rumors true, darling?" He smiles at her, his eyes crinkling at the corners.

"Yes." With a huff that's half annoyance, half affection, she brushes her fingers through his mustache to flatten the stray hairs.

Matteo turns to the group. "The key to a happy relationship is to show your woman she's loved. Every day. It's more than gifts or flowers. It's showing her she's taken care of. When she's tired, make dinner without being asked. Put the kids to bed. Those kinds of things make all the difference in a happy marriage."

Around the room, most of the women look at their partners in a *see? I told you* kind of way.

"If you come back, there'll be more lessons where that came from." He wags his finger, then holds a hand out to his wife. "Today, though ... we dance."

As if it's been cued up to start at the exact moment in their little display, music plays, and Frederica and Matteo begin dancing to the quick tempo. After about a minute, it cuts out, and they turn to us.

"That is called the foxtrot. It's a bit more advanced than what you'll be learning today," Frederica says, smoothing down her skirt. "But if you stick with dance, you absolutely could learn it. Today, though, we'll start with the basics of a slow waltz. Turn to your partners, please."

I face Caleb, rubbing my lips together like the motion alone will get rid of my nerves.

"The two of you should decide who leads. When you have, that person should extend their left arm like this." Matteo holds his arm out to one side. "Partners, you're going to take their hand in your right, then gently place your left hand on their shoulder."

I do as instructed, and as I'm getting settled, I catch the flicker of nerves in Caleb's gaze. That alone is enough to take away some of my anxiety.

"Light fingers," Frederica scolds. "No need to hold on for dear life."

I give Caleb a sheepish smile and relax my grip. "Sorry."

His answering smile urges the sticky fingers wrapped around my chest, squeezing, to loosen a smidge more.

"It's okay." He brushes his nose lightly against mine, sending a thrill through me.

"Hold this pose," Matteo calls out. "We're going to come around and make corrections to your posture."

I don't dare move, soaking in Caleb's proximity. "I'm not hunched over, am I?"

He chuckles. "No."

"My shoulders aren't up to my ears?"

His laughter deepens. "Your shoulders are fine."

"Okay." I swallow. "Just checking."

When Frederica makes it over to us, she taps our arms. "Elbows up, darlings."

We obey, lifting our joined hands slightly.

"More. There you go. And dear, fingers like this." She adjusts the way Caleb is holding my hand. "Perfect. Hold that and scoot a little closer." She urges us to close the awkward distance we've left between our bodies. "Act like you know each other. You do know each other, correct?"

"Yes, we're just nervous," Caleb replies as he takes a step closer, eyes locked on mine.

"No time for nerves," Matteo scolds from where he's helping the couple beside us. "Only fun."

Frederica nods succinctly. "Dance should first and foremost be enjoyable. It can be intimate, but it doesn't have to be. It's the expression of our bodies. They're designed to move, you know?" With a wink, she spins gracefully and moves on to another couple.

The class runs for just over an hour. By the time it's finished, I feel like I've done an entire workout. The waltz is slow, but that doesn't mean it's easy. Not for me, anyway.

Before we leave, Caleb guides me to the refreshments table and pours water into two small cups. "What did you think?"

Honestly?

"I loved it."

His smile is radiant and instantaneous. "Does this mean you'll do it with me again?"

I sip at the water and nod. "Sure. Why not?"

If the twinkle in his eye is anything to go by, he's pleased at the prospect. "Good. I'll sign up for the next class before we leave. They're every two weeks."

Without my permission, that insecure part of my brain rears its ugly head, whispering *what if he's already sick of you by the time the next class rolls around?*

"Sounds great," I say, shoving those thoughts down deep.

Frederica breezes over just as I'm tossing the empty cup in the trash. "It was a pleasure to have you in class today. I hope to see you for the next one. I see some talent here, and the chemistry you share is strong."

She probably says that to everyone, but the comment does bolster my confidence.

Once our thirst is sated, we say our goodbyes, sign up for the next class, and head out to the car. Caleb holds my door before rounding the hood and climbing in. He cranks the engine immediately but doesn't put the vehicle in reverse. "I planned to take you to a nice dinner after this, and we can absolutely do that if you'd like, but I'm starving after all that dancing. What do you think about grabbing dinner somewhere close instead?"

I sigh in relief. "I'm ravenous."

His lips kick up on one side. "I know just the place."

SEVENTEEN

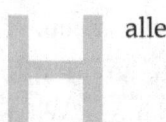alle

I never could have imagined Caleb choosing a bar with white and red checkered tablecloths and a whole room filled with pool tables, but this restaurant is surprisingly perfect.

It's loud, but the booth we've settled into in the back corner, away from the main bar and pool tables, is surprisingly private and cozy.

"How do you know about this place?" Straightening, I take in the dark paneled walls and the random memorabilia tacked to them. "It doesn't seem like your kind of place, Mr. Fancy-Pants."

It's hard to picture Caleb in all his clean-cut glory ever stumbling across a restaurant like this.

I swear he blushes. "The owner was a client. I'd meet him here sometimes so he didn't have to come to Boston. The food is great, so I come back when I'm nearby."

"That's…" Not the answer I was expecting. "Very kind of you."

He dismisses my compliment with a wave of a hand. "Anyone would do the same."

That's the thing, though. They wouldn't. Caleb might be the most considerate person I've ever met. And despite his job, despite the horrors he's no doubt encountered, he remains unfailingly positive and believes in the good of others.

Unable to hold back a smile, I pick up the menu. It's sticky, the way menus are in places like this. Ignoring the sensation, I open it and give it a cursory glance. "What's good here?"

He doesn't bother to open his own menu. "Everything."

A breath of a laugh escapes me. I don't doubt that he's spent enough time here to try every last item on the menu.

"All right, then." I scan the choices, surprised by the variety. The salmon with beurre blanc sauce looks incredible, and the crab rangoons boast the use of real crab meat. The pasta selections all promise that the noodles are homemade.

I can't help but survey our surroundings again, just to be sure I wasn't transported to a much finer establishment while perusing the menu. But no, it's still the same dive bar with the same cringy décor.

"Ty was working toward becoming a classically trained chef when his girlfriend got pregnant. They got married, and he quit the program so he could support his family. You can probably guess how that ended up. But he saved up and bought this place a few years ago. It allows him to cook what he wants, so…" Caleb taps his fingers on the wooden tabletop. "We can go somewhere else if you want?"

"No, this is perfect." I snap the menu shut and set it down. "I'm going to use the restroom. If the server comes by, will you order a water and the BLT for me?"

He scrunches his nose and eyes our closed menus. "Are you sure that's what you want?"

It's the cheapest thing on the menu, and I'll never knock a good BLT sandwich.

"Yeah, I'm sure." I give him a reassuring smile as I slide out of the booth.

Before I can ask him where the restrooms are, he points to a hallway near the back.

With a grateful nod, I head that way. I don't really have to pee, but I want to wash the sticky substance from my hands.

When I return to the table, a tall, broad-shouldered Black man is chatting with Caleb.

I slide back into the booth and offer the man a smile and a quiet "hi."

"Halle, this is Ty." He nods at the man. "Ty, this is Halle."

Ty hits me with a gigantic smile. The expression radiates happiness, instantly putting me at ease. He's older than we are, maybe in his forties, and good-looking, with straight white teeth, kind eyes, and tattoos along his entire right arm.

"Nice to meet you." He claps Caleb's shoulder. "This one here's a good one. I promise you that. If not for him, I would never get to see my kids. He's my hero."

Caleb's cheeks pink adorably as the man gushes. It's endearing, really, the way this grown man refers to him as his hero.

"He's pretty great," I agree.

If it weren't for Caleb, there's no telling where I'd be right about now.

"I'll leave you to it. Holler if you need anything."

"Thanks, Ty." Caleb shakes his hand, and as Ty disappears through a set of doors behind the bar, he focuses on me. "I ordered our food."

"Thanks." I brush my hair back behind my ear, then unroll the napkin from around my silverware and fiddle with the strip of paper that once held the bundle together.

"Is something wrong?"

Caleb's deep voice startles me. "What? Why?"

"You seem fidgety." He looks pointedly at where I've wrapped the paper strip around a finger.

"Oh." I unroll it and set it on the table. "I just … I'm hoping my brothers aren't being menaces for Cynthia and Thelma."

His expression softens. "I'm sure they're fine, but you could call and check in if it'd make you feel better. Or I can text Thelma?"

I straighten. "You would do that?"

With a shrug, he pulls his phone out of his pocket. "If it would put you at ease, then yeah."

"Yes, please. If I check in on them, the boys will think I don't trust them."

And to be honest, I don't. Not after their school shenanigans. But if I know them, smothering them will do me no favors.

Caleb types out a text, his fingers moving quickly across the screen, then sets the phone on the table in front of him.

"I know you're probably feeling anxious after the school ordeal—"

A humorless laugh bubbles out of me. "You have no idea."

"But they're good kids," he goes on. "I hope you know that."

Elbow on the table, I rest my chin on my palm. This is the farthest thing from typical first-date conversation, but we know each other already, so I suppose it makes sense that we've skipped over most of the awkwardness of getting to know each other.

He's right. They *are* good kids, but good kids still do stupid shit. Maybe this is an inevitable part of growing up, but I can't help but worry that with the role models they've had so far, they'll take those things too far.

"They are," I agree, reaching for my glass and take a sip.

"I know what they did with the paint."

I nearly choke on my water. "Excuse me?" I sputter and cough, spraying droplets across the table.

If Caleb is bothered by the mess, he doesn't show it.

"How do you know?"

With a shrug, he picks up his own drink. "When I asked Thelma and Cynthia about keeping the boys tonight, I noticed the art supplies were there. Apparently Thelma mentioned that she used to paint and was considering doing it again but didn't have the materials. Then your brothers showed up with everything she needs." His lips twitch like he's fighting a smile. "There's no way she hasn't noticed the labels on every piece that make it obvious they belong to the school. Frankly, I think Thelma would do the same thing, given the opportunity."

Head ducked, I give it a shake. "I don't know whether to be angry about the stealing or glad that they have no nefarious plans for the paint."

His responding chuckle is more like a low rumble. "Personally, I think it's sweet. You don't often see teenagers taking an interest in the older generation, but it's obvious that your brothers like Thelma and Cynthia."

"It is sweet, isn't it?" My shoulders sag a little in relief, though the sensation is quickly replaced with dread. "Ugh, this means I'm going to have to ask for the supplies back and drag the boys' butts up to the school to apologize."

Our server appears then, but rather than drop off our meals, she sets an order of the most delicious-looking mozzarella sticks I've ever seen in front of us.

"Thanks so much." Caleb picks one up as she gives us each a polite smile and walks away. With a heavy hand, he dips the cheese stick in the marinara sauce and holds it aloft. "You don't have to."

I huff. Don't have to what? Return the supplies?

"Caleb." His name comes out as a scandalized scoff. "You're a lawyer. You're supposed to uphold the law."

He shrugs as he takes a bite. "Technically," he says when his mouth is no longer full, "they didn't break any laws, since the school didn't report it stolen."

"Stop encouraging this," I groan, burying my face in my hands.

Not even the temptation of the cheesy fried goodness can stop me from spiraling over the embarrassment that will surely come with speaking to the principal again. But I'm the adult, the parental figure, and it's the right thing to do.

"I'll take them to school after their suspension is over and make them return it." With a nod of determination, I finally pick up one of the sticks.

Caleb arches a brow. "Didn't say you could touch my stick, Hal."

I drop the mozzarella stick instantly, and it rolls across the plate. "I'm so sorry. I should've asked. I shouldn't have assumed. I—"

"Whoa." He wipes his fingers on a napkin and holds his hands up. "I was just kidding, Halle. I got them for both of us. Fuck." Head dropped, he practically growls. "I should've realized how you would interpret that."

"Oh." My cheeks heat, and not because of the suggestive comment I'm only now registering. Pushing down my embarrassment, I force myself to make eye contact. "My mom was really weird about food. Sometimes she'd pick up food from McDonald's, but only for herself. If I even asked to share the fries, it would trigger her rage."

The blue of Caleb's irises deepens. "Halle." My name is a soft exhale from his lips. "I'm sorry."

"Nothing to apologize for." I lift a shoulder. "You didn't do it."

He searches my face, lips pressed together like he wants to say more but is holding himself back.

I'm grateful for his tact. I don't want to talk about my crappy childhood. Not on our first date.

"Dig in." He gestures to the plate with a swish of his hand.

The trauma of the situation still clings to me, making my instinct to refuse hard to ignore. But I'm not that little girl anymore, and this is the perfect opportunity to work through one of my many trauma responses. So I reach for a cheese stick. It's delicious, as I expected, causing a little moan to slip from between my lips.

Relief washes over Caleb, his expression lightening and his posture straightening.

"This is delicious."

Smiling, he snags another for himself. "Ty makes the breading and sauce himself."

"This place is a serious hidden gem. I've never been to a restaurant much fancier than this one, but I imagine he could be working in one in Boston if he wanted."

Caleb nods, humming in agreement. "He could, but here, he can follow his passion while still having free time to spend with his kids."

The waitress appears out of nowhere, a plate in each hand, and the two of us snap back, only now realizing how close we'd drifted together.

When she's gone, I say, "Family means a lot to you, doesn't it?"

He dips a fry into some sort of sauce and pops it into his mouth. "It does," he says when he's done chewing. "My family is small. Just my parents and me. But Salem and Thayer, those kids, Laith … they're my chosen family."

"You don't talk about your parents much."

He gives a gruff sigh. "My mom is overbearing and pushy. My dad only really cared about me when I was playing football." He shrugs it off like none of it really affects him, but there's no hiding the sadness in his eyes. "You probably don't want to hear this. You've had it way worse."

On instinct, I lay my hand on top of his on the table. "That doesn't make your feelings about your own childhood any less valid."

He flips his hand beneath mine and rubs his thumb on the inside of my wrist.

He doesn't say anything. He doesn't have to. Sometimes validation is enough. There is no competition here. We both endured trauma; we've both been affected by it.

Thirty minutes later, we're on our way back home when my phone rings and Quinn's name appears on the screen.

My gut immediately sinks. It's not a normal response for most people, but I've been conditioned to assume that something is wrong when one of my brothers calls.

"What's up?" I ask, trying my hardest to keep my tone even.

"Could we stay the night with Cynthia and Thelma?"

Confusion swirls through me. *What?* "You guys want to have a sleepover with Cynthia and Thelma?"

He blows out a breath, the sound crackling through the line. "It's not a sleepover. We'd just stay the night. They're going to teach us how to make their secret cookie recipe and brownies."

"I…" I blink, still trying to wrap my head around the question. "Yeah … that's all right with me if they're okay with it."

"They are. Thanks. Hope your date was good." Without waiting for a response, he ends the call.

For a moment, all I can do is stare down at my phone in stunned silence.

"What was that about?" Caleb glances over but quickly focuses on the road again.

"My brothers want to stay the night with Cynthia and Thelma. They're getting baking lessons."

His laugh is loud in the small space. He rubs at his mouth to try to stifle the sound, but it's no use.

"I never in a million years would've guessed they'd become friends with two old ladies. Or that they'd be interested in learning to bake," I go on. "Especially not after Thelma cornered us in the grocery store the day we met her."

Caleb clears his throat, probably trying to swallow back more laughter. "I think it's because they're kindred spirits."

A smile twitches at my lips. "You have a point there."

It doesn't hit me until we're in the driveway that this means Caleb and I will be alone in his house.

Does he expect—

I stop that thought before it can gain any traction. If I know anything about this man, it's that I can trust him with my boundaries. In fact, I bet if I made a move, he'd stop me. That's just who he is.

He leaves the car idling and undoes his seat belt, shifting my way. "I enjoyed tonight."

I hold my breath, waiting for the *but*. When it doesn't come, I exhale in a gust.

"I did too," I finally say. Dancing was more fun than I expected, and the dinner was delicious. "This is kind of weird, right?" I whisper, smoothing my hands down the material of the dress. "Going on a date and coming back to the same place?"

He shrugs. "Doesn't have to be."

Right.

My stomach twists. *I'm* the one making it weird.

"I could walk you to the door and leave and come back, if that makes you feel better."

A laugh bubbles out of me, along with some of the tension in my muscles. "No need. I'm okay."

"Come on, then." He kills the engine and pushes his door open.

Before I can slip my shoes on again—of course I took them off; as fun as dancing was, it did a number on my feet—he's at my door, holding out a hand.

I accept the help, even if I don't need it, wishing the night didn't have to end.

Worried that when I wake up tomorrow, I'll discover this was all a dream. A tease of what my life could be.

Caleb shuts the door and hits the lock button on his key fob, causing the SUV to let out a small honk.

"Don't look now," he whispers, lips grazing my ear. "But we have an audience."

Without thinking, I dart a look across the street. Sure enough, Cynthia, Thelma, and both my brothers sit out front, partially illuminated by the porch light.

I lift my hand in an awkward wave and let it drop.

"It's not just them," he warns. "Salem and Thayer are out too. With Laith."

"Oh, God."

If I wanted to bury my head in the sand before, the uncertain sensation has nothing on the mortification washing over me now.

Caleb pauses to unlock the front door, so I take the opportunity to peer over my shoulder. Like they've been waiting for me to look over, Laith salutes us and Salem claps giddily. Thayer shakes his head like he's embarrassed. Maybe for them, or maybe for us. I can't be sure.

Hand on my waist, Caleb ushers me inside. "Sorry about them."

"Small towns are so weird," I admit, face flaming.

He shrugs. "It's all I know. Maybe that's why it doesn't bother me. Besides, it's only because they care."

Lips pressed together, I nod. "When you put it that way, I guess it makes sense. And maybe once the embarrassment wears off, it'll feel good to know people care."

A soft smile grazes his lips. "It's hard for you to let people in, isn't it?"

I scoff a laugh. "You have no idea."

He really doesn't, because though we haven't known each other long, I've been more open with him than just about anyone in my whole life.

"But you're letting me in."

I swear he can read my mind. Maybe that's what makes it easier to be myself with him.

"Yeah," I whisper softly. "I am."

EIGHTEEN

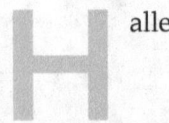alle

I awake suddenly, heart pounding, drenched in sweat. Blinking, I take in my surroundings and breathe deeply, willing the dream to release me from its clutches. Instead, it clings to me like dirt after a long day spent working outside. Eyes closed, I inhale slowly, then exhale again, willing my pulse to steady.

The dream felt so real. Probably because it was more memory than a storyline created by my brain.

The man's fingers had roved my skin despite my protests. My mom was still working at the time, one dead-end job or another, and the boys were just toddlers.

"Since your mom ain't around, it's up to you to make me feel good."

I shudder at the memory and blow out a breath.

That night, I managed to knee him in the balls and lock myself and my brothers in my room. I don't know how I did it, as scrawny and malnourished as I was, but I pushed my dresser in front of the door. It's a good thing I did too because he tried his hardest to get through while screaming dirty profanities at me.

After a dream like that, there's no chance I'll get back to sleep, so I slip out of bed and pad to the bathroom.

With each step, I work to ground myself.

I'm in Hawthorne Mills, Massachusetts.

I'm in Caleb's house.

My brothers are across the street with Cynthia and Thelma.

Everyone is safe.

After washing my hands, I twist my hair into a messy bun at my nape, then ease my bedroom door open and tiptoe to the stairs.

In the kitchen, I discover my stealthy movements were in vain. Caleb is awake as well, heating water on the stove.

"Hey." I keep my tone soft so as not to startle him.

He turns around, hair mussed and shirtless. His sleep pants hang low enough to show off a tan line and the divots that lead below the band.

"Hey," he echoes back, voice gruff. "Couldn't sleep?"

I focus on his face, trying my best to ignore the gorgeous body he's got on display. "Bad dream."

He dips his chin. "Want to talk about it?"

"Nope."

With a ghost of a smile, he turns to the counter and the tea bag lying next to a single mug. It's wild, how easily he accepts my responses. He makes it clear he's available to listen, but he doesn't push.

While he fiddles with the teakettle, I pilfer through his cabinets, searching for the yellow cake mix I bought a few weeks ago and the two accompanying containers of chocolate frosting. I was saving it for a rainy day, but after that dream, I could really use a big slice of cake.

Before I can even set them on the counter, Caleb has pulled out a bowl and is digging through the drawer for the beaters.

"Thank you," I say when he sets them on the counter next to me.

He hums. "What temperature for the cake?"

"Um." I squint at the back of the box. The light is dim, but I prefer it this way. Like it's easier to keep my demons hidden. "Three-fifty."

While he preheats the oven, I dump the mix into the bowl, then pull the eggs from the fridge and the oil from the cabinet.

The kettle whistles, the shrill sound causing me to wince, but he pulls it off the heat quickly, and the room falls silent again.

"Do you like tea?" he asks, filling a mug.

I frown as I stick the metal beaters into the mechanism. "I don't think I've ever had hot tea."

Without a word, he snags another mug from the cabinet and dunks a tea bag into it. While they steep, he pulls out a set of round cake pans and greases them for me, even adding flour so they don't stick.

It's strangely intimate, working in tandem with him.

Once the batter is ready, I pour it into the pans and slide both into the oven, then set a timer on my phone.

Caleb adds a dash of milk to each mug and sets them in front of the stools at the counter. Then he eyes me, silently signaling that I should sit.

Without anything else to keep me busy, I quietly settle beside him and wrap my fingers around the cup.

Almost immediately, the warmth that seeps into my palms soothes me.

"Tea, huh?"

"I've never been the best sleeper," he admits. "My mom would always make a mug of tea for me when I couldn't sleep." He takes a careful sip. "Couldn't stand this shit for the longest time, but now when I have trouble sleeping, it's my go-to."

"My mom would sing to me sometimes," I say quietly, focus fixed on my ceramic mug. "When she was sober and holding down a job, she was..." I smile as some of my better memories flit through my mind. "Really great."

"Tell me something else about her. Something good."

"Once," I say, the recollection coming to me instantly, "she picked me up early from school. She'd packed a whole lunch for us. Sandwiches and Cheetos—my favorite at the time—and brownies. We went to a nearby park and sat at a picnic table. We watched squirrels and just ... talked." My smile fades, and the ever-present ache in my chest pangs. "It was nice. Really nice."

Caleb gives me a soft smile in return. "That sounds like a great day."

With a sigh, I take a tentative sip of my tea. "This is pretty good," I admit.

He lifts his mug to his lips. "Glad you like it."

"What's your deal? Is there a reason you have trouble sleeping?" I ask. Maybe the question is too personal, but I'd rather not sit in silence.

He sighs, the sound weary and unexpected from someone who's generally so upbeat, and draws his index finger around the rim of his mug. "I've been this way for as long as I can remember. My mom always told me it's because my mind never quiets. That I feel like I'm wasting my life away with sleep when there are things to be done."

I wet my lips, savoring the flavor of the tea. "Do you agree with her?"

"She had a good point." He rubs at his jaw where a light dusting of stubble is beginning to grow. "I think it's worse now—with my job," he adds. "I'm always thinking about how many people out there need help, wishing I could just work more hours. Knowing that if I could, I could do more good. Don't get me wrong, I realize that there will always be people in need, and I know that if I don't take breaks, I'll burn out, but sometimes, especially at night, my brain forgets all that."

I take another sip of the warm tea, surprised by how much I enjoy the herbal flavor. "So," I prod, "when you can't sleep, you get up and make tea, and then what?" I'm suddenly curious about what his life is like when he's alone.

He shrugs. "I *try* not to work, figuring that since my mind is consumed with it, giving in would only make the sleep issue more difficult."

"But sometimes you do?"

"Yeah," he sighs, running long fingers through his already mussed blond hair. "But usually, I make tea and watch a movie, and eventually, I fall asleep on the couch."

"Do you want to do that now—"

Before he can respond, the timer on my phone goes off.

"Hold that thought."

I pull a knife from the utensil drawer so I can ensure the cake is done, but Caleb slides a bottle of toothpicks my way.

"This will be easier."

With a small smile, I pluck out a toothpick. Then I slide an oven mitt onto my left hand and pull the oven open. When I've confirmed they're baked thoroughly, I set them out to cool.

"Do you really want to watch a movie?" Caleb asks, rinsing his empty cup out in the sink.

"I wouldn't mind." I finish my own tea and rinse mine as well.

He strides out of the dim kitchen, his gait languid, but in the middle of the living room, he turns and gestures for me to get settled first. Once I'm curled up in the corner spot of the sectional, he sits beside me, though he keeps a respectable distance.

Honestly, I find that bit of space rather annoying. He's attracted to me, I know that, but then he does things like this that make me wonder if he actually wants me.

"Any requests?" he asks, scrolling through his movie app.

"Something lighthearted." I'll never go back to sleep if we watch something super heavy or scary.

He chooses a rom-com, and once he's pressed Play, he slides the blanket from the back of the couch and spreads it so it covers both of us.

Within minutes, I'm stifling a yawn.

His responding chuckle rumbles through me. "Ready to fall asleep on me already?"

"My body is, but my brain isn't."

With a low hum, he nods and focuses on the screen.

Pulling the blanket up to my chin, I sink farther into the cushion. In doing so, I slip a few inches closer to him. I hold my breath, thinking he might scoot away, but he doesn't. In fact, he doesn't seem to notice at all.

Though I try my hardest to focus on the movie, it's no use. About thirty minutes in, I give up and blurt out, "Why didn't you kiss me tonight?"

He goes rigid and whips his head around so fast I wouldn't be surprised if he has whiplash. "What?"

Fuck.

I don't want to say it again.

"Why didn't you kiss me tonight? After our date? If you..." I swallow down my pride. "If it wasn't what you were hoping for ... if you've realized you don't like me like *that* ... it's okay. But please tell me. I won't hold it against you, if that's what you think."

He shakes his head harshly, his hair falling over his forehead. "It's none of that. I'm doing my best not to push you too far too fast. You come across as a skittish kitten most of the time, claws out and hissing, but behind that you're a little unsure and scared. And that's okay. I just don't want to make you uncomfortable, and I don't want you to feel like you have to spend time with me out of obligation. I don't want you to feel pressured into doing anything you're not fully on board with. I want it to be your choice."

I blink. Then blink again. It's downright terrifying how quickly this man has seen through me. All of my carefully constructed walls, built brick by brick since I was a little girl, are nonexistent to him.

"So you're ... what? Waiting for me to make a move?"

He meets my eyes and holds my attention. "That's exactly what I'm doing."

Oh.

Somehow this man only gets more incredible.

"And if I kiss you right now, what will you do about it?" I challenge.

A lazy smile graces his lips. "Kiss you back."

Fuck.

Heart in my throat, I get up on my knees and toss my right leg over his body so I'm straddling him.

He doesn't move, but his Adam's apple bobs and his pupils blow out, and through his pajama pants and my thin cotton shorts, there's no denying that he's hard beneath me. With the willpower of a saint, he keeps his hands firmly at his sides.

I swish my hair over my shoulder, hands finding his cheeks. The rasp of his stubble against my palms sends electricity arcing through me. It's quickly followed by apprehension, but I shove my nerves aside and ignore my sky-rocketing heartbeat. His breath catches a millisecond before I press my lips to his. I don't know if it's because it's been a while or what, but that little sound from him sends me hurtling nearer to an orgasm than seems possible.

The kiss is tentative at first, while I explore his mouth. His lips are soft and plush beneath mine, which shouldn't come as a surprise. His mouth is just as perfect as the rest of him. I swear he's too good to be true. I'd be convinced he was a robot created to say all the right things if it weren't for the insistent press of his erection between us.

Caleb Thorne is human, after all.

"Caleb," I whimper, wanting more than soft and sweet. "I thought you'd kiss me back."

As if my words snap the tether he'd used to restrain himself, he grasps my ass, his fingers digging into the globes, and meets my kiss with an intense fervor.

Oh, God.

I've never been kissed like this before. With desire and passion and *feeling*.

No kiss I've ever experienced has come close, each one merely an exchange—an obligation, part of a routine that led to the better stuff.

He kisses me like I'm air and he needs my mouth in order to survive. I'm *consumed* by him.

He nips at my bottom lip and I gasp, opening for him, rocking against his straining erection as our tongues tangle and he grasps my hips and ass hard enough to bruise.

"Fuck," he growls. "Halle."

My name in that low guttural tone melts my insides. God, I want to record it so I can play it on repeat.

Halle.

Halllle.

Haaalllleee.

Between one heartbeat and another, I'm on my back, a small squeak escaping me. With my feet planted on the cushions, I let my legs fall open, making room for Caleb. And like a puzzle piece slotting into place, he presses his body to mine. With a growl, he pins my hands above my head and covers my mouth with his. The growl turns into a low moan when I grind my hips up into him.

Please, I swallow back the word.

I want to beg him to strip me bare and fuck me senseless, but we're not there yet. God, is this a tease—to feel him *right there* and force myself to resist going for more.

I wiggle my hands free, devouring his mouth.

Pulling back, he narrows his eyes on me. "Keep wiggling like that, and I'll have to find something to tie you up with."

My heart stutters to a stop, then pounds out a furious rhythm in my ears.

Oh my God.

Would it be wrong if I begged him for exactly that?

Probably.

Right?

Most definitely.

"I'll be good," I say instead, my voice a breathless whisper.

Eyes still locked on mine, he grins. "Or you could not and see what happens?"

Stick a fork in me. I am *done*.

Chuckling, he locks my wrists together again and brings his lips to mine, keeping me from responding.

Though I'm tempted to see how far we can take it, it's clear already that when it comes to sex, kind, considerate Caleb turns into a beast. And I'm thrilled at the prospect of finding out.

"Listen to you," he croons, kissing his way down my neck. "So worked up already. If I slid a hand into those tiny shorts, you'd be soaked, wouldn't you?"

I whimper in response, the ability to speak fleeing me, along with all rational thought.

"I bet all I'd have to do is stroke your clit once and you'd go off."

My core pulls tighter. I so would.

"Tell me, Halle"—he sucks my bottom lip into his mouth and lets it go with a pop—"do you want me to touch you? It'd be cruel to leave you so achy and needy, wouldn't it?"

Head dropped back, I pant, "Touch me."

How we went from our first kiss to this is beyond me, but I'm not mad about it. The two of us have been a spark just waiting to ignite. Now that the flames have been fanned, we're going up in an inferno.

"Ask nicer."

Ask … *nicer?*

"You want me to beg?" The words are breathless; I can't seem to get enough air into my lungs.

"Hmm." He strokes his nose along the curve of my neck.

Until this moment, I never knew the skin there could be so sensitive. But each brush of his nose or his lips sends shivers racing down my spine.

"Don't tempt me," he grits out. "I don't know that I could resist if you begged me."

"Please." If I could touch him, I'd claw at his shoulders, scratching at his bare skin like a cat in heat. I've *never* felt like this before, so unhinged. My whole life, I've fought to remain in control. With Caleb, I feel safe to let go. "Please, touch me. I want you to."

"Such a sweet, tempting offer." He slips his free hand beneath my shirt, skimming across my belly and teasing at the waistband of my sleep shorts.

So close but so far away from where I want him.

"Caleb." My voice is shaky, my heart thudding wildly. "For the love of God, touch me. If you don't, I'll have to go upstairs and take matters into my own hands."

His eyes flash like he's intrigued by the idea.

Pulse thrashing, I shake my head back and forth. "You won't be allowed to watch."

He leans over my body, and I whimper at the press of his weight against me—not because it hurts, but because it feels so damn good. Mouth at my ear, he nips the lobe, then whispers, "You might think you're in control here, but you're wrong."

He releases his hold on my wrists, and then his weight disappears, taking all his body heat with it.

I scramble to sitting, every nerve ending lit up. "Where are you going?"

I'm all worked up, and he's, what? Walking away?

He looks back at me over his shoulder, his blue eyes lit like flames. "Teaching you some manners. Night, Halle." Halfway up the stairs, he peeks over the railing. "Don't even think about touching yourself. I'll know."

Jaw unhinged, I sputter, unable to string a coherent thought together. My thoughts are nothing but a tangled knot I can't even begin to pick apart.

For several minutes, I don't move, certain he'll come back. He doesn't.

Eventually I gather my wits and head back into the kitchen. I wash my hands, ignoring the aching between my legs, and frost the now very cooled cake.

When that's finished, I turn the TV off, head upstairs, and fall into bed.

What the fuck was that?

Caleb Thorne is not at all what I expected.

NINETEEN

Caleb

"Can you take us to the store?"

"Uh…" I slowly set the knife beside the cutting board of diced onions. "For what?"

Casen and Quinn exchange a silent look Halle refers to as "fucking twin telepathy."

"Halle's birthday is Friday," Quinn explains, using his finger to trace a line in the marble countertop. "We wanted to get her something."

"Hold on." I brace my hands on the cool surface in front of me. "It's her birthday?"

"Yep." Casen slides onto one of the stools facing me.

"She didn't tell me." My chest pangs at the realization. Why wouldn't she mention her birthday? It's been two weeks since our first date, and since that night, we've gone to another dance class and to a movie. Granted, the twins came to the movies with us, so I guess it wouldn't be considered a date. Yet she hasn't even hinted about the special day.

"She wouldn't have." Quinn shrugs, sliding his hands into his pockets. "She doesn't like her birthday."

"Why not?"

They exchange another silent look, and eventually Quinn sighs. "Mom forgot her birthday a lot."

"And if she remembered, she usually made it miserable for her," Casen adds, shoulders drooping.

I blink, then blink again, processing the information.

Out of the side of his mouth, Quinn whispers, "I think we broke him."

Casen's eyes plead with me. "Can we do something special for her?"

I snap myself out of my stupor. "Of course. Let me finish this and get it in the slow cooker, and we can go."

"Do you need help?" he asks.

Surprised, I look from one boy to the other and back again. "You want to help?"

"Sure, why not." It's Quinn who answers.

With their help, I get the onions chopped and in the slow cooker quickly. It's a good thing too. I meant to have this done an hour or so ago, but when the boys showed up at home just before lunchtime—due to a half day none of us realized was scheduled—our routine was thrown off.

"I'll let your sister know we're going," I tell them after they've washed up at the sink. The scent of onions is still strong, and that won't change now that they're simmering in preparation for French onion soup.

I swipe my keys off the sideboard and jog upstairs. As I step into my office, I nearly stop dead. It happens every time I find her in here. I can't help but stare. Halle sits behind my desk with a pair of blue-light glasses perched on her nose. Her dark hair is pulled back in a ponytail, even though, when I left the room, it was down. She has one foot planted on the chair cushion and her chin resting on her knee as she types.

"What's up?" she asks when she notices me.

"We're running to the store, so we'll be back in a little while."

Brows furrowed, she slips her glasses off. "Why?" Knowing her, she's not thinking about the possibility that we're making birthday plans. She's worried about what kind of mischief the boys might be up to.

"They, uh, want a new video game or something," I stammer.

Narrowing her eyes, she says, "Why do I feel like you're lying?"

Probably because I'm bad at it.

"We'll be back in a little while." I turn and dart out the door before she can question me further.

"Caleb!" she calls after me, but I steadfastly ignore her.

At the mall thirty minutes later, I give the boys cash so they can pick out gifts for Halle as well as purchase the video game we're supposed to be getting.

Naturally, they're all too pleased by how my little white lie benefits them.

"Meet me back here in an hour. You got me?"

With matching nods, they're off.

Once I'm alone, I blow out a breath and scan the nearby stores. Halle isn't very materialistic, but that has more to do with her upbringing than her natural desires. Even so, I don't have the first clue about what she'd like. Since I don't know where to begin, I figure I'll browse for a bit, hoping I'll find inspiration.

In a stationery store, I pick up a pack of pastel notepads decorated with cute animals and a set of pens. Surely she'll like these, since she's always scribbling down notes in my office. They're way more fun than my plain notebook paper or Post-its.

Next, I pop into the bookstore across the way. At our last dance lesson, she mentioned wanting to get back into reading and talked about how, when she was younger, borrowing books from the library was one of her favorite things to do.

I browse the aisles, not sure what genre might pique her interest. I settle for two romance novels off a display table and two from the fantasy bestsellers. Then I venture toward the poetry section. Pretty quickly, three catch my eye, so I snag them all and add them to my stack. On my way to the register, I pick up a non-fiction, a mystery, and a thriller to ensure I've covered all my bases.

As I'm exiting the store, lugging an overloaded bag of books, I realize I probably should have saved this stop for last.

A few stores down, a pair of overalls with flowers embroidered on the legs catches my eye, so I head inside. I have to guess at her size, but I feel like I'm close enough.

She's going to accuse me of going overboard, and maybe she'll be right, but I don't care.

I'm determined to make up for all the shitty birthdays she's endured.

I stop off at a few more shops, adding a perfume, two candles, and a decorative container of matches the girl at the store told me was a must to go along with the candles. It's a good thing I only gave the boys an hour. Given longer, there's no telling what I might've purchased.

When I make it back to the door closest to where we parked, Quinn and Casen are waiting where I told them to be, each with a bag in hand, along with one from the video game store.

"Find what you wanted?" I ask.

"Yeah," Casen answers, his lips twitching. "Did you?"

I hold up both bag-laden arms. "Found maybe a little too much."

Quinn snorts. "We can tell."

As we step outside, I say, "I thought we could stop by the party supply store before we go home. What do you think?"

"Really?" Casen asks. "You'd do that?"

"It's her birthday." I shrug. "We should have balloons and stuff, right?"

Quinn laughs. "She's going to hate us for making such a big deal of it."

I set one armload of bags on the ground so I can dig my keys out. "I think it'll mean a lot to her that you guys care enough to make her birthday special."

"She's our sister," Quinn says softly as we load all of our bags into the cargo area of my SUV. "She is special."

"Speaking of our sister." Casen climbs into the passenger seat, then turns to face me, eyes narrowed. "What are your intentions with her?"

I choke on my own saliva. "Uh…"

Behind his twin, Quinn snaps his seat belt into place and leans forward. "I know she's strong, but she's sensitive too."

"In other words," Casen adds. "Break her heart and you're donezo." He slices his hand across his neck.

"Noted." With a wince, I pull out of the spot. "Your sister and I … I like her a lot. A whole lot. I'm trying to take it slow with her, though. She's a little…"

"Skittish?" Quinn suggests.

"Exactly."

Without my permission, my mind drifts to the night a couple of weeks ago when neither of us could sleep. To the way she came alive beneath my touch. Those memories have replayed over and over, and every time, I curse myself for not getting a taste of her. But I push that thought down each time too. Because I want to give her the time and space she needs to feel comfortable and safe. And maybe, selfishly, I want to be sure that she's choosing me because she wants to.

I don't want to be chosen out of obligation or convenience. I've been someone's second choice before. This time, I want to be Halle's *only* choice.

"She's never had a boyfriend," Casen says, eyeing me in the rearview mirror. "But don't tell her I told you."

I glance at him as the car rolls to a stop at a stoplight. "Never?"

He shakes his head. "She's been out with guys here and there, but she's never had a real boyfriend."

"I think she's scared." Quinn speaks up. "She doesn't want to get comfortable or open up, just for a guy to turn around and leave her."

Lips pressed together, I assess them both. They're far more perceptive than I've given them credit for.

"I can't guarantee what will happen in the future," I tell them. "But I like her a lot."

"That's good enough," Quinn says.

Casen clears his throat. "For now."

I'll take it. I don't want to let them down. I don't want to let *her* down. But I don't stand a chance if she doesn't let me in fully.

TWENTY

aleb

I haven't let on yet that I know today is Halle's birthday. I made pancakes, bacon, and eggs for breakfast this morning, but since I often make breakfast, I don't think that tipped her off. But now that I've got her and her brothers in the car, after telling her I want to take the three of them somewhere but not getting into details about the location, she's been eyeing me suspiciously.

Only days away from October, the weather has begun to turn. This afternoon, there's already a slight chill in the air. As a teen, I'd wanted so badly to leave this state. To leave behind the crisp falls and frigid winters. I did leave for a while. Salem and I moved to California, but it didn't take long for the two of us to want to return.

I pull up to the park and kill the engine. When I enlisted Salem's help, she lit up like a Christmas tree, then eagerly got everything set up for us. I couldn't exactly haul a picnic, balloons, cake, and presents in my car and hope for any kind of surprise at all.

"The park?" Halle asks, fiddling with the necklace she always wears. The gold chain is dainty, and the small teddy bear charm may seem childish to some, but to me it's perfectly her. "This is what you were so excited about?"

"Come on, Hal," I cajole. "Give me more credit than that."

I eye the boys in the back—they're both grinning like lunatics—and push my car door open.

Halle and the twins follow, and when the gazebo I reserved comes into view, there's no mistaking the balloons and happy birthday sign taped haphazardly to the side. Halle freezes, her shoes squelching in the wet grass.

"Wha—how?" She turns to me, then her brothers, her eyes narrowing. "You told him?"

Suddenly second-guessing my plan, I study her, trying to read into her expression and her body language, worried she's angry or sad or ... God, I don't know what. I just want to make sure she's okay with this.

"It's your birthday," Casen says simply.

"You always make a big deal out of our birthday," Quinn shrugs a bony shoulder. "We wanted to do the same for you."

Halle slowly meets my eyes, and immediately, the truth

shines there, impossible to miss. She's not angry or sad. No, all I see there is gratefulness. "Thank you," she whispers, the hint of tears clinging to her words.

"You're welcome."

The three of us follow Halle into the gazebo. I considered inviting Salem and Thayer and the kids. Cynthia and Thelma too. But if I know Halle, she wouldn't be comfortable with that much attention focused on her. So it's just the four of us.

"You got cake?" She sucks in a lungful of air and blows it out slowly, doing all she can to keep from crying.

"Your favorite," Casen says.

"Lemon." Quinn smiles. "Cynthia made it."

Halle's lips tremble, her eyes misting over. "She d-did?"

It astounds me, how little affection this woman has received in her life. It's been clear since day one, but this makes it all the more heartbreaking—watching the surprise that comes with realizing that the people in her life would do the most basic of things to celebrate her.

"Yeah, and we helped."

She takes in her brothers, mouth agape. "That's why you two were over there so late last night?"

"Yep," Quinn laughs. "And to think you tried to ground us for it."

Eyes narrowed to slits, she rounds on me. "That's why you convinced me to let them off the hook. You knew."

With a nod, I slip my hands into my pockets.

"And gifts." She sniffles, wiping discreetly beneath her eyes. "You didn't need to do this. None of you."

"We wanted to." Casen sits at the table and leans forward on his elbows.

"Can we eat now?" Quinn asks, taking a seat beside his brother. "I know you're all emotional and shit, but I'm hungry."

This at least pulls a laugh from Halle's chest. "Food too?" She eyes the basket off to the side.

"Yeah," I say, nerves skittering through me. "But it's nothing super fancy."

She lifts the edge of the basket and peers inside, her dark hair spilling over her shoulders. "Sandwiches and … Cheetos."

Straightening quick, she drops the lid and turns, the dam finally breaking. "Damn you, Thorne," she says, her throat thick with tears.

I open my arms. "C'mere."

To my shock, she does so easily. I wrap my arms around her and let her cry into my chest, mouthing "it's okay" to her brothers, who look on with horror-filled eyes.

They relax quickly. Halle needs a little more time to recover. I hold her until her sniffles subside, and when she gives me a gentle nudge in my stomach, I reluctantly let her go.

She inhales deeply, then lets it out slowly, eyes locked with mine. "This is the nicest thing anyone has ever done for me." Smile watery, she rounds the table and throws her arms over her brothers' shoulders, pressing kisses to their heads. "Thank you for thinking of me and making today special. I'm the luckiest sister ever. I love you."

"Ew," Casen laughs, pushing her off teasingly. "Don't go getting all soft on us now."

"Yeah, Halle. If you're gonna be so ooey-gooey on the inside, we might try to get away with more shit."

"Don't even think about it," she warns, ruffling their hair.

I set out the sandwiches, then open the giant Cheetos bag and set it in the middle of the table.

Once Halle and I are seated across from her brothers, bottles of water in front of us—soda for the boys—she slowly, damn near methodically, removes the plastic wrap from her sandwich like she's afraid it's not real.

"I still can't believe this," she says more to herself than me.

"What I can't believe is you weren't going to tell me it's your birthday." I stare her down, feigning offense.

"I've never liked my birthday," she admits.

"We told him." Casen pops the tab on a Mountain Dew.

Head tilted back, she sighs. "Of course you did."

"We want you to like your birthday," Quinn says. "You're the one who always told us birthdays are special."

Halle's eyes drop to the table. "They are, but—"

"But you don't think yours is?" Casen cuts her off, wearing a sharp look he clearly learned from her. "We disagree."

I can't help the amusement curling over my lips as they bicker. I used to want siblings more than anything. Not only for the company, but because I was sure my mom wouldn't be so overbearing if she had more than one child to obsess over. But after getting to know this family, I'm not sure I could have handled witnessing a sibling suffer in any way. It's so obviously hard on Halle. She's shouldered the brunt of so much so they didn't have to—so they could have a better childhood than she did.

"From now on"—Quinn says around a mouthful of food, unbothered when a chunk of lettuce falls out of his mouth—"we're celebrating your birthday. Got it?"

Halle lowers her head, trying to hide her amusement, but her smile can't be stopped. "Got it."

She can continue to insist she doesn't want to celebrate her birthday, but by her reaction, it's obvious this has meant a lot to her.

When we've all devoured our sandwiches, the boys insist on gifts.

"This is too much. Way too much," she says through laughter as we pile wrapped gifts in front of her.

"Caleb's a show-off," Casen says, feigning annoyance with a sigh.

Quinn laughs, a dimple popping in his left cheek. It—along with the matching one Casen has—doesn't appear often. "He went way overboard."

"You're telling me," Halle says, eyes widening when I set yet another present down.

"It's not as bad as it seems," I insist. Though as I go over the mental list of items I bought, I realize that's a lie.

Halle tears into the gifts with a fervor I wouldn't expect from a person who supposedly hates her birthday. She opens the books first, and when she takes more time to look over the fantasy and romance titles, I make a mental note.

She opens the perfume next, eyeing me in amusement.

"Are you trying to tell me I smell?"

"What?" I blanch. My voice higher than normal. "No. I just thought—"

"I'm kidding," she says, quickly putting me out of my misery. She carefully picks at the plastic wrapping, then eases the box open gently and plucks out the glass bottle. Eyes closed, she takes a sniff, and with a hum, she sprays a bit on her wrist. "Mmm, that smells really good."

I sag in relief. So far, my gifts have been winners.

After she murmurs happily over the notepads, she opens Casen's gift. From a pink gift bag, she pulls out two adult coloring books and a pack of markers.

"I saw you looking at coloring books a few months back," he explains. "So, I thought..." He trails off with an awkward shrug of his lanky shoulders.

"Case..." Her voice is thick, clogged with emotion. "This is so great. Perfect, actually. I love it."

That leaves Quinn's gift for last. The first thing she pulls out is a grumpy-faced storm cloud.

She laughs as she sets it down. "That's so cute."

"You're kind of grumpy sometimes," he says, his tone all tease. "Figured it suited you."

Next she pulls out a beaded bracelet that reads *Be Fucking Nice*.

Laughter bubbles out of her, carefree and easy. "Wow, Quinn. I'm sensing a theme here. Should I be offended?"

His cheeks pinken. "I just ... you don't take shit from anyone, so..." He scans the gazebo, suddenly looking unsure. "Was it a bad choice?"

"No!" she blurts out. "No," she says again, softer this time as she slips the bracelet on. "It's perfect. I love it."

"There's one more thing in there." He nods at the bag.

She digs through the tissue paper again, and this time she pulls out a tiny stuffed frog. It's fluffy and no bigger than her palm, but the emotion it inspires in her is big enough to fill the gazebo.

"I love it," she says, voice cracking as she cradles the tiny frog to her chest. "So much."

Her reaction makes my chest tighten and my eyes burn. Fuck. I think she's going to cry again.

I look between the siblings, clueless as to the significance of the frog stuffie but still moved by the gesture.

"I know it's not the same one," Quinn says, voice quivering. "But I thought it was—"

"Perfect, Quinn. It's perfect." She squeezes the tiny frog to her chest, a tear leaking out of the corner of her eye. "Best birthday ever. Thank you. All of you."

She leans over and presses a kiss to my cheek—though it lands closer to the corner of my mouth—shocking the hell out of me.

She sets the little frog on the table in front of her and studies it. "I love him." With a sigh, she eyes me. "Growing up, I had this stuffed frog I took everywhere with me. Even when I was a teenager, I couldn't sleep without it." She wets her lips. "My mom said she donated it when she was cleaning things out, but I think she threw it away. It was shortly after I told her I'd found an apartment and was moving out. I'm pretty sure it was her way of getting back at me for daring to leave. I looked everywhere for that stuffed animal. Checked every thrift store nearby for months and never saw it."

My heart pangs with sympathy, but also with a huge serving of respect. She doesn't see just how much she's done for her brothers. They may like to wreak havoc, but she's raising two thoughtful boys with good hearts. Pranks and petty theft aside, a person couldn't ask for more than that.

She inhales a shaky breath and reaches for the cake cutter. "Let's have cake. That sounds good, right?"

Casen gently grasps her wrist, stopping her. "Candles first, sis. You have to make a wish."

"A wish?" She echoes with a nod. "Right."

The boys load the cake with twenty-four candles. I suggested getting the candles shaped like a 2 and a 4, but they wanted twenty-four individual candles.

Once they're lit, the three of us sing happy birthday. And when she leans over the cake, ready to blow them out, I hop up and pull her hair back, scared it might catch on fire.

It takes three tries to get all the candles out, and as the smoke rises between her and her brothers, she tilts her head back, giving me a suggestive look that makes me want to know what she wished for.

TWENTY-ONE

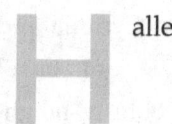alle

With a groan, I remove my microphone headset and stretch my neck. Scheduling for a doctor's office isn't the hardest work, but here and there, some of the people I have to deal with make the job exhausting. Especially when they argue about paying the no-show fee, unwilling to accept that I can't reschedule them until they do.

"Why can't you just waive the fee? Every time I'm there, I sit in the waiting room for an hour before I'm seen, anyway. Maybe I should charge the doctor a late fee. How about that?"

I just want to say "Dude, I get it. But I just work here, and I can't help you if you don't follow the rules."

Laptop powered down, I close it and slide it to one side.

My brothers won't be home for another hour, and Caleb is in Boston until the weekend.

What should I do with my rare free time?

Take a long, hot shower and sing at the top of my lungs? Maybe. I don't have one iota of singing talent, but that won't stop me.

It only takes a heartbeat to decide to go for it.

I even take extra care to blow my hair dry with a round brush. I'm not a girly-girl by any means, but occasionally, I enjoy primping.

Downstairs, I check the time, realizing that the boys should be home by now. Concern suddenly rolling through me, I peek out the front windows, searching for signs of them, then laugh when I find them sitting on Cynthia and Thelma's porch. They've made friends at school, but I swear they prefer the company of the two elderly neighbors. It's the cutest thing I've ever seen.

I unlock the door and open it, ensuring the screen door is unlocked too, then search the fridge for dinner ideas.

I've just pulled out the ground beef and lettuce when the door creaks open. "I'm making tacos for dinner," I call out. "Hope that's okay."

"Tacos sound fantastic, but I'm not here for dinner."

I turn at the sound of the female voice, finding Salem, who gives me a sheepish smile. "I knocked, but I don't think you heard me."

"I didn't." I set the supplies down, then pull a pack of tortillas from the pantry, needing a moment to collect myself.

Salem is genuine and kind, yet her presence—and maybe her beauty—makes me uneasy. Maybe it's my general lack of trust in people, or maybe it's because she knows Caleb in a way I don't yet. She knows him intimately. In a way that drives me insane, since the man is always wandering around the house with no shirt and those slutty sleep pants slung low on his hips. Sleep pants I'm almost certain he doesn't actually sleep in. Or maybe that's wishful thinking on my slutty brain's part.

"Right." She smiles widely, a ball of sunshine overpowering the rain cloud that's formed over my head. "I figured I'd pop over and invite you and your brothers to our Halloween party. Has Caleb mentioned it? It's the Saturday before Halloween. Dressing up is optional but preferred."

I frown, though I keep my tone even. "He hasn't said a word."

Does he not want me to go? It's hard to picture, knowing him, but why else wouldn't he invite us?

She plays with the ends of her hair, the move making me think it's a nervous tick. The same way my mom tapped her fingers against the side of her leg when she was lying to me.

"No, I'm not using again, Halle-girl."

She was.

"I paid the rent. I don't know why the landlord dropped off an eviction notice. He must've gotten the wrong apartment."

He hadn't.

"Maybe he didn't think you'd be interested and didn't want you to feel obligated?"

"Is he going?" I ask, the question a little more forceful than I mean for it to be.

She bites her lip, her eyes darting around like she realizes she's said something she shouldn't, but it's too late to backpedal. "I assume so, but he hasn't given me a straight answer, so please don't..." She scrunches her lips. "Just forget I said anything, okay? Pretty sure I just threw Caleb under a bus I didn't even know was there." She blows out a breath. "I don't know much about your relationship, whether you guys are serious—"

"We're not." We must not be if he hasn't bothered to mention a party that, from the sound of things, will be attended by all the people he cares about.

With only three weeks until Halloween, I can't imagine costumes will be easy to come by. I don't have the money for costumes, anyway, but I could pull together some pieces from my closet and the thrift store if necessary. But my brothers? That's a different story. At fourteen, I have no idea whether they'd even want to dress up.

Inhaling deeply, I force the thoughts to settle. There's a good chance I'm being too sensitive. The man went out of his way to make my birthday special—a birthday I hadn't even told him about. There's probably a perfectly reasonable explanation for why he hasn't mentioned it, yet I'm the one over here jumping to conclusions. Just like always. It's my fatal flaw, the instinct to immediately distrust a person's motives. To assume Caleb didn't want me to know about it in the first place.

Shoulders sagging, I blow out a breath, forcing my toxic thoughts to go with it.

"I'm sorry," I say. "I'm letting my insecurities get to me." The moment I voice that truth, I feel surprisingly better. It feels oddly empowering to admit that out loud.

"Insecurities?" She scrunches her nose in the same way Seda's does when she's confused. "About what?"

"You," I admit.

"Me?" she scoffs. "Why?"

"Look at you." I wave a hand up and down, gesturing to her soft curves and tanned skin, and perfect blond hair. I'm the complete opposite of her. Tall and curvier, dark hair and dark eyes. And though there's clearly been some hiccups in her past, she's living what looks like the perfect life. "You just seem like you have it all together."

She laughs, the boisterous sound pinging off the walls. "Trust me, Halle, I don't have anything together. My life has never been rainbows and sunshine. I can promise you that. But where I'm at now? I'm happy. Even on the hard days." She steps up close and grips my hands. "Come over for coffee and cupcakes sometime this week. That way we can get to know each other. I'm pretty much always home with Samson. He's a little terror, more so than either of the girls was at this age, so it's better to limit his exposure to the general public."

"Okay," I agree, surprising myself with my easy agreement. "I'll come over tomorrow around noon, if that's okay."

Normally, I'd brush off her offer, but I really like Caleb, and this is the mother of his child. She'll always be in his life, so I should get to know her.

"That's perfect."

I nearly yelp when she throws her arms around my shoulders and squeezes with more strength than someone her size should have.

She beams, eyes crinkling at the corners. "I have a feeling we're going to be great friends."

I smile back. When she smiles, it's impossible not to return the expression.

As I'm ushering her out, my brothers appear, stomping up the porch steps.

"Hey, Casen. Quinn." She greets them with the same effortless smile she had for me.

"Hi, Salem," they echo back.

"I'm making tacos for dinner," I tell them as they dart around us and into the house. "Get your homework done."

They grumble, but they head straight for the dining table and unpack their stuff.

The insurance company still hasn't had the damage appraised. The longer it sits without repairs, the more I worry about mold, but despite my dozen or so calls regarding the matter, the process is slow-moving.

Once Salem has descended the porch steps, I lock the door and get back to work on dinner.

Hours later, I climb into bed, determined to read one of the books Caleb got me for my birthday. No matter how many times I start, I get interrupted or doze off. And like every other attempt, my phone rings just as I'm finishing the first page.

Though my first response is one of annoyance, when I realize it's a FaceTime request from Caleb, the sensation quickly turns to dread, my stupid brain automatically assuming something is wrong.

With a shaky finger, I swipe the screen to accept the request. "Is everything okay?"

Caleb blinks back at me. "Um ... yeah. Why?"

Heat floods my cheek. "You haven't called me like this before," I say.

"I've been gone for days. I thought we could catch up." He swallows, and I swear concern flashes in his eyes. "I miss you. Is that okay to say?"

"You miss me?"

With a nod, he sets his phone down.

Unable to help myself, I peek at his surroundings. He must be in his apartment. The space behind him is small and outfitted with a couch, ottoman, and TV. Behind him is a set of doors that I assume lead to a balcony.

"Yeah, Hal," he murmurs. "I miss you a lot."

I press my lips together and consider the best way to respond. I miss him too, but I'm also incredibly frustrated with him. The desperate-for-sex kind of frustrated. I respect his thoughtfulness. Putting the ball in my court is honorable, regardless of what he knows about my past. But being the one saddled with the pressure to initiate even a kiss is a lot harder than I expected. As much as I want to ask for exactly what I want, each time I consider it, my dreaded self-doubt rears its ugly head.

Mocking me with thoughts like *What if his feelings aren't as strong as I've come to believe and he just said that because he knows I'll be too chicken to act on it again?*

I remind myself time and again that when I did act on it,

he was very much into it. Yet the memory hasn't freed me from my fear.

"It's okay if you don't miss me," he says, humor in his eyes.

God, has anything ever ruffled the persistent, perfect in practically every way Caleb Thorne? I can't imagine it.

"I do," I admit quietly, heart in my throat. "And that's weird for me. The only people I've ever missed are my brothers. And maybe my mom."

Although I haven't missed her once since she was sentenced. I've only felt relief in that respect.

"It's okay to let people in." He crosses his arms over his chest, the soft heather gray fabric stretching around his biceps in the most perfect way.

He's so annoyingly *fit*.

The thought has just popped into my mind when a grin splits his face. "You're staring at my arms."

"I am." No sense in denying it when I've been caught red-handed. "So, you called just to talk to me, or…?"

He sits back, and the stool he's sitting in scrapes against the floor. "Salem called."

"Ah." I lower my focus to the comforter covering my lap. "I see. You're only calling because of her."

"No." The firmness in his tone is a shock, causing me to whip my head up and assess him. "I've wanted to call you every day since I left, but I was afraid I'd make you uncomfortable." Sighing, he runs his fingers through his hair. It flops right back in his eyes. "I don't—fuck, Halle. I'm afraid of coming on too strong. You can be so skittish, and I don't want to scare you off." His shoulders sag like all the wind has been taken out of his sails. "I'm trying to give you space. I don't want to be overbearing. The kind of guy you can't shake. Okay? You're living in my house, and it's fucking killing me not to touch you, but I worry I'll make you uncomfortable, and—" He drags his hand over his jaw. "Fuck, I'm just really confused, okay?"

I bite down on my lip a little too hard, head bobbing. "I understand."

This whole thing *is* confusing. The day I chose to move to Hawthorne Mills, I couldn't have imagined meeting a man I'd be interested in, a man who also showed interest in me, let alone a man like Caleb—the kind of person who could absolutely ruin me if I let him. The kind of person who has reminded me again and again that there *are* good people in the world.

"I don't think you do."

The pain in his voice makes my stomach twist.

"Explain it to me, then."

He exhales, his whole body sagging and his gaze averted. "I've never felt like this before, and it ... fuck, Halle. I want you like I've never wanted anyone before, but I don't think you believe me."

I know I shouldn't ask, but the words leave my mouth before I can stop them. "Not even her?"

He holds my gaze, his attention never wavering when he says, "Not even her."

I keep my eyes locked with his for another moment, but eventually, my nerves get the best of me, and I duck my head. I have to let go of the Salem thing. He says he's over her, and he's never given me a reason not to believe him.

My stupid insecurities are to blame in this situation. I've let them get the best of me, so concerned that I'm not the kind of woman a man like him deserves.

He's gentle, kind-hearted, and caring, but couldn't I say those things about myself too? So why can't I be the kind of woman he deserves?

Caleb clears his throat, pulling me from my thoughts.

"The Halloween party slipped my mind. Salem mentioned that they were considering throwing one again this year, but I didn't realize it was set in stone. Then I left for Boston, and we really haven't spoken since then."

I nod. "I understand."

I really do, and I'm annoyed with myself for jumping to conclusions and performing Olympic-worthy gymnastic stunts in my brain.

He cocks his head to the side. "Do you?"

"Yes."

"Good girl."

My core tightens not only in response to the words but the tone in which he says them.

"I'll be home tomorrow," he says, stretching his arms above his head.

Here I go again, staring at his biceps and squinting at the tattoo peeking out from beneath the edge of his shirt sleeve, the one I've yet to get close enough to in order to identify.

"Okay," I say softly. "I need to run to the grocery store tomorrow. Want me to pick up anything in particular?"

"If I think of something, I'll text you." He leans closer to the camera, his wide shoulders blocking out the apartment behind him. "And Halle?"

"Yeah?" The word comes out as a nervous quaver. This man has a unique way of unsettling me. Though not in a bad way whatsoever.

"If you want me to take the reins, just tell me you're in."

For a second, all I do is stare, processing the words. It takes longer than it should, but eventually, understanding dawns.

"O-oh," I breathe, pulse suddenly pounding. "Okay."

"Have a good night, Hal."

"Night," I echo.

Once he's ended the call, I turn on the TV. There's no way I can focus on a book now, yet there's no way I'll be sleeping anytime soon. Not when I'm a live wire, one second away from exploding.

It's after two a.m. when I send the text message.

> I'm in.

TWENTY-TWO

Halle

I take a deep breath, giving myself one last pep talk before I knock on Salem's door.

She's there in an instant, swinging the door open with a quick smile before she darts off, chasing a little boy with dark hair who's sprinting away shockingly fast for a human being with such short legs.

"Samson!" she chastises. "Put that marker down now."

While she battles with the squirming toddler, I let myself in and shut the door behind me.

"I didn't even know we owned any Sharpies," she gripes as she holds the marker in her right hand and wrangles him with her free arm. "But leave it to Samson to find one."

"Kids are good at that."

My brothers were terrors from about the ages of two to six. They never failed to get their grubby little hands into the things they shouldn't.

"This way," she says with a nod. "Want a cup of coffee? I made turkey sandwiches for lunch. If that's not okay, I have—"

"That's great," I say, not wanting to inconvenience her. She's got her hands full as it is.

"Have a seat, and I'll grab everything." She motions to a long dining table.

Rather than leave her to do the work, I wring my hands and take a step closer. "Can I help?"

I'd much rather feel useful than sit here and do nothing.

She plops the squirming toddler into a highchair and scoots it to the table. "The sandwiches are on the second shelf in the fridge. If you want a bottle of water, grab one."

With a grateful smile, I obey, pulling the sandwiches out and setting them out of Samson's reach.

She sighs and drops into a chair beside her little boy. "Keeping tiny humans alive is a full-time job." Perking up, she snags a sandwich, and as she unwraps it, she keeps her attention downcast. Finally, she clears her throat and peers up at me. "I'm the one who invited you over, and now I don't really know where to begin."

I let out a nervous laugh. "It's weird getting to know people as an adult, isn't it?"

"Yes." She holds a quarter slice of her sandwich up to Samson's mouth.

He tries to yank it from her hand, but she's faster, pulling back before he can get his hand on it.

He grunts. "I feed myself."

She levels him with a stare. "You're capable of it, yes. But are you actually going to do it, or will you throw it on the floor?"

His answer comes in the form of a mischievous little grin.

With a sigh, she says, "I'll hold on to it for now, I think."

He frowns but leans forward and takes a bite without argument.

With a soft smile at me, Salem slips a lock of blond hair behind her ear. "I think you have the wrong impression of me, Halle."

"I—what—no," I sputter, my heart plummeting.

Laughing, she squeezes my hand where it rests on the table. "I'm not accusing you of anything. It's human nature to form preconceived notions, but I'd rather get to know each other so our impressions of one another can be informed by fact."

I nod. I should probably respond, but my brain has suddenly emptied, unable to scramble twenty-six letters into any kind of sentence structure.

"Did Caleb tell you that I grew up in the house he lives in now?"

Another nod, and finally, a few words. "He told me."

"I didn't have the best childhood. He hasn't given me any details—please don't think he's betrayed your trust—

but he hinted that maybe you and I share similar experiences."

My brows knit. "Similar experiences? Was your mom an addict too?"

Before she's even responded, I wish I could take the question back, certain she'll laugh. But, to my relief, she doesn't. "No, but my dad was abusive. It..." She gives her son a soft smile, her eyes full of pain. "It was horrible, to say the least, and it played a large part in shaping me into who I am today."

"Is he in prison?"

She shakes her head. "No, he died years ago. And maybe it's wrong, but I'm relieved. I don't think I would be nearly as okay as I am now if he were still alive. Even if he were behind bars."

She takes a deep breath, stretching her fingers out in front of her.

"More," Samson demands, smacking his hands on the highchair. "More, Mommy."

With a tender sigh, she brushes his hair back from his face, only for it to flop right back into his eyes. She holds the sandwich out to him. Instead of taking a small bite, he leans his body forward and snatches the sandwich from her hand with his teeth like a piranha.

"Samson," she scolds, but she can't keep the laughter out of her voice. Quickly, her attention veers back to me. "Do you want kids?"

I frown, mulling over the question. It's one I haven't put a lot of thought into. "I don't know. I practically raised myself and my brothers. For now, that's enough, but I think maybe one day I'd like to have a family."

Lips pressed together, she nods. "I always liked kids, but I used to think…" Eyes misting over, she considers her little boy. "I don't know." She clears her throat. "That maybe I wasn't worthy of them. Of being a mother. That I was too broken. Too tainted. For a long time, I couldn't put those sensations into words. Seda was a surprise, and honestly, it's best it happened that way. I don't know that I could have convinced myself that I deserved the love of a child." She inhales deeply, surveying me. "I hope the two of us can be friends."

For a moment, I'm overwhelmed by the depth of this conversation, unsure of how to respond. But I shake off the uncertainty—I'm overthinking this like I do most things—and force myself to speak. "I would like that. I … I'm not big on sharing, but I think … I think I'd like to tell you a little about my past, if that's okay?"

Salem nods, giving me a soft, encouraging smile. "Tell me as much or as little as you want."

So I do.

This may be the longest trip I've ever taken to the grocery store. Not because I'm buying an abundance of food, but because Caleb is home, and I'm a big, fat chicken.

He texted not long after I got here, but the message remains marked unread on my phone.

> I'm home. Where are you? The store? It's a bit late for a trip to the grocery store, don't you think?

Now that I've given him the go-ahead to take control, I'm nervous. He'd never take advantage of me. That's not the issue. But the anticipation might kill me.

I take one aisle after another with methodical precision, crossing off each item on my list and adding plenty more. By the time I check out and head to my car, the sun is beginning to set.

As I load the groceries into the trunk, I mentally consider every reason I might need to stop on my way home. I come up empty. It's time to stop stalling. I'm being ridiculous.

In the driveway behind Caleb's Mercedes SUV, my beaten-up Honda is an eyesore. Stray pieces of gravel scattered clumsily on the asphalt crunch beneath my sneaker as I step out and turn at the sound of the screen door closing.

Caleb leans against the column, his body lithe, his arms crossed over his chest, his gaze appraising.

"Need help?" he calls out, lips lifting into a dangerous smirk.

"No, I'm good," I lie, heart thudding in my ears, as I pop the trunk.

Why he even asked is beyond me, since he jogs down the steps and strides for me as if he didn't hear my response. He's there in an instant, arm brushing mine as he picks up all but one bag. One bag. With how effortless the move was, he easily could have gotten that one too, but he left it for me, knowing I would've fussed.

With a sigh, I pluck the last one up and slam the trunk, then follow him inside.

As I close the door behind me, I can't help but ogle him, practically drooling over the way his bicep bulges as he lifts his arm and sets the bags down. From the look of concentration on his face, he isn't focused on his muscles the way I am. Knowing he isn't flexing for my attention makes it worse. He gets to work unloading the bags, organizing the items into sections as I set my lone sack on the counter and search the main floor for the twins.

"Where are my brothers?" I ask, concern seeping in and dousing the desire that hit me at the sight of Caleb. They were working on homework when I left. I figured they'd be finished and playing video games by now.

Gallon of milk in hand, Caleb turns to me. "They're across the street. Cynthia's teaching them how to make quiche, I think. And they've gotten into watching some reality show together."

A scoff escapes me. "Seriously?"

Nodding, his lips kicked up on one side, he slips the milk onto the shelf in the fridge. "Mhm."

I pick up two boxes of cereal and put them in the cabinet. "I feel like we've slipped into an alternate reality. My obnoxious brothers have become besties with the nosy elderly ladies across the street? I can't wrap my head around it."

Caleb laughs behind me. "I can. They're alike in a lot of ways."

Head tilted, I mull over his statement. "Huh. You have a point, actually."

And spending time with the neighbors means my brothers are staying out of trouble. I think.

Just as relief hits me, my heart drops, taking the sensation with it. Because this means I'm alone with Caleb. Unless...

"Is Seda coming over for dinner?"

He shakes his head, stuffing one plastic bag into another. "She came over when I got home, but she's staying next door for the rest of the night."

I frown. "She hasn't been here much lately. It's not ... it's not my fault, is it?"

"What?" He snaps his head up, eyes wide. "No. She's just being a preteen. She's dealing with her first crush, and she gets flustered around your brothers. For now, I think she'd rather be with her mom."

"Oh." My stomach twists. "I'm so sorry. I didn't realize that we were keeping her away. We can—"

"Halle." His firm tone causes me to snap my mouth shut. "It's okay. Seda knows she's welcome here any time she wants to be."

"Yeah, but if our presence is taking your time away from her, then maybe it's better if we figure something else out."

He lays his hands flat on the stone countertop and narrows his eyes on me, his stare so intense I swear he can see right through me like my flesh and bones are nothing. "Has anyone ever told you that you're incredibly stubborn and self-sacrificing?"

I frown. "No."

"Well." He leans toward me, and there go my eyes again, taking in the flex of his forearms and biceps. "You are."

"Oh."

"Mhm." He spins, giving me his back again as he puts the bag of apples in the fridge. "What are you in the mood for?"

My brain short circuits. *What am I in the mood for?*

What kind of question is that?

And obviously, the answer is him.

He peers over his shoulder and adds, "For dinner."

I busy myself putting away the box of pasta, hoping he can't see the way my cheeks heat. "Oh, um…" I rack my brain, but it's pointless. I'm all out of sorts. "I'm not that hungry, actually."

"Well, I am." He steps closer and looks me up and down. At least I think he does, but maybe my horny brain is making stuff up now.

"What about a grilled cheese?" he asks.

"Grilled cheese?" I stutter out in surprise. "For dinner?"

"Sure." He pulls out the packages of cheeses he just put away. "I love a good grilled cheese."

I eye the selection. "I've only ever used Kraft American cheese."

He groans, his head tossed back. "You haven't *lived*, Halle. It's decided. I'm making grilled cheese for dinner."

Seriously? This man is seriously talking about a grilled cheese right now, and all I can think about is whether he has any plans to get me naked.

"Slice this up for me?" He points to a loaf of sourdough.

"When did you get that?" I bump his hip with mine so I can get a knife from the drawer.

"Seda brought it over with her. Apparently, Salem is trying her hand at making bread."

My chest tightens a fraction at the mention of his ex-wife. "I had lunch with her today."

"Yeah? How'd that go?" He pulls out the grater and gets to work on the cheese.

"It was good." I slice the bread carefully, ensuring each one isn't too thick. "I like her."

"Salem's pretty hard not to like. I think you two could be friends."

"I'm not good at making friends," I admit, keeping my focus fixed on my task.

He goes still, his gaze boring into me. "Could've fooled me. Aren't we friends?"

"Yeah, but that was all you." I throw a smile his way. "You're kind of persistent."

"Only about things that matter," he says, expression earnest.

"And I matter?"

He wets his lips with a small swipe of his tongue, his attention dropping to my mouth. "You know you do."

Caleb takes the bread from me and butters one side of each slice. He adds a sprinkle of shredded parmesan cheese on top before putting it that side down in the preheated pan. Without looking up, he adds a selection of cheeses to it, then finishes by setting a second slice of bread on top.

"That's an interesting concoction you have going there."

Spatula in hand, he lifts the sandwich just a little to see

how it's browning. "You're going to be begging me for it every day."

My silly, touch-starved brain takes that sentence and runs with it, my core pulling tighter and a thrill zipping through me.

He flips the sandwich, the fresh buttery side sizzling in the pan. "I can feel you staring at me." He peers over his shoulder, his blue irises a deeper shade than usual.

I don't bother to look away. "Guilty."

Though I've been apprehensive about being alone with him all day, I'm instantly thankful my brothers aren't here. I need this man to kiss me and put me out of my misery, and I'm not sure I would allow him to do that if they were around.

I've never … They've never seen me with a boyfriend. If that's even what Caleb is. I guess I wouldn't know. I've never had one. I've had flings and one-night stands, but never a relationship that warranted an introduction to my brothers. But they already know Caleb. Not only that, but I'm not just their sister anymore. I'm their guardian. I want to set a good example for them. I don't want to be like Mom, bringing home all the wrong kinds of guys, allowing virtual strangers near the boys.

This situation with Caleb is the farthest thing from it. Even so, it's hard to shake the fear that I might be like her.

Caleb slides the finished grilled cheese onto a plate and passes it to me and says "let it cool a bit" before he gets to work assembling the next sandwich. As he places the second piece of bread on top of the first, he side-eyes me. "What's on your mind?"

Ugh. This man. This sweet, kind, annoyingly perfect man sees through *all* of me. I can't hide a single worry from him.

"Nothing," I lie, tracing my finger along a line in the stone countertop.

A low rumble starts in his chest. "Halle."

My name is both a plea and a warning.

I should know better than to lie to him.

But the trauma that's clung to me my whole life makes keeping my thoughts and vulnerabilities to myself feel safer. I'm afraid to divulge the insecurities of my mind, but the truth is that if I *want* this thing with Caleb, I have to learn to open up. But, God, is it harder than it should be.

"I just … what are we?" I ask, hesitantly meeting his gaze.

He slides the spatula under the second grilled cheese and puts the sandwich on a plate. Then he turns, leaning back against the counter, and zeroes in on me.

"What do you want to be?"

My stomach flips at the intensity in his tone. "I don't know, but not because I don't like you. I don't know how to do this." I wave a hand between us. "I've never dated before. I don't know the rules. I don't know what signs to look for to determine whether this is serious or when to determine it's not worth pursuing."

His lips tip up slowly, his smile as breathtaking as the sun slowly rising in the sky. "If I'd thought you'd be okay with me calling you my girlfriend, I would've started already."

"Caleb." I drop my face into my hands to hide my embarrassment.

"Hey." His tone is gentle, as are his hands when he carefully pulls them away. Standing in front of me, he says, "We don't have to put a label on this yet. Not if you aren't ready. We've only known each other a few months. I understand your hesitation."

"You do?" The damn question comes out watery, the threat of tears close. What is it about this man that rattles me this way? I've never been much of a crier, but it's like he knows exactly how to hit those most sensitive parts of my soul.

"You're scared and—"

"I'm *not* scared," I grit out, trying to wriggle my way out of his hold.

He holds on tighter, but not so tight that I couldn't actually get away if I wanted. "You are scared, and it's okay, I'm scared too."

My heart stutters. "You are?"

"Mhm," he hums, blue eyes warm and deep as he surveys me, no doubt cataloging my freckles or the small mole on my lip. "Downright terrified."

"Why?" The question comes out small. Meek. Like a little mouse squeaking in fear.

"Because"—he angles in, his lips finding the curve of my ear—"I'm not sure I could survive losing you."

I close my eyes and grasp the front of his hoodie to keep myself upright.

Falling in love is, without a doubt, the most terrifying thing I've ever done. Even if I'm not ready to admit that's what this is, deep down, I know it. I'm not fully there yet, but I am in the free-fall phase. And even though he's right here with me, I'm not ready to fully trust he'll be there to catch me when I land.

"I'm going to kiss you now," he whispers against my ear. "If that's okay."

I nod, and just in case that's not good enough, I beg him with a soft, pathetic "please."

He obliges instantly, his left-hand delving into my hair as he devours me.

I melt at his touch, like butter in a hot pan.

He deepens the kiss, fingers tightening on my hair until the sensation borders on pain.

I had my first kiss at thirteen. I've kissed plenty of guys since.

But Caleb?

He doesn't just kiss me. He *claims* me.

With a whimper, I try to pull him closer, even though he's as close as he can get unless he could melt inside me.

I'd welcome it if it were possible.

He chuckles, the sound warm and husky against my mouth. "Look at you. Fucking desperate for me. You can't deny it anymore, can you, Halle?" With a groan, he peppers kisses down the column of my throat. "You *want* me."

"Y-Yes," I whimper. There's no denying it anymore.

Delicately, he slides his hands down my sides. Between one heartbeat and another, his touch turns rougher, more demanding, and he grasps my hips and lifts me up from the stool abruptly, pulling a squeal from me. He deposits me on the countertop, lips finding mine once more.

My heart beats out of control as our tongues tangle. The roar of ocean waves crashes in my ears as Caleb envelops me, every part of him threatening to pull me under. His smell, his taste, his sounds. It's all too much; it's *too good*.

I don't do *good*. All the good I've ever experienced has been taken from me. The smart thing to do would be to push him away, grab my shit and my brothers, and get the hell out of here. But I *can't*. Leaving Caleb would create an open, gaping wound in my side.

Besides, I'm so tired of running. For once, I can't help but wish that something in my life would go right, and I want that thing to be him.

"If"—he nips at my earlobe—"at any point you want me to stop, just say stop, and I will."

A shudder works its way through me, heat pooling in my core. "I'm not going to ask you to stop."

He pulls away a fraction, and already, the air has chilled. "Regardless, I need you to know that, if you want me to, I will."

I nod my response.

But he shakes his head. "With words, Halle."

With a long exhale, I release my hold on his hoodie and twine them in the hair at his nape instead. "If I want you to stop, I'll ask you."

I hope I don't sound as desperate as I feel. I *need* his lips on mine again. His hands all over me. My earlier reservations and insecurities have quickly been overtaken by the much stronger need to be possessed by him.

He smiles. "Good. I like that you listen." With renewed

fire in his eyes, he presses his open mouth to my neck and sucks.

I should be concerned that he'll leave evidence behind, a mark on my skin, but all rational thought has fled my brain, and my body has taken over. My hand against the back of his head presses him impossibly closer, begging for a closeness, a connection, I can't put into words.

"Can I make you come?" He whispers against my skin. "Please."

The heat in my low belly simmers. *Fuck*.

Did this man seriously just *beg* to give me an orgasm? Have I reached some sort of pinnacle of heaven I didn't know existed?

"Yes," I breathe, tipping my head back so he has better access to my neck. "God. Yes, please."

He lets out a gruff chuckle, finding my mouth and stealing a kiss that leaves me reeling. "So fucking eager." We don't separate as he finds the button on my jeans. Then the zipper. When his fingers slip beneath the band of my underwear and he finds my soaking wet core, I cry out.

He moans, the sound low and guttural, and as he pulls back, his hazy eyes hold mine prisoner. "All this for me, Halle? I'm so fucking lucky."

He slips a finger inside me and curls it, sending a zap of electricity through me.

"More."

As he breaks into a grin, he buries his face in my neck like he wants to hide the expression from me. "You're so fucking perfect, Halle. My girl wants more?"

I nod over and over again, my breaths choppy. "Yes."

"Yes, what?" He bites at my collarbone.

"Yes, please."

I'm rewarded for my obedience with a soft kiss to my lips. "Such a good girl," he murmurs, adding another finger to the first. I'm stretched, though I'm still not full enough, but I'll take what I can get.

He pumps his fingers slowly, thumb pressed to my clit. The sensations, coupled with his soft words of praise, send me hurtling toward the urge far more quickly than I could have anticipated.

"I'm—"

He cuts my words off with a kiss.

His tongue is still tangling with mine when I come apart on his fingers. I shatter into a million pieces, yet, somehow, he holds every one. It might be the most intense orgasm I've ever had. If I'm still mostly clothed, then I can't imagine what—

In one quick move, he pulls my jeans and underwear off and drops them to the kitchen floor. They look out of place in his neat space, melted onto the floor like a popsicle.

"Prettiest pussy I've ever seen," he whispers, eyes glued to my center.

Hit with a bolt of insecurity, I bring my knees together.

With two warm, gentle hands on my thighs, he stops me, pushing me open wider for his viewing pleasure. "Did I tell you to close your legs?"

I don't respond, the combination of desire and relief and trepidation making it impossible to form words.

Ducking so we're eye to eye, he prompts me again with a stern "Halle?"

Words shaky, I finally breathe out, "No. You didn't."

"So"—he arches a brow—"why did you try?"

My cheeks heat. "I don't know."

"Hmm," he hums. "Is it because you don't want my fingers inside you again?"

Heart stumbling, I squeak. "That's not—"

"Or my mouth?"

I whimper, the sound pulling a cocky grin out of him.

"Ah, so you do want my mouth on this sweet cunt?"

"Yes." My abdominal muscles flex, warmth flooding me again.

"Yes, what?" he teases, smirk growing. "Come on, Halle. I thought you knew the magic word by now."

My breath hitches. "Please."

Eyes darkening, he murmurs, "That's my girl."

Caleb drops to his knees with a groan, parting my folds with his fingers. "Fuck." His eyes flick up to mine. "I can't wait to taste you, sweetheart."

Sweetheart? I'm at risk of melting into a puddle on the floor beside my pants. No one has ever called me that before. Prickly? Sure. Stuck-up bitch? Plenty of times. But sweetheart? Never, and I … I hate that I like it.

Without warning, his mouth is on me, his tongue flicking my clit. I cry out, lying back on the cool marble. The little bundle of nerves is already sensitive, so almost immediately, I'm wiggling against him, a whimper falling from my lips. He presses a hand to my pelvis to hold me still, the move making the sensations all the more intense.

He works his tongue against me, licking and sucking, bringing me to the edge and pulling away just as the waves of pleasure crest. Each time, I cry out in protest, and each time, I swear his smug grin gets bigger. Before I can catch my breath and curse him out, though, he dives back in.

Caleb Thorne eats pussy like it's his life mission. Like there's nothing more important than bringing me pleasure. His enthusiasm only heightens the sensation.

When he finally gets tired of edging me and lets me come, I scream, my thighs shaking. Then he's there, standing between my legs, his mouth on mine to silence me.

When I finally come to, he backs away, eyes hooded and his erection straining against his sweatpants impressively. Damn, I'm going to be *sore*.

"Fuck me," I beg. "Please." I reach for him, but he grasps my wrists and shakes his head.

The rejection is like a knife to the chest, making it hard to breathe.

But his words are tender, his eyes soft. "Not yet."

"Why not?" I protest, sitting up on my elbows. My pussy is still on full display for him, but suddenly I don't feel so shy about it. "Do you want me to beg?"

He breaks into a slow grin and cups his erection. "I love it when you beg, but no, that's not the reason."

Eyes narrowed, I sit up. "Then what is?"

"When I finally fuck you, Halle, I'll have all the time I need. I'm going to make it perfect for you. You'll be screaming my name for the whole neighborhood to hear. Do you understand?"

I nod like a bobblehead, heart hammering again.

"I don't want to worry that your brothers are gonna walk through the door. Got me?"

How is it possible this man can render me so speechless? I stick with nodding. It's all I can manage.

Rubbing at his jaw, he snags my discarded jeans and underwear. Then, with ease, he slips my underwear up my legs and pulls me off the counter so he can situate them on my hips.

"I've got this," I say, reaching for my jeans.

"No." He pulls them away. "I undressed you. I'll redress you."

"Oh." The word is barely audible, my face once again heating.

He taps my right calf. "Leg up, sweetheart."

I do as he says, placing a hand on his shoulder to steady myself. He works my jeans up both calves and thighs and over my hips. Then he buttons and zips them up with an ease I envy.

When he steps away from me, I shiver at the loss of his body heat.

With a final smirk, he spins on his heel and starts for the stairs. "I need another shower."

His antics break the intensity of the moment and pull a laugh from deep within me.

"Hard as a fucking rock," he adds, dragging his feet up the first few stairs.

He turns and winks, then he disappears from sight, making my stomach stir with that feeling that only seems to appear around him—the one that terrifies me.

TWENTY-THREE

Caleb

I adjust the mask across my eyes and step back to assess the full outfit in the mirror. Every year, Seda dictates the family's theme. This year, though, while the rest of her family is dressed as *Toy Story* characters, she talked me into something different. And since *The Princess Bride* is her current obsession, this makes sense.

Can't say I wasn't ecstatic when she asked me to dress up as Westley.

Down the hall, Casen and Quinn bicker, like always, though their annoyance today has more to do with dressing up than anything else. But they're being good sports about it after Seda broke down in tears when they told her they weren't planning to dress up. I'm not sure what costumes they decided on, but based on the ruckus coming from their room, it's safe to say I should be worried.

A soft knock on my door pulls me from my thoughts, and I'm almost knocked on my ass when I pull it open and come face to face with Hot Pirate Halle.

"Can you help me with my corset?" she asks, turning around and dragging her hair over her shoulder to reveal the ribbons in the back.

"Yeah," I stammer, hands shaking at the thought of touching her.

I've been a taut bowstring since our moment in the kitchen. My current case load is kicking my ass, so I've been in Boston more than I'd like. Between that and the boys, Halle and I haven't had a second of time alone. Unable to resist the temptation, I dip my head and kiss her bare shoulder.

She lets out a tiny gasp that lights me up on the inside.

Stepping back, I study the corset, then tug on the ribbons. "Tight enough?"

She peeks over her shoulder at me. "Tighter."

I make some adjustments to the way the ribbon runs through the eyelets, then pull a little harder. "How about now?"

"Mm," she hums. "Just a little more."

Again, I tighten it, wrapping each end around my fingers.

"That's perfect."

Careful not to let out any slack, I secure the ribbon and tie it into a bow. Then I release her.

With a sigh, she lets her hair fall down to cascade over her back and turns to face me.

God, she's so fucking pretty. She has no idea how weak she makes me.

"What are you supposed to be? Zorro?"

I shake my head and adjust my mask when it slips a little. "Westley from *The Princess Bride*."

Nose scrunching, she tilts her head. "Is that a book?"

My heart about gives out. With a hand to my chest, I give my head a solemn shake. "Halle, Halle, Halle," I chant her name. "You're telling me you've *never* watched *The Princess Bride*?"

She winces. "Considering I assumed it was a book? No."

Leaning against the doorway, I let out a deep sigh. "A shame, truly. You're missing out on a masterpiece."

This time it's her lips that scrunch. "Why do I get the feeling you're exaggerating and it's actually terrible?"

Groaning, I pinch the bridge of my nose. "Not exaggerating. And no, it's not terrible. It's a classic. It's Seda's favorite movie at the moment, so she asked me to dress as Westley. She's going as Buttercup."

She narrows her eyes, like she thinks I'm fucking with her. "And who or what is Buttercup? A fairy? A flower?"

"She's ... you know what? We'll have Seda over this week, and you can watch it with her. She'll quiz you after, so be prepared."

She chuckles. "Sounds—"

A loud crash from down the hall cuts her off, and she darts away.

"Shit," she curses as she bangs on the door. "Are you two decent?"

"Um ... I guess," one of the boys calls as I catch up.

Halle throws the door open, and we're instantly greeted by the sight of a broken lamp. It's lying on the floor, the base smashed and in several pieces.

Halle covers her face, muffling her groan. "What did you do?"

"It was him," they say simultaneously, pointing to one another.

It's like they planned it on purpose, like they're imitating the Spiderman meme, since they're both dressed in Spiderman costumes.

As tense as the atmosphere is, it's hard not to break into laughter.

"I don't care who it was." Halle drops to the floor and carefully picks the lamp up by its neck. "Both of you, tell Caleb you're sorry and that you'll replace it."

"Hal," I say before the boys can speak. "It's just a light. It's no big deal, I promise." I unplug it from the wall and take the broken pieces from her. "No one's hurt. That's what matters."

She frowns up at me, still on her knees, brushing her fingers over the carpet subconsciously.

"Halle?" I prompt when she doesn't speak.

Her breaths become jagged, choppy, like she's struggling to get air into her lungs.

"Halle?" I repeat. When she still doesn't respond, I hold the lamp pieces out to Casen. "Take this down to the trash."

He takes them, looking from me to his sister and back, brows pulled low in concern. Eventually, he shuffles from the room. Quinn hasn't moved, his expression full of just as much worry.

"I've got her," I assure him, nodding at the door. "I promise."

He dips his head in acknowledgment before quietly slipping out of the room.

Halle slowly raises her head, her eyes welling with unshed tears.

"Baby." The word falls from me as I get down on my knees in front of her and gently cup her rigid shoulders. "What's wrong?"

"I just..." Her face contorts with a pain I wish I could take from her. I wish we could go back to moments ago when I was tying the corset. "I remembered something."

I cup her cheeks, trying not to get too excited about the way she relaxes at my touch. "Do you want to talk about it?"

She shakes her head.

I nod. I can respect that. One day, I hope she'll open up to me, but for now, I won't push.

With a sharp inhale, she blinks and straightens a little. "Actually, I do."

I stay quiet, waiting for her to fill in the blanks when she's ready.

"I knocked a lamp off the table once. I was dancing, just being a kid, you know? It broke, and the guy my mom was seeing back then backhanded me. Gave me a black eye. My mom told the school I fell off our front porch steps. I..." She trails off, attention dropping to the floor between us. "I don't know how I managed to forget that until now."

"The brain is capable of some pretty incredible things." I smooth her hair back from her forehead. "Including repressing memories in order to protect us."

"I didn't scare them, did I?" Lips tipped in a pained frown, she eyes the open door.

I give her a gentle smile. "I think they're just worried about you."

She sighs. "Can't say I blame them."

"Ready to get up?" I'll stay down here on the floor with her for as long as she needs me to, but moving on from this moment may do her some good.

She nods, so I stand and hold my hands out to her.

Even when she's steady on her feet, I don't let go. "How do you feel?"

She gives me a small, barely there smile. "Like I almost had a panic attack, but I'm better now. Promise."

My chest tightens. "You sure? We can stay here if you want."

Her eyes soften, gentle fingers grazing my jaw. "I appreciate the offer, even more so because I know you'd do it without complaint. But we need to go. Seda's waiting. I'm fine, I promise. And if I'm not, I know my way back over here."

I inhale, relishing the flutter of her pulse beneath my fingers. "You mean it? If you're upset, you'll tell me?"

"Promise." She stretches up on her tiptoes and kisses my cheek. "Let's go."

I can't help but catalog her every move as we go downstairs, where her brothers are sitting on the couch, waiting. I worry the party will be too much for her after her near panic attack, but now that the moment has passed, she really does seem to be okay.

Though that doesn't mean I won't continue to keep an eye out for her.

I snag the candy I left on the table near the front door, then usher the group out.

The whole way there, the boys watch their sister carefully. I'm not the only one who worries about her.

Next door, the party is already going, so rather than knock, I walk right in.

"Heck yeah," Laith, who's standing in the foyer nursing a beer, says. "Give me that." He snatches the candy bag from my hand and peers inside it. "You always bring the good stuff."

"Those are for the kids," I reprimand my friend. "And what's with the word *heck*?"

The two Spidermans head past us and into the family room.

Laith groans, scratching at his scruff. "Thayer might've already given me a warning about language. I'm trying to be on my best behavior. My brother's scary when he wants to be." His focus drifts from me to Halle, like he's only just now realized she's here, and as he looks her up and down, he breaks into a Cheshire smile. "Nice costume. We'd make a great couple."

I instantly bristle. I've never been one prone to violence, but I've never wanted to punch someone in the face more. Not even Thayer back in the day.

Halle giggles. She *giggles*. *What the fuck?* Have I been dropped into an alternate reality?

"I guess we would."

My stomach fucking drops.

"Dude." Laith claps my shoulder. "I'm talking about our costumes. Relax. God, your face is priceless."

I glare at my—now—former best friend.

He tips his beer in Halle's direction. "He really likes you."

Halle gives me a soft smile. "That's okay. I really like him too."

"Ugh." Laith groans, head dropped back. "I'm surrounded by couples now. The universe hates me."

"I'm sure there's a lucky girl out there just waiting for you," Halle says, her fingers finding their way to mine.

"Whatever." Grumbling, Laith holds up his beer. "You guys want a drink?"

"We can get them." Chin lifted, I look around for any sign of Seda.

"Sure, sure." He cradles the bag of candy against his chest. "I'm gonna go eat these till I'm sick and cry about my singleness. It's fine. I'm fine." With that, he turns and strides toward the back of the house.

"Is he okay?" Halle asks, squeezing my hand. "Should you go talk to him?"

"He'll be fine." I squeeze back. "He can be a little dramatic at times."

Knowing him, he's probably already digging into a Kit-Kat, having already forgotten his woes.

"Are you sure?" she asks, as I lead her back to the kitchen in search of food and drinks. "He seemed genuinely sad."

Her concern is sincere and not inappropriate at all. My jealousy, on the other hand, is ridiculous. "If it makes you feel better, I'll check on him after we get drinks and find Seda."

"Okay," she agrees, smiling at me.

That expression is like an arrow to the heart. All she has to do is point it in my direction, and I'll be on my knees for her. It's never been like this before.

Though there was a time I didn't believe it, I now see what Salem meant when she said that even though she loved me, what she felt for Thayer was different. This sensation is so much more than I knew was even possible.

Around the kitchen, tubs of ice hold a variety of drinks, and there are platters full of finger foods.

"What do you want to drink?" I bring my lips to her ear to be heard over the music—some kind of rendition of "Monster Mash."

"Just a Coke or Sprite."

I dig through a tub, then pop open a can of Sprite for her and another for myself.

Then, with her free hand in mine, I lead her through the crowd as I search for Seda. It seems like half the residents of Hawthorne Mills are in attendance. I even spot Cynthia and Thelma among them, dressed as witches.

"Daddy!"

Before I can find her, her little body crashes into mine, and she loops her arms around my waist. My heart lurches as I soak in the affection. Every time she greets me like this, I worry it'll be the last.

She pulls away, smiling up at me. "You dressed up as Westley."

"You asked me to." I ruffle her blond hair. "Did you really think I wouldn't?"

She bats my hand away. "I knew you would, because you love me." My girl turns to Halle, her smile just as bright as when she was assessing me. "Hi. You're a pretty pirate."

"Thank you." Halle does some sort of curtsy maneuver that has me fighting a laugh. "And you're a beautiful…"

"Buttercup," I finish for her.

She snaps her fingers, giving me a grateful smile. "Right."

Seda settles her hands on her hips, head cocked, full of attitude. "You've never seen *The Princess Bride*, have you?"

Halle cringes. "No, I haven't."

With a huff, Seda says, "We'll change that. Soon."

Halle leans into me, her mouth at my ear. "I feel like I'm in trouble."

"You definitely are."

"Come on, Daddy." Seda tugs at my sleeve. "Come say hi to everyone."

I need to check on Laith like I promised, but I don't want to run out on my daughter yet either.

"Mom, look! Daddy's here!"

Salem passes over a wriggling Samson to Thayer and

approaches. "I'm so glad you guys could make it. Casen and Quinn too."

"Nice costume," Halle tells her as the two women hug.

Salem adjusts her red cowgirl hat.

She's dressed as Jessie, while Thayer's Woody and Samson is Buzz. I haven't seen Soleil yet, but I can guarantee she's dressed as Slinky Dog or maybe Bo Peep.

"Are you okay here?" I ask Halle. "I want to check on Laith."

Halle nods, offering me a reassuring smile. "I'm okay."

I press a kiss to my little girl's head. "I'll be back in a few."

"Okay," she replies absently, her attention already zeroed in on the twins, who are conspiring in the corner.

God help me there. I knew she'd one day be interested in boys—or girls; that would be okay too—but I'm not ready. And I'm wondering if any parent ever is.

TWENTY-FOUR

Caleb

Laith isn't on the back porch, so I make my way down the steps and past the covered pool. At the base of the treehouse, I tilt my head back and squint into the darkness.

"Laith?" I call up. "Please tell me your sorry ass isn't up there sulking?"

He pokes his head out the open window. "Define sulking."

With a groan, I drop my head back. "I'm coming up."

The treehouse is sturdy, but it's not large, so as I climb the ladder, I ready myself for the tight quarters.

I pop my head through the door, then wiggle my way through.

"Jesus, it's tight in here," I groan, practically rolling over to sit. "And don't you dare make a joke out of that statement."

The glint in his eye dulls. "If you came out here to ruin my fun, you can go," he gripes, digging through the candy bag.

"When Salem asks where the candy I was supposed to bring is, don't think I won't throw you under the bus."

"Whatever," he grumbles, ripping another Kit-Kat open. "I'll buy a bag tomorrow."

I arch a brow. "Halloween is over, my guy." Town-wide trick-or-treating was held last night, so come tomorrow, Salem won't have much need for chocolate.

"Whatever," he gripes.

"Dude," I say, lowering my voice. "Are you actually upset right now?"

"No." He looks out the window, his face drawn. "I'm fine."

"Could have fooled me." I've never seen him look so forlorn.

Laith heaves out a sigh that I swear rattles the entire treehouse. "She's getting married."

My heart sinks. "Who's getting married?"

The glare he levels me with is sharp enough to slice right through me. "Don't make me say it."

"Daisy?"

He flinches. "Yeah." He unlocks his phone and slides it my way. "She looks happy."

I study the picture on the screen. I've never met her. In fact, I don't think I've ever seen a photo. She's blond, with a round, kind-looking face. In the image, she's smiling at the camera, showing off her engagement ring, wrapped in the arms of a man I presume is her fiancé.

"I don't know what possessed me to check her socials today, but I did, and..." He gnaws on another piece of chocolate. "Part of me is glad she moved on when I couldn't, but I'm angry too. Pissed that she could forget me so easily."

Laith has given me bits and pieces over the years. They grew up next door to one another. They were friends, and maybe a little more. When he left for college, they stayed in touch. But when he returned home for his first break, she was different.

"Mixed emotions are normal, man." I hand him his phone back and he tucks it into his pocket. "Maybe it's time for you to get back out there and date."

He opens his mouth, likely to argue with me, but I hold up a hand to stop him.

"*Not* hook up."

"I guess I could try." Head bowed, he digs through the candy bag again.

"Give that here." I snatch it from him.

"Rude," he huffs, holding up a handful he managed to keep.

Silence descends, only the muffled sound of music from the party permeating the air around us.

"Do you want to talk about it?" I ask when he's silent for a long moment.

He sighs, shoving the chocolate into his pocket.

I cringe. As a parent, I have firsthand experience with what happens to chocolate that finds its way into a person's pocket, but I don't say anything.

"What's there to talk about? She moved on and I'm still here." He lifts one shoulder, failing miserably at looking unbothered.

"Laith," I prompt.

He sighs again, deeper this time, the sound tinged with an edge of sadness. "I don't want to talk about it, Caleb. I shouldn't be hung up on her anymore."

"Maybe you should talk to Thayer."

He snorts. "I don't want to talk to my brother about my ridiculous pining."

"Why not?" I zero in on him. "He pined after Salem for, like, six years. If anyone understands, it's him."

Face lowered, eyes fixed on his hands, he deflates. "It really doesn't bother you, does it? Him and Salem?"

I scrub a hand over my jaw. "It did at first," I admit. "I didn't take my marriage vows lightly. But it was hard to stay mad once I saw them together."

Laith groans, dropping his head back. "Why do you have to be such a good guy? Can't you have some sort of flaw?"

I rest my head against the plywood wall and roll my eyes in his direction. "We all have flaws, man. Even me."

For a handful of minutes, we sit like that, neither of us speaking.

"You gonna hang out here a while longer?" I finally ask,

ready to get back to the party. On hands and knees, I crawl to the edge. My back is stiff, the bare floor causing my knees to ache. Is this what getting old feels like?

"Nah," he says, following me. "I better head back in."

I climb down the ladder and wait. Once he's beside me, I grasp his shoulder. "If you ever need someone to talk to, I'm here. You know that, right?"

"Shit, Caleb." He shrugs out of my hold. "Don't go getting all sentimental on me now."

I shove my hands into my pockets. "Dude, you were the one crying in the treehouse."

"I wasn't crying," he huffs.

"Maybe not," I give in. "But you were definitely sulking."

He heaves out a sigh, his whole chest rising and falling. "You've got me there."

The house is packed, making it impossible to find Halle or Seda.

"Where have you two been?" Thayer asks from behind me.

"Just catching up," Laith side-steps me to grab a fresh beer.

Thayer homes in on me. "It's like you two have a secret club, and I'm not invited. I don't know whether to be hurt or glad I'm not getting dragged into Laith's bullshit."

With a shrug, I turn, anxious to find my girls. "Don't know what to tell you, man."

Before I can make it more than a step, he grabs my shoulder. "Hey," he says in a lower voice as I spin back to face him. "If Casen and Quinn are comfortable with it, they can stay the night. Salem and I talked about it."

Suspicion has me narrowing my eyes. "Why?"

He shrugs, looking anywhere but at me. The two of us have come a long way over the years, but that doesn't mean that things don't get awkward at times. "Salem thought you and Halle might appreciate some alone time."

I bite back a laugh. Sometimes I'm reminded of just how strange this arrangement is. My ex is meddling in my love life, and I'm not the least bit offended by it. In fact, I'm amused. Not only because she thinks I need her help, but because she might be right.

"Thanks." I nod. "I'll keep that in mind."

A man I don't recognize taps Thayer on the arm, so while he's distracted, I slip away, going back to my search.

I nearly groan when I find Seda talking to the two Spidermans. If I know anything about adolescence, it's that there's no way this crush won't lead to my daughter getting hurt. And there's not much I can do about it.

Annoyed or not, I leave her where she is and go in search of Halle. When I've scanned every room downstairs and come up empty, I check the front porch. Despite the chill in the air, she's wrapped in a blanket, feet pulled up, swaying lazily in the porch swing.

The door clicks shut behind me, garnering her attention. Her head swivels in my direction, a look of surprise on her face. Though when she recognizes me, it morphs into one of relief.

"What are you doing out here?" I ask, the wood creaking beneath my weight as I cross the porch.

She pulls her legs in to give me space, but when I sit beside her, I grasp them and put them in my lap.

"Just needed to get away for a few," she says softly, her eyes glowing in the orange and purple lights strung around the porch. "It was getting a little too crowded for me."

"There are a lot of people in there," I agree, finding her foot beneath the blanket. I press my thumb into her arch and move it in slow circles.

The moan she lets out goes straight to my dick. Holding myself back has been hard, but it'll be worth it in the end.

"Thayer and Salem said the boys could stay the night if they're comfortable with that."

Brows knitted, she peers over at me. "Why would they offer that?"

I cock my head to the side, lips twitching with the threat of a smile. "Why do you think?"

Her mouth slowly morphs into a precious O, and her cheeks go pink. "Oh."

"We don't have to even mention it to them if you're unsure." The last thing I want is for Halle to feel pressured in any way. The two of us are the real deal, and I'll wait for as long as I need to.

"I..." She smooths out the blanket, her attention averted. "I'm okay with asking them."

I put a hand on her ankle, rubbing softly. "Are you sure?"

"Yes." She looks up then, holding my gaze.

The moment stretches on, the intensity growing between us. It's only more clear in this moment that when I finally have her, there will be no going back for me.

Halle ducks her head. "Should you hang out with Seda a while longer tonight?"

I snort, a mixture of heartache and amusement washing over me. "She was busy chatting with your brothers when I came out. Pretty sure the last thing she wants is for any of her parents to invade her space."

"Ah." Halle smiles softly, nostalgia deepening the brown of her eyes. "First crushes are something. I'm just sorry it had to be my brothers she's crushing on."

I shrug—going for nonchalant and probably failing. "The good news is that the age difference means nothing will come of it. But"—I sigh—"her heart is probably going to get broken anyway."

Her lips tug down into a frown, a line forming between her brows. "I hope not."

With a squeeze to her foot, I lift her legs as I stand. "I'll check on them. If they're done chatting, I'll see if Seda wants to dance with me. It's only a matter of time before she won't want anything to do with me."

Halle's frown deepens. "Don't say that."

I lift one shoulder and let it fall. "I'm just being realistic. Preparing myself for the inevitable, you know."

She presses her lips together, toying with the blanket on her lap. "I would like to think that if I'd had a dad like you, I would've always valued his love and opinion, even when I was a moody teenager." She cracks the tiniest of smiles, dark eyes carefully meeting mine.

I duck my head, holding her gaze. "Thank you. That means a lot."

I've tried my best not to repeat my parents' mistakes. To

love Seda rather than smother her. To encourage her but not overwhelm her. I'm here because I want to be, not because I'm chasing some sort of recognition or clout through my kid.

"I think I'll head back to your place. I'm all partied out." She shoves the blanket off and carefully extracts herself from the swing.

I nod, thankful she came at all. I wasn't sure this would be her kind of thing.

"I won't be long. Salem and Thayer will probably kick everyone out soon so they can get the kids to bed."

"Would you mind taking this back for me?" She holds the blanket out. "And could you give Salem my thanks?"

I drape the offered blanket over my arm. "I will."

Halle holds my eyes, and my stupid heart skips a beat. The air between us thickens, though it's tinged with awkwardness. Dammit. Maybe I shouldn't have mentioned that her brothers could stay the night.

I'm still cursing myself when she clears her throat lightly and says, "I hope they stay."

I blink, taken aback, frozen in place as she descends the stairs to the pavers lining the front walkway.

She's halfway across the yard when I find my voice. "What?"

Peeking over her shoulder, she gives me a smile that's equal parts nervousness and excitement. "You heard me."

My heart takes off as she turns back and makes a beeline for my front door. Only once she's tucked safely inside do I go back in.

I toss the blanket over the back of a chair and catch a

glimpse of Seda. I can't help but grin. She and several other partygoers are dancing to "Thriller." My little girl is doing the dance mostly wrong, but she's waving enthusiastically for me to join.

Without hesitation, I join in, soaking in the time I have with her. Seda's giggles are almost as loud as the music, each one lighting me up inside. The first time I heard her laugh, I was certain I'd never love another sound more. That hasn't changed. Her laughter is infectious.

When that song ends and a ballad begins, she grabs my hands and sways to the music. My heart pangs at the joy in her expression as I shift gears just as seamlessly. Lately, I can't stop thinking about how fast she's growing up. I fucking blinked, and she's ten. I worry that I'll blink again, and she'll be off to college. I want time to slow down so I can cherish every moment. Once these days are gone, there's no going back.

"I'm tired." She wipes the back of her hand against her forehead. "And thirsty."

Before I can reply, she scurries off.

I could use a bottle of water myself, so I head to the kitchen. Halfway there, A Spiderman steps into my path, stopping me. It isn't until he pushes his mask up, revealing heat reddened cheeks, that I can tell it's Quinn.

"Have you seen my sister?" he asks.

Before I can answer, Casen is there too, taking his mask off entirely, his hair a sweaty mess.

"She went home."

They frown at one another, like one person looking into a mirror.

It's so wild how identical their movements and expressions can be. Yes, they have their differences—Quinn prefers syrup on his pancakes while Casen sticks with butter only, and while Casen isn't a big fan of scary movies, Quinn is borderline obsessed—but their synchronicity is a bit jarring at times.

"She's okay," I say. "Just tired."

And probably waiting for me.

I leave that part out.

"Salem and Thayer said you guys could stay here tonight if you want."

Again, they exchange a look, communicating in that silent way they do, this one more considering than concerned.

"Actually"—Casen's the one to speak up—"Thelma and Cynthia invited us to stay the night with them. They're going to teach us how to make pancakes."

"Yeah," Quinn adds. "And we want to keep working on our crochet project."

Pancakes.

Crochet.

I bite back a chuckle.

Halle's twin brothers are turning into little grandmas. It's kind of cute, actually, considering the mischief they can get into. At least Cynthia and Thelma are keeping them occupied.

"What are you crocheting?"

Quinn shrugs. "Just the basics for now."

I have no idea what the basics of crochet are, but good for them.

"That's fine with me. I don't think Halle will care, but I'll let her know."

"Cool. We're going to head over with them now, I think. If Halle isn't okay with it, tell her to text us."

Once they've said their goodbyes to Salem and Seda, they shuffle to the door, where Cynthia and Thelma are waiting.

I give them all a wave. Honestly, between Thelma's sassiness and Cynthia's nurturing personality, it makes sense that the twins have taken up with them.

In the kitchen, I swipe a water from a tub of ice and guzzle half of it in one go. Just as I'm recapping the bottle, Seda pops around the corner, snacking on a cracker.

"Whoa. I am *beat*."

Salem, who stands at the sink rinsing a bowl, bursts into laughter. "Is that so? Your dad just took Soleil and Samson up. Why don't you head to bed too? I'm getting ready to shoo everyone out of here, so you won't be missing anything."

"All right." She stifles a yawn, cracker crumbs slipping from her mouth. With a laugh, she brushes them off. "I'm going to bed. Good night, Daddy." She throws her arms around my waist.

I hug her back, holding on a little longer than necessary. "Good night, princess."

Salem dries her hands on a dish towel. "Are the boys staying?"

Hands shoved into my pockets, I shake my head. "No, actually, they asked if they could sleep over at Cynthia and Thelma's."

Salem's melodic laugh resonates off the walls in the kitchen. "that may be the most unlikely friendship in the history of friendships. But it's cute. At least you still get the night kid-free." She winks.

"Ugh." Groaning, I turn away. "Stop."

"Have fun," she singsongs as I stride for the door.

TWENTY-FIVE

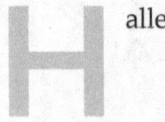alle

Waiting for Caleb to get home just might be the death of me. I'm *nervous*.

A man has never made me feel this way before.

My palms are clammy and anticipation swirls in my stomach. We've been tiptoeing around this for so long. It's surreal to think the moment is finally here. I swallow down my nerves and fill a glass with ice and water. Taking slow, measured sips, I will my heart rate to go down.

Long ago, my grandmother told me that when I found the right one, I'd know. That just seeing him would bring a smile to my face. That I'd want to tell him everything. That my heart would race just thinking about him.

I never believed her before now. My mom acted like that with every man she brought into my life. Yet one after another, they turned out to be assholes, and none of them lasted. So how could love be anything but pain and disappointment?

Eventually, I realized that she was chasing the high and not the person, but she'd been fooled over and over again, so how could I be sure the same wouldn't happen to me?

Once I've finished the water, I dump the ice in the sink and put the glass in the dishwasher—which I'm still not used to having.

This dreaded corset, while perfect for a pirate costume, is massively uncomfortable. But I need Caleb's help to get out of it.

That thought sends a new round of jitters through me. His hands on my body, his breath on my neck...

This feels like my first time all over again—all nerves and anticipation and fear that I'll do something wrong or stupid, and Caleb isn't even here yet.

The longer I wait, the more heat rises inside me. Panting, I lift my hair off my neck and pace the room.

"Stop it," I scold myself two or three laps in. Stopping, I bury my face in my hands. "You're being ridiculous. It's just Caleb."

Once he's here, all my nerves will melt away. But there's no tempering the anxiety while I wait.

I can't stay still. Now that I'm not pacing, my hands

have taken over the nervous movements, fluttering around my body, searching for ways to be useful.

With an audible groan, I drag myself upstairs. Rather than going to my room, I go to his. Caleb has been beyond patient with me thus far. If he senses any reservations, I worry he won't sleep with me tonight. The man is frustratingly perfect. Seriously, can't he have *one* flaw? I'm full of them.

I flick one of the bedside lights on, casting the room in a warm glow, then ease onto the end of his bed, crossing my legs. Instantly, I fidget again, crossing and recrossing and smoothing my hair back from my face.

For what feels like hours, I wait there. And when the front door opens and closes, my heart rate ratchets up once more.

Each beat sounds like *Ca-leb* in my ears, his footsteps on the stairs reverberating through me.

I hold my breath, like that will help this situation at all. Over my thundering heart, I can just make out the creak of a door down the hall. He's peeking into my room, finding it empty.

I didn't think my heart could beat any faster, but there it goes, proving the impossible possible.

My breathing is ragged when the door I left unlatched lets out the tiniest of squeaks as he eases it open.

He doesn't startle when he sees me. If anything, he sags a little, relieved. He closes the door behind him—but doesn't lock it—and leans against it, arms crossed, sizing me up.

"What are you waiting for, Halle?" His voice sounds deeper, huskier than normal.

My heart leaps into my throat. "You."

His lips tip up into a smirk. "And what are you going to do with me?"

The question instills a confidence within me. One I've never possessed when it comes to men.

Carefully, I stand. Then I pad across the room.

His Adam's apple bobs as he takes me in, the only sign that maybe he's a little nervous too. Eyes raking over my face, he drinks me in, the look full of desire but also concern, as if he's searching for any hint of unease. He'll find none.

My instinct is to press up on my tiptoes and kiss him. Instead, I tug my hair over my shoulder and turn around, giving him my back.

"I can't get this off on my own." I peer back at him, and when the need in his eyes registers, my knees nearly buckle.

His fingers tremble as he grips the knot, working it loose. When the ribbon falls to the ground at my feet, the entire corset goes with it. Though he can't see my chest from where he stands, I instinctively reach up to cover myself, but before I can, his hands are there, cupping my breasts.

The heat of his body radiates through me, but despite the warmth, a shiver makes its way down my spine. In response to my shudder, he holds me a little tighter and places a delicate kiss on my bare shoulder, his thumbs moving in slow circles over and around my nipples until they're sharp peaks.

"Caleb," I whimper, begging for more.

"Yes, baby?"

Baby. I've always hated that term of endearment. I used to find it downright patronizing. But from Caleb's lips? It's my new favorite word. Rather than cheap or generic, it's reverent. Like a prayer.

"Don't hold back."

With a growl, he releases my breasts and spins me around. He takes a step back, his gaze dipping to my bare chest, heated, hungry, like I'm something worthy of worship.

As if he can read my mind, he drops to his knees, head tipped back, pure adoration in his expression. His focus doesn't leave my face as he finds the zipper on the right side of my skirt and tugs it down. The skirt falls to my ankles, and he gingerly lifts my right foot, then the left, so he can get the fabric out of the way.

"I've been dreaming of eating this pussy again, Halle. You have no idea how good you taste." He skims his fingers up the inside of my thighs, causing a shiver to work its way through me. He smirks, clearly pleased that he has such an effect on me. "Are you wet already, baby?"

I nod, a quiet little, "Mhm," leaving my lips.

"Spread those legs for me, love. Let me see that perfect cunt."

Buzzing with need, I do as he asks.

His hum of satisfaction is low, rough. "My girl is such a good listener. Aren't you?"

I nod, dropping my hands to his shoulders to steady myself.

With two fingers, he parts my folds. "So fucking wet, and I haven't even put my mouth on you."

"Caleb." His name is a plea.

He grins up at me, clearly enjoying my desperation. "Yes, sweetheart?"

"Hurry up," I beg, my fingers digging into his shoulders.

Rather than hurry, he rubs his fingers back and forth lazily, taunting me, the smug bastard grinning again. Waiting.

"Please." I finally give in.

Rather than reward me, he removes his hand. I cry out in protest, grasping his wrist.

He chuckles. "Don't worry, baby. I'm just taking my mask off."

"No!" I squeeze. "Leave it on."

The way his face is partially hidden behind the mask lit a fire in me that's been burning low all night.

Carefully, he lowers his hands. "You like the mask?"

With a nod, I loosen my grip on his wrist.

"Noted." Lips kicked up, he pops up to his feet. The move is so quick, it startles me, and I take a step back, nearly tripping over my own feet. But before I can go down and completely embarrass myself, he catches my waist and holds me steady.

He dips his head toward me. "You good?"

I nod, unable to find my voice when he's this close. He towers over me, and he smells good. Between his scent and the mask, he's scrambling my brain.

With ease, he lifts me. I, naturally, am not nearly so

graceful. When my feet leave the ground, I let out an embarrassing squeak and wrap my legs around his waist. Instantly, the fabric of his pants provides much-needed friction to the sensitive place between my thighs.

He lays me on the bed, slipping his hands down to my thighs to keep them spread. He takes me in slowly, appreciatively, and all traces of embarrassment melt away. It's impossible to feel anything but empowered when he looks at me like that.

He steps back, eyes never drifting from me, as he undoes the buttons on his black shirt. When he shucks it, letting it fall to the floor by his feet, I nearly groan in relief.

His belt is next. Then he flicks the button of his pants. I'm panting in anticipation now, so damn needy. But instead of lowering his zipper, he stops there, his hands falling to his sides.

"Take your clothes off," I beg as he climbs over me, his hands on either side of my head, his body hovering over mine. God, he's huge and warm and consuming and … *everything*.

"You're cute when you beg." He nips my bottom lip. "But no. Not yet. Not until I get a taste of this sweet cunt again."

He trails kisses down my neck, then sucks a nipple into his mouth. Once he's thoroughly ravaged that one, he moves to the other. I'm writhing, hands buried in his hair, when he finally works his way lower. As his breath fans against my stomach, my skin pebbles and my back arches. The warmth in my core has heated to a full boil, every nerve ending hypersensitive.

When he finally reaches his destination, he drapes my legs over his shoulders and settles in. A lazy flick of his tongue over my clit has my back bowing off the bed.

"So responsive." He rubs his fingers over my slick opening, then slides them inside, his focus fixed solely on my center, his eyes widening as I tighten around him. "God, look at you."

He presses a firm hand on my pubic bone to keep me from wiggling. But I can't help it. My body is primed, set to chase the orgasm already building.

"Patience," he croons. "I promise I'll make it worth the wait."

I growl out my frustration. I've *been* patient. We've been tiptoeing around this moment for weeks.

He works his mouth against me and all thought melts away. My hands are in his hair again, fingers raking over his scalp, tugging the strands, holding on with all I've got. The moan he lets out in response is hands-down the sexiest sound I've ever heard. It's powerful, the realization that going down on me turns him on.

It doesn't take long for my orgasm to crest. It's within reach, growing, on the precipice, when he stops.

The sensation ebbs quickly as his tongue and fingers disappear. "What are you doing?" I protest, my voice laced with annoyance.

He works his pants down his legs, and at the sight of a tattoo on his upper right thigh, all my frustration evaporates. It's so … unexpected. Caleb is a clean-cut kind of guy. The small tattoo on his arm is one thing, but high on his thigh like this? I never would have guessed. But there it is, and it's beautiful. An intricate tangle of vines and flowers with a single butterfly.

"I didn't know you had that," I blurt, pointing at it.

He chuckles, kicking his pants out of the way. "You never asked."

"Is there meaning behind it?"

"Nah. Just thought it looked cool."

Laughter bubbles out of me unexpectedly. Caleb doesn't strike me as the kind of man who'd do anything just because he thinks it looks cool, especially mark his body permanently. But the evidence is right there in front of me.

I hum. "Is there a little bit of rebel lurking under all those button-down shirts?"

Snorting, he grabs my ankle, pulling me farther down the bed. "It's the tattoo that makes you think that? Not my stress smoking?"

Honestly, I'd forgotten about that.

He doesn't expect an answer, evidenced by the way he leans down and kisses me until my breath is gone.

I slip my hand between us, sliding it past the waistband of his boxer briefs and wrapping it around his length. Jesus, he's thick and so, so hard.

"Halle," he grits out.

In response, I work my hand up and down his shaft.

"Fuck." The word is a long drawl. "Baby, I—" The muscles in his neck go taut and he closes his eyes. "Fuck, I'm embarrassingly close to coming. Hold on a minute, babe."

He pulls away from me, sitting up on his knees. I mewl

in protest at the loss of him. He's only gone long enough to grab a brand-new box of condoms and rip the top open. He passes me a single foil wrapper, then tosses the box to the head of the mattress.

He takes the packet from my fumbling fingers with a grin. "Nervous, love?"

I shake my head, and his smile only grows as he rips it open and pulls out the condom.

"Liar."

Once he's sheathed, he lines himself up with my center. I expect him to take it slow, to tease me. Instead, he slides in with purpose, gliding easily against my slick channel.

"Oh, God." My back bows off the bed. Full. I'm so fucking full of him.

He grips my chin, forcing me to look at him. "Don't scream out for him. He's not listening, but I am." He releases me and cuffs my wrists, pinning them beside my head.

The move sends a thrill through me, making my breath catch.

He works himself in and out of me in a slow, measured rhythm, managing to rub against my clit every time he thrusts in, hitting me in all the right places.

In an embarrassingly short amount of time, I'm a panting, needy mess beneath him.

By the rigid set of his jaw and the tendons straining in his neck, he's holding back. I don't call him on it. Right now I'm not sure I can handle more. This moment is overwhelming. *He* is overwhelming. I've never had sex with someone I care about the way I do Caleb, and it's far more transcendent than anything I've experienced.

Without slowing, he releases my hands and finds my clit. He rubs it in tempo with his strokes, sending me hurtling toward the edge.

"Caleb," I whimper, head tipped back. "I'm gonna—"

"Come, sweetheart. Show me how much this pussy likes my cock."

I squeeze my eyes shut as pleasure thunders through me.

I think I scream "holy fuck," but I can't be sure. My entire being has reached a new plane.

It's not that I've never had an orgasm, but for the most part, they've been self-induced, and the presence of this man—his thoughtfulness, his patience, his passion—magnifies the sensation tenfold. The way he touches my clit and whispers my name over and over again like I'm something to be worshipped only extends the pleasure.

As I return to this plane of existence, I force my eyes open and cup his jaw. The awe in his expression is enough to have me nearing that boiling point again. Though he's stripped himself out of all of his clothes, the mask still covers the upper part of his face. I don't know what it says about me that I find it so fucking hot, but I do.

Just drinking him in like this makes my core tighten.

"Jesus fucking Christ," he curses in response. "You feel like you're ready to come again."

I can't respond. I'm incapable of proper speech at the moment. I'm purely moans and whimpers.

He pulls out of me and flips me over like a rag doll, pulling me up onto my knees and slamming back into me.

He fucks me hard and fast, murmuring words of encouragement as he does.

"Good girl. Fuck, you're so fucking hot. I wish you could see how your pussy squeezes my cock. So perfect, baby. So fucking perfect."

My body is still languid from my first orgasm, so I press my chest to the mattress and stretch my arms out in front of me.

"I'm close, baby," he warns. "Think you can come again before I do?"

I mumble something like *maybe*, but it's followed by *if I do, I might die*.

"I think you'll survive," he promises, bowing over me. He winds a hand around my throat and positions me so my back is flush with his front as he pumps into me.

"Almost there, baby," he croons. "God, you're so fucking pretty. Are you gonna let me come all over you? Please say yes. Please."

Oh, God.

Did he have to beg? And why is it so damn sexy?

The heat in my veins flashes. "Yes."

He pulls my head back against his shoulder, his mouth finding mine, swallowing my cries as he works my clit and slams into me, sending a third orgasm barreling through me.

When I go boneless in his arms, he guides me back down onto the bed. I mewl in pathetic protest as he pulls from my body.

I can't see him, but the sound of his hand working against his cock has my pussy clenching in need all over again. Hot streaks of cum hit my lower back and ass as his moans fill the room. My heart lurches at the sound. It may be the sweetest thing I've ever heard.

The mattress jostles, and then he's on his back beside me, pulling my limp body over his, kissing me, long and slow, like we have all the time in the world.

"I knew it would be good," he murmurs between kisses. "But I didn't know it would be like that."

A strange mix of excitement and contentment washes over me. I know exactly what he means.

He wraps his arms around me, pulling me even closer. I'm almost certain my hair is covering part of his face, but he makes no move to push it off.

We lie like that for a long time before he carefully moves from under me and pads to the bathroom. My eyelids are heavy by the time he returns, and when he presses a wet cloth to my back, I startle. Though it shouldn't—this is Caleb, after all—the gesture surprises me. Quickly, though, I relax against the mattress and close my eyes again.

The press of his warm lips to the back of my shoulder has me slowly blinking back to reality.

When I catch sight of him, I pout. "You took the mask off. I liked that."

Chuckling, he presses his teeth into the spot he just kissed. "I know you did, baby. I'll save it for another time. I'm not sleeping in that thing. Come on. I'm going to lift you up and tuck you in."

I'm too tired to protest as he scoops me into his arms

and balances me with ease while he yanks the bedcovers back. Once I'm cocooned in his soft bedding, he climbs in behind me and pulls me close.

I could get used to this.

And though it terrifies me, maybe I already am.

TWENTY-SIX

Caleb

My dreams have become extra vivid. Some so real I've been downright disoriented when I wake up. So, at first, I'm certain the feel of a warm mouth around my cock is all in my head. But as awareness creeps in, I quickly realize it feels a little *too* good.

I open my eyes and scan the dark bedroom. According to the clock on the nightstand, it's just after three.

And Halle's very real mouth is wrapped around my cock.

"Fuck." I draw out the word, covering my face with a hand.

She uses one hand to jack me as she licks and sucks and moans around me. Groaning, I gather her hair and hold it out of the way so I can watch her work in the light of the moon. She's so fucking beautiful. She has no clue how easily she brings me to my knees.

"God, look at you."

She moans at the praise, the sound vibrating against my dick and straight to my balls.

"Fuck," I curse again, gripping the sheets with my other hand.

It's been about a year since I've had sex. I'd love to blame the way I come hard and fast, unloading into her mouth without warning, blood rushing in my ears, on my lack of a sex life, but the reality is that Halle is really fucking good at this, and I can't fucking resist her.

She swallows down my cum and wipes a thumb over her lips, not the least bit bothered by the lack of warning. In my defense, I didn't get any warning either.

She pops up on her knees and crawls closer.

I grasp her hips and hold her in place, scrutinizing her expression. "Are you sore?"

Her brow wrinkles. "Just a little."

With one hand still holding her still, I stroke the base of my once again hard cock once, twice. A third time.

"Ride me."

Her eyes widen in surprise. "But you just—"

"Ride my fucking cock, sweetheart. Don't make me ask again."

Heat flashes in her eyes, maybe from the steel in my voice, or maybe she likes being called sweetheart.

Without hesitation, she positions herself over me and slowly sinks down.

"Shit. Fuck." I curse as I reach blindly for the box of condoms. "Shit, baby."

As if spurred on by my cursing, she rolls her hips against me.

I put a hand on her thigh, pinning her to me. "Let me get a condom."

"Hurry," she whimpers as I finally locate the box and rip out a condom.

"My last tests were negative," I promise, releasing her.

She pushes up onto her knees, letting my cock slip free.

"Mine too," she says as I roll the condom on. When it's in place, she grips my shaft and lines herself up, then lowers herself in one hard movement.

With a shuddering breath, she leans back and rests her hands on my knees, then rolls her hips slowly.

It's pure torture.

The feel of her.

The view.

I want more. I want all of her. Every day. For the rest of my life.

Never could I have imagined falling like this, but it's like my soul recognized hers from the moment I laid eyes on her. I knew—I fucking knew right then and there—that this girl would be everything I've been searching for, for so long.

I cup her breasts, rubbing my thumbs around her peaked nipples. Every fucking inch of her is so goddamn perfect and I'm going to enjoy every second of exploring her body.

Chest heaving, she straightens and presses her hands into my stomach, rocking against me with more force.

"Caleb." The whimpered sound of my name sends me barreling toward release. Knowing I make her feel this way fills me with the best kind of pleasure.

I know what she's going to say. I feel it. But she's not ready for those words. She'll second-guess herself once they're out. So I quiet her with a kiss. I don't want her to regret it later, to blame it on the sex.

"I know, sweetheart," I murmur, kissing along her jaw. "I know."

She drags her nails down my chest, leaving scratches in her wake, as she comes. Holding her thighs, I flex my hips, pumping inside her until my own climax shatters through me.

We cling to each other for a long moment, chest to chest, my arms wrapped tightly around her torso. Eventually, she peels herself off me and sinks into the mattress. I don't want to move, but I force myself to get up and throw away the condom. I use the bathroom and wash my hands, returning to find that Halle is sprawled out on her stomach, arms wrapped around my pillow.

I smack her ass. "Get up and go pee. I let it slide last time, but I won't have you getting an infection on my watch."

She groans into the pillow. "I don't want to move. Your bed is so comfy."

I arch a brow she can't see with her face buried like that.

"You want me to carry you in there and set you down on the toilet myself?"

"God no." She darts up and scurries to the bathroom, closing the door behind her like she's scared I'll come in and watch her.

Laughing, I adjust the pillows and climb back into bed.

When she emerges, wrapped in a towel, the laughter returns. She's covered herself up, as if afraid to let me see her. As if I wasn't just buried inside her. She stands in the doorway, hesitation written on her face, eyes darting from the bed to the door and back again.

"Hal?" I question when she doesn't move. "What's going on in that pretty head of yours?"

She worries her bottom lip, indecision warring on her face. "I was thinking … I can go back to my room if—"

I'm up and out of the bed before she can finish that sentence. I yank the towel off her body, eliciting a small squeal of protest from her, then pick her up and carry her to the bed.

"Caleb." She wiggles in my arms.

I don't slow. On a mission, I set her on the bed, climb in beside her, and pull the covers up.

"I swear, it's no problem," she murmurs. "I'm fine to sleep in the other room."

I wrap an arm around her waist and tug her against me so her back is pressed to my chest.

"Halle." I nip her shoulder. "Have I given you any indication that I want you to leave my bed?"

"No, but—"

"Go to sleep, baby."

With a sigh, she wiggles against me. If she keeps that up for long, I'll be hard all over again. But she's had enough for tonight.

Within minutes, her breaths even out and her body sinks against mine. I stay awake longer than I should, watching her. Maybe that makes me a creep, but I can't take my eyes off her when her face is soft with sleep, when all the worry lines have faded and peace has overtaken her expression.

I smooth her dark hair back from her forehead.

I just want to make everything all right for her. If only she'd let me.

TWENTY-SEVEN

Halle

I wake slowly, feeling as if I completed a vigorous workout in my sleep, and stretch my arms overhead before gradually peeling my eyes open and surveying the room around me. Where I expect to find Caleb, I'm met with cool sheets. The room is bright already, the kind of light that means the sun has been up a while.

Clutching his sheets to my chest, I peek over at the clock.

Nine-thirty.

I grimace. It may not be *super* late, but I never sleep in like this.

On my feet, I relish the sensation of the plush carpet beneath me for a heartbeat before I scurry around and gather up all the pieces of my costume. With them clutched to my chest, I ease his bedroom door open and listen for my brothers. When I'm met with nothing but silence, I sag in relief. They must not be back yet.

I dart across the hall to my room with my clothes clutched to my bare body, exchanging them for a simple pair of jeans and a long-sleeve tee, then head for the shower, where the warm water does wonders to soothe my aching body.

Apprehensive about seeing Caleb, I take my time applying a light base of makeup and swiping mascara onto my lashes.

Finally, when I've run out of tasks to occupy myself with, I creep down the stairs and into the kitchen.

I freeze when I catch sight of Caleb. He's shirtless, and his sweatpants sit low on his hips as he moves around the kitchen with calm efficiency.

I gather myself before he catches me gawking and shuffle to the island.

"Hey." I leave it at that. Otherwise I'm bound to make it awkward.

He looks up from the griddle, where he's pouring pancake batter, and smiles. "Hey, hope you're hungry."

At the mention of food, my stomach growls. Thankfully between the sound of bacon popping in the pan and music playing low in the background, he doesn't hear it.

"Starving."

He wipes his hands on a towel, then strides over and

kisses me. It's so easy. Natural. Like we always openly kiss like this, PDA has been nonexistent.

"How are you feeling?" he asks when he pulls away and goes back to his tasks.

I wring my hands, unsure of what to do with them. "Okay," I finally reply.

He cocks his head, lips pressed together, eyes dancing with amusement.

"Did I fuck the English language out of your brain? Are you only capable of one-word responses after last night?"

"No, I just…" Cheeks heating, I inhale deeply. "Last night was … it was intense." I look down at my bare feet. Intense probably isn't the correct word, but yeah, maybe he did scramble my brain.

With a finger hooked through my belt loop, he tugs me close. When I don't look up, he lets go and uses that same digit to carefully raise my chin. "It was for me too."

"I've never…" My throat closes up, making it hard to breathe, but I force the words out anyway. "It's never felt like that before."

"I know, baby." With a soft smile, he angles in and kisses me. It's just a peck, but it's oddly intimate. Maybe it's the quickness of it, the simplicity, like we have all the time in the world and therefore he doesn't need to linger. "Get the plates out," he directs as he turns back to his food.

Thankful for a task to put my mind to, I set out the plates and utensils at the kitchen table. We normally eat at the counter, but after last night, this meal is one we should sit at the table for.

"Orange juice?" I ask as I pluck the carton from the shelf on the fridge.

"Orange juice is great." He nods. "This is almost ready."

I swipe two glasses from the cabinet and set them on the table, along with the juice. "Need any more help?"

He shakes his head. "I think all we need now is coffee. Want to pour?"

Coffee sounds like an excellent idea. While I slept more soundly than ever and Caleb let me sleep in, we were up late, and our middle-of-the-night activities mean I didn't quite get a full night. I snag a mug from the cabinet, then another, bobbling it when it slips from my hand. Before it can crash to the floor, I grasp it firmly and set it on the counter, sighing in relief.

"How is it possible that you're still nervous around me after last night?" He appears at my side, his hand steadying my shaking fingers. "I know it's not because you're afraid of me, Halle. So, what is it, exactly?"

"I'm scared," I admit.

He carefully plucks the mug from my hand, then fills both with coffee.

"Scared?" He shuffles to the fridge and grabs creamer. "Of me?" He pours until the coffee is more beige than brown, just the way I like it.

"No." I tuck a piece of hair behind my ear and take the mug from his outstretched hand. "Of…" I drop my gaze to the steaming liquid, taking a moment to gather my thoughts.

Thankfully Caleb doesn't press me.

He's still waiting with a patient expression on his face

when I force myself to look at him. "I never thought I'd meet someone that makes me crave a normal life."

Brows knitted, he picks up the spatula and slides pancakes off the griddle and onto a plate. They're a little too done but not burned.

He greases the griddle again, then pours batter for another batch. "What does that mean?"

I take a sip of coffee, savoring the contrast between it and the sweetness of the creamer. "My whole life, my mom bounced from one man to another. Like if she could just find *the one*, that love would fix her. But I swear each guy was worse than the last. It made me wary of traditional relationships—marriage and babies, the whole thing. I've told myself since I was old enough to see what was happening that I wouldn't let anything keep me from being my own person. That I wouldn't get lost in someone else the way she did."

Hurt flashes in Caleb's eyes. "Are you saying I'm a waste of time?" He swallows audibly, the spatula in his hand trembling. "I'm a little confused here, Hal."

"No." Heart lurching, I shake my head. "God, no. That's not what I meant. I … God, I suck at explaining things. I just meant that I never thought I'd meet someone who'd make me want to settle down. To think about the serious things."

A slow smile spreads across his face. "So, what you're saying is you see a future with me?"

I shrug, trying not to appear *too* eager. Regardless of how I feel, we haven't known each other long, so that makes me cautious. Then again, my grandma was eighteen when she met my grandpa. They were married a month later and had a loving marriage. I guess, as ridiculous as it can sound, love at first sight really does exist.

Head bowed, I peer up at him. "Yeah, I do."

Caleb grabs the back of my neck and pulls me in, kissing my forehead. "Don't overthink it."

My first instinct is to bristle at the accusation, but I'm evolving, allowing myself to grow and lower my walls, so instead, I allow myself to appreciate just how well he knows me.

I wrap my arms around his middle and stay like that as he works around me to remove the last batch of pancakes from the griddle. Physical touch has never been my thing. My mom was never overly affectionate, even when things were good, so I suppose it has more to do with what I'm used to. But as my comfort level grows, I find myself wanting to touch Caleb any chance I get.

He rubs his fingers idly against my arm, completely at ease, as he works around my koala hold.

It's only when he picks up the dishes of pancakes and bacon that I finally let go and follow him to the table.

I'm perfectly capable of plating my own food, but when he does it for me, I choose not to protest. More and more, I'm discovering that Caleb enjoys taking care of me.

"You haven't been up too long waiting on me, have you?"

He shakes his head and moves on to plating his own breakfast. "No, I was just pulling out ingredients when I heard you get in the shower. I figured you'd rather have breakfast here than go out."

He thought right—because I'd be convinced that every person we encountered in this tiny town would take one look at my face and know exactly what we did last night.

"I was thinking about asking the boys if they wanted to spend a day in our hometown and visit with friends soon. Would you want to come?"

Asking Caleb to come to my old stomping grounds is a big move for me. I'm not proud of where I came from, but it did shape me into the person I am today, and though I don't have much experience with relationships, I do understand the importance of sharing pieces of oneself, both good and bad.

He surveys me quietly, like he's giving me a chance to take it back.

I won't. I sit straighter, looking him in the eye so he can see the certainty there.

"Yeah." He takes a bite of pancake, his lips curling up on one side. "I would love to come. Would you want to stay the night there? I'm sure I could—"

"Uh, no. The only places to stay are janky motels where questionable activities tend to go down," I mutter.

"No staying the night." He dips his chin. "Got it. But yes, I'd definitely go."

"I'd like that," I whisper, my chest tight.

A raucous peel of laughter spills out of him. "Why do you sound like you're saying that under duress?"

"Because my old town sucks," I gripe as I stab a piece of pancake. "It's not like this place."

He points his fork at me. "It's not full of nosy busybodies?"

"Oh no, it has that too. But it doesn't have any of the charm. This place is cute. Happy. Yeah, it's small, but it's full of life. Arlo Hollow isn't like here. It's small, sure, but it's far more run down and—"

He reaches across the table and presses a finger to my lips. "I've been there before."

"You have?" I squeak, stomach twisting.

He nods. "Yep. You don't have to explain anything to me, Hal."

"I talk too much when I get nervous."

"I hadn't noticed," he jokes.

I stick my tongue out at him, but at the sound of the front door flying open, I bolt out of my seat.

My brothers tumble in, all long limbs and loud voices.

"Did you have fun with—"

Without even acknowledging us, they scramble up the steps, leaving the front door wide open.

"I'll get the door." I'm halfway across the room when Thelma and Cynthia let themselves in. With a sigh, I shuffle back to my seat and pop another piece of pancake into my mouth.

"Hey, lovebirds." Thelma smirks at us as she pads into the kitchen. "You both look freshly fucked and ready to conquer the world."

Those words—*freshly fucked*—coming from this little old lady, make me want to crawl beneath the table, never to be seen or heard from again. Yet at the same time, I have to hold back uncontrollable laughter.

"Thelma," Cynthia scolds, batting at her wife. "Watch your mouth. You're embarrassing her. Look at her face.

She's so red." To me she says, "Breathe, hun. There are only two of us in this house who are old enough to go. Let's not resort to dramatics, okay?"

Caleb snickers and sets his fork down. "You two want any breakfast."

Scoffing, Thelma pulls out the chair beside me. So much for our quiet morning in. "Breakfast was hours ago. I eat at eight sharp every morning. You should try it. It's great for your digestive system."

Despite her speech, she plucks a piece of bacon from my plate and bites into it.

Caleb gives me a look, lips pressed together but twitching, as if to say *can you believe her?*

Yeah. Yeah, I can. If there's one thing I've learned since moving here, it's that Thelma marches to the beat of her own drum.

"The boys were great," she goes on, as Cynthia eases into the fourth seat at the table. "Though I'm sure you were too busy to think about them."

Cynthia heaves a sigh, placing her hands in her lap. "Stop with the guilt trips. We offered." She turns to me with a soft smile. "I hope you both had a lovely night."

I have never wished to be sucked up into a tornado or fall into a sinkhole, but right now, either would be preferable to this.

"It was great." Caleb sends a smirk my way, his chin lifted.

Kill me now, please.

"Good, good." She pats him on the cheek. "Happy to hear it. You deserve it."

I shove my plate away. Nothing kills an appetite like being congratulated for having sex by a pair of elderly neighbors. I might hate my hometown, but there are far more strange people here.

Though I suppose the town and the people in it are growing on me.

Like a weed.

"Well." Thelma smacks the table hard enough to rattle the cutlery. "We better be heading out. Headed to the flea markets today."

Cynthia gives us a gracious smile and eases to her feet. "Your brothers are lovely. We love having them over."

My heart pangs with gratitude. "Thank you. They're really fond of both of you."

I'm not sure I'll ever understand the friendship they've developed, but it's adorable anyway.

They let themselves out of the house, and we're once again alone, since the boys are nowhere to be seen.

Caleb picks up his fork again, eyes dancing. "You're not running away screaming, so I'll take that as a good sign."

Head lowered, I laugh. "Your town is crazy."

"My town?" He tosses a piece of bacon at me. "It's your town too, now."

I pick the bacon—which has landed in my hair—out and drop it onto my plate. "But it isn't named after me."

His eyes darken with heat. "It could be. One day."

My heart stops, my chest pinching painfully. "What did you say?"

"I said"—his smile grows, like he's not the least bit concerned about freaking me out—"it could be yours one day too. If you want it." He shrugs, as if it's no big deal to casually mention that he thinks about marrying me one day.

Yes, I just told him I could see a future like that with him, but this is so much bigger. He's talking about sharing a last name. As I process it, my pulse takes off, my breaths coming shallow.

Halle Thorne.

As the name echoes in my mind, a strange sense of peace sweeps through me. I have to admit, I like the sound of it.

The sounds of my brothers' feet on the stairs, thankfully, kill the conversation. When they step into the kitchen, they stop in their tracks, taking in the spread.

"Can we have some of this?" Casen asks, shoving his hair from his eyes.

"Sure. Help yourselves," Caleb replies, leaning back in his chair. "There's plenty."

They dart across the room and pull out plates, then pile them high with the last of the pancakes and bacon.

"Did you not eat breakfast with Cynthia and Thelma?"

"We did, but we're teenagers," Quinn throws over his shoulder. "We have to eat."

"Like all the time," Casen adds, chewing a piece of bacon.

I sigh, resting my elbows on the table and my chin in my hands. "They're going to eat through my paycheck."

"Good thing your boss pays well." Caleb shoots me a wink that has my stomach doing a somersault.

Before my mind can drift to how he looked above me

last night, naked save for the mask, I clear my throat and focus on my brothers. "Would you guys want to go back to the Hollow next Saturday to see your friends?"

Those of us from Arlo Hollow never use the town's proper name. To us, it's just the Hollow.

Using the twin telepathy they're so good at, they exchange some sort of silent communication.

"Sure," Casen says. "We'll check to see who's free."

Before I can respond, they're looking at each other again, and I swear the temperature drops, telling me that I'm not going to like what they have to say next.

"Could we see Mom?" Quinn asks, his gaze averted.

My stomach plummets.

They haven't asked about visiting her since I took them shortly after she was convicted. The visit was okay, but they haven't asked again until now, and I didn't push the issue. And now that we've moved, I figured … I don't know what I figured.

I *don't* want to see her, but I won't stop them if that's what they want. They haven't been as hurt by her actions as I have. I didn't have an older sibling acting as a buffer the way they do.

It would be cruel of me to say no, no matter how badly I want to.

"Yeah," I say, hoping they don't notice the tremor in my voice. "We can do that."

Based on the sympathetic look Caleb sends my way, I'm not fooling anyone.

"We'll see Mom while we're there."

I just hope I can stomach it.

TWENTY-EIGHT

Caleb

Arlo Hollow isn't as small as Hawthorne Mills, but it's in much rougher shape. The buildings are all run down, and the paper factory at the edge of town makes the whole place reek.

"I don't remember it smelling this bad," Halle says, white-knuckling the steering wheel. She wouldn't let me drive, insisting that if we brought my Mercedes, it would end up vandalized. I didn't bother arguing that I've been here just fine on my own. If I had to guess, she wanted to drive so she could feel like she had some sense of control over what today will bring. "I'm sorry."

I bite back a smile. "Why are you apologizing for the smell? Did you personally build the factory with your bare hands?"

She chokes on a breath. "No, but—"

"Stop apologizing for shit that's not within your control."

Quinn and Casen snicker in the back. Even if I can't get her to lighten up, it's good to hear the sound from them. As soon as we got in the car, Halle began chatting anxiously, and from the worried looks they keep giving one another and me, they're concerned about her.

I had to pull a few strings to schedule a visitation with their mom on such short notice. Honestly, I was hoping my request would be denied for Halle's sake, but she'd never tell her brothers no in a situation like this. She's selfless like that.

Since we have time to kill before their visitation, the boys suggested that Halle show me around.

"That's where I went to high school." Halle points to a building that looks more like a bunker than a school. "And that's where I worked after school."

I take in the hole-in-the-wall diner, trying to picture Halle behind its doors working.

"Were you a waitress?"

"Yep. And after I graduated, I waited tables at…" She grows silent, glancing in the rearview mirror.

"At?" I prompt, scrutinizing her apprehensive expression.

"Atthesapphirelounge," she whispers.

"I'm going to need you to repeat that," I laugh. There's no way I can separate the words she just slurred together.

"The Sapphire Lounge," she says, clearer this time, though her voice is still low.

Before I can ask her about the place, Casen flings himself forward, his head between our seats. "Oh my God, you were a stripper?"

"What?" Halle shouts to the rearview mirror. "No. I waited tables there."

"What was the dress code? A bikini top and thong?" This from Quinn. "Wait." He shakes his head. "Don't answer that. I don't want to know."

"No!" she shrieks. "A crop top and skirt or shorts. I wear less to the beach. Calm down."

"If you had been a dancer, there's nothing wrong with that," I say, tapping my fingers on my leg.

"I was *just* a waitress. The owner asked me constantly, but it wasn't for me. I respect the hell out of the girls who could get out there and do it, though. My tips weren't bad, but they made bank."

"We didn't know you worked there," Casen says, his tone dripping with accusation.

Halle narrows her eyes at him in the mirror. "Are you already forgetting your reaction from five seconds ago? Why do you think I didn't tell you? Besides, you were too young to know."

"What other secrets are you keeping from us?" Quinn asks, the words full of annoyance. "Anything we should know?"

Halle sighs, her grip on the wheel tightening, making the material creak. "No, nothing."

She turns off the main road and onto a side street, breathing deeply. A few turns later, she says, "This is where I lived until I was ten."

The townhouse is small and run-down, with crooked shutters and peeling paint.

"Do you see that black smudge there by the door?" Halle asks, slowing in front of the home.

I squint out the passenger window. "The blob that sort of looks like a heart?"

"Yes." She laughs quietly. "I was five when I did that. I was mad at my mom for ignoring me after she promised to paint with me, so I made that spot. I don't think she ever even noticed it, but it made me feel better."

From there she drives from one apartment complex to the next, pointing out all the places they lived in over the years. From my count, she moved more than once a year after her mom lost the townhouse. My parents have lived in the same house since before I was born. I can't imagine having to be uprooted so often.

It makes sense now, even with as rundown as the house is next door, that she bought it. She was looking for at least a small sense of stability.

As the visitation hour looms, Halle drives toward the prison in another town about twenty minutes north.

We're silent the whole way, but I keep my hand on her knee, trying to instill as much comfort in her as I can.

We stop at the security gate and are directed to park in

the visitor lot. Then we make our way inside, stopping for the scanners and other checks.

"I can go with them," I whisper when the boys wander to the vending machine. "You don't have to see her."

With a sigh, she wraps her arms around herself and rocks back and forth on her heels. For a moment, she doesn't speak, but eventually, she drops her arms and says, "She's my mom. I should see her."

"*Should* doesn't mean you have to," I say as the boys argue over which kind of soda to choose, even though I gave them enough cash for two.

"I know," she says, voice small, as she curls in on herself. "I know," she repeats. "And I don't want to, but who knows when I'll be back here, you know? I owe it to her to—"

I press my hands to her cheeks and force her to look at me. "You owe her nothing. You owe *no one* anything."

"I'll be okay," she says in a whisper, eyes misty. "Promise."

Still, I persist. "If, at any time, you're not okay, then go. I won't judge you if you have to step out."

"Thank you." Her eyes are still watery, but they're full of relief.

The pain radiating from her guts me, but thank fuck I'm here to support her.

The room is filled with a loud buzzing sound, snagging our attention. A door on the far side opens, and a large man in a dark blue uniform appears. "Emerson family? We're ready for you."

The boys dart across the room, soda cans in hand.

"You'll have to leave that here," the corrections officer says to the boys.

Unsurprisingly, they chug their drinks and toss them into the trash.

"Do you want me to wait here?" I don't want to force my presence on Halle when she's already stressed, but I'll gladly go and continue offering her all I can.

She grabs my hand, silencing my worries. "No, I need you with me."

Without speaking, the four of us follow the corrections officer back to an empty private room.

"You guys take the chairs," Halle tells her brothers, shooing them toward the two chairs set up to face the door her mother will be brought through.

They look at her with narrowed gazes, like they're going to insist that she should sit, but she gives them a parental look she's just about mastered, and they slump into them without argument. The two of us find a spot against the wall a foot or two behind them and wait.

About five minutes later—five minutes of nothing but tense silence—the door opens, and a female guard ushers their mom in. She's thin, her dark hair the same shade as her kids', though hers has gray streaks. Her face is gaunt and heavily lined, though she's only in her early forties. I guess it goes to show how much a rough life can affect a person's appearance.

"Kids." She smiles at the twins, opening her arms wide.

Casen and Quinn are up and out of their chairs with their arms wrapped around her within seconds.

She squeezes them tight, kissing the tops of their heads. "My boys."

Beside me, Halle fidgets, but she doesn't make a move for her mother. I give her hand a squeeze to remind her that I'm here and I'm not going anywhere.

Freya Emerson lets go of the twins, and when she turns her attention to her daughter, her smile drops and her eyes flash with an anger that inspires me to straighten and adjust my stance so I'm slightly in front of Halle, shielding her.

"Halle." Her mom's tone is brusque. "Nice of you to finally visit."

"The boys wanted to come," she mumbles, releasing my hand and crossing her arms over her chest.

The loss of her touch is almost painful, but I let her do what feels safest for her without argument.

"Well, how kind of you to allow them to see their *mother*." Freya scratches the side of her nose. "It's good to know I haven't been entirely replaced."

Halle flinches but says nothing in response.

The boys, thankfully, dive into conversation with their mom, asking how prison is and whether she thinks she'll be released early.

All the while, Halle silently suffers beside me, looking like she'd gladly melt into the wall behind us, never to be seen or heard from again.

Every now and then Freya's gaze flickers to her, but she keeps her attention fixed on her brothers.

Halle is tough, there's no denying that, but she's been hurt time and again—particularly by her mom. It seems contradictory for a person to be both tough and vulnerable, but in reality, a person can gain a great deal of strength while being exposed to actions and words that cut the deepest.

As the hour-long visitation winds down, Freya hugs the boys and asks them to step out so she can talk to Halle.

"You can leave too," Freya says to me, her expression hard.

I glare right back at her. "I'll stay with my girlfriend, thanks. I'm an attorney."

Halle blinks up at me, her lips parted in surprise.

Freya barks out a laugh, the harsh sound echoing off the walls. "Good for you, kid," she sneers. "Bagging a Richie Rich. Try to lock it in soon, though, hun. Kids help you do that."

Halle's dark eyes ignite. "That sure worked out for you, didn't it, Mom?"

Freya's cruel smile morphs into a glower. "You took my kids from me."

Halle sighs heavily, as if she's had this argument before.

"You lost them all on your own when you ended up in prison. The courts granted me custody when you were convicted. Would you have preferred they go into foster care?"

"Yes!" She pounds a fist against a table. "At least I could've gotten them back that way."

Halle shakes her head, her jaw working back and forth like she's trying not to cry. "They'll be eighteen before you get out of here."

"That's not true," Freya huffs. "This place is overcrowded, and my crimes are minor compared to a lot of the women here. I'll be out of here early. You hear me?"

Halle scrubs at her face. "Whatever you say, Mom. It's been fantastic seeing you." She turns and stalks to the door.

I follow and knock, signaling that we're ready to go. While we wait for the guard, Freya takes advantage of our inability to escape.

"Mark my words," she says, her tone frigid. "I'll make you regret taking them from me."

While my blood runs cold, Halle's shoulders sag with heaviness, as if she's used to the threats. "Whatever you say, Mom."

Blessedly, the guard opens the door, and as it shuts behind us, I pull Halle into an alcove with a water fountain.

"Are you—"

She wraps her arms around my middle and buries her face in my shirt, her silent tears quickly dampening the fabric.

I palm the back of her head and kiss her crown, wishing I could take the pain away.

Eventually, she gathers herself and pulls away, face splotchy from crying.

I rub my thumbs beneath her eyes, clearing away traces of mascara and smeared eyeliner. "You're okay. I've got you. You know that, right?"

She nods, her eyes downcast.

"Good." With two fingers beneath her chin, I tilt her head back and press a soft kiss to her lips. "Let's go."

TWENTY-NINE

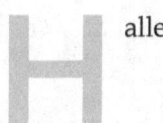alle

The abandoned drive-in on the edge of town may not seem like the kind of place one brings her boyfriend for quality time, but this is where I always ran when things got tough.

"How'd you find this place?" He reclines the passenger seat a couple of inches now that my brothers aren't squished in the back.

We dropped them off with friends, so we've got a little time to ourselves.

"When I was little and the place was still open, Mom would bring me for two-dollar Mondays. It's ... it's another good memory. When I was older, I came here, I guess, to remind myself of the good times."

He probably thinks it's strange to come here after how the visitation went. I'm still reeling from her downright threat. That's all it was. She's not going anywhere for years. Even so, it shook me.

Caleb leans back against the headrest, his hair rustling against the fabric as he turns to face me. I can feel his scrutiny, but I keep my focus fixed on the giant, tattered screen beyond the windshield. I don't want to look at him right now. I can't bear to see the sympathy in his eyes. It'll only cause more tears. For now, I just want to be here with him. I want to exist in this quiet place where it's just us.

"Do you want to talk about what she said?"

I scoot my seat all the way back and recline it as far as it will go. "No."

"All right."

Surprise flutters through me. I was sure he'd push the subject.

We're quiet for a long moment. Eventually I break the silence by saying, "I hate it here."

"Why?" he probes.

"This town is the kind of place where dreams go to die. Most people never get out." I rub at my tired eyes. The mascara I put on this morning is long gone after my crying sesh. Most of it is on Caleb's shirt. I cringe at the thought.

"You got out. And you got your brothers out too."

I slowly turn my head. "I did, but did I really take a step up by purchasing that money pit of a house? It was falling apart before it flooded."

"You're doing the best you can with what you have. You're a fighter. It's how we persist through the hard shit that defines who we are, and from where I'm sitting, you're pretty fucking tough."

My heart splits wide open and pure affection oozes out. How is it possible that this man always knows just what to say?

I lay my hand on his smooth cheek, brushing my thumb back and forth.

"Where did you come from, Caleb Thorne?"

Grinning, he puts his hand over mine and drags my palm to his lips, where he places a soft kiss. "The Hawthorne Mills hospital after a fifteen-hour labor and one failed epidural."

I laugh, surprised at how quickly the weight has eased from my shoulders.

Leaning in, I press my mouth to his.

In return, he palms the back of my neck, pulling me closer and working his mouth against mine. Surprised but suddenly needy for more, I open my mouth and lick into his, savoring the taste of him.

Just as enthusiastic as I am, he tangles his tongue with mine, his chest vibrating as a moan works its way out of him.

The sound alone sends my heart galloping and my core tightening.

"Come here." He clutches my hips and lifts me from the driver's seat with ease. When he settles me in his lap, there's no missing the ridge of his cock at my apex. Gasping, I rock my hips against him, helpless to stop. My hair forms a dark curtain around us, making it feel as though we're the only people left in this world.

Caleb slows the kiss, like we have all the time in the world and not like we're making out like teenagers in the abandoned drive-in parking lot.

My body aches for his. We haven't had a chance to fool around, let alone have sex, since last weekend. Between work and my brothers, it's been next to impossible to find time for anything more than a kiss every now and then.

I've got him all to myself for the next while, so why not take advantage?

"Have you ever had sex in a car?" I ask, tugging at his shirt.

Eyes hooded, he breaks into a lazy smile, not even bothering to help me divest him of his t-shirt.

"Yes," he says, finally lifting his arms so I can yank the fabric over his head. Humming, he brushes my hair out of my face and tenderly tucks it behind my ear. "But I've never had sex in a car with you."

"Smooth recovery," I quip.

He chuckles, lips ghosting over my cheek. "Is this your way of telling me you want me to fuck you in your car?"

An electric current sparks to life inside me. "God. Yes. Please."

He wets his lips, his eyes dark with amusement. "So fucking eager. I like that."

"You bring it out in me." Sex has always been a release, nothing more. Last weekend, Caleb opened my eyes to how much deeper the connection can go.

He cups my jaw, kissing the underside of my neck. "Is that so?"

I nod, my breaths coming faster. We may be new at this, but he's already discovered several sensitive spots like this one.

"I hate to be the bearer of bad news." His tone turns serious as he pulls away. "But I didn't bring a condom."

I bite my lip, but there's no hiding my smirk. "I guess that makes me the bearer of good news. I picked some up when we stopped for gas this morning."

He laughs, his body shaking beneath mine and causing the seam of my jeans to rub against me in just the right way, creating a mix of pleasure edged with the tiniest bit of hurt.

"You planned this," he accuses, pressing his thumb into my bottom lip.

Without my permission, my pelvis rolls over his, sending arcs of desire through me. "No, but I—"

He cocks a brow and forces my hips to still.

With a sigh, I mutter, "I hoped."

"Naughty girl." He nips at my neck. "Where are they?"

I scramble back to the driver's side and pull the plastic bag from beneath the seat, then dig out the small package and hand it to him.

He looks them over, his entire face lit up in a combination of need and amusement.

"You make me horny," I whine. "Stop judging me."

With a groan, he adjusts himself in his pants. "I'm not judging, sweetheart."

I pout, head lowered. "It feels like you are."

His eyes narrow and his nostrils flare. "Get back over here so I can show you just how nonjudgmental I can be."

I don't have to be told twice. Quickly, and a little awkwardly, I maneuver my way back over and settle into his lap.

He opens the box and sticks a condom wrapper in the empty drink holder, then tears my shirt off over my head. With nimble fingers, he pops the button on my jeans and lowers the zipper. When he slips his hand past the waistband of my panties and finds my pussy already wet for him, he groans.

"All this for me, baby?" he asks, stroking his fingers through my folds.

My hips rock against the friction, desperate for more.

He slaps my ass with his other hand, and I cry out, bracing my hands on the seat on either side of him, cheeks burning from the combination of pleasure and pain.

"I asked you a question, Halle."

"I..." My brain spirals. *What did he ask me?*

All this for me, baby?

As his words replay in my head, the warmth in my belly turns up a notch. "Yes. All for you. Only you."

"Mmm," he hums. "Such a good girl. You look so pretty riding my fingers, but you want my cock, don't you?"

"Y-Yes," I whimper, head thrown back. "Please."

He sucks at the sensitive skin of my neck. "I really like it when you beg." With a thumb, he presses against my clit.

Eager, desperate, so turned on, I rock against his hand once, twice, a third time, and then I come.

He silences my cries with a kiss, working his fingers into me until the orgasm fades.

"You're so pretty when you come, Halle. You have no idea."

He grasps my hips, urging me up onto my knees, then works my pants and underwear down, steadying me while I lift one leg, then the other, to get them off entirely.

With both hands, he grasps my bare ass cheeks and puts me right where he wants me, so my core is lined up with the thick length still encased in his jeans.

Reaching behind me, I unclasp my bra, and when I slip it down my arms, he drops his head back against the seat, groaning, and takes in my bare breasts.

"It should be against the law to be this perfect," he rasps, throat thick with desire.

I'd argue that they're too small, too pointy rather than gently rounded. But when he looks at me like this, it's hard not to believe every word he says. He cups my breasts, fitting them easily in his big hands.

"Caleb," I whimper.

He rubs his thumbs against my pebbled nipples. "What do you need, baby?"

"You." I drag my hands down his bare torso to his belt. "That's all."

"You have me, Halle." He kisses me, his hands cupping my jaw. "You've had me far longer than you realize."

"Fuck me," I beg, yanking on his belt. "Please."

He grins, kissing me again. "Whatever my girl wants."

I add the belt to the pile of clothes on the driver's seat and pop the button on his jeans, then slowly slide down the zipper. I'm taking my time the way he always does. Like I did as a kid, opening the few presents I received. I always cherished every part of the process.

Impatient, Caleb lifts his hips, sending me wobbling, and shoves his jeans and boxer briefs down to his knees, freeing his cock.

God, it's beautiful. I never thought this part of the male body was all that great to look at, but Caleb has changed my mind, and he doesn't even know it.

I trace my finger along a vein in his shaft, and he bucks his hips in response.

"Baby," he warns. "It'd be awfully embarrassing if you made me come that easily, and believe me, I'm dangerously close."

I lean in, mouth against his ear. "I think you mean *hot*. It would be insanely *hot* if you came that easily."

He zeroes in on my face, the intensity in his expression causing my skin to pebble with goose flesh.

"Grab the condom," he commands.

Without hesitation, I snap it up and tear open the wrapper.

He takes it, and I watch with eager fascination as he fits it onto his thick cock.

"Halle?" he whispers, encouraging me to lift my hips.

"Yea—"

He wraps his arms around me and drives up into me in one smooth, hard thrust.

I scream, grasping the head rest to steady myself. "Holy fuck!"

He rolls his hips, grazing my clit with every upward

thrust, the deliciously violent moves causing colors to dance behind my closed lids.

"Fuck, baby. You're squeezing my cock so tight. Keep that up and I won't last long."

"Can't help it," I pant, barely holding on.

He grasps my throat, holding just tight enough to disrupt the flow of oxygen as he drags my mouth to his.

Never did I think that the straitlaced man in the suit, with the tidy home and responsible car, would be this intense.

"You ride me so good," he praises, eyes hooded. "Such a good girl."

I whimper at the praise and gasp for air. "Caleb."

"Tell me how good it feels." He loosens his hold on my neck for a moment, then tightens it again. "Tell me how much you love the way I fuck you."

"It's so good," I cry out. "You have no idea. You fuck me so good."

"That's right," he growls. He slips his hand from my neck to my chest, his palm flat on my sternum, and guides me until my back rests against the dashboard. "No one can fuck you as good as I can."

He finds my clit with a thumb and rubs it in time with his thrusts.

"Caleb. Oh, God." I rake my nails down his chest, only coming to a stop when they land on his abdominals. How is he so ripped? I swear he must live at the gym when he's in Boston. That or he works out so damn early I've never caught him doing it.

The hand on my hip tightens, his thumb digging in hard enough to leave a bruise. "Tell me what you need, baby."

"To come. I need to come again."

It's right *there*. I'm teetering on the edge. All I need is—

He presses his thumb firmly into my clit, and I detonate, an intense orgasm taking over, making my vision go black and my body lose all control. I crash into his chest, biting into his shoulder to quiet my scream.

Caleb doesn't slow, his frenzied movements dragging out my orgasm far longer than seems humanly possible.

"Fuck, fuck, fuck." I lean back, bracing my hands on his knees, watching the way he fills me, whimpering at the sight of his length disappearing with each roll of his hips.

"That's it, baby." With his hands firm on my waist, he guides me. "Ride my cock."

He swells inside me, his length dragging perfectly against my inner walls, ratcheting up my need again. If I keep this up, I'll be rewarded with yet another orgasm.

I've never been this responsive to a man. It's about so much more than just attraction. With Caleb, I have a connection unlike anything I knew existed.

A fourth orgasm sweeps me away, pulling a long, low cry from my throat. His low moans echo in my ears as his hips stutter and he pulses inside me, filling the condom.

Our breaths are out of control, our bodies sweaty. I don't make a move to get off him, and he doesn't encourage me to move. In fact, he wraps his arms around me like that's the last thing he wants.

Gradually, our breaths even out and sync up. I rest my ear over his chest, letting his heartbeat settle me.

Eventually, he releases me, but I cling to him like a baby monkey, not ready to let go. He chuckles and maneuvers around me to pick up our garments from the driver's seat.

He holds my bra up first. "Time to get dressed, baby."

With a sigh, I lean back and reach for the bra, but he yanks it away and shakes his head, insisting on dressing me again.

I let him clasp it behind my back and slide my shirt on, but there's no way I'll get back into my underwear and jeans while I'm on his lap, so I slide back into the driver's seat to finish dressing.

Caleb finally removes the condom, tying it off and shoving it into his pocket as he yanks his jeans and boxer briefs back into place.

Once we've mostly righted ourselves, I start the car, ready to pick my brothers up and get home. Before I can put it in gear, though, Caleb grabs the side of my face, pulling me in for a long kiss. When he pulls back, he gives me a long, steady look.

He doesn't have to say anything.

I don't either.

But it's there between us, those three words I'm not ready to speak or hear. The words that just might ruin me.

THIRTY

Caleb

At the sound of a creaking step, I spin and find Halle padding into the room. The sun is high in the sky, the kitchen, where I'm working today, lit up with natural light.

I straighten from my slouched position on a barstool when the defeat in her expression registers.

"What's wrong?" Without waiting for a response, I'm up and out of my seat and striding for her.

She tucks her phone into her back pocket, shaking her head like she can shake off the look.

"I ... that was the guy who's going to repair the flooring.

He said they had a cancellation, so they can start on my place early. They'll be there tomorrow."

"Oh." The news hits me like a ton of fucking bricks to the chest. It's *good* news, I suppose. Halle and her brothers can return to their home and their normal lives. But I've loved having people in my house. It's made it feel like a home again. I've loved having *Halle* here even more. Her brothers too. They feel like family. "That's good news."

"Yeah, it is." Despite her agreement, her words are full of dejection.

I cup her cheek, rubbing my thumb along her smooth, soft skin. "You don't sound happy about it."

Her whole body deflates. "I'm being stupid."

I angle her head back, forcing her to look at me. "Whatever you're feeling, I promise it's not stupid."

She bites her lip, her eyes darting away from mine.

"Shh." I move my hand down to her neck, relishing the way her pulse flutters against my palm. "Just tell me."

With a groan, she lifts her arms and lets them drop to her sides. "What if we move back home, and you … we … What if with the distance is too much?"

It takes effort to hold back laughter. It's ridiculous. "Distance" in this respect is a quarter of an acre at most. But if I laugh, it'll only confirm, in her mind, that her insecurities are silly.

"Baby." I pull her in close.

She's stiff at first, but I hold tight, and like I knew she would, she eventually melts into me.

"I hate to break it to you." I bury my face in her hair.

"But you live next door. I don't think you need to be worried about the distance. What's the real issue?"

She rests her chin on my chest and pouts up at me. It's fucking adorable. A quirk I never would have expected from her until a few weeks ago. She's gotten comfortable with me. More and more, bits and pieces of the true Halle peek out, like the sun appearing between the clouds on a rainy day.

"I don't know."

I rub my finger down her temple, then her cheek. "I think you do know. There's nothing to be ashamed of. I can't make you feel better if you don't tell me what's really wrong."

With a sigh, she tries to pull away, but I hold her there. "What if when I'm not here all the time, you realize I'm not really that great and you don't want to see me anymore?"

This time I can't help but chuckle. With a hum, I trace the slope of her nose. "That's not going to happen, pretty girl. I've been enamored with you since the moment your brothers whacked me on the head with a soccer ball."

She scrunches her nose. "Ugh. Don't remind me."

Laughing, I drag my hand down the column of her neck. "You're worrying about things you don't need to, but I'm glad you're talking to me about it. I can't help you through it if you keep your thoughts to yourself." I tap the side of her forehead, driving home my point. "Now that we've handled that, are you ready for lunch? I was thinking about making sandwiches."

"Yes, please." This time when she pulls away, I let her

go. "I'm starving." Likely knowing I won't let her help, she hops up onto the counter. "You spoil me."

I pull out lunch meat, then a loaf of bread. "Making a sandwich for you isn't spoiling you. It's called providing for you."

"Ah." She sways her feet back and forth. "Is that what we're calling it?"

I pop four slices of bread into the toaster. "Yep. If I'm going to spoil you, it'll be with more than a simple turkey sandwich."

Her expression softens. "I'm not the kind of girl who needs anything lavish."

My chest warms. "Maybe not, but you deserve it."

She drops her head back with a groan. "Can you stop being so perfect? Your existence alone has got to be a sore point for the rest of the male population."

I nearly choke on a laugh as I twist the lid off the mayo. "Maybe the rest of the male population needs to learn that they'd be nothing without women."

She opens her mouth, but before she can respond, her phone rings. With a huff, she pulls it from her pocket. "Watch it be the contractor calling to say that instead of starting early, he'll actually have to delay the project." With a finger hovering over the screen, she frowns. "It's the school." She answers, her expression stony, but after the space of a couple of heartbeats, her eyes go wide and her lips part in horror. "I'm on my way."

That's all she says before she leaps to her feet and pockets the device.

"What happened?" I ask, grabbing the ingredients so I can shove them back in the fridge. "Are they okay?"

Her hands flutter at her sides, her mind a million miles away. I throw all the items onto the top shelf, slam the fridge, then cup her cheeks, worried she'll have a panic attack.

"Halle, breathe. Tell me what's going on."

Her eyes dart frantically about the room. "Keys. I need my keys."

"Not like this, you don't," I argue. "I'll drive you wherever you need to go."

Her anxious gaze finally meets and holds mine. "The hospital. I need to get to the hospital."

Halle all but slams her body into the desk just inside the entrance.

"Casen Rose. I'm here about Casen Rose."

The bored-looking receptionist takes her time looking up. "Are you family?"

"Yes." Halle blows out a frustrated breath, making the hair around her face flutter. "I'm his sister and guardian."

The receptionist taps on her keyboard, still taking her sweet-ass time. "It looks like he's still in the emergency department. If you head through those double doors there"—she points to our left—"follow the hall to the end and turn left. Then look for the ER sign. It'll be on your right."

Halle takes off in that direction, and I give a muttered, "Thank you," before following her.

Once we find the emergency department, we're stopped at yet another reception desk.

"I'm here for my brother," Halle says without preamble. "Casen Rose. I'm his guardian, Halle Emerson. He was brought in by ambulance from his school."

This receptionist is much more reactive than the first. She has a pass filled out before Halle has finished rattling off this information.

"Bay twelve on your left," she says, handing the visitor sticker to Halle. "Are you gonna need a pass too?" The receptionist peers over at me.

"Yes, ma'am," I answer, as Halle bounces in place beside me.

"Name?"

"Caleb Thorne," I answer. "Go," I tell Halle. "Don't wait for me."

She bites her lip, brow furrowed like she doesn't want to leave me. But her worry for her brother wins out, as it should, and she takes off.

"Here you go."

I stick the badge to my shirt, heading in the direction Halle disappeared in.

A minute later, I find her in room twelve. Casen lies in a bed that takes up the majority of the space in this small room, his normal olive-toned complexion replaced with an ashen pallor.

Halle's hands flutter around his body like a frightened butterfly unsure of where to land.

"Case," she whines. "What happened?"

He winces. "I fell wrong during gym glass."

"Your leg is broken!" Tears pool in her eyes. "That's a big thing."

He groans, covering his face. "I know."

"Have they given you anything for pain yet?"

He nods, his bottom lip wobbling in a way that's rare for fourteen-year-old boys. "I overheard the doctor saying I'll need surgery to set the bone. I don't want to have surgery, Hal."

"Fuck," she curses, taking a step closer. "It's okay. If that's what has to be done, we'll get through this. I'm here for you, no matter what you need."

"Where's Quinn?" he asks.

The question isn't a surprise. Of course he'd want his twin here.

"Still at school," she answers.

"Is he going to come?" Casen asks.

Halle sighs, clearly too overwhelmed to process how to handle the situation.

"School will be out in an hour or so," I say, squeezing Halle's shoulder. "When he gets off the bus, I'll have someone bring him straight here, okay?"

Casen assesses me, his expression full of more emotional intelligence than a kid his age has any right to possess. "Thank you."

I dip my head in acknowledgment and pull out my phone. I shoot off a quick text to Salem, who responds almost instantly, more than happy to help out.

"Can I hug you?" Halle asks her brother. "I don't want to hurt you, but I just … I really need to hug you, okay?"

Casen opens his arms. "It's just my leg, sis. My arms are fine for a hug."

With a watery laugh, she dives in to hug him. "When the school said you were being transported by ambulance, I was so scared. I don't want anything to happen to you."

"Back at you, Hal." He pats her back and lets go.

"What happened?" she asks him, plopping into the chair on his left.

He sighs, scrubbing a hand over his face. "We were playing football outside. I was running for the ball, and my feet got tangled." He holds out one arm, his hospital bracelet slipping down his wrist. "Now I'm here."

Halle laughs, though the sound lacks humor. "You were a clumsy baby, so I guess I shouldn't be surprised that you're a clumsy teenager too."

"Hey," he laughs. "Don't kick me when I'm already down."

She leans over and squeezes his hand. "I love you, Case. Don't scare me like that again."

"Love you too, Hal. And no promises. Accidents happen."

With a sigh, she looks up at me. "Yeah, they do."

THIRTY-ONE

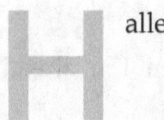
Halle

Even as infants, it was nearly impossible to keep my brothers apart. They'd cry any time they were out of sight of one another. Identical twins are like that. They're still thick as thieves, so it doesn't surprise me when Quinn insists that he's staying the night at the hospital and that he has no intention of going to school. He needs to be here while Case is in surgery, and I can't blame him for that. I couldn't imagine being anywhere but in this room with my brothers.

Caleb, who's sitting in an uncomfortable chair in the

corner, rubs his jaw. Casen was moved to an overnight room an hour ago, so we have a lot more space.

"You should go home," I tell him.

"I'm not leaving you." The words are firm, automatic.

I sigh. This man thinks I'm stubborn, but he's just as bad.

"How about you pop into the house and grab a few things we might need?" I suggest instead.

This time he nods, his face fixed in a thoughtful frown. He doesn't do well if he doesn't have something to *do*. He always needs to be helping.

"I can do that. I can bring dinner too."

"Yes, please, God!" Casen cries from the bed. "Don't subject me to hospital food."

Caleb laughs. "Text me what you want. I'll be back." With that, he heads for the door.

Just as he's slipping out, I hop up and scurry after him. "Hey," I say, grasping his wrist.

"Yeah?" He looks me over, his face a mask of concern.

I pop up on my tiptoes and press my mouth to his.

He kisses me back, soft and slow. Sweet.

With a sigh, I let him go. "Thank you."

"For what?" he asks with a scoff. "Picking up a few things?"

"No." I shake my head. "For being you."

Caleb Thorne has a heart of gold. I can't imagine there's another soul on earth who is as truly good at their core as this man is. If he has a serious flaw, I haven't come across it yet.

He pulls me in for another quick kiss. "Don't forget to text me your food order too."

With that, he turns and heads to the elevator bay.

I watch him until he disappears from my sight, then head back into the room. As the door closes with a soft click, I find two pairs of eyes fixed on me.

Quinn leans back in his chair, arms crossed behind his head, a smirk dancing at his lips. "Did you have fun kissing your *boyfriend*?" He sings the last word in a playfully taunting way.

"Shut up," I grumble, cheeks heating.

"Are you going to marry him?" Casen teases from the bed.

I sigh, eyes narrowed on him. "It's good to know you're still capable of taunting me, even with a broken leg."

Case laughs, his expression much more relaxed than it was when we first settled into the room. Likely because of the second round of pain medicine the nurse brought by about half an hour ago.

"In all seriousness," Quinn says from his chair. "We're happy that you're happy."

There's no stopping my smile. I don't need my little brothers' approval, but that doesn't mean I don't appreciate it. "Thank you."

"Caleb's a cool guy," Casen says. "Aside from his taste in women, that is."

"Hey." I scoff. "Now is not the time to be ribbing me. I *cried* over you."

"Aw, come on, Hal. It's just—"

I point at him in warning. "If you say it's just a broken leg one more time."

"All right, all right," he cajoles, both hands held up in front of him.

"Can I trust you here alone?" I ask Quinn.

He rolls his eyes like my question is the most preposterous thing he's ever heard.

But I know my brothers. There's a good chance that if I leave, I'll return to find all the drawers rifled through and the two of them making balloons out of gloves.

"Yes. I'll be fine, and it's not like Casen is going anywhere."

I take a deep breath—still not fully convinced that I won't come back to discover some sort of shenanigans have happened in my absence, but I'd give just about anything for a coffee from the snack station the nurse showed me earlier.

Though Casen's room is equipped with an en suite, I stop by the restroom at the end of the hall. Once I've relieved myself and my bladder has thanked me for finally listening to it, I wash up and head to the snack station on the other side of the wing.

I grab a soda for each of the boys and a water and coffee for myself. I even snag a couple of protein bars and bags of chips. Case must be starving. He missed lunch, just like I did.

Juggling the drinks and snacks, I manage to get the door open. Inside, Case and Quinn are discussing a new video game they're excited about.

With a huff of a breath, I set all my finds on the tray.

"Sweet, is that for me?" Casen asks, pointing at my haul.

"All for you, kid." I hold out a can of Coke and a protein bar.

"Hey, what about me?" Quinn gripes.

I flick my finger at the assortment of goodies. "Help yourself."

Quinn snags a protein bar and a Coke for himself while I settle into a chair with my coffee and a bag of Little Bites muffins. I'm so hungry that I could easily be convinced the slightly squished, almost soggy pastries are gourmet.

"What do you want for dinner?" I ask. If I don't text Caleb soon, he'll be hounding me for our order, I'm sure.

They each rattle off three or four places, talking over one another.

I shake my head at the blending of their voices. "I got none of that. Discuss among yourselves and let me know what you decide."

Once they have their orders figured out, I text the extensive list to Caleb.

Tired doesn't even begin to describe how I feel. Exhausted barely scratches the surface. The moment I answered the phone call from the school, my body went into fight-or-flight mode and still hasn't quite returned to normal.

I sip at the coffee, hoping it gives me the spark of energy I desperately need to make it until Caleb returns and I can change into more comfortable clothing.

As I take another sip of coffee, I will myself not to panic about Casen's upcoming surgery. It's a challenge to keep my knee from bouncing and my breaths from getting shallow. Surgery is a big deal. Getting put under, cut into—

Blowing out a long breath, I put a stop to my thoughts right then and there. I can't go down this path. I won't let myself spiral. Not when I need to be strong for him. He's the one who has to endure it. My job is to provide support.

After what feels like years, Caleb returns, arms weighed down by supplies and food.

Quinn sits with Casen, using his brother's hospital bed as a shared table, while Caleb and I sit side by side across the room.

"Thank you for this," I say quietly. "I'll give you money for dinner."

Caleb levels me with a sharp look that stops me cold—not because I'm scared of him, but because it heats my blood. It seems impossible that my libido would stir to life so easily when I'm dead on my feet, yet here I am, practically panting for him.

"You're not giving me money for dinner."

Hackles rising, I straighten. "Sure I am. This couldn't have been cheap. They each got two burgers and—"

"Let me provide for you, Halle." He ducks in close, his voice low, vibrating through me. "It gets me hard."

I snort a laugh. It feels good to find a little humor after such a shit-tastic day. "Providing for me makes you hard?" I mutter. "You're ridiculous."

"What? A guy can't get off knowing that he's providing for his woman?" He takes a bite of burger.

I arch a brow, fighting a smile. "Oh, and now I'm your woman?"

"Yep." With his free hand, he picks up his soda. "That's right."

Head lowered, I give it a shake. "I think I like this side of you."

"What side?"

"All…" I wave a hand. "Possessive. It's very hot."

"That's what makes you hot? When I call you mine."

I bite my lip, heat pooling in my belly. "Yes."

Thank God my brothers are too busy talking about friends and crocheting with Cynthia and Thelma to be eavesdropping on our conversation. Otherwise, they'd be traumatized. They don't want to hear about my sex life any more than I'll want to hear about theirs when they're older.

That thought stops me cold, and the food I've just consumed turns to lead in my stomach.

Did Mom ever give them a proper sex-ed talk? Doubt it. And school only does so much.

The ball of dread in my gut grows. Fuck, fuck, *fuck*.

I'm going to have to give my teenage brothers the sex talk.

I'd rather be put under the knife in Casen's place.

"Hey," I say to Caleb, heart thudding. "Would you give my brothers the sex talk?"

Caleb blinks, his hand paused in midair, fries dangling from his fingers, and bursts into laughter. Casen and Quinn look our way but shake their heads and return to their conversation.

"Oh," he blurts out when all I can do is stare at him. "You were serious." He clears his throat and drops the fries back into the bag. "Can I ask *why* I would need to do that?"

"B-because ... I'm their sister," I say, stumbling over my words. "That would be the most awkward conversation of my *life*. I can't do it."

"They're almost fifteen. I'm sure they know—"

I grab Caleb's wrist. "Yes, I'm sure they do, but I need to ensure they understand how to be responsible. That if they're going to have sex, they'll use condoms, Caleb! They need condoms!"

It's only when I snap my mouth shut that I realize that the room has gone eerily silent.

Oh, crap.

I slowly turn and find that a doctor has come into the room. He's looking at me, wide-eyed. So are my brothers.

I want to crawl in a hole and die, though the embarrassment may kill me first.

"Hi." I give the doctor a forced smile. "Just talking about safe sex! You know, normal stuff."

He frowns. "I gathered that."

I keep smiling, even when the expression feels more like a grimace.

"I'm here to do my rounds and check on your son."

"Brother," we all respond with scary precision.

"Brother." He nods once. "He's scheduled for surgery tomorrow at eleven. Is that correct?" He zeroes in on me, brows lifted. "You'll meet the surgeon in the morning, and they'll go over the details then."

He's finished with his checks in a matter of minutes. In that time, I pray the sex-slash-condom conversation has blown over. I should know better.

"So..." Quinn angles his chair toward us. "You think we need the sex talk?"

I let out a sigh and sink low in my chair. "Listen, you're probably old enough to be interested in girls, and you might be curious about sex. And I just..." My heart lodges itself in my throat. "Don't come to me with details, please, but if you have questions, I'm here. And please, for the love of God, be safe. As much as it pains me, if you won't go buy condoms yourselves, then tell me, and I'll handle it."

Quinn snickers, bringing a fist to his mouth. "You look like you swallowed nails."

"Feels like it too," I gripe, wanting to sink through the floor. "Just promise me you'll come talk to me if you need to, okay? Then I'll never bring this up again."

"Sure," Quinn agrees with a shrug.

Case nods and gives me a salute. "Yep, you got it. Safe sex. Great talk, sis."

Beside me, Caleb watches the entire exchange, his lips curled in amusement.

"Stop smiling," I groan. "It's pissing me off."

His grin only gets bigger. "My smile is making you angry?"

I frown, annoyance rolling through me. "Yes. So, stop it."

He flattens his lips into a straight line, but it's no use. In a matter of seconds, they're twitching again.

"I hate you," I mutter.

"No, you don't," he volleys back.

I shove another bite of food into my mouth to keep from saying more. Because he's right. I don't.

I think I'm very much in love with Caleb Thorne.

THIRTY-TWO

Caleb

"I'll be in the waiting area the whole time, and as soon as they give me permission to be in recovery with you, I promise I'll be there." Halle smooths Casen's hair back from his forehead.

I lean against the wall, watching the exchange, my chest aching. It's all too easy to imagine a much younger Halle caring for her baby brothers.

"Everything's going to go fine."

"I know it is," Casen says. He may be wearing a stoic expression, but there's no hiding the fear in his eyes.

"I'll be there too." Quinn gives his brother a pat on his shoulder.

"All right, guys," the nurse says from the door. "It's time to head to the OR. You know where the waiting room is?"

Halle nods, then kisses Casen's head. "I love you. You're gonna do great." She gives his hand a squeeze and steps away.

Quinn takes her place, saying goodbye to his twin, and then the team wheels Casen out of the room.

Once we've gathered our things, we shuffle to the designated waiting room, and Halle sinks into one of the uncomfortable plastic chairs, covering her face with her hands.

"Are you … crying?" Quinn asks as he plops into the seat beside her.

She lowers her hands, revealing her tear-stained face. "Yes, I'm crying. I'm supposed to keep you two safe. It's my job to protect you, and now Casen has a broken leg and needs surgery. That's my fault."

Quinn frowns, his brows knitted together. "How is it your fault? He ran and fell wrong. At school. It was a freak accident."

"It doesn't matter." A breath shudders out of her. "This kind of shit didn't happen when you lived with Mom." A sob escapes her as she cups her hands over her red, splotchy face again.

I sit beside her and silently take her hand, wishing I could take the pain away.

Quinn snorts. "Sure it did." He rolls up the sleeve of his shirt, revealing a scar on the underside of his bicep. "I fell on the steps outside of that house on Cellar Road. You remember the one? Needed stitches."

Halle frowns. "I ... how did I not know about this?"

With a shake of his head, he rolls the sleeve back down. "Mom made us swear not to tell you. She knew you'd be pissed, but it was an accident. Just like this was. If you're to blame for anything, it's caring a whole lot, and I don't think that's so bad."

A small, watery laugh leaves her. "Thank you."

"You're welcome." He nods once and hops to his feet. "I'm going to the vending machine. You guys want anything?"

I shake my head, and Halle gives a small, pathetic "no."

When he's gone, she gives my hand a squeeze. "I don't know how people do it."

"Do what?" I frown.

"Raise kids. This part of it is so hard, and I'm not even their actual parent. It's painful to know that I can't protect them from everything."

"Maybe not everything, but at least you can protect them from STDs and unplanned pregnancy," I joke.

"Caleb," she groans, dropping her head back against the wall. "That mortifying memory was just beginning to fade from my mind, and you had to go and bring it back again."

Amusement washes over me, but I school my expression as best as I can. "Sorry."

Arms crossed, she glowers. It's so damn cute. "No, you're not."

No, I'm not.

My phone vibrates in my pocket. Though I've cleared

my calendar today, I automatically reach for it, concerned it's a client or colleague who needs my help.

Instead, the name on the screen makes my stomach sink.

My relationship with my mom is the definition of complicated. Once I started seeing through her bullshit and recognized her manipulation tactics, it became impossible to ignore them. I've put up a wall between myself and my parents to curb her meddling. My dad isn't the meddling type, but he never steps in. In fact, he's content to go along with my mom's scheming most of the time.

"I better answer this," I tell Halle as I stand.

I've ignored my mom's last few calls, which means if I don't, there's a chance she'll show up at my house unannounced in the very near future.

Though my parents live in Hawthorne Mills, it's surprisingly easy to avoid them. All I have to do is avoid their usual haunts, and that's simple, since they keep to the schedule they've had for years. My mom goes to the grocery store every Monday at eleven. She visits with her friends at the local tea shop every Wednesday at noon. On Fridays she volunteers at the local thrift shop. My dad still works during the week, and on the weekends the two of them frequent the country club a few towns over.

I step out into the hall and quickly find a quiet corner, sliding my thumb over the screen before the call goes to voicemail.

"Hello?"

"You are alive? I was getting worried."

Biting back a groan, I close my eyes and pinch the bridge of my nose. "Yes, alive and well."

"So, just ignoring me, then?"

"I wasn't ignoring you." *I definitely was.* "I've been busy with work."

"Clearly if you're too busy to answer when your parents call. I worry about you, you know? You may be grown, but I'm still your mother."

She's laying it on real thick. I'm not surprised. "Do you need something, Mom?"

Her sigh gusts over the line. "Why must I need something to call my son? Maybe I just wanted to hear your voice," she argues, her tone high-pitched and haughty. "But yes, I called to ask if you'd come for Thanksgiving dinner—"

"I have plans, but thanks. I'll be spending the day with my daughter, like usual."

This sigh is laced with disapproval and annoyance. "Caleb, she's not—"

"She *is* my daughter," I hiss.

We've been having this conversation for years. It's disgusting. For a long time, Salem didn't want anyone to know that Seda was Thayer's child, and I was fine with claiming her as mine, because she *is* my daughter in all the ways that matter. But since the truth came out, my parents have been dead set on convincing me to cut ties. Like blood has anything to do with the love I have for my child.

"I will not continue to have this asinine conversation with you."

"I just don't understand—"

Anger rushes through me, hot and vicious. "You don't have to understand."

"Is it so wrong to want to spend Thanksgiving with my son?"

"Yes," I snap. "It is when you insist on denying my daughter. I spend my holidays with her now. I've told you before, you're welcome to come to Salem—"

"I will do no such thing." She scoffs, as if my suggestion is preposterous.

Defeated, I slump against the wall. "Then I don't know what to tell you." I scrub a hand over my face. I'm so tired of having this argument with her. Why the hell can't she accept Seda as my daughter? Love and family are about so much more than DNA.

"Perhaps," she hedges, "your father and I will stop by after we have our own Thanksgiving meal, since you won't join us."

Somehow, she makes it sound like *I'm* the one being unreasonable.

I bite back another retort. "Sure, sounds great."

Sounds more like torture, but whatever. I can't avoid my parents forever.

The line grows quiet, but I know her well enough to know she's not done, so I wait.

"What is this I hear about a girl and her kids living with you?"

Stomach twisting, I drop my head back against the wall. Keeping the situation from my parents has nothing to do with shame. I haven't talked to them about Halle because I know my mom will find some way to spin the situation.

"My neighbor and her brothers are staying with me, yes." But she knows that already. The people of this town are nosy. By now, everyone knows that they're siblings. "Their house flooded and the flooring has to be repaired. I offered them a place to stay." Again, it's not shame that keeps me from telling my mom that Halle and I are ... what we are. I keep it to myself because I can guarantee she'll try to sabotage the relationship. "That's all."

She makes a displeased sound, a cross between an *mhm* and a *well*. "Did her insurance not provide her with money for temporary housing?"

"It provided some, but not enough to cover a place for an extended period, and I have a big empty house. Why wouldn't I offer it up?"

I check the time on my watch, annoyed that this conversation has dragged on for this long already.

"Because from what I hear, they're not good people."

I bark out a sardonic laugh, shaking my head. "Not good people?"

"Did you know her mom is in prison?"

Jaw clenched, I rub my eyes with my thumb and index finger. I like to think I'm a fairly patient person, but my mother manages to bring out my very *im*patient side every time. "Yes, I'm aware."

"I hope you're being careful."

"Mom," I grit out. "I'm seeing her."

"Seeing her?" she parrots, her tone high, like she's genuinely confused.

"Halle, the woman who's staying with me. We're ... dating."

That word, dating, doesn't even come close to encompassing what we have. Though I've only known her for a few months, it was obvious right away that this connection was different. More. When you know, you know. That's the saying, right? Maybe it would sound absurd to others, but I'd marry her tomorrow if I didn't think it would scare her off.

"Caleb Henry Thorne. Surely, I didn't hear you right."

I grunt. "You heard me just fine, Mom."

"Oh, good heavens." I can imagine what she looks like right now, clutching her literal pearls. "You sure know how to pick them."

She means it as an insult, but I'm not bothered by the implication.

"I do, thank you. I gotta go. This conversation isn't getting us anywhere."

"You're such a disappointment at times. A smart, brilliant boy. Talented, a good job—"

"You're a disappointment too, Mom. Bye." With that, I end the call and shove my phone into my pocket. My heart pounds, my blood pressure at an unhealthy level, I'm sure. For several minutes, I walk the halls, working the annoyance out of my system.

Though I've calmed quite a bit by the time I return to the waiting room, Halle studies my face, gaze narrowed, like she can see right through me. "Is everything okay?"

I scrub a hand over my stubbled jaw and drop into the chair beside her. "Just decompressing from a call from my dear ole mom. She's got a talent for ruining my day."

She takes my hand, her palm cool thanks to the blasting AC. I understand why they keep it so cold, but the temperature is damn near arctic during the winter months.

"I'm sorry."

I lift a shoulder. "It's just how she is." It's not an excuse, just a fact. "I'm used to it."

"Do you want to talk about it?"

No, I really don't, but Halle should know. "I told her we're together."

Nose crinkling, she deflates a little. "I take it that didn't go over well."

"No." I rub my free hand on my knee. "She ... she doesn't handle change well. Honestly, no woman could ever live up to her impossible standards, so when you finally meet her, please know that her judgment has nothing to do with you. It has everything to do with *her*."

Her frown deepens. "I'm sorry it's like that for you."

"It could be worse." It's the same excuse I always use when it comes to the woman who raised me.

"Yeah," Quinn snorts from Halle's other side. "Your mom could be in prison."

Halle giggles, and despite my best effort, I laugh too. His comment brings some much-needed levity to the situation.

"I don't know," I say. "She might be worse. She's pretty unhinged. Just wait until you finally meet her."

Quinn leans forward, elbows on his knees. "Is your dad cool, at least?"

I stifle a snort. "No. He goes along with my mom, regardless of the situation. It took me a long time to see that he does that for his own sanity."

"Women," Quinn says, his tone knowing, like he's feigning way more experience than he actually has.

"Hey," Halle scolds playfully, batting at his arm.

"What?" He raises his hands, brows high on his head. "You can't deny it. You women can be—"

I throw a hand up in warning. "Trust me, you don't want to finish that statement."

Dark eyes twinkling, he mimes zipping his lips.

Halle gives my hand a squeeze. "Should have left him to dig his own grave."

"Us guys gotta stick together, right, Caleb?" Quinn barks a laugh.

"I'm just trying to help, and here I am getting in trouble," I gripe, all tease. "Hate to break it to you, though, man, but I'm going to pick your sister's side every time."

"Traitor," the kid mumbles.

"So, even though we've never met, your mom already hates me?" Halle asks, bringing the conversation back around.

The tightness in my gut worsens. "She doesn't hate you. She doesn't even know you."

Lips pursed, Halle slides lower in her seat. "It feels like she hates me. I can feel the hatred burning through your phone."

I groan. "She's a miserable person. It's nothing personal."

"You know…" She pulls her hand from mine and plays with the frayed fabric at the knee of her jeans. "If we're … you know … together … I'm going to have to meet her eventually."

"There were an awful lot of pauses in that," I point out,

chest constricting half in elation that she's considering it and half in fear that she'll change her mind.

"It feels weird to call you my boyfriend." She wrinkles her nose at the word. "It sounds so middle school."

"I'm pretty sure there's a chaplain walking around here somewhere." I lean forward, like I'm going to stand. "Maybe we could convince him to marry us."

She stares at me, open-mouthed. "I can't tell whether you're joking."

"I'm not."

"Don't bother," Quinn interjects. "Casen would kill you for getting married without him."

"Well"—Halle gestures to her brother—"there you have it."

"I can wait until he's out of surgery."

Her eyes widen. "Caleb."

"What?" I blink, feigning innocence.

"It's too soon."

I ignore the disappointment that hits me and smile. "When it's the right person, it's never too soon."

Some might argue that I don't know what I'm talking about since I've been divorced, but I *know*. My gut has never steered me wrong before, and I'm certain it isn't now.

Halle is going to be my wife the moment she's ready.

THIRTY-THREE

Halle

"Could you carry him?" I beg Caleb as a crutch slips out from beneath Casen and he barely catches himself from falling. We haven't even made it into the house, and already, I've sprouted gray hairs. "I think I'm going to be sick."

It hurts, knowing he's in so much pain, and I can't help but worry that if he takes a tumble now, he'll end up with another injury.

"I'm not letting your boyfriend carry me into the house." Case, whose leg is now in a cast, pauses at the bottom of the porch steps and frowns in concentration. After a moment, he shoves one crutch at Quinn, and when that hand is free, he clutches the railing and hops up the first step. His twin stays by his side, braced to catch him if he loses his balance.

"I don't know how I'm going to survive this," I grumble as Caleb drapes an arm over my shoulders.

A gust of wind whips my hair around my face, making me curl in on myself. The sky is an ominous gray, and according to the forecast, it's going to snow this afternoon.

So, along with the other items on my long list of worries, I'm stressed about Casen having to navigate snow and ice with a broken leg. Whether he likes it or not, I plan to drive them to and from school until the cast comes off and he can put weight on his foot. If he'll let me, I'll even walk him to the door of the school to ensure he doesn't slip and fall. But something tells me he'll fight me on that.

"One day at a time. I think that's how most people survive things."

"It's going to be at least six weeks." It'll be well into December by that time.

"Again," he says with a soft laugh, holding me tighter. "One day at a time."

"You probably think I'm insane."

Case finally makes it to the porch, his free arm lifted in triumph.

I let out a breath of relief, my lungs deflating.

"No, I think you're a concerned sister and guardian. I'd be more worried if you weren't acting this way."

"Daddy!" Seda darts across the lawn, straight into Caleb's arms. "How's Casen?"

"He's doing okay, sweetie."

She throws her arms around me next and squeezes with a surprising amount of strength.

I take a small breath. It's all I can manage when she's holding me so tightly. "You can go in and see him if you want."

She doesn't have to be told twice. A heartbeat later, her feet are thundering up the stairs, and she disappears into the house.

I hate that she hasn't seen much of her dad since he insisted on staying with us at the hospital, but I can't deny his presence was a huge comfort.

How on earth do people do it? The stress alone is enough to have me questioning if I even want children.

"I'm going to order pizzas, if that's okay with you," Caleb says, guiding me to the porch.

It's nearly five already, and after sleeping in Casen's hospital room for two nights, I'm far too tired to think about cooking. More than anything, I want a hot shower. While Casen's room was equipped with all the facilities, the water pressure was pathetic.

"Pizza sounds perfect."

"Seda? Boys?" Caleb slides his phone out of his pocket and sidles over to where the kids have gathered on the couch. "Pizza?"

"Yes, please," Casen groans, his head resting on the back of the couch. "Pizza."

"I'm down." This comes from Quinn.

"Pizza?" Seda sits up straight, face alight. "I love pizza."

With a nod, he taps at his phone's screen. "I'll put in an order."

"Case, are you all good for now?" I ask, hands clasped in front of me. "Do you need a drink or—"

"I'm fine." He chuckles. "Stop acting like a mother hen."

Lips pressed together, I lower my head a little, blinking back tears. It's hard not to act this way. It's my job to keep him safe, and though I realize it was an accident, I still feel like I failed him.

"I'm going to shower," I say, and without waiting for a response, I pad through the house.

Upstairs, I grab a clean set of clothes and shut myself in the bathroom. While the water warms up, I wash my face and brush my teeth. I've done both already today, but they go a long way to perking me up.

I drop my dirty clothes into the hamper, eager to be rid of the chemical smell clinging to me. If I never see another hospital, it will be too soon.

The frosted glass is fogged by the time I slide the door open and step inside, the hot water an immediate balm to my skin. In seconds, my stiff muscles begin to relax. For a moment, I stand in place, eyes closed, and relish the sensation. Despite the fight he put up, I insisted Quinn sleep on the couch in Casen's hospital room. Caleb and I roughed it in uncomfortable chairs. I told him he could go home, but he insisted on staying.

At the sound of a creaking door, I freeze beneath the spray, holding my arms in front of me like that will protect me.

"Hello?" I carefully raise my hand and swipe at the fog on the shower door. I nearly scream when a figure near the sink comes into view. Luckily, Caleb's form registers quickly, and I choke back the instinct.

Eyes on me, he tears his shirt off and shoves down his pants. Then he slides the shower door open and steps inside.

"What are you—"

He buries a hand in my hair and yanks me forward so my mouth collides with his.

Oh, fuck.

Just as quickly, he spins, and my back hits the tile, the cold of it jarring against my skin. The combination of that sensation and the instant desire sparking to life inside me causes my nipples to pebble against his bare chest.

He kisses his way down my neck to my right breast and swirls his tongue around my nipple, dragging a moan from my throat. He gives the other breast the same attention. That alone is enough to ignite a fire in my core.

"Need to fuck you so bad." He drags his tongue back up my neck and cups my jaw. "My cock is aching to be inside this pussy, baby," he murmurs against my lips. "You have no fucking idea."

I whimper. It's the only sound I'm capable of making at the moment.

"Do you need me too, baby?"

Though he still holds my face firmly, I manage to nod.

"Good." He slides his fingers down my shower-slicked body until he finds my pussy and spreads me open. "Jesus Christ, Halle. You're soaked already. This sweet cunt was aching for me too, wasn't it?"

Head pressed back against the tile, I give a small cry in agreement.

"I'm going to fill you up so good," he croons. "Don't you worry, baby. I'm going to take care of you."

My heart races, my breaths coming quick. God, yes. Please.

He lifts me up, holding me with ease in one arm, and guides his cock inside me.

I close my eyes, relishing the sensation. He feels so fucking good. "Caleb," I whimper as he fills me.

He's so big and I'm so full. My pussy quivers, adjusting to his intrusion.

He buries his face in my neck, cursing. "This isn't going to last long."

I grasp his wet shoulders, searching for purchase. "Don't care."

Blue eyes lit with need, he keeps his focus fixed on me as he pumps into me, hard and fast. His intense gaze bores into me, straight to my soul, seeing everything. It's too much. I have to close my eyes, or I'll lose all control.

"Uh-uh." He grips my chin. "Look at me, Halle," he demands. "Look at me when I fuck you."

I bite down on my lip, my whole body shuddering. What does it say about me that his bossiness is such a turn-on? Is it wrong? If so, then I don't want to be right.

"Do you like that?" He punctuates the question by grinding his hips into mine. The stimulation against my clit has my nails digging into his back. "You like it, don't you? When I tell you what to do?"

"Y-Yes—*ohmygod*." I shudder, my release looming.

Before the wave can crest, though, the bastard pulls out and roughly sets me on my feet.

"Suck my cock," he demands.

Without hesitation, I drop to my knees in front of him, the shower spraying against my back, and take him into my mouth, one hand on his shaft. His skin is hot as I pump him and suck, finding my rhythm. I maintain eye contact as I take him deep, knowing it makes him lose his mind.

Chin tucked, he pushes my wet hair out of my face, gathering the strands. Hand fisted, he tugs. Not enough to hurt, but enough to silently convey that in this moment, I'm his to do with as he pleases, and fuck, it's hot.

"Look at you," he croons. The sweet tone and the way he gently strokes my face with his other hand are in complete juxtaposition to the demands of a moment ago. "So fucking pretty." He pushes his hips forward, his grip tightening in my hair so I'm forced to take him to the back of my throat. "You can take more than that, baby. I know you can."

I whimper, my eyes watering, and relax my jaw to take him deep. I hold him there until I gag. In response to the sound, he releases me and drags me up to his body, holding my limp frame against his. When I've found my balance, he switches places with me so his back is now to the showerhead.

"Hands on the wall and spread those legs, baby."

I do as he says, legs shaking in anticipation.

With a bruising grip, he spreads my cheeks and fills me with his cock.

A scream works its way up my throat, but before it can leave me, he clamps a hand to my mouth, silencing me.

"Yes, yes, fuck yes," he chants in my ear. "So fucking good, baby."

He finds my clit, and it only takes a few strokes of his fingers over the sensitive bud to set me off. It's embarrassing how easily he controls my body.

Moaning, he pulls out of me, and an instant later, warm spurts of cum land on my ass.

"Look at that." He rubs the globe of my right ass cheek, then gives it a sharp smack. "You're like my own little piece of artwork."

Boneless, all I can do is press myself to the tile and suck in gulps of air.

He turns me around easily and kisses me, then drags me back to the shower head.

"Let me wash you up, baby?"

I nod. I barely have the strength to stay standing, let alone scrub myself clean.

Caleb takes his time lathering my hair with shampoo. He scrubs my scalp, massaging as he goes, each step more intimate than the previous. While the conditioner sits in my hair, he squirts a dollop of body wash onto my purple loofah, then gently swipes it over my neck and shoulders, working his way down and around.

When he's finished and he's rinsed the conditioner out of my hair, I grasp his arms and urge him to shift.

"My turn," I tell him, switching places.

He has to crouch so I can lather his scalp with shampoo. While he rinses it out, I use my loofah on his body. He's seriously gorgeous. Muscular, but not overly so. Toned in all the right places. The dusting of hair on his arms and legs is darker than the blond on his head.

When I reach the back of his knee with the loofah, he startles.

I look up at him, fighting a smile. "Ticklish?"

"Yes." Eyes blazing and cock half hard already, he pins me with a look.

No longer holding back a grin, I rub the loofah there again, and he curses.

I choose not to torture him further, moving on from that spot. Once he's rinsed off, he steps out and passes me a towel. While I dry my body, I watch him do the same, only pouting a little when he wraps the towel around his waist, cutting off my view of his lower half. Swooping in for a kiss, he renders me speechless. With a wink, he backs out of the bathroom, leaving me alone with the memory of the way he touched me.

I exhale a shaky breath.

This man makes me a wild, crazy mess.

I make quick work of combing my hair and dressing in a pair of black leggings, an oversized crewneck, and socks. I swipe Chapstick on my lips and twist my damp hair into a bun at my nape.

Downstairs, my brothers and Seda are still lounging on the couch. They've turned on *Lord of the Rings*, and the chatter from earlier has vanished. In the kitchen, Caleb is filling a glass with water. As if he can sense me, he turns and smirks as I shuffle close to the island.

The man seriously just railed me in the shower, yet here

he is, looking so domesticated, sipping a glass of water like it was no big deal.

Suddenly parched myself, I pass him, headed for the cabinet. His fingers brush my wrist as he reaches past me and plucks a glass from the shelf. Lips grazing my ear, he murmurs, "You smell good."

I'm breathless again when he hands me the glass, but I find the wherewithal to fill it with ice and water from the dispenser in the fridge.

"Pizza should be here soon," he says, loud enough for the kids to hear.

"Sweet." Casen tips his head back, eyeing us. "I'm *starving*."

It's so, so wrong, but as I look at Caleb, all I can think about is being on my knees, taking him into my mouth.

"Can we have brownies for dessert?" Quinn asks.

Seda hops up, abandoning the movie. "We have brownie mix in the pantry."

"Sweet. I'll help." Quinn hauls himself up and follows her.

"You guys are seriously abandoning me here? I can barely walk."

"Good," Quinn teases. "It means you can't get in the way."

Taking pity on Casen, Caleb and I settle in the living room, leaving Quinn and Seda to work on the brownies without our interference.

It's hard to miss the way she smiles at him and blushes. Girl has it bad for my brothers. Crushes at her age are so intense and not always logical.

When the doorbell rings a few minutes later, Caleb hops off the couch to greet the delivery person, and my stomach rumbles, reminding me that the granola bar I scarfed down this morning was hardly sufficient for a snack, let alone a replacement for multiple meals. But I kept thinking we'd be discharged at any moment, and I wanted real food rather than chips or another protein bar. But it was well into the afternoon before we were finally given the go-ahead to break out of the place.

Caleb and I divvy up the pizza, and I take Casen a plate first.

"Thanks, Hal." He gives me a soft smile. His normally bright eyes are dull and ringed with dark circles. He's exhausted, and it's almost time for more pain medicine, so I can imagine he's hurting. We're being strict with his dosage because of our mother's addiction issues. Case was just as concerned as I was, and even suggested going without, but after a discussion with his surgeon, we created a plan to keep him out of pain.

"Thanks for dinner," Case says to Caleb as the two of us return with our own plates. Seda and Quinn are still working on brownies, so they elected to eat in the kitchen.

"No problem." Caleb nods, a slice held aloft. "How are you feeling?"

"Sore," he answers without hesitation. "Tired."

"You should go on to bed soon." I tap my phone screen to check the time. "Maybe after you eat?"

"I might." He stifles a yawn.

None of us have had much sleep. Not between all the beeping machines and alarms and nurses checking in throughout the night. I'm just grateful they let us stay with Casen.

I've never watched the *Lord of the Rings* movies, but I find myself being sucked into the story. Once he's finished his pizza, Case sets his plate on the coffee table and slides the blanket off the back of the couch. He's asleep, head resting on my shoulder, before the brownies come out of the oven.

Caleb peers around me. "Poor kid's exhausted."

"I should stop by the school tomorrow and pick up his work so he doesn't fall behind."

"I can do it." Caleb flashes a grin. "The office ladies love me."

"You know how to work your charm, don't you?" I joke.

He peers into the kitchen, where Quinn and Seda are washing dishes. "Of course."

I follow his line of sight. "I like it when she's over."

With a smile, Caleb sets his empty plate on top of Casen's. "I do too."

"I don't know how I'm going to get this one upstairs for bed." I frown at my sleeping brother. There's no way I want him to hobble his way up the stairs.

"I can carry him up," Caleb volunteers.

"While I don't doubt your prowess, I'd rather not put you at risk of breaking your neck or injuring him more."

"Baby," he laughs. "That's definitely doubting my prowess."

"Whatever," I mumble.

"I have an inflatable mattress. We could set it up down

here. It's not as comfortable as a real bed, but it would keep him from having to deal with the stairs for now."

I hate for Casen to be displaced longer, but it's probably the best option. The doctor said this wouldn't be an easy process, but until now, I didn't understand just how hard it'll be. Even after the cast comes off, he'll probably be required to wear a boot, and he'll need physical therapy.

"I'll go get it now." Caleb eases off the couch so as not to wake Case and takes our dirty plates with him.

He's just returned with the air mattress—still in the box, like it's never been used—and a set of sheets, when the oven timer goes off.

Casen startles, shooting up straight beside me. "What's that?" he looks around, eyes bleary. "Alarm?"

I can't help but smile at his confusion. "Timer for brownies."

"Ooh, brownies." He drops his head back, his face slack with exhaustion. "I want one."

"Once they cool down, you can have one. Caleb's going to inflate a mattress so you can sleep down here rather than tackle the stairs tonight. Is that okay?"

Casen agrees without hesitation, which can only mean he's really hurting. "That's fine. I need to pee."

Standing, I help him find his balance and get the crutches under his arms. Then, hands clasped, I force myself to remain where I am rather than help him while he makes his way slowly to the bathroom.

Once the door clicks shut behind him, I help Caleb move the coffee table to one side of the room and spread out the deflated air mattress. And when Casen returns, he bypasses us, heading straight for his brother and Seda in the kitchen.

Seda smiles up at him with hearts in her eyes as he approaches.

Caleb turns on the mattress's built-in air pump and follows my line of sight, huffing. "I really thought I had a few more years before the crushes started."

With a laugh, I take the fitted sheet from him, and we work together to put it on the mattress. It keeps popping off the bottom corner on my side. Caleb gently nudges me over and fixes it with annoying ease.

"Show-off," I tease.

He shakes out a soft blanket and lays it across the bed. "I'll grab his pillow."

While he jogs up the stairs, I join the kids in the kitchen so I can rinse the plates and put them in the dishwasher. I've gotten used to the damned appliance and I'm going to miss it when we move back into our house.

That thought has my stomach sinking, though I'm quickly distracted by Quinn.

"I'm going to sleep on the couch so I can be close to Case."

"I can sleep on the couch too," Seda volunteers.

I have to bite my lip to hide my smile. "Your dad would probably prefer it if you slept in your bed," I warn her.

Lips pursed, she shrugs. "It can be like a sleepover."

I arch a brow at Quinn in silent question.

He shrugs, mouthing, "I don't care."

"If it's okay with your dad, you can sleep on the couch." I'm not her parent, so it's not up to me to make that decision, and I have no interest in stepping on toes. Though I can't imagine Caleb being upset if I did make the call.

The dishes in the dishwasher rattle as I close it and press start. And as it begins its cycle, it makes a whirring sound so quiet, I can't always tell whether it's actually going. So like I always do, I lean down and double check.

Okay, I may be getting used to it, but clearly, I'm still skeptical.

As Caleb descends the stairs with Case's pillow tucked under one arm, Seda strides his way, already going in for the kill.

"Daddy?" she says, her tone extra sweet. "Can I sleep down here on the couch with Quinn and Casen?"

Caleb's eyes widen as they dart to his daughter.

I have to turn away, otherwise his frightened expression will send me into hysterics. He looks like a wild animal caught in a cage.

"No," he answers without hesitation.

She pouts, hands shooting to her hips. "Why not? I have sleepovers all the time."

"With girls," he mutters, dropping the pillow on the mattress.

"Are you going to marry Halle one day?" she counters.

I blanch. How the hell did I get dragged into this?

Caleb meets my eyes, wearing a tiny, devilish grin. "Yes," he replies without hesitation.

"Then Casen and Quinn will be my stepbrothers, right?" She lifts her chin, waiting for him to respond. When he nods, she says, "So what's wrong with a sleepover on the couch?"

Caleb lets out a beleaguered sigh. Clearly, he doesn't want to agree, but she's backed him into a corner.

"Fine," he says, his face a mask of defeat. "If they're okay with it."

Ah. My chest tightens in anticipation of how this is going to play out.

He figures they won't want her to hang around. What Caleb has forgotten is that my brothers rarely do what's expected of them.

"I don't care," Casen says, stifling a yawn. "I'm crashing as soon as I get one of those brownies any way."

Quinn shrugs. "Seda can hang out. I don't care."

Caleb turns away to hide his frustration.

"If that's settled," I say, "I know it's early, but I'm exhausted, and I have to work in the morning." I kiss Casen on the top of his head, hit with a memory of when they were little and I'd do the same thing. I kiss Quinn on the head next. They're much closer to being grown men now than to those tiny versions of themselves. "Sleep tight." I hug Seda, then shuffle for the stairs.

It's only a little after seven, but I've barely slept in days, and I'm close to delirium.

On autopilot, I change into pajamas, brush my teeth, and climb into bed.

I've barely dozed off when my bedroom door eases open and Caleb is hovering over me, his lips on my ear.

"You're sleeping in my bed."

I groan in protest. "I'm so comfy."

"You'll be comfier in my bed."

"Fine." I fling the covers off.

Before I can even sit up, he scoops me into his arms.

I push against his chest weakly. "I can walk."

He chuckles, the sound vibrating through me. "I know, baby. But I have to prove to you that I'm strong enough to carry you, since you doubted my capabilities."

"Show-off," I mutter as he steps out into the hall.

He toes his door open and then pushes it shut gently with his elbow. Once he's laid me on the bed, he pulls the covers over top of me.

As tired as I am, I manage to keep my eyes open so I can watch him ditch his shirt and sweatpants before climbing in beside me.

"I know I'm hard to resist"—he loops an arm around me and pulls me in tight—"but no funny business. Just sleep."

I don't bother replying, because sleep is already pulling me under.

THIRTY-FOUR

Caleb

Thanksgiving snuck up on me. Between Casen's injury, my heavy caseload, and trying to carve out time with Halle, the month has flown by.

Salem and Thayer's house is filled with a cacophony of voices, clanging dishes, and the upbeat music that goes along with a very interesting competition of *Just Dance* in the family room.

I love it.

As a kid, I craved a large family to spend the holidays with. Instead, each one was lonely—just me and my parents. This chaos? This is what the holidays should be about.

Thelma tries to get in on the *Just Dance* game with the kids while Cynthia scolds her about potentially breaking a hip. Laith nurses a beer by the back door, ignoring yet another one of Salem's attempts to set him up. Salem is yammering on, undeterred, while she flits around the kitchen.

With Samson in one arm, Thayer mixes the mashed potatoes one-handed.

"Let me take over." I grab the hand mixer and wave him off so he can deal with Samson.

"How are things with you and Halle?" he asks.

For a minute, I'm frozen, wondering whether he's asking because he's my friend or because Salem put him up to it.

Truthfully, it still blows my mind that the two of us are friends. I so badly wanted to hate him, but he made it impossible. He's a genuinely good guy, and it's obvious he loves Salem and his kids with everything he has.

"Good, really good," I answer, working the beater around the edges of the bowl.

"It seems pretty serious."

"It is." I don't elaborate, keeping my focus fixed on the potatoes.

"It's only been a few months."

The implication there rankles me. Irritation seeping into my veins, I arch a brow in his direction. "How soon after you met Salem did you fall in love with her?"

He nods, head bowed. "Touché."

Samson wriggles in his arms, demanding to be put down. Thayer obliges and the toddler takes off, no doubt looking for trouble.

"It's good," he goes on. "Seeing you happy, I mean."

"Was I unhappy before?" I turn the mixer off and nod at the bowl, urging him to check the consistency.

"That's not what I meant. I—"

I hold up a hand. "I know the two of you worried that I wouldn't move on, but that's silly. I've dated in the past, but until now, I hadn't found the right person. I wasn't going to rush into anything just to ease your guilt."

Thayer flinches, but he holds eye contact. "Understood."

Yeah, we're all good, but that doesn't mean I want them prying into my love life.

"Pass me that bowl." He takes the mixer out of my hand and points to the island.

I heft the large serving dish and set it on the counter so he can fill it with the potatoes.

He clearly doesn't need my help now that both hands are free, so I go in search of Halle. When I don't find her downstairs or on either porch, I head up to the second floor. I can't imagine she'd venture up here on her own, but it's possible Salem sent her to grab something, and I think she would have checked in if she was running next door.

The noise from downstairs fades as I hit the top landing. Only then can I make out the sound of voices down the hall.

Near the end, I peer through Soleil's open bedroom door, finding Halle kneeling on the floor with the little girl, each with a Barbie in hand. Neither of them notices my presence in the doorway, so I take a moment to just watch.

Halle interacts easily with Seda's little sister, playing along with the story she's creating for the dolls.

"You stole my purse," Soleil says in a high-pitched tone.

Halle mock gasps, moving her doll's arm up in time with the sound. "I didn't steal anything. I got this from the mall."

"If by mall," Soleil says, "you mean my closet."

A laugh slips out at the sass coming from such a tiny human.

The two of them turn in unison, eyes going wide.

"Go on," I tell them. "I want to know what happens next."

"Caleb," Soleil groans. "You ruined it."

"We can play again later." With a soft smile, Halle unfolds her legs and stands.

"Dinner's almost ready. I hope you're hungry."

"Starved," Halle groans, hand on her stomach.

"Piggyback ride?" I ask Soleil.

Giggling, she bounces to her feet. "I'll never say no to that."

I crouch down so she can hop on, then zoom out of the room. I'm careful on the stairs, but when we hit the first floor, I spin in a fast circle, causing Soleil to screech in my ear. Once I set her on her feet, she grins and takes off, joining the other kids in the family room.

Halle brushes my arm as she passes me at the bottom of the steps, but I snatch her hand and tug her into me.

"You're good with her."

She shrugs off my praise, gaze averted. "I always wanted a little sister."

"Dinner's ready!" Thayer hollers from the kitchen. "Make your plates in the kitchen and sit wherever you want."

As a stampede of kids makes its way past us, with Cynthia, Thelma, and Laith bringing up the rear, I hold tight to Halle, then guide her in behind them.

We settle into the makeshift line behind the crowd that also includes Thayer's parents and Salem's sister and her family. All day, everyone has commented on my goofy grin, but there's no tempering it. This right here is what I've always wanted.

The kids take over the table in the kitchen, so the adults end up in the dining room.

Beside me, Halle takes a bite of macaroni and cheese and moans softly.

"Good?" My voice is heavy with humor.

"You have no idea." She goes in for another bite.

"How have you been?" Georgia, Salem's older sister, asks me. "I haven't seen you in a while."

It's the first quiet moment we adults have really had, and like every other gathering we have, it won't last long.

"I've been good, G. Thanks for asking."

Georgia leans forward, eyeing Halle. "I hear you're the girlfriend."

Halle's eyes flare wide and the mac and cheese falls from her fork onto her plate. "Uh…"

"Georgia's a bit intense, but she won't eat you," I promise.

"Yeah," Halle says, voice small, looking to me for reassurance.

I wink, hoping she can sense how at ease I am with these people. If that's the case, maybe she'll feel the same way.

Georgia hums. "Good. He's a keeper."

"Thanks, G." I shake my head, biting back a smile.

Georgia barely tolerated me when Salem and I dated in high school. She warmed to me a bit when we got back together, but that was stamped out when the two of us split and the truth came out.

"Halle," Georgia says. "What do you do for a living?"

"Oh." She wipes her mouth with her napkin. "I work for a medical office answering calls from home—scheduling appointments, getting insurance information, stuff like that. And then before … um … before we"—she looks to me—"started seeing each other, Caleb hired me as his assistant."

"That's our Caleb," Georgia croons. "Always so charitable."

"Georgia," I snap. The word is harsher than I mean for it to be, but knowing Halle, G's comment is going to hit her the wrong way.

"Oh." Georgia pales. "I'm so sorry. I didn't mean it like that. I was just—" She blows out a breath. "You know what? I'm going to stop talking now. I just keep putting my foot in my mouth."

"It's okay," Halle says softly, looking at me. "Caleb has been really good to me and my brothers."

I tilt close and press my lips to her temple. The move inspires an annoying chorus of *aw*s.

We're finished with dinner and the kitchen is mostly picked up, though we haven't had dessert yet, when the doorbell rings.

"Were we expecting someone else?" Salem asks over her shoulder, rinsing a dish.

Thayer presses a kiss to her cheek. "I'll get it."

He disappears, and when he returns thirty seconds later, he's wearing a grimace. "It's for you."

It takes me a moment to realize he's talking to me, but when I do, confusion swirls in my mind. "For me?" Everyone I know is already here.

"Yeah." His lips twitch. "It's your mother."

Shit.

THIRTY-FIVE

Halle

Across the kitchen, Caleb's eyes go wide. He darts over to me and mutters a panicked "don't listen to a word she says. Take it with a grain of salt," then shuffles off to greet her.

I blink at Salem, my heart in my throat. "Is she really that bad?"

With a snort, she arranges a serving dish on the bottom rack of the dishwasher. "Oh yeah."

My breath gusts out of me. Dammit.

Straightening, she gives me a sympathetic smile. "I could lie to you, but it's better if you're prepared. Mrs.

Thorne is a hard pill to swallow. If it makes you feel better, there's no way she could hate you more than me."

That comment only makes my stomach twist. If she doesn't like Salem, one of the nicest humans on this planet, I'm doomed.

As if every being here has been alerted to an alien presence, the house goes silent. Even the kids and loud-mouthed Thelma don't make a sound.

She's sitting at the table with the whole gaggle of children, playing what looks suspiciously like poker, glowering at the couple entering the house.

I swear the room drops several degrees when Caleb ushers them into the fray. "My parents decided to stop by." Despite his best efforts to keep a neutral expression, he grimaces. "Mom brought tiramisu."

"Apology dessert," Salem huffs beside me. "Bet it's as bitter as she is."

I cover my mouth to hold back surprised laughter.

"Mom, Dad, I'd like to introduce you to Halle and her brothers."

Oh no, oh no, oh no. They're coming my way.

Caleb steps away from his parents and sets the dessert on the island. Then he sidles up beside me, his shoulders pulled back and his head high. "This is Halle, my girlfriend."

I plaster a smile on my face and extend my hand to his mother. "Hi, nice to meet you."

She takes it, delicately grasping my fingers rather than my whole hand. "I'm Katrina," she says in a bored tone, her focus drifting around the room rather than fixed on me.

"Thomas." Caleb's dad's handshake and tone are at least polite.

"Salem," Katrina says in a snide tone.

"Always a pleasure," my new friend croons.

Thayer appears at her side, arm around her waist, stepping slightly in front of her like he might have to physically defend her from the frigid woman who just arrived.

"Likewise," she drawls, moving away.

"And over there by Thelma and Cynthia," Caleb says, pointing at the table, "are Casen and Quinn. Halle's brothers."

Katrina assesses them with an unimpressed look, her only response a "hmm."

At her side her husband shoves his hands in his pockets, looking like he'd rather be anywhere else. From the way he rounds his shoulders, it looks like he's the kind of man who lets his wife dictate things and prefers not to rock the boat, lest it disturb whatever kind of peace he's carved out for himself.

"Are you hungry?" Caleb asks them. "There are plenty of leftovers. I can warm up a couple of plates."

Katrina's lips pinch, her expression sour. "We already ate. Just thought we'd drop by for dessert."

"I'm glad you're here." His expression looks kind enough, but based on his reaction when Thayer informed him of their arrival, I get the impression this statement is very much a lie.

"We're having dessert in a bit." This comes from Thayer, his voice deep and rumbly. "Feel free to find a seat and make yourselves at home."

Katrina gives him a hard look, then makes her way out of the room.

With a heavy sigh, Caleb's dad turns to Thayer. "Got any whiskey around here? I need a drink."

I think we all might.

Outside on the porch, watching the kids play kickball in the street, I pull my coat tighter around me, trying to stave off the chill. While I'm shivering, the kids act like it's the middle of summer, not a single one bothering with a coat or even a sweatshirt.

Casen sits on the front steps beside me, lips downturned as he surveys the game.

I bump his good knee with mine. "You'll be back and better than ever before you know it."

"I know," he groans, his expression still flat.

He's much better with the crutches now, and he's figured out how to navigate most tasks, but I can imagine it's still hard for him to sit on the sidelines so often.

I rest my cheek on his shoulder. "I love you, kid."

He gently drops his head to mine a moment later. "Love you too, sis."

We're still sitting like that, watching Quinn chase after Soleil, letting her stay ahead of him, when a shadow falls over us.

I know who it is before I even look.

"Could we have a chat?" Katrina asks, peering down at me with an expression of pure judgment.

"Yes, of course." I feign a smile and stand, dusting off the back of my jeans.

I follow her down the stairs and onto the sidewalk to the end of Caleb's driveway.

Caleb catches my gaze from where he's refereeing the kickball game. He's tense, poised to run over, like he wants to play referee with us too, but I shake my head. Katrina might intimidate, but I'm used to people like her. At the end of the day, they're just big bullies.

She turns to me, arms crossed in a defensive stance. I mirror the move, a shiver running down my spine that has nothing to do with the temperature.

I barely know this woman, but I don't like her. It was clear the moment she stepped into the kitchen today that she's cold. Calculated.

I can see it in her eyes—how much she dislikes me as well.

She nods her head to where Seda, Quinn, Soleil, and Georgia's boys play.

"She's not his, you know."

Frowning, all I can muster is a confused "huh?"

The comment is so sudden and unexpected that it catches me off guard.

"Seda. He calls her his daughter, but she's not his. Has he told you that?"

Though it's a question, she doesn't wait for me to respond before continuing to spew the venom I have a feeling she saved for this moment. As if this is her true reason for showing up today. To intimidate me, to try to scare me off. If that's the case, I pity her. I can't imagine being so miserable.

"Salem was his high school girlfriend. I always knew she was trouble. Ended up knocked up by the older guy living next door, yet somehow manipulated my son into marrying her. And Caleb? He was more than happy to swoop in and make it all better for her." Every word that comes out of her mouth is dripping with disdain.

Face stony, she looks me up and down like I'm the dirt beneath her shoes. "That's what he does. He takes in the strays and tries to save them."

She's chosen these words carefully, with the intention of wounding me. I know that, yet it doesn't erase the sting they cause.

"He deserves better," she goes on. "Someone right. Someone proper. A woman from a good family. A woman deserving of the Thorne name."

She studies me once more, lip curled in disgust, silently relaying that, in her eyes, I'm not that person. After a heartbeat, she strides toward Caleb to say goodbye. From there, she heads straight to the Mercedes her husband has already started. Neither of them even acknowledges Seda.

That alone guts me more than any other part of today's interaction.

When I turn back to check on Caleb, he's watching me, a hand raised to shield his eyes from the sun and worry deepening the lines on either side of his mouth.

Her words shouldn't cut me, but they do. And she's right in a lot of respects. I'm not proper, nor do I come from a good family. In the past, her words might've been enough to have me breaking things off, but I'm stronger now, and I won't let a woman who's so obviously miserable in her own existence dictate how I feel about myself and those around me.

I walk over to Caleb, who engulfs me in a hug when I get close.

"What'd she want?"

Chin resting on his chest, I give him a small smile. "Nothing important."

His eyes flit across my face like he's trying to read me. "You sure?"

My chest pinches at the concern there. "Yep."

"Halle?" he prompts, clearly unable to let it go.

With a sigh, I say, "It wasn't nice, but it doesn't bear repeating. I know how you feel about me and I'm not going to let your mother get in my head."

He sags. "You shouldn't be trying to keep peace between me and her."

I bristle, straightening. "She's still your mother."

With a kiss to the top of my head, he heaves out a breath. "You're too good for me."

He's wrong. It's the other way around. But I keep that to myself.

Though I didn't grow up in the best of places or under the best circumstances, I *know* Caleb is my person.

I meet his eye, ensuring he can see the truth behind my next words. "I love you."

For an instant, he stiffens, his eyes going wide, but as the words sink in, he groans and presses a kiss to my mouth, his hand warm on my cheek despite the chilly air. "'Bout damn time you got on the same page as me. I love you too, baby."

THIRTY-SIX

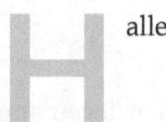

Halle

With the floors ripped out like this, the house looks even worse than it did before the damaged carpets and linoleum were pulled up. Though on occasion, I get the urge to regret the purchase, but it fades quickly each time, because it brought me to this town. To Caleb. To Cynthia and Thelma. Even to Salem and Thayer.

This is where I'm meant to be.

Men dressed in bright t-shirts and stained jeans haul the damaged flooring and floorboards out of the house and toss each piece into the dumpster out front.

Thelma had some choice words for me when the ugly

dumpster arrived. When I told her that I couldn't do anything about the look of it, she went off on a tangent about starting her own dumpster company. If she did, apparently she'd paint them pink and make them glittery. As long as my brothers aren't stealing paint for her again, then she can do whatever she wants, and I wouldn't put it past her to start a dumpster company in the near future. Eventually, she ran out of steam and waddled back home to do more research into the matter.

At the sound of a soft cry, I whip around and scan the street. Seda, head bowed, darts up the steps into Caleb's house.

"Seda?" I hurry after her, the floors a secondary concern now.

I don't catch up to her until she's throwing herself across her pink bedspread.

"Seda, sweetie, what's wrong?"

She wraps her arms around her pillow, her face damp with tears.

"He ... h-he was k-kissing another g-girl," she chokes out between sobs.

"Who was, sweetie?" I smooth her tangled hair back from her forehead. She looks like she ran all the way here from her bus stop at the end of the block.

"Q-Quinn." She wipes at her face.

Oh, God.

"Well, he's almost fifteen," I hedge. "He's about the right age to start dating, I guess, and—"

"They're supposed to wait for me," she wails.

I cover my face with my hands and focus on breathing

while I sort through that statement. "You like both of them?"

"Yes," she sniffles. "They're so cute and nice and—"

Shit. I figured she was sweet on one of them, and I mean, they're identical, so I guess I kind of get it, but she's really gone all in on her first crush … crushes.

Why did it have to be my brothers?

"Well, they're a good bit older than you and—"

"I don't care." She wipes her eyes with the backs of her hands.

My heart aches for her. Young love and first crushes don't always make sense, but the emotions that accompany them can be strong.

"Casen doesn't have a girlfriend, does he?" she asks, her voice rising in panic.

"Um…" Chest pinching, I shake my head. "Not that I know of."

Then again, I didn't know Quinn even liked a girl, let alone was close enough to one to be kissing her. Though since the awkward condom conversation that I'm sure will haunt me for the rest of eternity, I've steered clear of asking about their love lives.

"Why couldn't he kiss me first?" she cries, eyes pleading.

"Umm…" I worry my bottom lip, wishing Caleb were here to handle this. "You're ten, and they're almost fifteen, so—"

"And I'm almost eleven."

"Yeah, but right now, a four-year age difference is a big

deal. Once you're adults, age gaps like that aren't as big an issue."

Her eyes widen in a mix of excitement and horror. "You mean I still have a chance with them, but not until I'm twenty?"

I'm not going to touch on the *them* part of that question, deciding to assume she means that she might have a chance with one of them. Surely that's what she means, right?

"Um, yeah." I heave a breath. It's better to reassure her than crush her spirit even more, right?

Still sniffling, she says, "My mom is running errands. Is it okay if I hang out here until she gets home?"

"Yeah, sweetie. That's fine. Do you want a snack?"

"No," she sighs. "I just want to lay here and listen to sad music."

"Oh." I stand slowly. "Just holler for me if you need anything."

"Thanks." She gives one last sniffle. "And thank you for talking to me."

"Mhm," I hum, easing out of the room. "You're welcome."

I shut her door quietly behind me and let out a deep breath. Then I pray that this crush passes quickly. For all our sakes.

Despite my better judgment, the second Quinn steps into the house, I blurt out, "Who's the girl you were kissing?"

"Jesus." He slaps a hand to his chest. "Where did you come from?"

"Do you have a girlfriend?" I ask.

Casen shuffles in behind him. He's doing much better with his crutches, but they still slow him down. He refuses to let me take him or pick him up from school anymore, but from the look of things, getting home from the bus stop is a chore. He makes it over to the couch and drops down onto it, backpack and shoes still on. When the crutches clatter to the floor, no one bats an eye. It's a regular occurrence anymore.

"Sort of," Quinn answers. "How do you know?"

"Seda saw you kissing a girl."

Shit, the words are out before I can stop them. The last thing I want is to throw her under the bus, but it's too late to backpedal now.

"Oh," he breathes, his dark eyes going soft. "Is she ... okay?"

Casen snorts, sprawled out like a starfish. "Probably not."

I wince. Looks like they're not oblivious to her crush.

"She came home crying. She's upstairs right now."

Quinn rubs his jaw. "Crap. I should probably go talk to her."

I frown, stepping in front of him. "Do you think that's best?"

Casen hauls himself up to one foot. "Nah, I'll talk to her."

Hands thrown up, I surrender to their discretion. "Do whatever you guys think is best."

I leave them to work it out while I start dinner. Caleb's in Boston, so we're on our own. I've always fought the idea of becoming dependent on a man, and I like to think I'm still self-sufficient, but I *miss* him when he's not around. Being in love can be quite annoying in that way.

I'm halfway through making dinner when Seda comes downstairs without the boys.

"Hey, sweetie." I blow an errant hair out of my eyes. "How are you feeling now?"

"Better." She gives me a small smile. Though her eyes are puffy, her face is no longer blotchy.

"Do you want to stay with us for dinner?"

She pulls out one of the barstools and clambers up onto it. "What are you making?"

I peek into the oven, then straighten and turn to her. "Pork chops with mashed potatoes, green beans, and rolls."

With a shrug, she traces a line in the marble countertop. "Sounds good, sure. My dad is staying in Boston tonight."

"Yeah, I know." I turn my back to take the mashed potatoes out of the microwave and give them a good stir. No homemade potatoes here tonight. I don't have time for that. When they're fluffy, I set them on a potholder and face her again.

"Do you miss him?" She balances on her knees, elbow on the counter with her chin in her hand. She looks so much like her mother it actually stuns me for a moment.

I give her a soft smile. "Of course I miss him."

"Good."

I can't help but laugh. "What would you do if I said I didn't miss him?"

She doesn't hesitate. "I'd tell him."

A louder laugh escapes me. "You're protective of your dad, aren't you?"

"Yeah," she says easily. "He's one of my favorite people."

My chest warms at the sentiment. It's incredible that, despite the unusual circumstances, Caleb, Salem, and Thayer have managed to come together to raise this spectacular child.

When dinner is ready, I make up plates for all four of us and call for the boys to join us.

As Casen comes down the stairs on his butt—finding it much easier than hobbling precariously from one to another—it's hard not to wish time would move more quickly so he can be cast-free again. At his follow-up, the doctor was hopeful he could be in a walking boot before Christmas.

Christmas.

The holiday is only a few weeks away, and I haven't bought a single gift. My brothers will be easy enough to shop for, but Caleb? I've yet to figure out what to get the man who has everything.

Seda heads home after dinner and my brothers shock me by asking me to watch a movie with them. Armed with bowls of ice cream, we lounge on the couch to watch a racing movie I've never heard of. It's not my kind of thing, but I'm happy to be included.

Rather than focus on the movie, I study them. They're turning into pretty decent young men, and with any luck, I won't fuck this whole thing up.

They're at a pivotal point in their lives, and they're stuck with their older sister as their only parental figure. I'm not sure how well that bodes for them.

When the movie is over, the boys settle in for the night, and after I've washed my face and changed into pajamas, I check on them, standing in the doorway, close to tears. I might not be a mother yet, but I've played a part in raising my brothers since they were newborns. In a month, they'll be fifteen. Before I know it, they'll be driving. Then eighteen is around the corner. And with these milestones will come girls, cars, jobs, maybe even college. They'll live entire lives.

Casen catches me in the doorway as he adjusts the pillow behind his head. "Oh no, Quinn. She's doing it."

"Doing what?" Quinn asks, rolling over and groans. "Halle, stop reminiscing. It makes you all teary, and we're not good with tears and shit."

"I'm fine," I say, the choked words belying the sentiment. "Just thinking about how quickly you guys are growing up."

"Yeah." Quinn throws his arms out to his sides. "You're reminiscing."

With a sniffle, I say, "Good night, losers. Love you."

"Love you," they echo as I close their door.

Down the hall, I step into the room I've been staying in. But halfway to the bed, I turn on my heel. Then I head straight to Caleb's. Tucked beneath the covers, I pull his pillow against my chest, letting his scent engulf me like a cozy blanket, and fall right to sleep.

THIRTY-SEVEN

Caleb

Halle isn't answering her phone.

Or emails.

Or texts.

And in my gut, I know something is wrong. She's supposed to be working today. It would take a catastrophic event to keep her from doing her job, and even then, she'd let me know.

When yet another call goes to voicemail, I shove away from my desk. Until I hear from her, I won't get anything done. I'm too fucking out of my mind with worry.

I stop by the senior partner's office to let her know I'm leaving, then I speed all the way to Hawthorne Mills.

Before I get on the highway, I try Halle one more time.

And by some miracle, she answers.

"Hello?" she croaks, sounding so unlike herself.

"Are you okay?" I bark out, white-knuckling the steering wheel.

"I'm sick," she mumbles. "I've thrown up so many times. I think it's the flu." She gasps, and then there's muffled rustling on the other end of the phone. "Oh my God, I'm supposed to be working. I'll get logged—"

"You'll do no such thing," I grit out. If she's sick, she should be in bed. "I'm on my way home."

"Why? What happened?"

I tap my thumb against the steering wheel. Is she serious?

Who am I kidding? Of course she is.

"You, Halle. You happened."

Her quiet "oh" nearly crushes me.

"I'm going to stop and pick up a few things for you on the way. I'm getting on the highway now."

"You really don't have to come home," she whispers. "I'll be okay. I can take care of myself. Wouldn't be the first time."

"Things are different now," I remind her. "You have me."

"I gotta go," she says, her tone panicked. More rustling, followed by a whimper, and just before the line cuts off, she retches.

Heart hammering, I press harder on the accelerator.

At home, I have plenty of Tylenol and Advil to help with her fever, as well as broth I can use to make a simple soup, but I'm pretty sure the boys have finished off the sports drinks, so I grab several of those, as well as a box of crackers, at the pharmacy on the edge of town.

As I head toward the checkout, the sign above another aisle catches my eye, and my gut clenches.

No.

But it *is* possible.

I swipe a pregnancy test from the shelf and drop it in the basket. Then, for good measure, I add two more. Better safe than sorry. We haven't been the most diligent about condoms, but on the occasions that we haven't used them, I've pulled out. Even so, the technique is called pull and pray for a reason.

I check out, knowing full well that the cashier who's known me my whole life will call my mother and give her a list of the items I purchase as soon as I'm out of here.

Oh well.

The house is quiet when I let myself inside. The boys are at school, and if Halle isn't in bed, she's gonna hear it from me.

As I make my way upstairs, I loosen my tie and the first few buttons of my shirt.

When I ease her bedroom door open, all I find is an empty bed, made up with throw pillows and everything.

I close the door and continue down the hall. Finally, I find Halle passed out in my bed, mouth hanging open and dark hair a wild halo around her head. There's a glass of water on the nightstand, as well as the Advil, and there's a trash can beside her on the floor.

As quietly as I can, I set the plastic bag on the bench at the foot of the mattress, then toe off my shoes and check her forehead. She's warm, but I don't think she has a fever.

At my touch, she stirs, blinking bleary eyes open.

"Caleb? You really did come?"

I sit beside her, easing onto the mattress to keep from jostling her. "I told you I was on my way, baby. Did you think I made it up?"

"I thought I dreamed the whole thing," she mumbles. "I've been up and down since three. Or maybe it was two? Four?" She prattles on. "I can't remember."

"How are you feeling now?" I tuck a piece of hair behind her ear.

"Like my mouth is gross, and if I move, I might die."

I chuckle. "That bad, huh?"

Groaning, she squeezes her eyes shut. "You have no idea. Everything aches, and after all the puking, it feels like I've done the longest core workout of my life."

"Do you think you can sit up?"

"Maybe." She inhales a shaky breath and braces herself. When I lean in to help her, she holds up a hand. "Don't get too close. I haven't brushed my teeth. I tried, but it made me throw up again."

"Baby," I croon, chest aching. Fuck, I feel helpless right now.

As she slowly works her way up to a sitting position, I crack the lid of a Gatorade, and when she's settled again, I hold it for her, tipping the liquid to her lips. She takes three meager sips before she guides my hand away.

"Think you can drink some more?" I probe.

She shakes her head. "I'm so—"

She retches, lunging for the trash can. I reach it before she does and hold it while she vomits the Gatorade right back up.

She takes the basket from me, wrapping both arms around it, and while she heaves again, I set the bottle on the nightstand and pull her hair away from her face, rubbing her back, wishing I could do more to comfort her.

When she finishes, she groans. "That's what happens every time I try to drink."

I touch the back of my hand to her forehead again, swearing she's warmer than she was moments ago.

Or maybe my paranoia is getting the best of me.

"Let's get you into a cool shower."

"No," she whines. "I'm too tired and achy. And I'm *cold*. I need a hot shower."

I shake my head and stand. "Not a chance, pretty girl."

I leave her long enough to start the shower, and when I return, I find her with her legs slung over the edge of the bed, hands planted firmly at her sides. From the concentration scrunching her face, I assume she's working up the nerve to stand.

"Let me get you, baby," I plead.

She shakes her head, as stubborn as ever.

I crouch in front of her, tapping her bare knee. When I realize the over-sized shirt is *my* shirt, I'm filled with a ridiculous amount of satisfaction.

"If I carry you to the bathroom, I promise it won't make you less of a badass."

"I'm afraid I'll puke on you."

I clench my jaw to keep from smiling. "I took care of a newborn. I've been peed on, pooped on, and thrown up on. I'll survive."

"Yeah, but newborns are cute."

I tap her knee again and wait for her to look at me again. "And you're my girl and you're beautiful. Let me take care of you. All I want is to be your person, Halle. Let me be that."

Her lower lip wobbles, her eyes going misty. "It's really unfair for you to be so sweet when I smell like throw-up and sweat."

"Come on, love." I scoop her up. "I've got you."

She wraps her arms around my neck, giving in, and rests her head on my shoulder.

I don't stop moving until we're in the shower, clothes and all.

"Ugh." She clings to me as I sit on the built-in bench. "I need it warmer."

"I can't make it any warmer if you have a fever."

"You didn't even take my temperature," she whines. "I might not have a fever."

"Better safe than sorry." I kiss the side of her forehead. For a moment, I hold her like that, soaking in the way she's letting me literally hold her up. Eventually, though, I clear my throat, preparing for the ire my next words will be met with. "I want you to take a pregnancy test too."

She goes rigid in my arms, but she doesn't try to escape me like I thought she would. "I'm not pregnant."

"You could be." I push her wet hair back, my dress shirt clinging to my skin. "We haven't been careful every time."

"I take birth control," she argues. "Never miss a pill."

"People get pregnant on the pill. Shit happens. Just take one."

She pulls back, her eyes tearing up in earnest now, the droplets mixing with the water clinging to her lashes. "I love you, but I don't want to be pregnant. I'm not ready now."

"I know, baby." I cuff her neck gently, massaging with my fingertips. Truth be told, as much as I want more kids, I'm not ready for a baby right now either. Selfishly I want more time with Halle first. Even if we've already got the boys and Seda. "I still think you should take a test."

"Fine," she grumbles. "But I probably don't have enough liquid left in me to pee."

That pulls a chuckle from me. "In the morning, then."

"Okay." She heaves a sigh and burrows into me again. We stay like that for another minute or two before she says, "I think I can keep it together if you're willing to help me wash up."

I stand, then ease her to the tile seat, wishing I could turn up the temperature when she shivers. Once I've removed her shirt, I step out of the shower long enough to grab a washcloth. I add my soap to the cloth, then glide it gently over her body.

Eyes closed, she lays her head back. This moment, despite how bad she feels, is one I'll treasure forever. For the first time, she's giving me her complete trust. This privilege, to care for her when she's her most vulnerable, is far more precious and intimate than sex.

I wash her hair quickly, and while I'm working the conditioner in, she goes peaked. Stomach sinking, I lean out of the shower and snag the bathroom trashcan.

But, stubborn as ever, she holds it together. She's stoic as I turn off the water and dry her off, and she's breathing deeply as I drag another of my shirts over her head.

"I need to brush my hair," she mumbles. "Or else it will tangle."

"I'll brush it for you."

I close the toilet lid and point for her to sit. "I'll get your brush."

Quickly, I dart into her bathroom to get it. When I return, she's gripping the trashcan.

"Did you get sick?" I ask.

"No, but my stomach started lurching again."

"Mmm. If you need to, I'm here to help." I divide her hair into sections and begin combing it out.

"How are you so good at this?" she asks as I finish the first section.

I pause, hand held in the air, on the verge of laughter. "How do you think?"

"Oh, yeah," she breathes, slumping. "You have a daughter." I'm almost finished with the last section of hair when she speaks again. "She came home crying yesterday. She saw Quinn kissing a girl."

My heart pangs. Though I hate the obsession she has

with the boys, I hate the idea of my little girl being upset. "She was heartbroken?"

"Unbelievably. Hopefully her next crush will be someone her age."

I grunt, jaw clenched. "I hope she never has another crush."

"Unlikely."

"I know." I lean over her, setting her brush down. As I move, I'm hit with a cool shot of air, and I shiver.

Halle peeks over her shoulder, frowning at my wet clothes. "You need to change, or you'll be sick too."

I pick up her towel and scrunch her hair, sure to get the excess moisture from it. "I'm okay."

"Caleb." The warning tone is one she usually reserves for her brothers. I'm not sure what she thinks she's going to do to me, since she can barely stand without help, but I like it when she tries to act bossy.

"Let me get you into bed, and then I'll change."

"No," she counters. "The water will soak into my t-shirt. Change first."

Admitting defeat, I take a step away and unbutton my shirt. I drape it over the towel rod, along with my pants. Then I toss my socks into the hamper.

"Take it off," she attempts to catcall when I'm in nothing but my underwear. The tease falls flat, her voice too weak.

With a smirk, I saunter into the closet. I shuck my underwear and pull a pair of sleep pants from the drawer.

"No funny business tonight, sweetheart," I say as I emerge, covered from the waist down.

Once I've got her situated in bed again, I hold the

Gatorade out to her. "Sip. We need to keep you from getting dehydrated."

"You're so fucking bossy," she grumbles.

"When it comes to your well-being, hell yeah I am."

She takes a couple of slow, tentative sips, and when it doesn't immediately come back up, I breathe a sigh of relief.

"I have a humidifier around here somewhere. I'm going to dig around for that and get it set up."

"I don't think I need a humidifier." She stifles a yawn. "I'm not congested."

"Google said it would help."

"Fine." She slumps back against the headboard, eyelids heavy. "Whatever you say."

I locate the humidifier in the hall closet and set it outside my bedroom door to set up later. Then I go downstairs and search the pantry for the can of broth I know is hiding somewhere. Once I've found it, I text Salem, warning her to keep Seda away for now. If Halle is contagious, the last thing we need is for Seda to end up with the bug and take it home to her siblings.

With that taken care of, I call Thelma and ask if the boys can crash with them for a night or two. Unsurprisingly, she and Cynthia are all too happy to take them. Next, I let the boys know the plan and ask them to text me a list of things to pack for them.

> Casen: Sweet. I can work on my whale some more.

> Me: Whale?

Casen: I'm crocheting a whale.

Quinn: My triceratops is cooler.

I shake my head, fighting a smile. I'll never understand the friendship that's developed between the boys and the elderly ladies across the street, but I appreciate it, nonetheless.

Me: I'll leave the bag by the door. Just pick it up when you get off the bus.

Casen: <thumbs-up>

Quinn: Wait. How do we know Halle's sick and you're not kidnapping our sister? You could be holding her hostage.

Me: Seriously? And didn't she tell you she was sick this morning?

Casen: She did.

Quinn: Doesn't mean you're not holding her hostage.

Quinn: Tell her to FaceTime us tonight. We need proof of life.

Casen: Stop being an asshole.

Me: Whatever makes you feel better.

Quinn: Cool.

Casen: Whatever.

By the state of the kitchen, it's obvious the boys fed themselves this morning. Cereal bowls with sugary milk sit in the sink, several cabinets aren't fully shut, and though the orange juice made it back into the fridge, its lid did not.

I want to check on Halle, but I'm hopeful she was able to go to sleep, so I putter around the house, folding and refolding the throw blankets in the living room. I dig a shoe out from under the couch—one of Casen's that went missing days ago.

I'm shoving the boys' video game cases back onto a shelf when there's a soft knock on the front door.

"How's she feeling?" Salem asks when I pull the door open.

"Better, I think, but I'm trying to let her rest."

She rolls her eyes playfully. "You've always been such a hover-er. This must be killing you. Anyway, I had leftover chicken noodle soup in the freezer. Figured it might help."

"Thanks." I take the container from her with a grateful smile.

"And a cupcake for you." She balances it on top of the container, then takes a step back. "Cupcakes make every day better. If you need anything, let me know."

Once she's gone, I put the soup in the fridge, figuring I'll be pushing my luck if I try to feed Halle anything other than plain broth tonight.

I disinfect the first floor, hoping like hell it'll keep the rest of us from getting sick. Then, unable to resist the temptation, I peek in on Halle. She's asleep again, her mouth ajar like it was earlier.

God, she's fucking adorable.

But she'd probably kill me for thinking so.

I pack a bag for the boys and set it on the front porch,

adding necessities, like toothbrushes and deodorant, they forgot to add to the list. I probably don't want to know what kind of shit they're going to get into with Cynthia and Thelma. Something tells me it'll be more than crochet.

With nothing else to do, I make myself a quick meal. I'm not all that hungry, but I figure it's better if I eat while Halle is still asleep.

It's weird, how quiet the house is now that I'm effectively alone. I've been on my own a while, but living with other people for a few months has left me spoiled. They've brought life into my home, and I dread the day they move out. It's selfish of me. I'm sure they're anxious to get back into their own space, but I … fuck, it's going to suck. Yeah, they'll only be next door, but the distance isn't the issue here. What eats at me the most is knowing I'll be alone again. I've found my people—is it so wrong to want to be with them?

I'm putting my plate in the dishwasher when the floor above creaks.

As much as I want to rush upstairs to help Halle, I hold myself back.

She's not the kind of girl to take kindly to my smothering.

Five minutes is all I manage to wait, though, before I force myself to take slow steps upstairs.

When I step into my room, she's propped up in bed, wearing a tired smile.

"Hey," she says softly. "Thank you for letting me sleep."

"You were out for a while." I look her over, wishing I could interpret how she feels. "You needed the rest."

"I'm sorry I took over your bedroom."

"Halle," I sigh as I shuffle closer. "The last thing I'm worried about is you in my room."

"Still, I'm sure you want your room back. I can—"

I quiet her with a look. "Nice try."

"Then you should stay in my room. I don't want to get you sick."

I shake my head. "Nope. I'm good here." I step up to her side of the bed and hand her the mug I've filled with warm broth.

Her lips turn down. "But what if you get sick?"

"Then you can take care of me." I wink. "Eat up. It'll help."

She scrutinizes the liquid for a moment, then, without argument, she takes a sip.

I settle into bed beside her and turn the TV on. "Anything in particular you want to watch?"

"Trashy reality TV? It's the worst, but I love it."

I laugh and flick through the channels until I find a show with several women sitting around in a fancy home with high ceilings and monochromatic decor. "This?"

"Perfect." She gives me a tired smile, but it falls quickly, her shoulders curling inward. "I'm really sorry you had to come all the way home to take care of me."

I shrug. "I'm not. There's no place I'd rather be."

Head tilted, she searches my face. "You really mean that, don't you?"

"I'm not in the habit of saying things I don't mean. You should know that by now."

She's quiet for a long while, slowly sipping her broth off a spoon. Eventually, she says, "I'm glad you came home."

I smile over at her. "Me too."

"I love you," she whispers, the words sticking in her throat.

It's hard for her to admit it, but that doesn't bother me. For Halle, love makes a person vulnerable. For me, love makes them stronger.

With any luck, she'll see it my way one day.

"I love you too."

With a smile, she sets the mug on the table. Then she wiggles her way to my side and snuggles into me, her head on my shoulder.

I can't help but brush my lips over her crown. The day this girl moved in next door, I couldn't have imagined she'd move into my heart too, but now that she's there, she's not going anywhere.

THIRTY-EIGHT

Halle

The stomach bug lasts less than twenty-four hours, but when I wake and shuffle to the bathroom, I still feel weak.

Before I've even lifted the toilet lid, the door opens behind me, and Caleb appears.

Shit. Why didn't I lock it behind me?

"What are you—"

He pulls his hand from behind his back, waving a pink box in the air.

Damn pregnancy test. With a sigh, I glower at the box.

"I'm *not* pregnant." We've been safe ... mostly ... and I

don't want to be pregnant, therefore I refuse to accept this as a possibility.

"Please." He waggles the box in front of me. "For my peace of mind."

"Get me a cup," I grumble, snatching the box from him.

Smiling in victory, he plucks a paper cup from beneath his sink and passes it to me. Then he just ... stands there.

"Get out." I shoo him toward the door. "Let me retain what little dignity I have left after yesterday, please."

He crosses his arms over his chest, leaning his butt against the counter. "You promise to take it?"

"Yes." I hold out my little finger as my bladder screams at me to get it over with. "Pinky promise."

He loops his pinky through mine, and with a nod, exits.

I flick the lock before he can change his mind and barrel back in.

Once I've relieved myself—and filled the cup—I wash my hands and pull the instructions from the box.

Why is this so complicated? I may not be puking anymore, but my mind is a mess.

A knock startles me, making me drop the instructions. "Can I come back in?"

With a sigh, I pick them up, then turn the lock and shove them at him.

"What does this even mean?" It's all gibberish.

He takes it and reads it over. Then, without a word, he removes the test and dips it into my urine. Totally at ease, he sets the stick on its wrapper on the counter, then turns to me and crosses his arms. "Now, we wait."

"It was really that simple?" I gripe.

Smiling, he steps in close and cuffs my neck, pulling me against his chest. "I notice that when you panic, you shut down. It's okay. You have me."

Yeah, I do have him, which is the wildest part of all of this.

This man needed to be in Boston, but he didn't hesitate to hop in the car and drive home to look after me.

While we wait, he keeps me pressed against him. Nerves rattle through me, causing my stomach to roll, but his heartbeat remains steady.

All too soon, he releases me and looks at his watch. "Time to check."

He presses his lips to the side of my forehead, then picks up the test. Eyes darting to it, he sobers, then studies me, as if gauging how I might react.

I cover my eyes and sink my teeth into my bottom lip. "Just tell me."

"It's negative."

A gust of air leaves me all at once. "Oh, thank God."

The possibility was almost nonexistent, but that didn't stop me from panicking. The last thing either of us needs right now is an unplanned pregnancy.

"I'm going back to bed and sleeping for a hundred years," I tell him.

With a chuckle, he grasps my wrist and tugs me gently back to him. For a moment, he just looks at me, as if studying my features. I open my mouth, itching to break the silence, but before I can, he says, "I love you."

I smile. Hearing those words from Caleb is *everything*.

He proves every day that he means them, whereas my mom used to use them as manipulation.

"I love you too."

"Get some more rest." He gives my ass a light swat. "I'm going to make toast before you doze off, though. Think you can get that down?"

I frown, but nod. Though my stomach is telling me no, my brain recognizes that I need to eat at least a little. "I'll try."

With a soft smile, he guides me back into the bedroom, and as he leaves, I settle back into his bed. The guestroom mattress is pretty great, but it's got nothing on his. It's enormous, and he has the softest sheets imaginable. The bonus? They smell like him. I never want to sleep in another bed again, and something tells me Caleb would be all too happy to give in to that fantasy.

While I wait for him to return, I channel surf. Eventually I come across a documentary on penguins, but within minutes, I'm tearing up over the real footage of a sea lion chasing one into the water and capturing it.

No, thank you. Instead, I settle on a Hallmark movie. Cheesy, predictable, and exactly what I need while I'm still recovering from this bug.

The stairs squeak beneath Caleb's feet, and when he appears, he proudly holds out a piece of buttered toast on a plate. "Your breakfast, milady."

I roll my eyes. "You're ridiculous."

"And a glass of water." He sets a glass on the nightstand and the plate in my lap.

"Don't you have work to do?"

He settles into the bed beside me, crossing his legs at the ankles. "No. I took the day off."

My heart lurches. "Because of me?"

"*For* you," he corrects.

Is there a difference?

He lifts his shoulders easily. "I have more vacation days than I know what to do with. It's not a big deal."

The toast is dry and crumbly, the last thing I want, but I take a bite and manage to get half the slice down, which makes Caleb smile with more pride than seems warranted.

As I set the plate on the mattress beside me, I realize that despite the dry toast and the whole puking my guts up thing, I'm truly, genuinely happy.

For so long, I wasn't sure it was possible—this feeling of contentedness, the belief that my life is going the way it should. I'm not saying my days are all rainbows and sunshine, but they're pretty damn incredible.

THIRTY-NINE

Halle

I *loathe* Christmas shopping. It has absolutely nothing to do with my lack of budget and everything to do with how obnoxious people can be.

"What do you mean you don't have this in a size nine?" the man in front of me complains. Again.

I just want to check out, and he's having a meltdown trying to get shoes for his wife.

The poor girl at the register sighs. "You can order them online—"

"But I need them now. I don't have time for shipping

and all that." He waves a hand wildly, nearly taking me out in the process.

Thankfully, another cashier comes over and takes pity on me.

"I can check you out over here, ma'am."

I set the boxes—sneakers for my brothers—on the counter with a grateful smile. When I asked them what they wanted for Christmas, they fought me. They're old enough to understand that money is tight, and they don't want to add to that burden. I could see it in their eyes. But they're crazy if they think I'm not getting them Christmas gifts. After more than one argument, I proposed the idea of a *want, need, wear, and read* Christmas, and they were on board with that.

Though I separated them and had them each write out a list of a few items for each category so I'd have options, the items they chose were nearly identical except for the book section.

Both requested crochet supplies. It was the last thing I expected, but pretty adorable, even if I've yet to see any of the projects they've been working on.

When the cashier gives me the total, I try to hide the cringe that overtakes me. Even on sale, the shoes are pricey. I dig in my purse for my wallet, and as I pull my hand out again, a piece of paper slips out and flutters to the floor.

"Crap," I mutter, bending over to pick it up.

With no recollection of what it is, I carefully open it.

Caleb's writing is scrawled across the page, and dammit if my heart doesn't beat a million times faster.

I can guarantee that I'm thinking about you right now.

Miss you.

—Caleb

I smile and tuck the note back into my purse. He's been in Boston since about two days after I got sick. It took that long to convince him that I was fine. He's working overtime to wrap up a couple of cases so he can spend several weeks at home over the holidays. I miss him more than seems possible. I don't like being this lovesick girl, but I wouldn't give it up if it meant losing Caleb.

Once I've checked out, I head to the bookstore and grab a comic book for Quinn and a fantasy for Casen.

Next is wrapping paper and a roll of tape, then I head back home to get this done.

I pull into Caleb's driveway, and when I catch sight of the men working next door, my stomach dips in dread. I don't want to go back there.

I'm so fucked.

Caleb's coming home tonight.

I wish I could say I'm not excited, but it would be a lie.

All day, I've teased him, and it's the most fun I've ever had.

> Me: I can't wait for you to bend me over your bed and fill me up with your hard cock.

> Caleb: Halle.

I smile, figuring he's probably sighing at his phone right about now.

> Me: I'm so wet already. You won't mind if I take care of myself while I wait, will you?

I snap a photo, a teasing taunt of my fingers slipping beneath the elastic of my leggings.

His text comes through seconds later.

> Caleb: Don't you dare touch yourself until I tell you.

I drop my head back and laugh. God, it's so fun to rile him up. I've never experienced this kind of comfort with another person. A feeling of safety that allows me to play.

> Me: But I really need to.

I'm actually at my desk, working, not in bed actually touching myself, but this is way more fun than a solo session—knowing *he's* getting worked up and can't do anything about it.

My phone rings, his name flashing on the screen. I send him to voicemail.

> Caleb: ANSWER YOUR PHONE.

> Caleb: So help me God, Halle. If you're touching yourself right now, I will spank your ass raw when I get ahold of you.

Giggling, I kick my feet, causing my chair to roll. I've

never been like this in my life, but Caleb makes me feel safe enough to feel happy and have fun. I'm not waiting for the other shoe to drop with him.

> Me: I have to get back to work. My boss is kind of a hard-ass.

> Caleb: I am your boss.

> Me: I know.

Snickering to myself, I set my phone aside, fully planning to torture him more later. It's too much fun not to.

At the sound of the front door opening, I turn to check the clock. After dinner, the boys asked if they could stay with Cynthia and Thelma tonight. I okayed it with the neighbor ladies first, and the twins left while I cleaned up. When I was alone, I took my time showering, then crawled into bed, knowing Caleb would be late.

Thunderous steps sound on the stairs, making my heart rate pick up.

Oh.

The door flies open, banging against the wall, startling me.

"Caleb?" I squeak as he enters the room. I shut my laptop and sit up, the move causing my loose t-shirt to fall over my shoulder. Caleb may have purchased the garment for himself, but it's mine now.

He shuts the bedroom door behind him and locks it. "Where are your brothers?" He undoes his tie with a violent yank. The intensity radiating off him has me scooting back.

Not in fear, but in anticipation.

I wet my lips. "They're with Cynthia and Thelma."

The tie drops to the floor. "For how long?" he asks as he works the top button of his crisp work shirt.

"They're spending the night. Caleb—"

"Good." He drops the shirt near the tie and leans forward, wrapping one hand around my ankle and pulling me down the bed.

I squeal as the shirt bunches beneath me. I'm not wearing a bra beneath. Only underwear.

"You thought you could tease me at work all fucking day, and I wasn't going to punish you for it?" His eyes flash with heat. "Do you like knowing I was stuck at my desk all fucking day because I was so hard? I couldn't even get up and get a glass of water."

I giggle. "Oh, that's what this is about?"

"Oh," he mocks, yanking off his belt. "You *wanted* this, huh?"

Excitement burns in my veins.

The metal buckle clinks as he drops the belt to the mattress. Then, before I know what's happening, he's got me flipped over so I'm on all fours.

He yanks my arms behind my back, and I cry out in surprise.

Oh my God. He's tying my wrists with his belt.

Heat floods my body as he secures them over my head. This act alone is going to leave me soaked.

Holy fuck.

He rubs the curves of my ass over my cotton boy short underwear, pulling a moan from me. The sound quickly turns into a sharp cry when he delivers a smack to each cheek.

"Caleb," I whimper, the side of my face pressed into the mattress.

My heart accelerates when he backs away. I can't see him, but his warmth has disappeared. I try to wiggle around, but before I can, he's there again, delivering another smack.

I huff, pushing back, because although my ass stings, I'm only more desperate and aching for his touch.

"So fucking naughty," he croons. He pulls my underwear down and off and massages my bare cheeks. "Taunting me all fucking day. I bet you sat in my office laughing at me, didn't you?"

"Only a little," I admit.

He chuckles, the sound dark and promising. "You're gonna regret that, pretty girl."

I wiggle in anticipation.

Deep down, I knew this side of Caleb existed, just waiting to be unleashed, and I'm glad I'm the one he feels safe letting his walls down with.

"I don't think I will."

Rather than respond with words, he startles the hell out of me by slamming inside me, burying his cock deep and grinding his hips against my ass. Thank God I'm already soaked.

"Holy fuck," I curse, my body going limp.

"Such." *Smack.* "A." *Smack.* "Tease." *Smack.* "Fuck," he curses lowly. "You like this, don't you?" He curls his body over mine. "You get even wetter each time I swat your gorgeous ass." He grips my chin, forcing me to turn and look at him. "My naughty girl."

"Yes," I gasp out.

The press of his body over mine as he drills into me is almost too much to take. I've never been fucked like this in my life. He's powerful, all-consuming. He's in complete control. His movements are rough, but every now and then I'll feel a gentle caress of his fingers over my hips or the curve of my breasts, as if he wants to remind me that, while this is the definition of fucking, he still *loves* me.

If I voiced even a moment of hesitancy over his roughness, he would stop. I have no doubt. But I don't want him to. I like him like this—unleashed and losing his ever-loving mind because of *me*.

I'm teetering on that delicious edge when he pulls out of me, taking the sensation with him. I cry out in annoyance as he flips me onto my back and cups my cheek roughly.

"Doesn't feel good to be edged, now, does it?" He taunts, licking his lips. "How long do you think I should make you suffer before I finally let you come?"

I whimper, my breathing shallow. "I don't know."

He lowers himself, his body heavy on mine, his lips finding my ear. "You made me suffer for *hours*, Halle. Should I make you beg for it?"

Yes.

It's wild, how quickly the word forms in my mind, how easily the excitement swarms in my belly.

"Touch yourself," he demands.

I yank on my restraints with a pained cry.

He grins wickedly. "Oh, wait, you can't."

With a light, teasing touch, he plays with my clit.

I gasp, back arching.

The move makes his smile grow. Then his fingers are gone. He's enjoying torturing me way too much.

I'm delirious with pent-up need when he slips his fingers inside me and curls them, once again bringing me to the edge.

When I'm sure I'll tumble over it, his touch vanishes and so does the feeling.

"Caleb!" I squeeze my legs together, desperate for friction.

He pushes my knees apart with firm hands. "Nice try, baby."

Eyes narrowed, I stare him down. "You're being mean."

With a hint of a smile dancing on his lips, he arches a brow. "So were you."

A bubble of laughter that seems totally out of place rises up and escapes me. Fuck, I can't help it. "It's fun messing with you."

He tilts his head to the side. "Worth the consequences?" With a little caress, he lets go of one of my thighs and wraps a firm hand around his dick. He strokes roughly, his focus never leaving my face.

I'm rapt, unable to look away from the way he touches himself.

"Want a taste?" he taunts.

My heart stutters. "Yes."

He helps me to my knees, easing my arms down so they're secured in front of me, and I kneel in front of him. It's vulnerable—the position and the inability to use my hands—but I know I'm safe with him.

He rubs a gentle finger over my chin. The sensation is in complete juxtaposition with his words when he grits out, "Suck it."

Without hesitation, I lean forward, taking him into my mouth. Instantly, the taste of the two of us bursts on my tongue, pulling a moan from deep within me. I'd give just about anything to touch myself right now, but I don't dare ask him to untie me. I already know what the answer will be.

I work my mouth over his length. Licking and sucking.

Every time I peer up at him, he's watching me with approval in his eyes, the blue of his irises nearly swallowed by his pupils.

Delving his fingers into my hair, he holds it back from my face.

Such a gentleman, even when he's destroying me.

When he pulls back, I mewl in protest. But when he picks me up, guiding my legs around his waist, I can't help but grind against him.

He lays me back down on the bed, and between one blink and the next, he's sheathed himself inside me.

"Oh my God," I cry out, pinching my eyes shut.

"Look at me," he commands with a roll of his hips. "Don't you dare close your fucking eyes."

I peel my eyes open, and God, am I glad that I do. The way he looks at me makes me feel *alive*.

He shoves my shirt up and over my breasts, wetting his lips as he takes me in.

In this moment, I may be the one tied up, but I feel powerful. In charge. I can bring this man to his *knees*.

The sound I make when he drags me to the edge and back again this time is a cross between a cry, a scream, and a moan. I'm frustrated, but I can't deny that I *like* the torture.

He grins down at me, rubbing the tip of his cock against my clit.

"Look at you," he croons. "You want this, don't you? You like it when I push you to the edge, then force you back. You like it when I taunt you. Don't worry, baby, it'll be so worth it when you finally come."

I whimper, digging my teeth into my bottom lip. My body feels like one giant live wire. All it needs is a spark to ignite it, and that spark is Caleb.

He spreads my legs wide and kneels between them, then places a gentle kiss to my clit.

A groan of pent-up fury rips out of me.

I *need* to come. My body is begging for it.

"Caleb."

"Shh," he hushes, rubbing his finger lazily around and around my clit. "Let me enjoy this."

Finally, he puts his mouth on me, and my back bows off the bed. My wrists strain against the belt. I want to touch him. *Need* to touch him.

He licks and sucks, driving me wild in the way only he can.

I'm so close to coming. Closer than I've been since this

started. For an instant, I'm certain he'll let me come this time.

But I'm so, so wrong.

Just when I start to fall, he pulls me back again but—

I go from empty, hollow, to fuller than I've ever felt in the space of one heartbeat.

"Caleb!" I scream his name so loud I fear the neighbors might hear. I should be embarrassed, but I'm too wound up. "I'm coming. I'm coming. I'm coming."

My words turn into a nonsensical chant as I lose touch with reality, my vision going spotty. Flashes of black and white against my closed lids.

The orgasm lasts for an incomprehensible amount of time. It could be a few seconds, it could be a lifetime.

"Holy fuck," he curses, keeping up his rhythm. "Your pussy is still squeezing the fuck out of my cock. Are you still coming?"

I can't answer him, because yes, I think I am.

"Fuck, baby," He pulls out of me in one rough move. That alone causes another, smaller orgasm to roll through me. He pumps his cock, and thick spurts of come shoot out, covering my abdomen. "So fucking hot," he pants. "So fucking *mine*."

He stares at me like I'm a masterpiece of his own creation. We're coated in sweat, panting wildly. He angles over me and unbinds my wrists, rubbing the raw skin from where I kept pulling against the belt.

"Are you okay?" he asks as he straightens.

I still haven't regained my composure, but I manage a tiny nod and a mumbled "yes."

"Good."

He picks me up, and I go limp in his arms. Every muscle is spent. He starts the shower and washes us both before dressing me in yet another one of his shirts.

"No panties," he warns when I reach for a pair.

My strength is slowly returning, but my brain is still fuzzy.

He tugs on a pair of boxer briefs and takes my hand, encouraging me to follow him downstairs to the kitchen.

"Hungry?" he asks, peeking into the pantry.

"Starving." How could I not be after all the energy I just used?

He pulls out a box of pasta and sets it on the counter, then plucks a lemon from the fruit bowl on the island and parmesan from the fridge. He sets a pot of water to boil before he turns my way with an arched brow.

"You okay?" he asks.

This man just fucked my brains out, and now he's standing here, all hot and sexy, cooking for me, and he worries that I'm not okay? Of course I'm not okay. I want to drag him to the floor and ride him right here.

"Just peachy," I tease.

He smirks like he knows exactly what I'm thinking. Who am I kidding? He probably does. Caleb seems to have a sixth sense for these kinds of things.

"What are you making?"

"Pasta." He grins, setting out two bowls and the strainer.

With a roll of my eyes, I prop my elbow on the counter

and put my chin in my hand. "I gathered that, but what kind?"

"Bow tie." His smirk grows. He's having fun annoying me.

"Caleb."

"It's nothing special." He turns to add the pasta to the boiling water. "Just a little olive oil, pasta water, and parmesan to make a sauce for the pasta. You'll see."

I squint at him, doubtful, but sit quietly while he prepares the meal.

When he sets a bowl in front of me, I dig in.

"Simple, my ass," I gripe. "This is delicious."

He laughs, pulling out the chair beside mine. "Glad you like it."

I devour the meal like I'm scared he might snatch it back. I ate about two hours before he arrived, but I'm pretty sure I burned all those calories off upstairs.

The Christmas tree in the corner is lit, putting off a soft glow. As I survey it, I smile. My brothers helped us pick it out, and then Seda joined us when we decorated. We ended the day with homemade hot chocolate far more delicious than I thought possible.

For a moment, I'm lost in my happiness.

I don't want things to change.

I'm happy. Just like this. What difference does it make to anyone else what I choose to do with my life? I can't live my life on some perfectly laid-out timeline. It's time to do the things that feel right.

"Caleb?" I prompt softly. Nervousness creeping into my voice.

His fork stills against his bowl. "Yeah?"

"Did you mean what you said in the hospital? About marrying me? That you'd have found a chaplain and done it there?"

"Yes." He arches a brow. "What are you getting at?"

I swallow past my nerves and clasp my trembling hands in my lap. "Let's do that."

Eyes narrowed in confusion, he studies my face. "Do what? Go back to the hospital?"

"No." I shake my head.

He's giving me an out. He's too smart to not know what I'm getting at. But I *am* sure.

"Let's get married," I breathe. "I love you. You make me happier than I've ever been, and I'm tired of always waiting for the other shoe to drop. Of thinking I'm not worthy of being happy. Of being loved by someone like you." Tears prick at the backs of my eyes. "I want to choose you. I want you to choose me. I want to know every day that you're not just the man I love but my husband. My partner. My—"

He's off the stool, hands on my cheeks, his mouth slanting over mine, before I can finish.

"Yes," he murmurs. "God, yes." He nips my bottom lip. "I would've married you the day I met you."

I laugh. "You're ridiculous."

He pulls back just enough to lock eyes with me as he shakes his head. "No, Halle. I *knew* from the moment I saw you that you were going to change my life. It was like the universe finally gave me everything I'd been begging for. When I saw you, I knew you were meant for me. I just hoped I was meant for you too."

Fuck. This man.

A single tear tracks down my cheek.

He cups my jaw, pressing his forehead to mine. "We're going to have a great life, Halle. I'll take care of your heart."

My chest squeezes in response to his promise. I know he will.

FORTY

Caleb

"Do you still want to get married?"

I can't help but ask the question first thing the next morning. And I fully expect her to back out. I'd be okay with that. It would be normal to have reservations, though I truly have none.

So it shocks me when she blinks back at me sleepily, and a slow smile spreads across her face. "I want to be your wife."

With a groan, I burrow beneath the covers and show her just how much that pleases me.

After, we shower and get ready, then head out to file for

our marriage license. We'll have to wait at least three days before we can actually get married, and if, in that time, she gets cold feet, that'll be okay too. I want this, but I don't want her to do it until she's ready.

As we exit the courthouse, Halle clings to my arm, smiling from ear to ear.

This might be the happiest I've ever seen her.

"You're going to be my husband," she says as we reach my car.

I cage her in against the passenger side, one hand on the frame on either side of her head. "And you're going to be my wife."

She bites her lip, dark eyes flashing. "Say it again."

Grinning, I lean down until my lips brush her ear. "Wife."

She shivers, and not because of the cold. "We need to tell my brothers. I want them to know. To be there."

"Of course." I straighten and nod. Pretty sure I'd agree to anything she says right now.

"And I want to get rings." She turns, eyeing my left hand where it's pressed to the side of the car.

I can't stop smiling, and fuck, my face already hurts. "You want the whole world to know I belong to you?"

"Yes." She tips her face up, shoulders back.

"I love that." I brush my lips over her soft cheek. "I love when you're possessive."

She rolls her eyes. "I'm not possessive. I'm…" She huffs out a breath. "Okay, maybe I am. A little." She pokes my chest. "I also want a dress. Not a wedding dress, but something that makes me feel pretty."

"We can do that." She can wear whatever the fuck she wants. With any luck, I'll convince her to do a real wedding one day. For now, I'll take what I can get. At the end of the day, all I want is her. Calling Halle my wife will be the greatest pleasure of my existence.

"Why do I feel like I could ask you for a car, and you'd say yes?"

"Because"—I grin, taking her cheeks in my hands—"if you haven't figured it out yet, baby, I'm incapable of saying no to you."

"You're really too good for me, Caleb," she says softly.

"No, I'm not." I stroke my thumbs over her smooth cheeks. "You've just never met anyone who put you first before."

That's the thing she doesn't realize. I'm nothing special, but I'm willing to do whatever it takes for the people I love.

"Let's go find you a dress, yeah?" I pull away and tug her gently so I can open the car door.

She nods, an excited smile taking over her face before she can stop it.

One day, maybe she'll learn that she doesn't need to hide her happiness. That it's okay to find joy in things.

"You don't have to stick with me," she says when we enter through the sliding doors and the soft mall music permeates the air around us. "I know most guys aren't into clothes shopping."

"I don't mind." I lace my fingers with hers and slide my other hand into my pocket. "I plan to stay with you unless you want me to be surprised by what you pick."

Her lips quirk up in amusement, making me curious about what she's thinking. In the end, I don't press her.

The first shop we pop into gets an immediate no from her.

The next is better, but she doesn't find anything worth trying on.

"We'll check a few more places, and if I don't find what I'm looking for, we can come back," she says, dragging me from the store.

I like that she hasn't dropped my hand yet. That she likes touching me as much as I like touching her.

When we step into the third shop, her eyes light up. In minutes, she's got several dresses draped over her arm, all ranging from true white to ivory to even a pastel blue option.

"Something blue," she says when I keep staring at it.

I smile, surprised to hear her say something so traditional.

"I like it." And I do. It's got a slight shimmer to it, with butterflies stitched around the slit in the side. "I'll go ask about a dressing room. Keep looking."

I take the dresses from her and leave her to browse the racks while I find an employee and secure a room for her.

By the time I locate Halle in the store again, she's found one more possibility.

I take it from her, then grasp her hand. "Dressing rooms are this way." I lead her through the maze of racks to the back and point out the room where the other dresses are waiting.

She comes to a stop, scrutinizing the little cubicles, her lip caught between her teeth.

"Go on," I encourage, parking my butt in an empty chair. "I'll be right here."

With a small smile, she disappears behind the curtain, the swoosh of fabric blocking me out.

A moment later, a muffled "oh my God" comes from the dressing room.

I straighten, eager to see her, but slump again when she adds, "Absolutely not. I'm not even showing you."

"Come on, Hal." I rest an ankle on one knee. "Let me see."

She snorts. "Not a chance, buddy."

"Halle." My voice is stern. "I'm about to be your husband. Don't call me buddy."

For a moment, I'm met with silence. But then her fingers slowly appear around the curtain, and she pulls it back just enough to poke her head out.

She doesn't say anything, just stares at me with her lips slightly parted.

"Something wrong, baby?" I ask, leaning back in the chair.

She shakes her head like she's clearing away the fog in her brain. "No, it's just … I'm not sure I'll ever get used to the sound of that."

"Sound of what?" I grin, already knowing what she means.

"Husband," she whispers, her eyes wide. "You're going to be my husband."

A thrill shoots through me. "Yes, I am, sweetheart."

She disappears back behind the curtain. The dress she tried but refuses to let me see hits the floor, and she tries another. This time she throws the curtain back and steps out.

It's flowy, with long sleeves and a slit up one leg. She looks stunning in it, but that's not what matters. I only care about how she feels in it.

"It's an option." She decides as she inspects her reflection in the wall of mirrors. "Do you like it?"

"I like you in anything you wear."

She rolls her eyes at my answer. "So diplomatic."

When she steps out again, wearing another long-sleeve option with a bow on the back, I know right away she's not a fan.

The frown is a dead giveaway, but she turns to me anyway. "What do you think of this one?"

"It's a no."

"Why?" she presses, tucking a piece of hair behind her ear.

"Because you don't like it."

Her mouth pops open. "How can you tell?"

I shrug. "Because I know you."

The third dress is the light blue one. She looks fucking stunning in it, but I rein in my reaction, not wanting to sway hers. It's not the traditional white, and that may be an issue for her.

She smooths her hands down the front of the dress, biting her bottom lip as she surveys her reflection. She lifts her hair up, angling her neck like she's trying to imagine it with an updo or maybe even with jewelry around her neck.

"Do you like it?" I ask.

She turns to me, letting her dark hair fall back into place.

"I really do. I'm just not sure about the color and ... do you think it's too summery? With the straps? It's December."

"You could get some kind of white shawl thing to put around your shoulders?" I suggest. "If it's what you want."

She turns, letting the bottom flare out a bit. "Let me try on the rest, and then we'll see."

She quickly vetoes an option with flowy sleeves, and the next one looks too matronly, according to her. By the time she's tried them all on, her shoulders are slumped and her face is drawn in defeat.

"Try the blue one again. We can always try more stores. You don't have to pick the winner here."

"I know." She disappears behind the curtain again, swishing it closed. "I just thought this would be easier, I guess. I'm not normally a picky person."

"This is a big deal. It's okay to be selective. But as long as you feel good in it, that's all that matters. If you want to do a big wedding down the road, you can go all out then."

She pokes her head around the corner, narrowing her dark gaze on me. "We both know I'm not the big wedding type, so get that notion out of your head right now."

I sigh and mutter, "Yes, ma'am."

She steps out a moment later, the blue dress fitted perfectly to her frame, and she's fucking *glowing*.

I say nothing as she looks at herself in the mirror, giving her full control over the decision.

"It might be silly with the color and the butterflies and

spaghetti straps and…" She lets out a sigh. "But I want this one."

I stand and pull her to my chest. "It's perfect."

She smiles up at me, and the pure happiness radiating from her nearly knocks me to my knees. Her eyes were so dark, so lost when I met her, but now there's no trace of shadows anywhere. I chased them all away.

"I love you," she says, leaning into me.

In response, I kiss her.

FORTY-ONE

Halle

"Married?" Quinn repeats. "You guys are getting married *now*? Like before the new year?"

My brothers exchange a glance. Casen sports a smug smirk.

"Yes, that's what I said. We'll go to the courthouse in a few days and do it. I want you guys there with me."

"You can't wait until the new year?" Quinn groans.

Why is he so hung up on the new year? We haven't even made it to Christmas yet. "Um ... I wasn't planning on it?"

"Pay up." Casen holds his hand out.

Grumbling, Quinn pulls out his wallet and slaps a few

bills into his twin's palm. The boys might not have proper jobs yet, but they've been doing odd jobs for the neighbors to earn money to buy Christmas gifts.

"Why are you two—" I gasp. "Wait, did you place bets on this?"

Casen laughs as he shoves the money into his pocket. "Sis, we saw the writing on the wall from the get-go. I had a feeling you two would be standing at an altar before the year was over. This one"—he tosses a thumb at Quinn—"thought you'd hold out a bit longer."

I blink at them, mouth still open, flabbergasted. "I honestly can't believe either of you right now," I mutter.

Quinn shrugs, resting his elbows on the dining room table. "It was obvious from the day Caleb helped us move in that he was interested in you. And you tried to hide it, but we could tell you liked him too, and if you haven't noticed, Halle, you don't like very many people."

"*That's* what led you to thinking we'd get married *now*?"

"Well"—Casen scratches his chin—"you are, so it's not like I was wrong. Why are you mad?"

"I'm not mad." I cross my arms. "I'm offended. There's a difference."

"Offended that I was right?" Casen gives me a confused frown.

Head dropped back, I groan. I should know by now that there's no reasoning with my brothers. "I just can't believe you guys thought we'd end up married that fast."

"Again, you are," Casen reiterates.

I swallow past the lump in my throat and inhale a deep breath. I'm glad now that Caleb agreed to let me talk to them on my own while he tells Seda. He'd never let me live this down.

Focus fixed on the table in front of me, I clear my throat. "Do you think I'm making a bad decision?"

"No," they answer in that synchronized tone that always jars me.

I snap my head up, my breath catching. "Why?"

"Because," Quinn answers, "Caleb looks at you like you're the only thing he needs in the world."

"Like he'd jump in front of a bullet for you," Casen adds.

"It's really soon, though, isn't it?" I press them.

They look at each other and break into identical shrugs.

Casen clears his throat. "When it's the right person, why wait? Do you have any doubts about him? Do you think there's someone else out there who's better for you?"

My stomach twists at the thought. "No."

"Then marry the guy." Quinn breaks into a smile.

"You guys are really okay with this?" I push. "You don't care if I put the house on the market after it's fixed and we make this move permanent?"

They make eye contact, communicating in their secret twin way.

Quinn is the one to answer. "We don't care. If you haven't noticed, this place is a lot nicer."

"Fast Wi-Fi," Casen adds.

Quinn snaps his fingers. "Thicker walls."

"Oh, yeah. That's going to be important," Casen muses.

I roll my eyes, my cheeks heating. "Oh my God."

"What?" They blink at me innocently.

"You guys are truly okay with this?" I'm not fishing for an excuse to back out. I'm just shocked they're so chill about it.

"Yeah." Casen taps his fingers on the table. "You're happy and that's all that matters to us."

"If we thought Caleb was a bad guy, we'd tell you." This from Quinn.

"He makes you smile," Casen says softly. "Most people don't do that."

His words hit me solidly in the chest, pushing me back in my chair. "I don't smile?"

"You do now," Quinn says, tone just as quiet as his brother's. "But for a long time, you didn't. I think Caleb makes you feel safe, the same way you've always made us feel safe."

Talk about a stab to the heart. I have to fight the urge to rub at my sternum. "You guys feel that way about me?"

It's hard, this role I've slipped into, where I'm their sister but also their authority figure. I've always taken care of them, but before Mom went to prison, I was careful not to step on toes. I didn't want to lose that sibling relationship, but I didn't have a choice.

"Yeah, Hal," Casen says, his irises dark, swimming with sincerity. "You've always looked out for us. We know how much you love us and how far you'd go to protect us. We might not always say it, but we love you, and you deserve to have your own life separate from us."

There goes the pain in my chest again. "I don't want it to be separate," I whisper.

Quinn laughs, shaking his head. "I guess it's more like two worlds becoming one, huh?"

I nod, giving a watery smile. Ugh. Leave it to my brothers to make me cry. It's not something I do too often. I've always had to keep my wits about me. I've rarely ever had time for a breakdown.

Once they start, I can't seem to stop the tears. The two of them get up and wrap their arms around me, only making me cry harder.

"I love you, guys."

"You're going to let us walk you down the aisle, right?" Quinn asks, rubbing my earlobe between his thumb and forefinger like he did when he was little.

My responding laugh is punctuated by a sob. "I'm not sure there's going to be much of an aisle. We're just going to the courthouse."

The boys sit again, and Casen laces his fingers together, laying them on the table like he's about to give me a very serious talking-to. "Whatever there is to walk down, we'll go with you. We have to stick together."

I reach across and take his hand and one of Quinn's too.

"Yes, we do."

I should've known our simple courthouse ceremony would be thwarted. But honestly, I can't say I'm mad about it. Salem, Thayer, Cynthia, and Thelma showed up, along with Seda and the boys, of course. For the first time in my life,

I'm surrounded by people who care about my brothers and me. That's worth more than any smidge of annoyance.

Family has always been important to me, and while none of these people are of blood relation, I know they'll be in my life for the long haul. In the lives of my brothers too.

Since it's warm in the courthouse, I pass my thick white shawl to Cynthia.

She drapes it over her arm and gives my cheek a tender pat. "Take care of our boy," she says before disappearing into the room where the ceremony will be held.

"You needed a bouquet," Thayer says, holding out a beautiful arrangement of flowers. His voice is deep and almost jarring after the soft sweetness of Cynthia's. "I put this together from my greenhouse."

Salem watches her husband with stars in her eyes. I fear if they're not careful, they might have another kid on the way soon.

"They're a mix of white roses and blue hydrangeas. Caleb said your dress was blue, so…" He shrugs and steps away.

It takes a minute to collect myself and find my voice after such a sweet and unexpected gesture. "Thanks. This is so kind of you."

Salem waves a hand in the air. "My contribution is cupcakes for after."

"After?" I ask, looking between her and her husband.

She sighs like she's exasperated with me. "You didn't think we'd let you get away without having a reception, did you?"

My heart trips over itself. "Oh, no. Really, that's fine."

Thelma lets out a noise that sounds like a combination of a laugh and a cough. "Get used to the meddling, girl. You're getting a reception."

"Oh," I say softly. "Okay." As I'm processing the suggestion, a horrifying thought occurs to me, "Oh my God, Caleb's parents aren't coming, are they?"

The day we applied for our marriage license, he called to let them know. His mother was none too pleased. I could hear her shrill raised voice through the speaker loud and clear as she told him how foolish he was. Caleb didn't expect her to be happy, but I don't think he expected such a nasty reaction either.

Despite her outburst, showing up at the reception sounds like the exact kind of thing she'd do.

Salem wrings her hands. "I didn't invite her."

"Oh, thank God," I blurt out.

With a laugh, she smooths a piece of my hair. "Yeah, she'll never win an award for mother-in-law of the year. Just remember, her behavior isn't your fault. She's miserable and takes it out on the people around her."

She steps back, and Thayer loops his arm around her waist. It's obvious in their every interaction that, after so many years together, they're still sickeningly in love.

I can only hope that's how Caleb and I will feel ten years from now.

"We're going to find our seats." Salem gives my wrist a squeeze as she passes.

The words make me chuckle. Like she's worried the place will be full. I don't need a roomful of people, though. All I need is the people who truly care about us.

"Good luck, sweetie," Thelma says, heading past me into the room.

It's perhaps the nicest thing she's said to me.

Naturally, the moment that thought crosses my mind, she ruins it by turning around and saying, "Oh, but dear, do make sure to close the blinds next time."

Horror washes over me. I cannot believe she's seen Caleb and me...no, I can't let my thoughts stray there before I meet this man at the altar.

Is there even an altar?

I suppose it's more of a symbolic altar?

Down the hall, the bathroom door squeaks open and my brothers step out wearing coordinating suits.

The breath whooshes from my lungs at the sight. They look so dapper.

"When did you guys get those?" I blurt out.

"We told Caleb we wanted to dress up, and he delivered." Casen adjusts the sleeve on his dark blue suit.

In this moment, they look so mature. Every bit of their almost fifteen years.

"How do we look?" Quinn turns, arms out, so I can see every angle.

"Like men." I swallow past the lump in my throat.

It's moments like this that remind me of just how close they are to graduating from high school and going to college.

"Don't you dare cry and ruin your makeup," Casen warns as he pulls me into a hug.

Quinn hugs me next. "All right, sis. Let's get you to your husband."

Husband.

My husband is waiting for me.

My brothers each offer an arm. I take one at a time, keeping a careful hold on the bouquet from Thayer.

This is so over-the-top for a courthouse wedding, but it couldn't be more perfect. When we turn and enter the room, my knees go weak. Caleb waits at the other end with Seda at his side. She's wearing a pink floral dress and tugging on his arm. He bends down so he can hear what she says, his eyes on me the whole time.

I head straight for him, maybe a little too quickly. Maybe I should be embarrassed by the way I can't get to him soon enough, but there's no shame in any aspect of how I feel about him.

As he takes my hand and we exchange our vows, the room melts away. It feels like it's only the two of us as we slide bands onto each other's ring fingers. When he kisses me, it feels like the promise of a new beginning.

The start of a new chapter.

One I can't wait to fill the pages of.

FORTY-TWO

Caleb

"Those dance lessons paid off, huh?" I ask as we sway to the song.

As meddlesome as our friends are, I probably should have expected the surprise reception they put together.

Halle lets out a laugh that ends in a snort. Her cheeks pinken, and she peers around like she's worried someone heard her. "Rub it in."

Grinning, I tuck a piece of hair behind her ear. "You're my wife." I can't stop saying it. Subconsciously, maybe I'm a little scared that if I don't, I'll wake up to discover this has all been a dream.

"You're my husband." She rests her chin on my chest, looking up at me.

The rec center is filled with people from town. I don't think Halle knows many of them, at least not well, but she has encountered them. That's how Hawthorne Mills is, though—one giant family.

Except for, ironically, given our ancestors were the founders of this town, my own family.

I've tried not to dwell on my mother's reaction. I expected it, honestly, but that doesn't make it hurt any less. There's no changing my parents. I learned that long ago. All I can do is keep reaching out, hoping to meet them in the middle. If they don't want to take the step to do the same, that's okay too. I'll never put my relationship with them above the ones I have with my wife and kid.

Salem appears from the kitchen, holding a carrier filled with cupcakes, and a second later, Halle sees her, her eyes lighting up.

"Cupcakes!" she squeals, pulling away.

The girl I met months ago never would've reacted so openly to a sweet treat. I'm so fucking thankful that she let me peer past those thick walls of hers, that she eventually let me dismantle them and that she's found a home with not just me, but with this entire town.

Before she gets far, I grab her hand.

She's mine now, and I'm not letting her get away that easily.

I do, however, let her drag me over to the table where Salem is carefully setting out an array of cupcakes.

"Do you have red velvet?" Halle asks with a little bounce.

Salem swishes her hair over her shoulder. "Duh. It's your favorite." She plucks one and hands it to Halle. "You want one too?" she asks me.

I hold out an eager hand.

With a playful eye roll, she passes me a cupcake of my own.

I swipe a plate, napkins, and a bottle of water before dragging *my wife* over to the table set up at the head of the room.

There's a good chance Halle will be annoyed by how often she's going to be hearing the word *wife*. It settled in my brain with ease, like that label was always meant to belong to her and only her.

Once we're seated, Halle peels the wrapper from the cupcake, careful not to get any red velvet crumbs on her dress.

"Today's a good day, isn't it?" she asks with a smile.

"The best day." I grin at her as she takes a bite and hums when the flavor hits.

It'll be a long time before a day comes along that can top this one.

I'm finishing my cupcake when Seda darts over to us. "Dance with me, Daddy?"

I smile at my girl. "Always." I wipe my hands, then stand and follow her onto the dance floor, looking back at my wife, who's watching us with a smile.

This kind of pure happiness should be illegal.

"I love this song," Seda says, smiling up at me.

"I know you do." It's from one of her favorite boy bands, a song I've had to listen to over and over again. Which is probably why Salem added it to the playlist.

"When I get married, I want to wear a big white princess dress."

The idea of Seda getting married one day momentarily crushes me. It's inevitable, but I want her to stay my little girl forever.

"You can wear whatever dress you want." I pull her closer.

"Will you *and* Dad walk me down the aisle like Casen and Quinn did with Halle?"

I give her hand a soft squeeze, my heart thumping in my chest. "I'm sure we could do that."

Her responding smile is blinding. "You're both my dads, so it only makes sense."

"That's right."

"And I want lots of flowers," she goes on. "And pizza for the reception. You can't go wrong with pizza."

I have to bite back a grin as she prattles on.

"I'm not wearing heels. Mommy always says heels suck."

With a chuckle, I kiss the top of her head. "You don't have to wear heels, sweetheart."

She continues on like I haven't said anything. "I think I'd like to get married outside too. Not in the summer. Too hot. But maybe in the spring or fall."

"Whenever you want."

"And"—she looks up at me, lashes fanning her cheeks—"I want to dance with you just like this."

Fuck, talk about a stab to my heart. I can picture it. "I'll always dance with you."

"I know you will, Daddy, because you love me."

When the song comes to an end, I scoop her up and hold her tight. I didn't know until this little girl came into my life just how much love a person can be capable of.

I hug her until she's wiggling in my arms.

"Daddy," she giggles. "You have to let me go."

The deeper truth in those words guts me.

I release her, and she runs toward Casen and Quinn, who are raiding the cupcakes. Though I'm still apprehensive about her crush on the boys, I turn and head to the table, where Halle is still sitting, elbow propped on the table, chin in her hand, smiling at me.

"Caleb." A small but firm hand grips my elbow, then Thelma is at my side. "Cynthia and I will take the boys tonight. And Lou at the inn said she's got a room set aside for the two of you. Free of charge."

Warmth blooms in my chest. "That's very kind of her, but I have a feeling Halle will want to go home."

Thelma shrugs, releasing my arm. "Once you talk to Halle, let me know your decision, and I'll pass it along to Lou."

I start toward my wife again—my *wife*—but just as I approach her, her eyes go wide, and she stands.

"Mom?" she blurts out.

I turn, following her gaze, and when I catch sight of her mother, I'm hit with a bolt of surprise.

The woman's posture is rigid, and she's heading our way.

"Mom?" Casen and Quinn echo, their tones full of shock. "What are you doing here?"

She ignores her sons, her eyes zeroed in on Halle. The room grows quiet, every eye in the place locked on her.

The air goes strangely still, like even the environment knows something isn't right. We're all frozen, except Freya, who's still making a beeline for Halle.

I shake my head free of the cobwebs and move, quickly putting myself between Halle and her mother.

"Move!" Freya demands. Her eyes are bloodshot, her skin waxy as her gaze jerks around the room.

"No." I put a hand behind my back and give Halle a nudge so she'll stay where she is.

She grips my arms, peeking around me, but her view is cut off when Laith and Thayer flank me, coming without hesitation to help me protect my girl.

"I need to talk to my bitch of a daughter."

"Why are you here? *How* are you here?"

Freya leans to one side, then the other, trying to see around us, but she can't see much of Halle. We've made sure of that.

"I told you I'd been on my best behavior." Her lips curl in a cruel smirk. Her smile has the slightly unhinged quality of a person who has nothing left to lose. "I asked around while I was on the inside," she goes on. "Talked to some people. Got me a lawyer. Cheap one, but he's decent. He told me it wasn't random that I got caught. Someone snitched on me, and who else would want to more than you, Halle girl?"

"What?" Halle wraps a hand around my bicep and gives

me a shove. I move a few inches, but only because she's freakishly strong.

Her grip on me tightens. "I didn't turn you in."

"Don't lie!" Freya's shout echoes through the event space.

"Hey, now. We don't need any of this fuss," Thelma says, stepping forward from where she and Cynthia have been standing on the side of the room. "This is getting out of hand."

Freya turns her way, reaching into her bag. "I'll show you out of hand."

In what feels like slow motion, she pulls her hand out and brandishes a gun. It takes a moment to register in my brain, but Thelma is already stepping back, hands in the air.

Thayer inhales sharply beside me. "Fuck." The fear in his tone has me zeroing in on Salem and the kids over Freya's shoulder.

"Hey." I raise my hands. "There's no need for that. Put the gun away, and we can find somewhere to talk. How does that sound?"

Eyes narrowed, she opens her mouth to respond, but snaps it shut again when Quinn shouts from behind her.

"Mom," he pleads. "It wasn't Halle. We did it."

I wince, silently cursing him for speaking out. She whips around, gun wobbling in her hand, making me think she doesn't even know how to use the thing. That only makes her more dangerous.

"I don't believe you," she snaps.

Dread washes over me. In the space of a heartbeat, the best day of my life has devolved into this.

Casen and Quinn slowly make their way toward us, hands raised. I do everything I can with my eyes to tell them to stop, to stay where they are, but they're too focused on their mother to notice.

Fuck. Why didn't I look into Freya more after she threatened Halle? I know better. But naively, I believed she'd be locked up for quite a while longer, and I never could have imagined she'd show up with a gun.

"Mom," Casen says softly. "I swear it was us. Halle didn't tip off the cops. We did. Someone had to do something, and Halle always protects you, so we did it."

"Boys," Halle gasps behind me. "I can't believe you'd do that."

"You cared too much to do what needed to be done," Quinn says, eyes full of silent apology as he focuses on his sister.

Halle sniffles behind me, her fingers flexing against my arm.

Freya sways, the gun wobbling in her hand.

"Let's put the gun down," Thayer says gently. "All of this was a mistake."

Freya cries, her face wet with tears. "I thought … I thought…"

"Come on," Thayer says, taking a slow step in her direction. "Just give me the gun and—"

A sharp crack echoes off the walls, so loud my ears ring.

It's followed by screams.

"Oh my God." Freya drops the gun, looking at … looking at *me* in horror.

"Caleb!" Halle screams, shoving in front of me.

As she looks down at my abdomen, I follow, only now noticing the blood staining my abdomen.

"Halle," I whisper. I touch the wound, my fingers coming away bright red.

My vision gets blurry, and then Thayer and Laith are grabbing my arms and laying me down.

"Caleb," Halle sobs, her hands cupping her mouth. "Oh my God. Caleb, please."

I reach for her, my movements sluggish. "I-I'm okay." My teeth start to chatter.

Halle kneels at my side.

"Y-Your dress. Don't g-get blood on i-it."

She brings a hand to my cheek.

Why does it feel so cold?

I try to put my hand over hers, but I can't seem to get my limbs to cooperate.

In the background, there's a muffled "someone call 911."

"They're already on the way" is the response.

"Caleb," Halle begs, her eyes full of tears. "Stay with me."

"I love you," I tell her.

I want her to know that.

I love her, and that makes everything worth it.

It's the last thought I have as my vision goes dark.

FORTY-THREE

Halle

"Open your eyes," I scream, patting Caleb's cheek. When that does no good, I do it again, a little harder this time. "Caleb! Don't you dare do this to me," I sob, my whole body shaking. "Wake up. Please, wake up."

The world around us is a blur. I have no idea what's happening with my mom, whether my brothers are safe, any of it. All I can focus on is the man I love bleeding out right in front of me.

I press my hands to the wound in his abdomen and put pressure on it. I'm not sure it's the right thing to do, but it seems like a good idea.

Thayer is on his knees beside me, probing Caleb's neck with two fingers. "There's a pulse."

"Where's the ambulance?" I scream.

I heard sirens in the distance before the shot even rang out, so help has to be on the way, right? Where are they? Caleb needs help now.

Across from me, Laith is hovering over Caleb too, his skin leached of all color.

"Caleb, can you hear me?" I give his cheek another tap. "I'm right here. Stay with me. Help is coming. I love you. I love you so much, and this is just our beginning."

I refuse to believe it's also our end.

It feels like hours pass before Thayer is pulling me away to make room for the paramedics.

"Let me go," I fight against him. "He's my husband. I have to stay with him. I need to hold him!"

"Shh," he hushes. "You have to let them help him."

Somewhere, in the logical part of my brain, I know that. I've been waiting for them, cursing their slowness. But I can't stand the idea of being apart from him.

"Caleb," I sob as they cut away his shirt, revealing the wound beneath and all the blood.

God, there's so much of it.

Red and vibrant and everywhere, staining Caleb's white dress shirt and pooling on the floor beneath him.

"I'm going to throw up," I blurt.

Rather than let me go, Thayer scoops me up like I weigh nothing and carries me to a trashcan. We've barely made it before I empty the contents of my stomach.

His fingers are gentle on my neck as he holds my hair back, but I recoil at the touch.

I want Caleb.

Thayer doesn't react to my flinch, and he doesn't let go of my hair until I've finished.

When there's nothing left to purge, I straighten, wiping my mouth with the back of my hand. When I turn and take in the room, I find that it's emptied of everyone but us and the paramedics and Caleb.

Another sob tears out of me.

The man who's taken over my world, who's larger than life, who's always there to make things better, looks so broken. They've moved him onto a gurney and strapped an oxygen mask to his face.

I find Thayer's hand and grip it hard, needing the hold to keep me from crumpling to the ground.

"He has to be okay," I whisper. My voice seems to have left me.

"He will be," Thayer says. "He's tough."

As they wheel him to the door, I run after them.

"Let me come with you. He's my husband. Please. I need to be with him."

One of the paramedics gives me a gentle nudge out of the way. "I'm sorry, ma'am," he says, his expression full of genuine apology, "but in the condition he's in, we need the space to work."

"No!" I shriek, running after them. "Please, let me go!"

Outside the rec center, the cold air hits me like a slap to the face, causing my steps to falter.

That's all it takes for the paramedics to get ahead of me.

Before I can catch up, they've got Caleb loaded and they're closing the doors.

"No!" My knees give out, but before they can collide with the concrete, Thayer's there again, scooping me up.

The world around me blurs. Thelma speaks to Thayer. Something about taking all the kids. Then I'm put into a minivan with Thayer, Salem, and Laith.

I shake uncontrollably in the back seat. Up front, Salem looks back every few seconds, tears in her eyes and lips turned down like she's scared I'll completely fall apart. Laith looks downright sick at my side.

Salem and Thayer talk as Thayer drives, but I'm too out of sorts to make out their words.

"Shouldn't we be at the hospital by now?" I ask after what feels like an eternity.

"They're taking him straight to the bigger hospital thirty minutes away," Thayer answers, glancing at me in the rearview mirror.

That makes my tears come harder and faster.

"My b-brothers?" I stutter. "Are they okay? They're okay, right?"

Fuck, it's only now occurring to me to think about them. I'm a horrible sister. I was too caught up in Caleb's injury to think about them.

"They're fine," Salem answers. "Shaken up, but fine."

I wrap my arms around myself, suddenly freezing, my whole body shaking and my teeth chattering uncontrollably.

I nod woodenly. They're fine. They're okay. That's all that matters. But Caleb…

A sob rips out of me.

I've always prided myself on being strong. On holding steady during difficult situations. But nothing could have prepared me for seeing the person I love most shot right in front of me. Especially knowing that shot was meant for me.

And the shooter was my own mother…

I can't think about it right now. How she got out, how she made her way there, what she was thinking … it's all too much for me to handle.

By the time we arrive at the hospital, I've detached from my body. Like my consciousness is floating outside my form and I'm viewing the scene like I'm watching on TV.

My body moves woodenly through the sliding doors into the lobby of the ER. Laith stays by my side while Thayer strides straight to the desk. He gestures to me, and when he says *wife*, another sob escapes me.

We're supposed to be celebrating our wedding. It's supposed to be the happiest day of our lives.

When I hear the woman mention *surgery*, I nearly crumble to the floor. Only Laith's arms around me keep me upright.

I hate this. I hate this. *I hate this*.

My breaths come in sporadic pants.

Is this what a panic attack feels like?

Laith drags me over to a chair. "Breathe," he commands, hands on my cheeks. "I need you to breathe, Halle."

Unshed tears burn my eyes. "Am I going to lose him?"

I've finally found the one person I feel safe with, that I can open up to, who sees all my flaws and loves me anyway, and now I could lose him. Did I do something in another life that's left me undeserving of even an ounce of genuine happiness?

Laith presses his lips together. "I don't know."

Though I'm grateful that he's not sugarcoating the truth, I hate his answer.

Thayer joins us with Salem in tow. Her face is red and splotchy, and stress lines bracket her mouth.

"Hey," she says softly, sitting in the empty chair to my left. "Come here."

She's not much older than I am, but the maternal way she speaks has me diving into her arms for comfort.

I've always prided myself on standing on my own, on not needing anyone, but I've come to realize there's much more strength to be had in finding people I can trust to shoulder some of my burdens.

Salem holds me, letting me cry on her shoulder.

"I'm so scared." The words come out broken. "I can't lose him."

"I know." She rubs my back. "I know."

Thayer steps away, his phone to his ear.

"M-My mom," I croak out. "What happened to her?"

Salem exhales a shaky breath. Every person we care about has to be traumatized. Talk about a horrifying situation. All because my mom has well and truly lost her mind.

"She put down the gun and went with the cops willingly."

"All this because she thought I ratted her out." Another sob rips out of me. "Am I going to lose him because of her selfishness?"

Salem touches my cheek, gently wiping my tears away. "Caleb is one of the toughest people I know. I don't think he's going anywhere."

"I can't lose him. I just … I can't."

"It's all going to be okay," she says, wrapping her arms around me once more.

When Thayer turns around, still on the phone, his face drawn and his eyes bloodshot, I'm not so sure.

FORTY-FOUR

Halle

It's dark out when a doctor finally comes to talk to us.

The moment I see him headed in our direction, my stomach sinks. I swallow down the bile quickly rising in my throat. My heart beats so hard that I can hear it in my ears as I try and fail to read the doctor's flat expression.

"Are you the family of Caleb Thorne?"

"Yes." Somehow, I find the strength to stand, though my legs are wobbly, and wrap my arms around my body, trying to hold the fragile, broken pieces of myself together. "I'm his ... I'm his wife."

Salem stands with me, looping her arm through mine.

"Is he okay?" she asks, since I can't seem to find the words to ask myself.

The doctor rubs at his jaw. "We got the bullet out and stitched everything up. He lost more blood than we'd like, but no vital organs were damaged. He's doing better than we expected already. He's still asleep in recovery, but as soon as he's moved to a room, family can see him."

I can barely see through my tears. "He's going to be okay?"

He dips his chin. "Everything is looking promising."

If it weren't for the way my friends support me, I'm fairly certain I'd fall to the floor. "That's good. That's really good." I struggle to catch my breath, my chest still tight.

"Just sit tight and—"

There's a commotion behind us, then a familiar voice pierces the air.

"My son," a woman says breathlessly. "My son was shot and brought in and—"

I turn, finding the receptionist pointing in our direction.

Caleb's parents jog over to us, and his mom stops in front of the doctor. "Oh, God. Please tell me my boy is okay."

The doctor repeats what he's already told us, and the older woman sinks to her knees. Her husband follows, though a little more gracefully, and cradles her.

I don't have much respect for the woman, but sympathy for her overtakes me anyway. If I wasn't still reeling, I might feel a little bad that it didn't even cross my mind to call them.

Salem, Thayer, and Laith lead me away, and I'm grateful

for it. Something tells me his mom would love nothing more than to spew more hateful shit my way, and I'm so emotionally strung out I'm not sure how I would react.

With each passing minute, the need to get out of this waiting room increases.

"I'm going to find a vending machine," I announce, standing.

Laith practically jumps up too. "I'll go with you."

We're quiet as we head down the long, empty hall away from the ER's waiting room.

"I hate hospitals," he says once the noise has faded. His voice is barely a whisper, but it still manages to echo off the walls.

"I don't have too much experience with them," I admit.

"Good. That's good," he mumbles, looking around.

At the end of the hall, I survey the contents of the vending machine. I'm not even thirsty or hungry, but I need *something* to keep me distracted.

Laith pulls out a wad of bills from his pocket and feeds one into the machine. "Pick your poison."

I choose a Dr Pepper. I can't remember the last time I drank one, but out of the options in front of me, it seems like the best choice.

The next machine has chips and candy. I point silently to the M&M's. Laith's lips twitch with amusement, but he obliges and hands me the chocolate.

"I'm not ready to go back," I confess.

"That's okay." With a sigh, he rests a booted foot against the wall. "We can hang here."

I sit on a bench a few feet away, and eventually, Laith joins me.

"Do you ever feel like you're being punished over and over for something you didn't even know you did?"

He blows out a breath, crossing his arms over his chest. "All the time. But sometimes we're just dealt shitty cards. Take my brother, for instance. I'd hate to think he lost his son because the universe decided he needed to pay for something."

I twist the soda cap off the bottle, then tighten it again. "You have a good point."

"You've made a lot of progress since you moved here. I'd hate to see you regress."

I drop my head at his words. "I think I needed this place. And I definitely needed him."

"The right place, the right people, make all the difference." He leans back against the wall, stretching his legs out in front of him. "You were so closed off when we met," he goes on. "You've changed a lot. Sure, Caleb has helped, but you wouldn't have made this much progress if you didn't want to."

"I didn't want to fall in love with him," I confess, head bowed. "But he's pretty impossible to resist."

Laith huffs out a small laugh. "If there's one thing I know for sure, it's that we have no choice when it comes to who we fall in love with."

As I peer over at him, I can see it in his eyes, a past that haunts him.

"Hey." Salem's voice interrupts us, her focus fixed on

me. "They said one person could go back now. I had to tell off his mom, but you're free to see him."

Heart pounding, I hop up and smooth my dress, ignoring the bloodstain on the hem. A shiver works its way through me as I follow Salem down the hall. It's frigid in the hospital and I'm not wearing enough layers.

As I enter the waiting area again, I ignore Caleb's parents. Frankly, I owe them nothing. If they apologized, then I'd consider playing nice, but until then, they can kiss my ass.

The nurse waits at the door, her expression soothing and sympathetic. "This way, sweetie."

Salem gives my arm a reassuring squeeze as I head for the double doors.

"He's doing well," the nurse assures me, her smile kind. "He's a little groggy and still pretty tired, so he might fall asleep."

"Is there … is there anything we should be worried about?" I don't dare allow myself to believe that, somehow, he's truly okay. I'm used to having the rug yanked out from under me.

"I can't give any false promises, but his blood work looks good and surgery went well."

I exhale a shaky breath, the tightness in my chest loosening a fraction. "Okay. Thank you."

She takes me to an elevator, and we head up to critical care. It's a step down from intensive care, but it still worries me.

At the end of the hall, she stops. "He's just in there."

"Thank you."

I hesitate outside the door, taking a moment to gather myself. It's pointless. The second I lay eyes on him, I burst into tears.

His skin is waxy, his blond hair in wild disarray, and his eyes are ringed in dark circles. The nasal cannula only adds to the pitiful sight.

"Baby," he says softly. "Don't cry."

"Don't cry?" I laugh, though the sound morphs into a hysterical hiccup. "You got *shot*, Caleb. Right in front of me."

He spreads his arms wide, wincing before he can hide the reaction. "I'm doing great. See?"

"Liar." I cross the small room, only stopping when I'm at his side. I slide my fingers into his hair and down his face. His skin is cool, but he's real beneath my touch, and that's all that matters.

He closes his eyes, placing his hand over mine. "I'm sorry about your mom."

A scoff flies out of me. "She shot you, and you're apologizing?"

"Yes, because I know she hurt you."

I shake my head. This man. He's impossible.

"Still the best day of my life," he yawns. "I got to marry my girl."

"You're insane," I laugh.

"Insanely in love with you."

I bite my lip to stifle another laugh. "I'm glad you feel well enough to be so cheesy."

"It's the drugs," he admits, slowly blinking, like he's fighting sleep. "They make me loopy."

"That's okay." I pull the chair up closer to his bed with my free hand and sit down. "Go to sleep. I'll be here when you wake up."

He gives me a half smile. "Promise?"

"I did make a vow to stick with you in sickness and in health," I tease.

"That's right." His hand grows weak against mine and falls to the bed. "I love you."

"I love you too," I say, but he's already asleep.

FORTY-FIVE

Caleb

Slowly, I blink into awareness.

The room around me is dark, but the beeping is loud. And it feels like I've been run over by a truck ... or shot.

Second by second, the details creep back into my memory.

Yesterday was supposed to be the best day of my life, and it was, until...

An image of Freya and the crazed look in her eyes appears in my mind. It makes my chest ache, knowing how angry she was at Halle. The boys. I'd take the bullet a million times over if it meant keeping them safe, but I know Halle and the twins must be feeling awful.

Halle.

It's then that I search for her. She's still holding my hand. No wonder it's warmer than the rest of my body. Eyes closed, she's slumped partially onto the mattress, still wearing that blue dress.

Fuck, she has to be cold.

Little by little, I work one of my blankets off and drape it over her. Each move, no matter how small, is excruciating.

Wincing, I push the button that's supposed to dispense more pain killers through my IV.

Less than a minute later, a nurse comes in. "Hey." She disinfects her hands at the antibacterial pump in the wall. "I noticed you pushed the pain button. I thought I'd check on you since you're awake. I take it you're feeling some pain."

"Yeah," I groan.

After the work I did to cover Halle, I've broken into a sweat.

Her eyes follow mine to my wife, and she sighs. "Let's try not to do anything strenuous, okay? You just had surgery."

"Can't help it," I mutter.

"I'm going to get your temperature and blood pressure. They should be coming by for blood work in the next hour or so."

I let her do what she needs to do, thankful when the pain medicine kicks in, even if it makes me groggy.

"Let me get another blanket or two," she says when she's done with all her checks.

When she returns, she lays one blanket over me and another on Halle.

I can barely keep my eyes open as I whisper, "Thank you."

"You're welcome. Hit the call button if you need me."

I'm out before she leaves the room, but Halle and I both stir when a phlebotomist arrives to draw blood.

When they're gone, Halle touches my cheek, looking at me like she can't quite believe I'm here.

"How are you feeling?" she asks.

"Like I'm not going to let a little bullet wound slow me down."

She rolls her eyes, even as they mist over. "Caleb."

"I'm serious." I grasp her hand, grateful for the feel of her fingers as she wraps them around mine. "This is nothing."

"You were *shot*. I wouldn't call that nothing."

With my free hand, I tuck a piece of hair behind her ear. "I'm still here, aren't I?"

"Yeah, after a lot of blood loss and surgery." She sniffles. "What if—"

"Let's not dwell on the what ifs. What-ifs are the thief of joy. All that matters is that I'm alive."

Halle gives a soft laugh. "I admire your ability to be optimistic in even the worst circumstances."

My lips twitch. "One of us has to be."

She shakes her head. "A couple of days ago, my brothers told me that you look at me like you'd jump in front of a bullet for me. I just didn't think you'd literally put that theory to the test, especially so soon."

I break into a genuine smile. I appreciate her attempt at levity. "Baby, when are you going to realize that you're my world? I'd do anything for you."

She leans over, pressing her forehead to mine. "I love you."

I don't say it back, because she already knows.

Seda's hug is downright bone-crushing. It's excruciating, really, but I don't dare let my little girl go. I can't even think about what kind of hell she went through yesterday.

She cries into my shoulder, my hospital gown wet with her tears.

"You gave us all quite the scare," Salem says from the end of my bed.

"You really didn't have to test how much we care about you by getting shot." Thayer levels me with a stern look.

"Seda, sweetheart?" I say when her tears haven't slowed. "Daddy's okay. I promise."

"I thought you *died*," she sobs.

I wince. I can't imagine what was going through my little girl's head yesterday, how hard it must have been on her, on everyone.

"I'm okay," I say, gently stroking her hair. "I had surgery and I'm good as new."

"I was so scared," she says. "But Casen and Quinn kept me safe. They shoved me behind a table."

My heart thumps heavily in my chest. I'll have to remember to thank them for that, even if it was incredibly stupid of them to try to approach their gun-wielding mother.

When Seda finally lets me go, she wags a finger in front of my face. "Don't you ever get hurt again, Daddy. Promise?"

I pull her closer and kiss her cheek, but I don't make that promise. Any number of things can happen to a person, and I don't want her to ever think I'd break a promise.

"I love you, sweet girl."

"Love you too."

When she hugs me again, I can't help the groan that slips out of me.

"Seda, I think you're hugging too tight." Salem gently tugs our daughter's shoulders, pulling her back. To me, she says, "Did Halle tell you your parents are here?"

I nod. Before my wife left to go home to shower and change—after much convincing on my part—she mentioned that my parents were in the waiting area. It might be selfish, but I have no interest in seeing them. But as a parent myself, I don't have it in me to turn them away.

"Should I send them back?" Salem asks.

I give a wooden nod. There's no telling how this will go.

"We'll see you when you bust out of here," Thayer says, giving my foot a light tap.

"I'll see you soon," I tell Seda. "I promise."

That's a promise I can keep.

She nods, wiping at her face. "Okay."

Once Seda has followed Thayer out, Salem rests a hand on mine. "I don't know what any of us would've done if we'd lost you. I hope you know how much we all care about you."

I turn my hand over and give hers a squeeze. "I know."

She gives me a watery smile. "Good. I'll let your parents know they can come back."

I nod and take a moment to brace myself for their appearance. Chances are, this visit will leave me feeling emotionally drained.

All too soon, they're both standing in the doorway, peering in.

Annoyance leaches into my tone as I adjust my position in the bed. "You might as well stop staring and get in here."

My mom rushes forward, a cry ripping out of her throat. She opens her arms wide to hug me, but I shake my head and weakly hold up an arm.

"No, don't."

I'm doing a kindness by allowing them in to visit. I don't owe them any affection. For years, I've put up with their shit, and I've been more patient and understanding than they deserve.

"I..." Her hands float down and rest listlessly at her side. "I guess I deserve that."

"You do." I don't bother to soften the blow. "You've been nothing but judgmental of my life choices for years. You ridiculed my ex endlessly, you've never accepted Seda, and now that I've met someone else, you're repeating the cycle. You never learn, and frankly, I'm tired of giving you second, third, and hundredth chances. You've shown me over and over that you'll never change, and I finally believe you. I won't continue to make the people I love endure your ridicule. It's gone on long enough."

"Caleb—" she starts.

I shake my head. "I'm serious, Mom."

Her hands hover near me like she wants to touch me but knows if she does, I'm likely to blow up. "I understand, Caleb, I do but—"

"You don't, or we wouldn't be having this conversation. There are no buts to be had. No more excuses. I mean it."

"I've just always wanted what's best for you." She sniffles.

"What makes you think you know what's best for *my* life? You're my mom. You're supposed to be there to support me. Not make my decisions for me. I decide who I want in my life. Not you."

She brushes her short hair behind each ear. It's a nervous tic. She only ever messes with her hair when she's uneasy.

"I'm not a kid anymore," I remind her. "I'm an adult, and I'm fully capable of making my own decisions. My life choices are mine to make."

"I…" She rubs her hands down her shirt. "You don't understand. It's so hard being a parent—"

Irritation washes over me, making every cell in my body hurt. Despite the pain, I bark out a laugh. "I *am* a parent. You may refuse to accept that, but I am. Seda is my daughter in every way that matters."

She winces. "Right. I..."

"Forget?" I supply for her. "Even though Seda has been my daughter for ten years?"

"It's just hard for me to accept," she admits.

"It shouldn't be," I argue. "All I've ever asked is for you to follow my lead, and you didn't."

"You lied to us for a long time," my dad interjects. "You said she was yours."

Annoyance flares in my veins. All I'm doing is repeating myself over and over and getting nowhere.

"Yes, because she is mine. I chose her. Do you not understand that? Blood is nothing. I lied, if you want to call it that, because I knew you'd behave like this. And let's be candid. You didn't exactly embrace her even when you thought she was my biological child because of your dislike of Salem. Both of you are pathetic."

My mom rears back like I've slapped her, but it's about time I told them. I've tiptoed around, avoiding outright hurting their feelings for too long. I should've stood up to them a long time ago.

"I'm tired of being nice," I go on. "Of always placating your feelings. What about my feelings?"

She exhales a shaky breath, and at the foot of my bed, my dad bows his head, his focus set on the floor.

"I'll give you guys one last chance to do things right even if, frankly, it's more than you deserve. But the second you insult my wife or her family or my child, I'll fully cut you out of my life without a second thought."

My mom nods and reaches for my hand. This time I let her touch me.

As much as I'd like to believe that things will be better moving forward, I'm not optimistic. But at least I've said my piece. That's all I can do. The rest is up to them.

FORTY-SIX

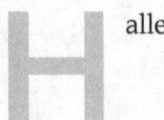alle

Caleb finally gets the all-clear to come home on Christmas Eve. It feels like he's been gone for weeks, when in reality it's only been a few days. All that matters is that he's okay ... and maybe that he gets to be home for Christmas. It's been hard not to look forward to spending our first holiday together as a family.

I'm still reeling from the events of our wedding day, and I have a feeling I will be for a long time. It pains me that my mother ruined what should've been one of the best days of my life. And it's impossible not to tear up when I think about how I nearly lost Caleb, all because she was hell bent on making me pay for something I didn't do.

My brothers were distraught, blaming themselves for the incident. But they're kids, and they did the right thing, regardless of the consequences. No one could've imagined things turning into the clusterfuck they have.

As for my mom, she's back in prison. That's all I know, and beyond that, I don't care.

I'm so tired of having to pick up the pieces for everyone else. If we're called to testify against her, then we will, but until then, I can't worry about it.

"Are you sure you're okay?" I ask, my hands fluttering uselessly around me.

"I'm sure," he gasps out. He takes the porch steps carefully, one hand on the railing and the other holding pressure against his side.

When he's made it to the top, I skirt around him and throw open the door.

"Welcome home!"

Caleb's eyes widen at the greeting from our friends and family. The lights strung around the stair railing and archways give off a warm glow, and the soft cadence of Christmas music brings a level of comfort I haven't felt in days.

"Wow," he says as he crosses the threshold. "This is quite the surprise."

"We're not going to stay long," Salem says, stepping forward to hug him. "We just wanted to see you."

It's wild to think that just a few months ago, I was jealous of this woman. Now, I consider her a friend.

"It's good to see you doing well." Cynthia pats his cheek.

"Thanks." He ducks his head. "I'm glad to be okay."

I shut the door behind me and set the bag I packed for the two of us when I came home to shower the day after Caleb was shot.

As I do, all my energy is sapped. Like now that he's home, my body can no longer function. But Seda is dying to stay the night here, which means we still have to make cookies for Santa. She still believes, and I'll do all I can to make the holiday magical for her. It's good to hold on to that childlike wonder for as long as possible.

I sit in the chair in the corner while Caleb greets and hugs everyone. He's exhausted too, dark circles under his eyes and a stoop to his shoulders. He hasn't been sleeping well in the hospital, what with the constant checks and machines beeping.

Thankfully, within an hour, it's just us and the kids.

Caleb settles on the couch with a yawn. "Seda and I watch *Elf* every Christmas Eve. Are you guys okay with that?"

"Yeah, we love that movie," Casen replies, settling onto the couch beside me.

"A movie sounds great," I say, even though I fear it might drive me even closer to passing out.

As the opening credits roll, Caleb captures my hand, rubbing at the ring around my left finger, a tiny smirk on his lips.

This man. He was shot a handful of days ago, and he's silently gloating over the ring on my finger.

"You like that, huh?" I whisper.

"Very much." His smile grows, his eyes warm and full of love.

I never dreamed of finding someone like him. I didn't think a love like ours existed. And I surely never thought I'd deserve it. But Caleb Thorne stormed into my life like a tornado, uprooting everything and putting it back as he saw fit, putting it back *right* and making me his in the process.

Later that night, when we play Santa and lay out all the gifts, when he kisses me in the glow of the Christmas tree, I know this is only the beginning of the rest of our lives.

EPILOGUE

Casen and Quinn's High School Graduation

aleb

"Are you crying?" Halle's tone is almost accusatory.

"No," I huff, even though that's exactly what I'm doing.

Every time I think about the boys heading to college in just a few short months, I get choked up. It's been a privilege to watch them grow and flourish over the past few years. I'm looking forward to seeing what they do in the future.

"You totally are," Halle laughs.

I wipe beneath my eyes. "Can't help it. Look at them."

Both over six-foot now, they tower over most of their graduating class.

When Casen's name is called, he crosses the stage to receive his diploma. Quinn is next.

It's going to be quiet when they're gone, but not for long.

On instinct, my hand finds the small swell of Halle's stomach. It's only just popped out, and it's the cutest thing I've ever seen. I drive her insane talking to the baby every night, but she humors me. We don't know yet if it's a boy or girl, and we aren't going to find out until delivery. Truthfully it doesn't matter to either of us. We just want a healthy baby.

The decision to have a baby wasn't an easy one. We've talked about it often over the past few years, discussing how perfect our family already was. The two of us, along with the twins and Seda. In the end, we decided one more just might make our family that much better.

"Daddy, you're such a sap," Seda says from my left.

The only reason she still calls me Daddy at this age is because she calls Thayer Dad, but I hope she never stops. It makes me feel like she's still a little girl and not like she's fourteen.

"I can't help it." I've probably always been a little too tender-hearted, but I'd rather care too much than too little.

"Are you going to cry at my graduation?" she asks.

Halle snorts. "He's going to sob like a baby."

Seda giggles, giving my knee a pat. "I'll make sure you have tissues, Daddy. Don't worry."

"Thanks, sweetie."

The ceremony comes to an end, and caps are tossed in the air. Then we head down the auditorium steps to meet with the boys.

Quinn is there first, scooping Seda up and spinning her around before setting her down and ruffling her hair. As a blush stains her cheeks, I count backward from ten to calm myself. I thought by now her crush on the twins would've faded, but if anything, it's only gotten worse.

"Congratulations," she says to him. "And to you too," she adds when Casen joins us, his fingers tangled with his girlfriend's.

Seda's face contorts with annoyance every time the poor girl is around. God help me. The only good thing about this crush is that it has kept her from going after other boys. But once they're gone for college, who knows what will happen.

Casen gives Halle a hug. "We wouldn't have gotten here without you, sis."

"What about us?" The question comes from Thelma. "Don't forget about us now."

Thelma and Cynthia sat in the bottom row so they didn't have to climb the stairs.

"We could never forget about our other favorite women." Quinn throws an arm around Thelma's shoulders.

"Yeah." Casen does the same with Cynthia. "We're going to miss you."

"Well, you're not leaving yet," Thelma gripes. "So stop trying to say goodbye. We have a few more months before we have to do that."

"Don't worry," says Casen. "We'll come back and see you as often as we can."

"You better." Cynthia pokes his side.

The boys' unlikely friendship with our elderly neighbors has never wavered. In fact, sometimes I think they spend more time over at their house than ours.

It's incredible to watch, and it's been good for them all.

"We're going to head out. We'll see you later." Cynthia hugs each of the boys and has to pry Thelma—who I swear is wiping away a tear—away.

"What are your plans?" Halle asks the twins. "Your party isn't until seven."

Quinn and Casen exchange a look. "We thought we could all get a late lunch together," Quinn answers.

"Oh." My wife's face lights up in genuine surprise. "I thought you'd want to hang out with your friends."

"We'll see them later," Casen says.

"I've gotta go." His girlfriend stands on her tiptoes to kiss him. "See you later."

Seda doesn't even try to hide her eye roll at the display of affection.

"Lunch it is then." Halle claps once. "We'll meet you guys at the car?"

The twins melt into the crowd, though it's still easy to pick them out with their heads sticking far above the rest, and with an eye on Seda and a hand on Halle's waist, I guide my girls through the crowd.

Outside, the sun is shining, and the air is warm. Seda, too cool to be seen with us when there are so many teenagers around, hustles ahead.

Halle strolls easily beside me, taking in the row of bushes and flowers planted along the walkway.

"What are you thinking about?" I ask.

She gives me a soft smile. "You."

"Me?" I laugh.

"I was thinking about how if you hadn't been so persistent, then we wouldn't be here right now. I wouldn't be this happy. You never gave up on me. Thank you."

"We never gave up on each other."

She often forgets all she did for me back then too. When we met, I was a scarred man who was barely clinging to a hope that I could find my person. Then she showed up, the light I was waiting for all along.

I pull her closer and press a kiss to the side of her head.

Every day she shows me just how important I am to her.

With Halle, I never question if I'm second best.

ACKNOWLEDGMENTS

I can't begin to tell you how special it was to revisit the town and characters of Hawthorne Mills. I've known for a long time that I wanted to return, but I wasn't sure if there would ever be a story. I was so happy when Caleb popped up in my head and started telling me all about this girl he was falling in love with. I knew right away that I had to start writing the story. The world of the wildflowers is incredibly special to me, and I hope you enjoyed the peek back inside. I hope we all get to visit them again soon!

Thank you so much to the readers who have loved and talked endlessly about the Wildflower Duet for the past few years. It's changed my life, truly. I've gotten to know and meet so many of you because of these books, and that's so incredibly special.

This book wouldn't have been possible without a lot of help.

Firstly, to my main girl, Emily Wittig, for always listening to my podcast-length voice messages and keeping me sane and taking Disney trips with me—I'm forever grateful you sent that message on Goodreads all those years ago.

Melanie, thank you for your valuable insight, as always. I value our chats so much. You have no idea.

Beth, I don't have words for how much I appreciate you. I hope you know how much I value your hard work and dealing with me when I'm late (like with this book, haha). I'm forever grateful Melanie sent me your way.

Valentine, it's been a wild ride this past year, and I can't thank you enough for giving me the strength to brave some things I wasn't sure I could do. Thank you for holding my hand through it and giving me a kick in the butt when I needed it. I can't wait to see what all we accomplish together.

Thank you to all the bloggers and early readers for taking the time to read this book and talk about it. I would be nowhere without you. You guys have all my love.

www.ingramcontent.com/pod-product-compliance
Lightning Source LLC
LaVergne TN
LVHW030312070526
838199LV00069B/6457